CHAOS LOOMING

THE LEGION OF PNEUMOS
BOOK ONE

H.B. RENEAU

VESALIAN PUBLISHING

Acknowledgments

This book would not have been possible without the help and input of untold family, friends, roommates, classmates, editors, and beta readers. Writing a book has always been my dream, and thanks to you all, it's now a reality.

Special thanks go to my mom, Mysti, and my brother, Noah, who read over the earliest versions and whose advice, discussion, and above all encouragement were essential to the writing and editing process. Additional thanks go to my editors, Alison Rolf and Lauren Smulski, whose insight and guidance helped turn this manuscript into the finished product before you. Thank you also to Natalia Junqueira for her gorgeous cover design. Seeing one's words brought into the visual sphere with such keen imagination and perspective has been an incredible experience.

In the end, I believe that Joss Whedon said it best:

I write to give myself strength. I write to be the characters that I am not. I write to explore all the things I'm afraid of.
—Joss Whedon

Thank you all for being the people I aspire to be.

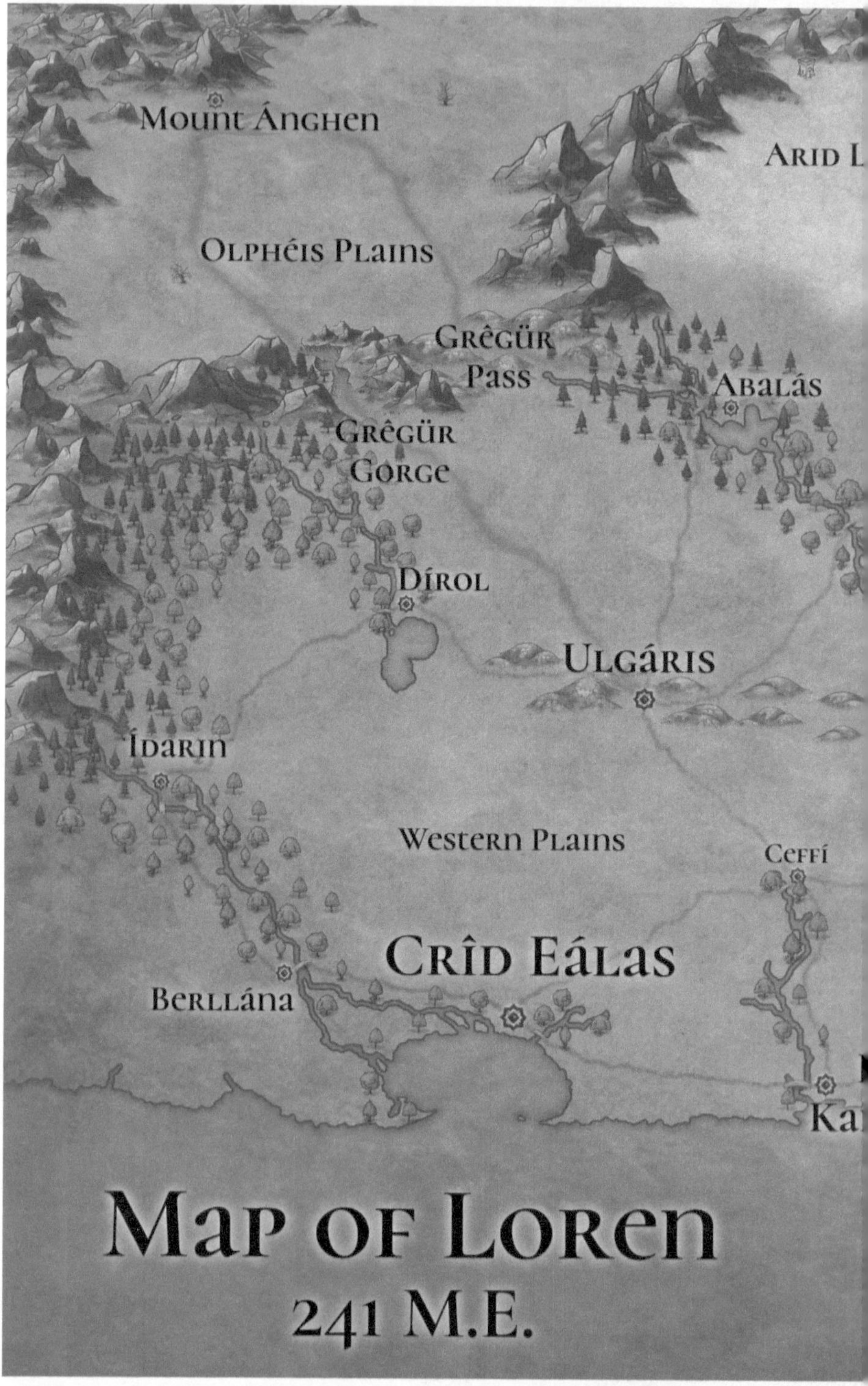

Mount Ánghen
Arid L
Olphéis Plains
Grêgür Pass
Abalás
Grêgür Gorge
Dírol
Ulgáris
Ídarin
Western Plains
Ceffí
Crîd Eálas
Berllána
Ka
Map of Loren
241 M.E.

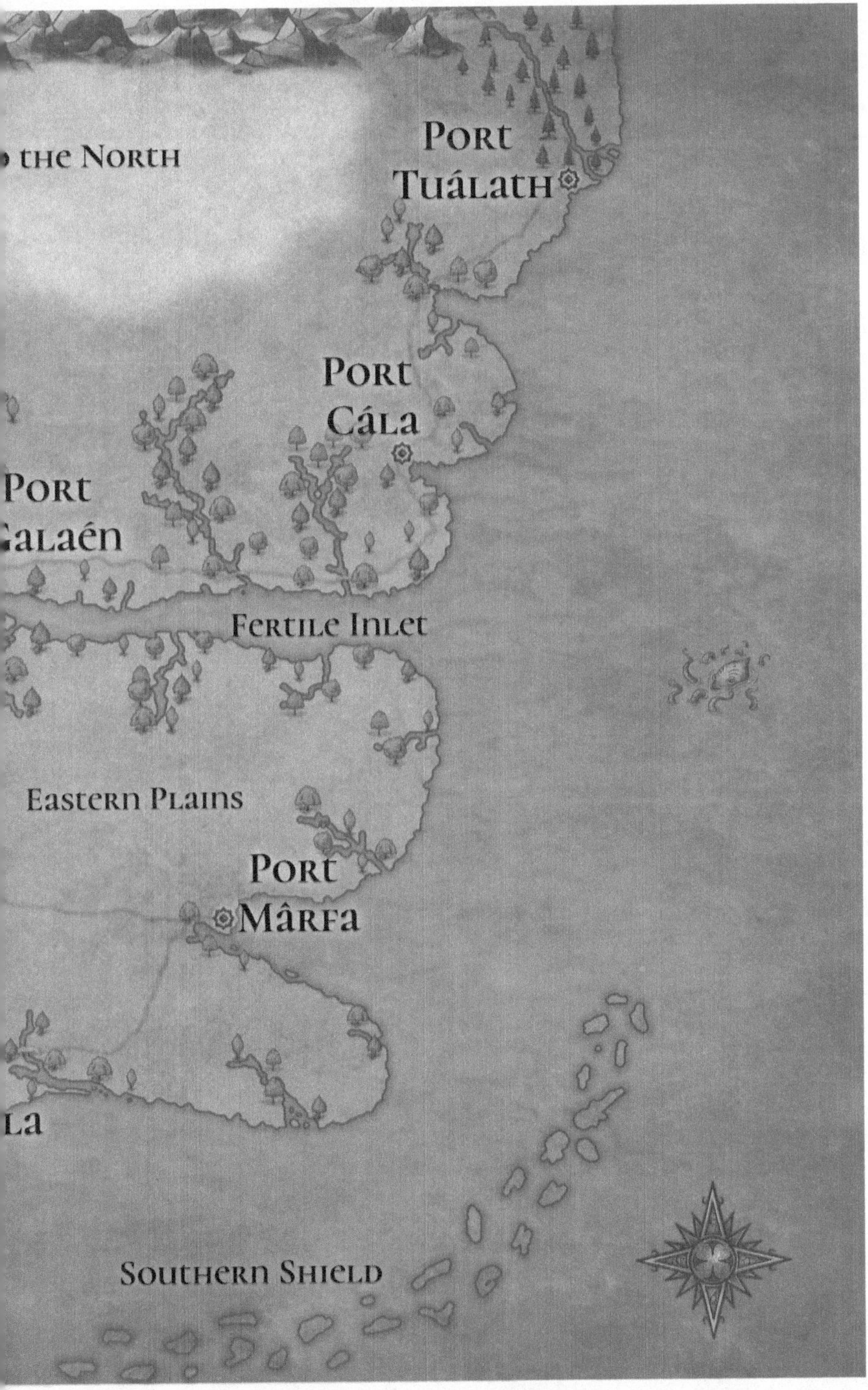

the North
Port Tuálath
Port Cála
Port Calaén
Fertile Inlet
Eastern Plains
Port Mârfa
La
Southern Shield

CHAPTER

ONE

In the silence of the moonlit forest, all seemed to be in order. Yet the cord of chaos thrummed beneath, heard only by those who cared to listen.

Keira Altman felt that cord in her bones and let its steady pulse ground her. She breathed in the air, thick with anticipation, as the legionnaires creeped through the underbrush, their footsteps light on the dew-laden leaves of the forest floor. Bringing up the rear, Keira followed suit. Barely daring to breathe, her legs moved double time to keep up with the others' loping strides.

When they'd crested the hill, she finally glanced up, sucking air through her teeth at the sight before her. Even in the dead of night, Marek Larghaen's manor cast a pall over the single-story wattle and daub buildings that gathered at the base of the hill, making up the small fishing village of Abalás. The shadow of the tax collector's extravagance stretched menacingly out over its surroundings.

Keira swallowed, refusing to let the others see the nerves that coiled like a nest of vipers in her belly, the way her traitorous limbs threaten to shake. No, she'd asked to be here, pleaded even. She'd been desperate to join this mission despite her mentor Nazor's protests that she was far too inexperienced. Well here she was, creeping around in the pitch black outside the house of possibly the most dangerous man in the uplands. She'd gotten exactly what she'd wanted. Now if only she could keep from screwing it up.

A hissed warning from the lead legionnaire shocked her out of her reverie. He'd dropped to his knees and was gesturing for them to follow suit. Keira dove for the nearest bush, heart pounding and unsheathed blade at the ready. She didn't dare move, instead listening hard for the source of the delay. A movement to her right caught her eye and she saw Danny motioning toward the manor. She inched around the shrubbery just in time to see a flickering candle disappear from the window.

She glanced at Danny, his pale green eyes just visible over the dark mask that covered his mouth and nose. They tightened in silent question and Keira shook her head. She couldn't imagine why anyone would be awake at this hour. In fact, their entire plan hinged on the element of surprise.

What if the old snake had been warned? The corrupt merchant had enough spies—helpless people indebted to him and willing to do anything to escape his grasp. What if they were walking into a trap? Keira squeezed her eyes shut, forcing her breathing to slow as she focused all her attention on the here and now.

You can do this, she reminded herself. Over a year of endless training and she was as ready as she'd ever be. No, this was her shot—maybe her only chance to be admitted to the rites that year. And if she became a full legionnaire . . . well maybe, just maybe, she'd finally find a way home.

Home.

The thought sent a ripple of excitement down her spine and sparked a flame of yearning deep in her gut. Without consciously thinking, her hand went to the gold locket she always wore around her neck—the one her mother had given her on the last day they'd been together. But that was in a world far away from this one—a world filled with everyday miracles like electricity and refrigeration. It had been over a year since her life had been turned upside down—since she'd lost everything and everyone she cared about. Well, this new world had given her a second chance, and she'd be dammed if she let that happen again. Turns out dying has a way of bringing out your determined side.

Danny's quick head jerk brought her back to reality and she creeped her head around the shrubs to see the two lead legionnaires crouched together, heads bent in whispered consultation. Keira's heart thudded a quick staccato.

Would they turn back? There'd be no shame in that. Even though she'd volunteered for this raid, if it ended in retreat, no one could blame her. Sure the rites would remain just outside her grasp, but so too would the humiliation sure to follow if she failed her first true test.

But before she could think herself in any more circles, the lead legionnaire rose to his feet, motioning them forward once again. They continued their slow progress up the hill, one by one, stepping carefully to avoid the loudest patches of underbrush. Keira watched as the other black-clad figures slipped off in pairs, each going to their assault points. A light brush on her arm brought her attention back to Danny, who nodded toward the cellar door at the rear of the lodge. Reminded of their assignment, Keira took a deep breath, steeling herself for the task ahead.

Come on, Altman, don't screw this up.

They reached the cellar doors all too soon and Keira glanced around nervously, scanning for guards who might come to investigate their activities. Danny tried the door handle gingerly, then more forcefully. As they'd guessed, it was latched from the other side. He turned to her expectantly.

Time for Plan B.

Keira wiped her sweaty palms on her trousers, fiddling with the mask that covered her face as her eyes darted around the clearing. Danny's brow furrowed.

"You all right?" He asked, the Boston Irish lilt of his voice barely above a whisper.

Keira nodded, not trusting her voice to come out any stronger than a squeak—not exactly the tone of confidence she'd hoped to convey.

She forced her leaden legs to move as she kneeled before the cellar door. A warm squeeze on her shoulder made her glance up to meet Danny's warm gaze. He gave her a small nod and she felt something warm and gooey fill her insides, filling and soothing the gouges her fear had carved into her in the way only Danny could. There was a reason he was her grounder after all.

She could do this.

She took a deep breath and turned back to the cellar door, feeling Danny move into position to guard her back. She'd be royally screwed if someone tried to sneak up on her once she began the binding process—not the way she hoped to end the night, or her short second life.

Reaching deep inside herself, Keira gently nudged the mass of energy that lay just behind her stomach. Sending it downward through her feet, she firmly anchored herself to the grassy patch she'd chosen. Then, reaching out for the latch, she let the energy flow through her fingers as her lips puckered in a whistle. Called pneuma, or "breath," she knew the energy was too high for normal ears to detect. She felt this energy being twisted and shaped to match the waves of sound, and she altered the pitch of her note, letting it guide the pneuma into the shape she needed —wrought iron. All materials, and even people, had a shape to their pneuma, an amplitude and frequency to the energy holding them together. While a person's pneuma could change over time, the pneuma of objects like this lock remained a constant, unalterable touchstone.

She willed her pneuma to first match the iron's, then alter slightly, slowly disrupting its tidy molecular structure. The latch felt cold in her hand as it pulled the heat from her body, disordering the molecules that comprised it until the metal was nothing more than a molten blob. Wiping the sweat from her brow, Keira grasped the ledge of the door, easing it upward until the metal bindings gave way with a dull *thunk*. Below them stretched earthen steps that led down into the cellar.

Danny began descending the stairs, longsword at the ready. They'd decided he'd go in first, to stall for time should they encounter anyone, and to give her the space to orchestrate a binding if needed. Following close behind, Keira nearly ran smack into Danny, as he he froze at the bottom of the steps. She halted, listening for the sound that had caught his attention.

Bringing a finger to his lips, Danny inched forward again, deeper into the dank caverns of the cellar. Keira gripped the hilt of her sword and balled her left hand into a fist to hide its shaking.

You can do this. Just keep moving forward.

They were almost to the far end of the cellar now, and Keira could just make out the outline of the promised ladder leading to the main floor above. She barely registered the creak of a door hinge before something slammed her against the wall, sending her sword flying. She dropped to the ground, breath ragged as she tried to keep from heaving onto the floor.

She shoved aside what looked like a chair and scrambled to her feet. Hearing Danny cursing nearby, and the clang of metal as he fought off his own seemingly more human assailant, she staggered forward.

Keira emerged into a filthy larder to see him locked hilt to hilt with one of the conniving Marek Larghaen's hired men. She swore under her breath. They'd hoped to catch him unawares, but it seemed the old bastard had been warned, and had upped his guard to prepare for their arrival.

Keira sprinted toward Danny, shouting his name. His gaze shot up and with a great *umph,* spun the man he'd been grappling with in her direction just as she reached them. She met his back with her blade and felt an unsettling *crunch* as it slid through him. The man slumped against her, and she briefly bore his weight before letting him slide to the ground. He gurgled blood as Keira pulled her sword from his back, then was still.

"You okay?" Danny asked, quickly scanning her up and down.

Keira nodded. She couldn't seem to look away from the man at her feet. He was definitely dead—his eyes had that blank, dilated look that corpses get and he smelled like he'd wet himself. Her mentor, Elliott, had told her the end wasn't pretty, but until this moment, she hadn't fully grasped the horror that would be her first kill. She swallowed hard, avoiding Danny's eyes. She wasn't ready for the understanding and sympathy she knew she'd find there.

Blinking furiously, Keira forced her gaze away from the body. "Fine," she muttered. "You?"

"I'll live."

She knew he wanted to say more, knew the moment he thought better of it. She was grateful for that—Danny always seemed to know exactly what she needed.

"We should keep moving," Danny said. "On account of it seems like the others have run into trouble too. We need to get to Marek before he pulls off another of his grand escapes."

Keira nodded, noticing for the first time the sounds of fighting echoing from elsewhere in the lodge. She wadded up her confusing mix of emotions and flung them to the back of her mind. She'd have time to deal with them later. Peering around for an exit, Keira noted that the larder had seen better days. A thick layer of dust and grease covered the chopping tables and cabinetry, but the still-smoldering embers in the grand fireplace betrayed the room's recent use.

Shouts and curses echoed from the front rooms, but Keira and Danny instead headed for the servants' staircase in the back of the larder. The steps creaked as they swiftly climbed, making for the bedchambers on the floor above. But when an echoing creak reached their ears, they both froze. Any sound was amplified in the tight quarters and Keira barely dared to breathe as the creaking grew closer and closer. Her eyes darted to Danny's to find he'd pressed himself against the far wall, one finger pressed to his lips. Keira similarly eased herself flat against the wall opposite and forced air through her nostrils. *Inhale.* The creaking was just around the corner now. *Exhale.* Keira and Danny leaped forward, swords at the ready.

Tiny squeals and muffled sobs met them as a woman dressed only in a sleeping shift pressed two small children to her.

"Please, oh please," the woman cried. "They're just children. A-and I'm their nursemaid."

Danny was the first to step forward, brandishing a torch from the wall as he quickly surveyed the woman. Her dress was plain enough and she didn't appear to be hiding any weapons, making her story seem plausible.

"What do you think, Keira?" Danny asked. "I wasn't aware Marek had any kids, personally."

Keira didn't answer, throat working silently as her eyes fixed on the two small children. The smallest was a boy, no more than two or three whose sandy brown hair stuck up at odd ends. Fat crocodile tears filled his eyes as he stared up at her and he quickly buried his face in his nursemaid's skirts. But his sister, only a few years older from the looks of it didn't cry but stared wide-eyed at Keira as if transfixed. Her blonde hair was neatly parted with braids framing her face on either side. *Just like Molly.*

"We should see them out," Keira said suddenly. She didn't know where the impulse came from, but once uttered it just felt *right.* She couldn't leave them.

"There isn't time." Danny hissed. "They'll be fine."

But she shook her head and thought about the man and dog they'd encountered in the cellar. There could be more. Staring at the wide-eyed children all she could see was Molly, the little sister who wasn't even truly related to her, and the car accident that meant she may never see her again. But this little girl was here, now, and she'd be damned if she let anything happen to her.

"There could be fighting outside," she whispered back at him. "I have to make sure they make it safely."

"The mission—"

"I'll catch up to you," Keira insisted, sliding one hand into the girl's trembling one as she led the three of them down the steps.

From behind, she heard Danny's whispered curse. But there was no time to worry about that. They were innocent, these three, caught up in something they likely could never understand. She'd been there, silently begging for help from strangers who merely averted their gaze from the uncomfortable or inconvenient. She would never be that person.

It took only a few minutes to see the children and their nursemaid safely out through the cellar—their path thankfully absent any unexpected encounters. When Keira returned to take the stairs two at a time, she nearly ran smack into Danny and swore in surprise.

"Y-you stayed." *Obviously,* she chided herself.

Danny steadied her with one hand, meeting her gaze with a single cocked eyebrow.

"Now when've I eva' left you behind?"

Keira flushed and could only offer a half-hearted shrug. He was right, of course. Danny was nothing if not steadfast and loyal to a fault. He'd sooner have chewed off his own arm than left her back unguarded. It was the thing she loved most about him.

That thought sent a warm tingly sensation all the way to her toes and Keira felt her blush deepen. Now was *definitely* not the time for such thinking.

Luckily Danny had already turned and continued their ascent up the back staircase. Keira hurried after him, hand tightening on the hilt of her sword as she forced herself to refocus. They paused when they reached the landing, and Keira motioned toward a room on their left, where candlelight flickered beneath the closed door. Someone was definitely inside.

They flanked the door, one on either side, and Danny raised his eyebrows at her expectantly. She closed her eyes and concentrated on the pneuma. Slowly, Keira cast it out on the back of an inaudible whistle, searching with her mind for the presence they sought. The pneuma she encountered was twisted, dark, and calculating, but tinged with something else—a nervous tension of sorts. It was definitely Marek, all right, but he wasn't alone.

She could feel him pacing on the other side of the door along with two others, most likely bodyguards. Coming back to herself, she caught Danny's eye and held up three fingers. His brow furrowed. They'd been told Marek had only one bodyguard he trusted to share a room with him as he slept, and the original plan had been for her to muscle bind Marek while Danny took care of the bodyguard. Two guards threw that notion out the window, as she could only cast one bind at a time, and the out-of-body requirements of casting made her useless in a physical fight. That's why Danny was there—to guard her back during the process, and to help bring her back if she lost control. This would be difficult for him to do while fighting off two assailants at once.

She shook her head, and he nodded in response. Though the mask covered half his face, she knew he was grimacing underneath. They'd have to do this the old-fashioned way.

Danny grasped the door's handle while Keira mimed the general location of each of the three targets. Her fingers counted them down. *Three*...her grip tightened on the hilt of her sword...*two*...Danny's calm, determined eyes met hers...*one!*

With a shove, Danny flung open the door and rushed the closest bodyguard. Quick on his heels, Keira sprinted into the room and slammed into the other, meeting his sword with the clang of her own.

She cursed their rotten luck—of course they had their weapons at the ready. No doubt they could hear the shouts echoing from the rest of the house.

She didn't have time to think about this long before she felt her sword drawn up and around in a giant arc, disentangling their blades and putting her immediately on the defensive. She barely blocked a crushing overhead swing. *This must be Rhondor*, she thought. *Marek's favorite.* Panic welled within her. *He's too big.*

She quickly squashed the panicked thought and forced herself to think rationally. *This is what you've trained for.* The man was enormous, and the broadsword he wielded nearly doubled his arm's reach. She needed to get some distance, or he'd skewer her for sure. After parrying his next slash, Keira snatched up a ceramic plate from the table behind her. When Rhondor advanced again, she blocked his stroke while simultaneously shattering the plate against his head. He stumbled backward, allowing her a few precious seconds to regain her bearings.

From the corner of her eye, she saw a huddled figure creep along the edge of the room, making for the open hall door.

Oh, no you don't, she thought.

Shifting her sword into her left hand, using the other to snatch up her hip dagger and sent it flying end over end into Marek's side. The man cried out and doubled over in pain.

Keira grinned in satisfaction. *That'll keep him from getting too far.*

Before she could revel in her minor victory, Rhondor was on her again, and he was angrier than ever. Keira, remembering everything her mentor Nazor had ever taught her, spun out of his way, letting his momentum carry him into the wall behind. As she turned, she brought her blade down in a sweeping arc, slicing the giant man collar to navel. It wasn't a deep cut—certainly not mortal—but it was enough to slow his movements as he forced her back on the defensive, hammering her with slashes and stabs. He was tiring, but so was Keira. Her breathing was shallow, and her sword felt heavier with every block.

Rhondor's wound was bleeding freely now, forming a small pool at his feet. Sensing an opportunity, Keira retreated slightly. Rhondor immediately pressed his advantage and leaped toward her, his foot slipping on his own blood. He didn't fall, but he definitely stumbled.

That was all Keira needed.

She lunged forward, cutting a single stroke in and up, wedging her blade between the giant's ribs. He exhaled sharply, then dropped to his knees, blood bubbling past his lips. She let him sag to the floor, then wrenched her blade free and spun to look for Danny.

He was in the opposite corner of the room, dealing the final blow to the other guard, a savage slice to the man's neck that left him in a gurgling heap. Danny turned toward her, and she saw a cruel cut down the side of his left arm. She started forward, brows knit with concern, but he waved her off.

"Just a scratch," Danny reassured her.

She nodded, not entirely convinced, but knew better than to argue just then.

"Where's Marek?" Danny asked.

Keira glanced around and cursed. "Well, he can't have gone far, not with my knife sticking out of his gut."

She saw a ghost of a smile cross Danny's face as he ran for the door. Out in the hallway, he bent to look at something on the floor before motioning her closer.

"Definitely blood. Seems you're not quite as hopeless at knife-throwing as Nazor says," he teased.

Keira scowled. "I told you I hit him. Honestly, I'm surprised he made it this far. From what they told us, I didn't take him for much of a fighter. His type always seems to have others around for the dirty work."

Danny's smile twisted darkly. "Never underestimate the survival instincts of a man like Marek. He didn't get to where he's at for lack of determination."

Keira nodded, gritting her teeth. She'd never met Marek Larghaen, but she knew enough about the snake to suspect that Danny was probably right. The slimy merchant had clambered over the backs of his fellow uplanders to become the local Tiarna's chief tax collector, keeping his power through threats, intimidation, and outright violence. *Yes*, Keira thought grimly, *he was certainly motivated, but that makes two of us.*

A clatter of metal hitting the floor brought their attention to a room at the far end of the hall. The two of them slipped down the hall toward the sound, careful to check each room they passed to ensure they wouldn't be ambushed. As they approached the far door, Keira heard voices coming from inside—laughing, it sounded like. Danny pressed his ear to the door, a puzzled look on his face, then sighed in relief.

Throwing open the door, he and Keira entered to find a cowering Marek, surrounded by four of their fellow Legionnaires. Though masks obscured their faces, Keira quickly recognized their mentors, Elliott and Nazor.

"Nice of you both to join us," Nazor growled.

TWO

"We were wondering where you'd gotten to," Nazor drawled, looking amused. Keira flushed, her face turning the deep shade of crimson for which it was famous.

"Well, at least we slowed him down. That's my knife sticking out of his hip," Keira shot back—too quickly, she realized. The tall woman's mouth twitched, and Keira's blush only deepened.

"You mean this?" Nazor's long fingers caressed the handle of Keira's blade and Marek whimpered. "Yes, we were just discussing it. Seems our friend here would very much like us *not* to touch it."

Marek nodded vigorously. "P-please. Just tell me what you want. Is it money? Jewels?"

His eagerness filled Keira's mouth with an acetic tang. Of course he supposed they were a band of thieves, after his hard-earned—or, rather, *stolen*—cash. Nazor must have had a similar idea, as her black eyes suddenly narrowed. In one swift motion, she yanked the dagger from Marek's side.

The man howled, and the two hooded figures standing by Elliott and Nazor laughed savagely. Keira felt sick as she stared at the blood flowing freely from Marek's side. She stepped forward out of reflex, but felt a firm hand grasp her wrist. Startled, she looked up to meet Danny's hardened face, his mouth set into a tight, immovable line. A small, almost imperceptible shake of his head reminded her it wasn't the time to offer a bandage.

Nazor's face was an inch from Marek's now, the point of Keira's blade pressed firmly into the scum's left jugular.

"You think I want your blood money?" Nazor's words were barely a whisper, and Keira felt an icy shiver course down her spine. "You think I don't know how you got it? The lowlife rats you scrounged up to feed on the common river folk, on your own people?"

Beads of sweat trickled down Marek's cheek, mixing with the droplet of blood that had materialized on his neck.

"N-no, please. I'm only a merchant, an honest, hardworking merchant."

The other Legionnaires guffawed—even Elliott chuckled quietly, to Keira's surprise. She'd almost forgotten he was there. Elliott eyed Marek, a doubtful look in his eyes, but Marek didn't notice, too busy backtracking to care.

"I mean, maybe I have to grease a few wheels to get things done, but who doesn't? You wouldn't blame a roan for that, would ya?" He'd clearly seen the venomous look on Nazor's face and was trying desperately to right a swiftly sinking ship. "Who am I to turn down honest business over some misplaced scruples, I—aaah!"

Nazor had seized him by the collar and hauled him bodily to his feet. "I don't give a damn about your scruples," she snarled. "The only thing I care about is the four people killed this month by highway bandits—bandits paid for out of *your* coffers."

"Bandits? Surely not! I employ lawmen for—"

"*Lawmen?* Is that what you call brutes and thugs who take what they want and brutalize anyone who gets in their way?"

"I-I really can't imagine—"

"You're either a bastard or a fool, and I daresay it isn't the latter," Nazor said coldly. "Now, tell me, who else has benefited from your idea of 'scruples'?"

Marek blustered and Nazor's grip on his shirt front tightened.

"Come on, worm, tell us who put you up to it."

The cowardly swine swallowed hard. "I-I can't. They'll see me dead."

"*We'll* see you dead if you don't tell us what we need to know."

Marek was sweating profusely by this point, his eyes darting from side to side like the cornered rat he was. He was almost pitiable—almost.

Nazor spat to the side in disgust. "Very well," she hissed, turning to Elliott. "Shall we bind him, then?"

Elliott shifted his weight from side to side, reaching up from crossed arms to rub the bridge of his nose, an old habit from his days of spectacle use. He gave Nazor an intent, searching look, and she matched it, unyielding in her question. They stood that way for a moment, their silence masking the intense flurry of activity going on behind those measured gazes.

Finally, Elliott sighed. "Indeed." He stepped toward Marek, leveling him with that same piercing gaze.

Before Keira could think, she felt her legs moving, heard her voice calling out.

"Wait!"

Six pairs of eyes turned to stare at her.

"Let me do it. I've been practicing spirit binds, and I could use the experience. It's part of the trial, right? During the rites?" Nazor wore a doubtful expression, but Keira pressed on, undeterred. "Danny can ground me—we've done it before."

Danny's wary gaze told her he knew as well as she did that *before* meant on animals and willing participants only. She ignored him.

This is my chance, she realized, trying to get her breath under control so as not to shatter the illusion of confidence. She watched as the others weighed her request. *This is my chance to prove myself.* As a Legionnaire-in-training, she knew there was precious little opportunity and this year's rites were quickly approaching.

It was Elliott who spoke.

"Very well, Keira. Prepare to perform the binding." Turning to Nazor, he explained, "If she's to perform the rites and become a full Legionnaire, she'll need the experience."

Nazor's face still showed her obvious skepticism, but she nodded, following Elliott's lead. Her grip loosened on Marek's collar, and she allowed him to collapse back onto his stool. She held fast to the dagger, though, and the look she gave him spoke all too clearly of her willingness to use it if provoked. Keira stepped toward Marek and assumed a wide-legged stance, rooting herself firmly in place.

"Slow your breathing, control it. In, then out." Elliott's voice was barely audible, but she calmed at once, feeling his support. She took a big breath in through her nose, out through her mouth, rooting herself into the floor. She could feel Danny's pneuma behind her—steadfast, grounding. For a moment she considered grabbing onto that presence, wrapping it around herself so tightly that nothing could separate them. He would see all of her—dreams, fears, and everything in between. The thought sent a small thrill coursing through her. There was a part of her that wanted that, that wanted him to really *see* her. But there was a larger part of her, one steeped in hesitation born from years on the move, relying on no one but herself. No. Danny was there to ground her if she needed him but she could do this on her own.

So closing her eyes, she reached firmly for the ball of pneuma at her core. It responded almost instantly, unraveling until it flowed freely from her fingers. On an inaudible whistle, she cast it in Marek's direction. The pneuma coiled around him, smoothing out until it matched the pitch and kilter of his own spirit—the spirit of Marek.

The feeling of leaving her body didn't happen all at once. It came on slowly, almost imperceptibly, until Keira realized with a start that she was becoming less *her* and more *them*.

She tasted his fear first and was struck by its metallic taste. He was afraid of the masked figures around him, but even more so, of—

The connection between them bucked and roiled as a wave of nausea threatened to overwhelm Keira.

He's fighting the binding, she realized almost absently, struggling to remain upright. A warm, firm hand grasped hers, and she felt herself flooded with familiar pneuma. *Danny.*

The nausea receded almost immediately. With Danny's pneuma tethering her in place, she could stretch out of herself, to wind around Marek more fully, settling into the exact shape and feel of his essence. Then the memories came, brutal and overwhelming.

A child held in the warm embrace of its mother.
Cold isolation as that same mother was lowered into a grave.
Harsh words and the violent slap of a drunken father.
Taking over the family business from that same abusive father.

Rising through the ranks of the merchant class, hiding his humble origins.

Being appointed a tax collector and finally getting the share he deserved.

Fear of the rumblings of a downtrodden peasant class.

Conviction that nothing and no one will take what is his.

The letter, threatening and veiled, yet oh so clear.

Leaving to purchase a larger ho—

The letter! Keira tried to stop the rushing tide of memories, tried to go back and get a better look. *What did the letter say? Who was it from?*

Marek's psyche rippled, as if realizing belatedly that it had an unwelcome intruder in its recesses. Keira was swimming upriver now, wading through memory and emotion, searching frantically for another glimpse of that letter. Marek fought her outright, trying to throw her off as the waves of his psyche tossed her about, ever more tumultuous in their fury.

Keira felt herself slipping and grasped desperately for some handhold in that sea of angry thoughts. Danny's hand tightened reflexively around hers, sensing her panic and seeking to draw her back. She fought him off, desperate to see what Marek was trying so hard to hide.

A muffled howl pierced her focus once more, and she realized they were up, standing, ready to make a run for it, knife in hand.

How did we get a knife? She thought distantly, still trying to hang on to Marek's mind. The gray-clad figures encircled them, and Keira felt Marek's growing panic, realized he'd risk it all in search of escape.

"Keira, come back!" someone yelled, fear filling his voice. "Keira, you've lost control! He's throwing you off! Unbind, so we can stop him! Do it now!"

Keira struggled to do just that, but she was bound too tightly with Marek.

"I'm stuck," she whispered weakly.

Danny threw his pneuma toward her again, and she latched on, binding herself to him as tightly as possible, letting him pull her back. She felt herself slowly untangling from Marek's mind, and all at once, she was in her own body once more.

"I-I'm back," she panted.

It was precisely at this moment that she saw, through hazy vision, Marek lunge for the door, slashing savagely at the figure who stood in his way—at *Elliott*. Nazor appeared out of nowhere, stepping between them, her claymore spiraling in an elegant arc, cutting Marek down as deftly as she'd skim cream from milk.

That was it—he was gone. All of their hard work, for nothing. Keira's nose burned and her eyes watered, not only for losing the information they'd counted on so dearly to help the locals. She was genuinely sorry for losing *him*—Marek. That no-good, slime-ridden snake had made her weep for him, or rather, for the boy she'd seen in his memories. Bindings were notoriously intimate affairs, and she now knew him, *really* knew him, his hopes and dreams. She'd just seen them come to a bloody end, no sooner than she'd realized them, and that was damn near worth crying over, curse him.

Somewhere in all of this, Keira had collapsed to the floor, a fact she didn't realize until she felt Danny's sturdy arms lifting her gently to her feet. She was still wobbly, and so leaned heavily on him as they approached the others.

"I'm sorry," she muttered. "I thought I had it, but he got away from me." She cast pleading eyes toward Elliott, searching his face for understanding, for forgiveness. In his eyes, she found exactly that and breathed out a sigh of relief. She avoided Nazor's gaze, knowing all too well what she'd find there.

"It's all right," Elliott assured her. "Bindings are no simple matters. What did you find out?"

Keira shifted through the jumble of memories she'd uncovered. "He received a letter a few months ago. There was something threatening about it, and I'm sure it has something to do with why he hired the bandits to loot the local trade routes."

"But who sent it?" Nazor's voice was icy. Keira glanced into her dark eyes, then quickly looked away, not wanting to deal with her disapproval quite yet.

"I-I'm not sure," she stammered. "The letter was marked with a purple seal, but I couldn't get a good enough look at it."

"Well, that's just excellent," Nazor snapped. "We've narrowed it down to everyone who's purchased purple wax over the last few years."

A familiar burning sensation prickled at Keira's nose and her eyes stung. *Don't you cry, Altman. Don't you dare,* she ordered herself. *Not now. Not here.*

Danny's grip on her tightened. "Keira did her best," he said defensively. "He was a slippery one—even I could feel that."

Keira thanked him silently, even as she knew Nazor would find this excuse utterly unconvincing. Predictably, her mentor snorted and turned away, barking a command at the other two Legionnaires.

"Come on, then, let's get *this*—" She nudged Marek's lifeless corpse with her toe. "—out of here."

Legs still wobbly and hands revealing a traitorous tremble, Keira let Danny help her down the stairs, heading toward their rendezvous point. For Keira, they couldn't get there fast enough. All she wanted in that moment was to curl up in her bed and let all the pent-up tears come. Because even after everything—the studying, the training, and the pleading to even be allowed on this mission—she'd blown it. Her one chance to prove herself ready for the rites this year and she'd done the exact opposite. Her free hand clutched at her mother's locket, the cool metal soothing to her own flushed skin.

I'm sorry, Mom.

And with that, Keira felt the first tear fall.

THE NEXT MORNING, Keira was up and out of the house well before dawn, desperate to avoid both the pitying looks from Danny and frank disgust from Nazor. She'd barely slept the night before, lying awake long after they'd returned to their farm, just outside the sleepy fishing village of Abalás. Looking back at the home she'd shared with Danny, Nazor, and Elliott these last five years—longer than she'd lived anywhere—Keira was struck by the familiar, gut twisting sensation that she didn't really belong here.

She made her way to the stable and was greeted warmly by her horse, Cerise, whose lips nibbled inquisitively at her ear as Keira began her daily grooming. Keira started at Cerise's flanks, methodically working on her chocolate brown withers with a round brush while trying hard not to dwell on the previous night's utter failure. She'd been so eager for this mission, ready to prove her worth to the Legion—and particularly to Nazor, who'd never hesitated to point out Keira's various deficiencies over the years.

So much for that, Keira thought ruefully.

She'd just started combing through Cerise's silken mane, carefully teasing apart the knots that seemed to magically accumulate mere hours after their last untangling, when Keira heard footsteps approaching. Stubbornly refusing to look up from her task, she attacked the knots with more vigor, determined that one thing in her life should be forced to cooperate as planned.

It was only when Cerise knickered in protest at her vigorous attentions that Keira looked up sheepishly to meet Elliott's gaze. One ruddy eyebrow was lifted in question.

"Be any rougher, and poor Cerise will require a wig fitting," he observed mildly in his clipped Oxford accent, "and I daresay that's not a good look on a horse."

Keira gnawed at her lip and slowed her frantic combing, rubbing Cerise's neck in apology. Never one to break a silence unnecessarily, Elliott selected a hoof pick and joined her labors in quiet camaraderie.

Grateful as ever for Elliott's comforting, non-confrontational demeanor, Keira continued her work in a more subdued fashion, still worrying at her lip. Eventually, though, Cerise and all the other horses had been groomed to perfection, the stalls mucked out, the tack room organized, and Keira realized with disappointed resignation that there was nothing left to distract her from the real task at hand. As always, Elliott seemed to sense her thoughts and had settled himself on a bench outside, the one they used for mending tack on fair weather days. His lanky legs stretched out before him as he leaned back against the fencepost to watch the rising sun. Keira joined him, sitting stiffly as she tried to find the right words. Finally, she settled for the obvious.

"I'm sorry."

Elliott didn't answer right away, and instead ran a hand through the shaggy, russet hair he preferred to leave untamed and falling past his ears on both sides. She'd begun to think he hadn't heard her when he suddenly spoke.

"I remember when you first arrived in Loren, Keira. So hurt and angry, confused about what it was we were even doing here. You're not alone, of course," he added, seeing Keira about to protest. "I've mentored dozens of Legionnaires over the centuries and through the various lives I've led. It's always the same—pulled so roughly from one world and dragged into another, it's only natural to be upset and disoriented. Pneumos may know the reason you were brought to this exact place and time, but we certainly don't."

Elliott shot Keira a crooked smile, and she met it briefly before kicking at some pine needles under her boot. He was right, of course. She'd spent just over a year in the small country of Loren, in this world they called Carnos, training to become a full Legionnaire, and she still found it difficult to grapple with the enormity of the Legion's calling. Hidden guardians who moved between worlds and whose tenure spanned multiple lifetimes, the Legionnaires' mere existence was a lot to take in.

"Do you remember the conversation we had about the nature of pneuma when you first arrived? You asked about the Legion, and I explained our mandate."

"Of course," Keira said. She'd heard that mandate repeated hundreds of times in the years since. "We create order from disorder, rebuild what has been destroyed, and heal what is broken."

Elliott nodded. "True, that is all true. But there is a qualifier. Do you remember it?" Seeing the quick shake of her head, he added, "We are to build *more* than we break and heal *more* than we destroy. It is a fundamental misattribution to believe that one can ever create order without *some* destruction. In fact," he continued, slipping smoothly into his nineteenth-century professor's voice, "as you know, everything in the universe trends toward greater and greater disorder. In your time, I'm told by other Legionnaires that the concept will be called 'entropy.' The universe is always expanding, leaving a void that must be filled, and the energy released by the creation of new worlds further fuels the universe's expansion. That is also how our pneumonancy works, of course. We harness the principles of entropy to disrupt the natural arrangement of atoms and molecules to create change in the world around us."

"My point," he emphasized, seeing Keira about to interrupt this endless monologue, "is that things naturally fall apart. Energy and matter delocalize, and order breaks down. The purpose of the Legion is, in many ways, to fight against entropy itself, to create order out of the chaos and prevent, or at the very least slow down, the gradual march of the universe toward inevitable chaos."

Keira rolled her eyes at the former Oxford professor, who was never one to forego a theoretical physics lecture tinged with philosophical implications. They'd had versions of this same debate before, but she played along anyway.

"So, what you're saying is that it's a doomed purpose," Keira challenged, slipping easily into their usual back and forth. "The universe will continue to expand. Disorder will increase because that's its nature, and all we can do is slow it down. Why even bother?"

Elliott cocked his head and grinned at Keira. "Who is to say what is truly natural? The world as it is now is not necessarily the world as it was meant to be. Besides, there is a purpose to any fight, even if the end is known. Even when progress cannot be seen, that doesn't mean it's not there."

"But why *me*?" Keira asked, not for the first time. "Why am *I* here? Why did I have to be the one to die in a car crash and show up in an entirely new world?"

Elliott shook his head sadly. "I don't know, Keira. I can't tell you what the hinge point was that brought you and Danny here, or what it is you're meant to do. All I can say is that there is a reason, a *meaning* behind everything you've gone through, and everything you will go through. Of that, I am certain."

Keira considered this, then remembered Marek's desperate struggle for control over his own mind, the way he'd fought against her—and won.

"It doesn't matter," she said miserably. "I *failed*, Elliott. I failed in the first important job the Legion trusted me with." She looked up at him, searching his face for some understanding. "All the practice and training—*years*, Elliott—and then I fail in front of everyone. How can they ever trust me as a Legionnaire now?"

How will I ever get home? This last question she didn't say aloud, but the force of it thrummed beneath her skin.

Elliott eyed her, and she knew he was choosing his next words carefully.

"You didn't fail, Keira. You merely didn't succeed."

Keira snorted, which Elliott pointedly ignored. "Binding is about ordering the world around us, and I would remind you that we cannot hope to master the chaos of the world until we first confront the chaos within."

Keira laughed openly at that. "You sound like a fortune cookie."

"A what?"

Grinning, Keira shook her head. "Never mind."

Elliott gave her a considering look before asking, "Why didn't you have Danny ground you from the outset?"

The question caught her off guard, and Keira flushed with embarrassment. "I—well, I didn't think I'd need it." She tried to shrug off his probing stare, but continued to shift in her seat, gaze averted.

"What I mean is, what keeps you from reaching out to him when you need help?" Elliott pressed, though not unkindly. "You know the dangers of ungrounded pneumonancy. Push too far, and you'll become *undone*, your pneuma dissociated, and your mind unable to return to your body. Why is it you wait for Danny to sense you're in danger before allowing him to intervene?"

Keira shivered at his words. Every Legionnaire had heard stories of the undone. Their bodies remained alive, but they were empty shells, utterly devoid of the people they'd once been. It was said that the Legion's council of elders could sometimes rejoin pneuma and body, but there was certainly no guarantee. Elliott was right—she knew the dangers.

She refused to meet his eye, refused to face the real question he was asking. When she didn't reply, Elliott cocked his head slightly, eyeing her intently. "Keira, I can't help but think there's something about the grounding process you're avoiding," he said gently. "You and Danny arrived in Loren within a year of each other. The two of you are bound as grounder and cantor, with a shared purpose here in Loren. There is no escaping it. I hope you know that."

Keira felt her face blush scarlet. She didn't like the direction this conversation was headed and certainly didn't want to be discussing it with Elliott.

"You're right, of course," she said, keeping her tone light, almost flippant. "I was too cocky. I need to work on my control of the bind, avoid being so drawn into it. I'll do better next time, Elliot. I promise."

She could see the disappointment on his face, the knowledge that she was avoiding his actual question. Keira waited for him to press the issue, but slowly released the breath she'd been holding when he remained silent. She didn't want to think about why she had such difficulty letting Danny ground her, why she resisted that level of intimacy. To be so exposed and vulnerable, your every hope and fear on display for your grounder, was something she just couldn't bring herself to do. Understanding why would require a level of psychotherapy that she suspected was not readily available in Loren.

The two of them sat quietly for a moment, listening to the chatter of birds in the trees. "You've come a long way since you arrived," Elliott said finally, his warm smile extending to his twinkling amber eyes. "I'm proud of you."

Keira felt her throat tighten, her eyes suddenly stinging. *How was it*, she thought, *that he always knew the right thing to say?* It was largely thanks to Elliott that she'd found a home here, unexpected though the journey had been.

She watched as he languidly stretched and climbed to his feet, waving at her as he sauntered back toward the house. Elliott might be proud of her, but it wouldn't mean much if she couldn't prove herself to the Legion as a whole. She had to find some way of qualifying for the rites this year.

It's been years, a voice in the back of her mind reminded her. *You think your life will be the same as you left it after all this time? Who knows if your mother even survived that car crash.*

Keira shoved the thoughts away. She refused to give up. She couldn't. Her mom needed her. All her life it had been just the two of them and heaven knows which among them had kept the train on the rails. She loved her mother fiercely but the woman regarded life skills like paying bills on time and avoiding non-toxic relationships as mere suggestions, and bothersome ones at that. Besides, time worked differently between worlds. How many times had Elliott told her that? If she could just find a way back, she knew she could set things right. And the Legion was by far her best shot at doing that.

So now to the task at hand. She knew she'd ruined their chances of finding out who was truly behind the recent thefts and violence in Abalás. And if fighting chaos was the Legion's mission, she'd have to show them she could contribute, that she was worthy of becoming a full Legionnaire.

Tomorrow, she decided. *Tomorrow, I'll put everything right.*

THREE

Crîd Eálas

The clipped *tap-tap-tap* of the page's boots on the cobblestone steps echoed through the halls as he lurched down the never-ending corridor that led to the Regio's personal chambers. Daryn's hands seemed to have attracted all the moisture his dry mouth lacked, and he nervously licked his cracked lips. He tried to keep the silver platter balanced during his ungainly scramble, the wax sealed letter at its center threatening to slip to the floor at any moment.

Please don't mess this up, he pleaded silently with himself.

Finally, the great oak doors loomed before him, and he paused, trying unsuccessfully to swallow the lump that had settled inconveniently in the back of his throat.

Now or never.

Reaching out a shaky hand, Daryn rapped smartly at the door. He could feel the sweat trickling between his shoulder blades, and he had just about convinced himself that he should knock again when a voice like liquid honey answered from inside.

"You may enter."

Taking a deep breath, the page lifted the latch gingerly, the platter firmly balanced in the other hand. He slowly entered, head bowed. The once-towering figure of Regio Claudius was dwarfed by the immensity of the four-poster bed he lay in. The old king's eyes were closed, but his shallow breathing made the page doubt he was actually asleep. His daughter, Lady Junia, sat beside him, book in hand, her dark eyes clear and calculating. Her raven hair was woven into a severe plait that pulled taut the olive skin around her eyes and mouth. Her eyes narrowed at his stare, and he quickly dropped his gaze to the floor.

Striding to kneel before her, he announced, "A letter for his regal majesty from the Council of Benadur, who from the holy lands of Ulgáris do ensure order in the name of Pneumos, protection to the sovereign realm of Loren, and peace to its citizens therein."

The unfamiliar words tumbled from him awkwardly, his tongue tripping over the traditional phrasing. His arms trembled as he held the platter aloft, fixing the cracked stonework beneath him with a terrified gaze, waiting for a word from her ladyship that would release him.

Or end my pathetic life, he thought. *One of the two.*

Languidly, he sensed rather than heard her move as she deftly plucked the letter from the proffered plate. He slowly climbed to his feet as she read its contents. Unsure what to do next, the young page shifted uneasily for a moment before finally standing at attention, the silver platter grasped tightly under one arm.

She scanned the contents quickly before speaking.

"It seems the old horse-hinds are convinced you're not long for this world," Lady Junia said, raising her voice so that the Regio could hear her. His eyes fluttered open in response, but he seemed wholly unconcerned with proving them wrong, offering only an apathetic glance in his daughter's general direction.

"They're asking for Landrianus to be brought to the hill country," she continued. "I'm sure they want to see for themselves what five years of tutelage have earned them in a future Regio." Her tone made it clear what she thought of her brother and the Council's likely findings.

Daryn had to physically grit his teeth to keep from gaping. He wasn't sure what was more shocking—to hear the holy Council spoken of with so little respect, or to hear Lady Junia talk so openly about her father's death. Daryn couldn't imagine ever being so bold.

The Regio grunted, which Lady Junia seemed to take for acquiescence. "Well, I suppose we ought to send for him," she said airily, refolding the letter. "Though, with rumblings of discontent among the peasantry, I certainly don't trust the Council to have our best interests at heart." Her mouth set in a thin line. "At the very least, it'll be good to have him home again—good for him to see you one last time."

Daryn thought he saw her eyes grow sad as she considered the shrunken figure of her father. Once standing nearly seven feet tall, Claudius was a legend in his own right. Daryn imagined it must be difficult to see him so reduced, and suddenly felt pity for the powerful woman who sat before him.

So engrossed in his own musings, he barely noticed that she'd started speaking again.

"—like to summon a Bellatori cohort as an escort through the hill country and home to Cr"d Eálas."

She swiveled her eagle gaze onto him, and he realized with a shock of panic that this last bit had been directed toward him. He stammered, trying to find the correct response, and he watched in amazement as her lips twitched, her eyes fully meeting his for the first time.

"You are to fetch me the scribe. Dismissed."

Not needing to be told a third time, Daryn bowed smartly before turning on his heel and striding purposefully out of the room. Once outside, with the door safely closed, he finally let out the breath he'd been holding and felt his anxiety fade. Shaking his head, he shuffled down the corridor in search of the scribe needed to compose Lady Junia's message.

"Damn you, Caryn," he said, cursing his pain-in-the-arse older brother. "You had to choose today of all days to get the pox."

~

Near Abalás

DANNY AWOKE WITH A START, sweat pouring off of him as he stared wide-eyed at the ceiling, trying to remember who and where he was. The shadows of the room stretched languidly in the predawn light as if just coming back to themselves after a night freed by darkness. Rolling out of bed, he stepped over the twisted sheets and padded over to the washbasin. He splashed cold water over his face, wincing as his arm rebelled against the motion. He glanced down and could see blood seeping through the bandage and his forearm but he ignored it, instead leaning heavily against the chest of drawers. Looking up, he met his own green gaze in the mirror's reflection, considering.

It had happened again.

He cast his mind back, trying to remember the details of the dream. He'd been standing on the side of a highway that twisted steeply up the mountain behind him, an embankment dropping off sharply to his left. Rain drenched him as he looked down the slope to an overturned car, perched precariously against a twisted metal railing that creaked and protested at the injury. The car itself was strange-looking, with larger wheels and a fuller cabin than those he'd once driven back when he had cars to drive. But the more pressing concern was the sound coming from the vehicle. Choked sobs cut through the night air, and he could just make out a young woman struggling against something inside, clearly trying to extricate herself from the vehicle. A slumped figure occupied the other seat.

Danny started running. He could feel his legs moving, but didn't seem to get any closer to the wreckage. All the while, the guardrail continued to creak and moan. Scared now, he tried to run faster, but the car seemed to get farther away.

"Oh, God!" the woman cried, her voice choked with tears. "Help! Please, God, someone help me! It's stuck!"

Danny tried to shout back he was coming, but he felt his throat muscles clamp shut. Her pleas turned to shrieks as the sound of groaning metal grew louder, and Danny gaped in shock as the guardrail suddenly gave way. The car lurched, disappearing over the cliff.

Danny had then launched into wakefulness, the woman's desperate screams still audible in his ears.

Danny stood still against the sudden spinning of his head and the nausea that rose unbidden to his gullet. Closing his eyes, he focused inward until he could feel that pulsing energy that lived deep in his gut. Gently nudging it with his mind, Danny felt warmth flood out through his limbs as pulsing waves shot from his feet, rooting him deeply to the earth. He felt tethered, stable, and immovable. The sensation was profoundly calming, and he felt his insides unclench. He breathed deeply and opened his eyes.

The dreams had begun not long before Keira first arrived in Loren. For months after they'd continued to come—hyper-realistic visions, each more lifelike than the next, and each leaving him sweaty and nauseous when he woke. The memories came from various points in her life, important moments and treasured secrets—some strange side effect of the grounding process, Elliott had explained. Danny still wasn't quite used to them.

As he worked to slow his breathing, something tugged at the edge of his memory. Thinking back, he realized with a start what he'd previously overlooked—that the car perched so precariously on the cliff's edge had had the words "Stanford Bound" etched across its back window, the interior overflowing with boxes.

"You never made it," Danny whispered. And the realization punched through him. Because she had never told him that. Never told him it was on her way to a brand new life that she had died.

THAT NIGHT AT DINNER, the four of them settled into their usual rhythm as they arranged heavy dishes on the table. Though the events of the previous night went unspoken, Danny could see their effects in the tense set of Nazor's shoulders, the forced cheeriness of Elliott's lighthearted chatter, and Keira's unusually muted demeanor. He tried to catch her eye, but she refused to meet his, seeming to curl further in on herself with every moment. The message in the room was clear. All may have been forgiven, but it certainly wasn't forgotten.

Eventually, even Elliott's forced cheeriness was extinguished under the heavy weight of unspoken disappointments.

"So, Nazor," Danny said suddenly, grasping at straws for something, anything, to break the silence. "I was reading through some of your old war journals the other day—the ones about the Tramorian

Uprising—pretty thrilling stuff." He paused, but was met only by Nazor's grunt of acknowledgement. He barreled onward, undeterred.

"I had a question, though. You talk a lot about ground maneuvers and formations to brace against the Tramorian charges. But I just don't understand why mounted maneuvers wouldn't be more effective. Aren't the Tramors nomads? Surely, having your own horses would have leveled the playing field."

Nazor snorted. "That's because you've never seen a dromedon up close. Monstrous creatures, twice the height of a man and skittish beyond reason. The Tramors swear by them, though. They claim there's no better steed for making one's way across the Arid Lands. They can go for days without water and are resistant to the bites of even the fiercest of desert flies."

"Flies?" Keira asked quietly. "As in the insect?"

Nazor said nothing for a long moment as she eyed Keira sternly. The tension between the two of them was palpable and Danny shifted uneasily in his seat.

"Yes," Nazor said finally. "Flies, the likes of which you've never seen. They can grow to the size of a small dog with bites that fester. They've brought down even the heartiest of men."

"Huh," Keira said finally, her gaze flicking to Danny. "Remind me to change our vacation plans." She grinned and there was a long moment as the tension held before Nazor finally offered a small smile in return.

"Indeed. I can't say I'd recommend it."

And with that, the spell was broken. And while the tension didn't completely dissipate, it settled down to a low thrum that could almost be ignored. Danny and Nazor continued debating the merits of mounted vs ground warfare as Keira and Elliott launched into an equally vigorous debate over the Tramorian understanding of Pneumos and pneuma.

"You see, the Tramors believe only in Pneumos." Elliott explained. "They believe she is the creator of the universe—her and her alone."

"But what about Séiro?" Keira asked. "Where do they think the chaos in the world comes from if not him?"

"They believe that as the creator of all things, nothing, including Séiro, could exist without Pneumos' explicit permission."

"So Pneumos, the goddess of order, is somehow also the cause of all chaos as well?"

"That is what they believe."

"Huh, that's fascinating."

This caught Danny's ear and he turned without thinking to ask, "Well, how do we even know Séiro exists?"

Three sets of blinking eyes turned to stare at him and Danny rubbed his suddenly damp palms against his pant leg. "I just mean, how do we know they're not right? It's already a stretch to imagine one divine being hangin' around before all existence. Wouldn't two be even less likely? And if Pneumos is more powerful, then what *made* her more powerful? How come Séiro isn't callin' the shots, pullin' people across worlds and all that?"

Beads of sweat materialized on his brow as Elliott continued to stare and Nazor barked a sharp laugh behind him.

"I—I was just wondering."

"Well, the key is balance, Danny. The cosmic balance between order and chaos. Pneumos cannot exist without Séiro just as Séiro cannot exist without her. One is no more powerful than the other, which is why it's up to us, her servants, to fight on her behalf—to fight in the name of order."

Elliott smiled kindly, though the faint scent of condescension wafted in the air. Or maybe that was just Danny's embarrassment.

"Ahh, yeah, I guess that makes sense." Danny quickly nodded, suddenly desperate for a change in subject.

"It was a good thought, though, Danny." Elliott said graciously. "A *perspective* I honestly had never considered before." Nazor only shook her head.

At that moment, Danny wanted nothing more than to sink through the floor. He'd never been one for deep philosophical conversations, after all. He'd barely made it through high school before the war had broken out. And as his uncle had so often reminded him, he wasn't exactly blessed in the brains department. In fact, he wasn't sure he really even understood what pneuma was or how his grounding even worked half the time. No, mysteries and metaphysics were definitely more Keira's area of expertise. Normally, he was wise enough to keep his ill-formed ideas to himself, sure that no one else had any real desire to hear them. Oh why did he have to open his mouth?

"I don't know. I think maybe Danny's got a point."

Danny's eyes shot to Keira's—relief and gratitude instantly flooding him. Her brows were raised and her chin jutted out at that stubborn angle it had as she looked between Nazor and Elliott.

"I mean, we don't really know how pneuma works or even what Pneumos's goals in all this are. Just because the Legion believes in this cosmic battle doesn't make it true. Who's to say the Tramors don't have more insight than any of us?"

Elliott nodded, considering her words thoughtfully before saying. "True enough."

Nazor only snorted, rolling her eyes as she declared. "Well, I don't know why we bother discussing such things. Greater minds than ours have long considered such mysteries and given answers only they can understand."

"Because it's *fun*, Nazor, dear." Elliott replied, eyes twinkling as he nudged her affectionately. "You know, that thing you find so disagreeable and, as you say, *trifling*?"

"To *you*, maybe, Obi'm. To the rest of us, it's merely dull."

The two of them burst into laughter then. Keira's eyes met Danny's and she sighed dramatically, shaking her head as if to say, *why don't they get a room?*

Danny tried to smile, but he was sure it came out all wobbly and forced. He glanced away, but not before he saw her own smile falter, brows knitting with concern.

He said nothing for the rest of the meal, his own embarrassment slowly gnawing away at his stomach. And at the first opportunity, he sprang to his feet, claiming to get a head start on the evening chores.

He fled the room, determined to make it outside, to the cool air that would clear his head.

"Hey, wait up!"

Damn it.

He didn't stop but slowed his pace slightly so Keira's shorter legs could catch up just as he reached the paddock gate.

"Hey, you ok?"

He said nothing as he leaned heavily against the fence, watching as his horse Boyd eyed him with interest as he chewed his cud. His silence did nothing to deter Keira, though.

"I just wanted to make sure, you know. You just—you seemed kind of quiet at dinner and I know Nazor can be kind of harsh. And really, I meant what I said. It was a cool idea. And we really *don't* know how Pneumos actually works . . ."

Danny turned then to eye Keira with amusement, as she rambled her way through in customary fashion what could have been a very direct question, getting more and more nervous as she went. It was pretty adorable, actually. Time to put her out of her misery though, he decided.

"I'm fine, Keira. Not the first dumb thing I've said. Definitely won't be the last."

Keira's brow furrowed at his words. "But it *wasn't* dumb, Danny. That's what I was trying—"

"It's fine Keira, really." He cut her off, not wanting to hear another word of false reassurances. "I'm not like you or Elliott. I know that, they know that, and really you know that, too."

Keira crossed her arms over chest, glaring back at him. "I don't know what the hell you're talking about."

Danny rolled his eyes even though his heart warmed a bit at her stubborn scowl, glaring up at him from barely five feet tall. Trying somehow to defend his honor. He chuckled.

"I'm just a bag boy from Boston, Keira. Only good for Nazi cannon fodder. I was never going to end up at some fancy college where I could read books all day and talk about philosophy and the meaning of life. Not like you."

Keira opened her mouth to argue and then closed it. A vice constricted in Danny's chest as he watched her search for the right words.

Finally she snapped, "So what?"

Danny blinked. "I'm sorry?"

"So what if you weren't going to college? So what if you never do? That doesn't mean you aren't smart and brave and loyal and perfect just the way—"

"Perfect?" He interjected, and her mouth snapped shut. "You think I'm perfect?"

He felt a slow grin spread across his face and his stomach flip-flopped as he watched the color flood her cheeks.

"Maybe not *perfect*," she muttered. "But you're *fine*."

"Fine?"

"Yes, fine."

Danny tried to match her scowl with a severe expression of his own, but utterly failed as a broad grin slipped past his defenses. Then he laughed and was rewarded by a crack in her frown even as she rolled her eyes at him.

"You know . . . when you're not being *completely* infuriating."

"I shall strive to do better, m'lady." He said this in a perfect imitation of Elliott's arched British accent, complete with courtly bow.

She threw her hands up then, shaking her head in exasperation. He laughed aloud and watched as a dark curly strand of hair escaped its top knot at the motion, falling across her face.

He didn't plan his next movement, didn't think through the consequences. On impulse, he reached out and tucked the strand gently behind one ear.

She froze, barely breathing as his fingers skimmed her jaw. Realizing his mistake, he yanked his hand away as if she'd burned him.

"Sorry," he muttered, rubbing a hand against the back of his neck as he eyed her tense posture.

"It-it's . . ."

"Fine?" He offered helpfully. She nodded.

"I think *that* has been established," he replied, trying to cling to the lighthearted banter that seemed to slip from their fingers with every moment.

"I should probably go," Keira muttered. "Promised Elliott I'd help organize some books . . ." Her voice faded and Danny raised his brows.

"Well, I definitely wouldn't want to stand in the way of the book organizing."

Keira tried for a small smile but it faded away as she turned too quickly to head back to the house.

Typical, Keira, Danny thought as he watched her jog back to the house.

One step forward, two steps back.

She was . . . complicated. He'd known that from the first days she'd come to live with them. Scared, confused, and fiercely determined to escape, to find a way home to the life she'd been torn from. That determination may have faded over the time she'd been there, morphed into a single-minded focus on finishing her training, proving herself, and completing the rites. At first, Danny had been pleased, glad to have a partner as committed to training and fulfilling their duty as he was. But as time passed, he wondered if there was something else behind it. Because that instinct to flee—to run and hide from anything that made her feel lost or out of control—that had never once faded.

But at the end of the day, Keira was who she was—smart and capable and a fierce protector of those she cared about. And there's nobody he'd want more in his corner when chaos finally arrived on their doorstep.

So it was better this way, he told himself. Better that they stay friends . . . partners. Because something was coming. He could feel it. And while he may not understand exactly how pneuma worked or the strange forces that had brought them both here to this place and this time, he knew it was for a reason. And he could feel it racing toward them, getting closer with every day.

CHAPTER

FOUR

*"*B*lue or green?"*

Keira pulled off her headphones, letting them fall to the bed along with the fading lyrics of the Lumineers' "Sleep on the Floor."

She glanced up from her calculus textbook to see her mother perched in the doorway, a giddy grin stretched across her face and a sequined scarf held in each hand.

"Green," Keira replied after a moment, turning back to the long series of integral equations before her.

"Because of my eyes, right?"

Her mother flounced forward then, collapsing dramatically onto the bed as she flung the green scarf across one shoulder and batted her eyes.

Keira snorted. "Yeah, that and I can't have you stealing my color," she replied, batting her own baby blues up at her mother.

Tammy giggled as she reached out a hand to gently stroke the back of Keira's head.

"I think he may be the one, baby." She crooned. "I really do."

Keira rolled her eyes. "You always think they're the one. Where'd you even find this guy?"

"Oh, you know . . . around."

Keira's eyebrows shot up. If Tammy wasn't telling, then he must be a real winner. Her mother wasn't exactly known for her sensible taste in men.

"Where, Mom?"

"Well, if you must know, it was at the laundromat."

"The laundromat."

"Yes, the laundromat. Well, technically, it was outside of the laundromat . . ."

"What was the guy doing hanging around outside the laundromat?"

"Well, he said he was waiting for some friends. But Keira you should have been there. He was such a gentleman. Offered to help carry everything out to my car. Can you believe it?"

"Did he offer to take the keys, too?" Keira muttered under her breath.

Her mother lightly slapped her shoulder. "Now you be nice. I told you, I have a good feeling about this one."

Keira met her mother's shining eyes once more—always too earnest, too trusting.

"Just be careful, Mom. Promise me."

"Oh, sweetheart," her mother said, wrapping her in a ferocious hug. "You know I always do."

"Just," Keira paused. "Promise me you'll take it slow? For real this time? Besides, it's my senior year. I'd really like to finish it out."

"You will, baby." She crooned, winking conspiratorially. "I told you, I have a good feeling about this one."

And with that, she hopped to her feet and practically sashayed toward the door. Keira shook her head, shoving down the rising wave of anxiety that pulsed in her belly. Then a thought occurred to her.

"Hey," Keira called after her. "Did you see the internet bill? I put it on your nightstand when I got home." She paused, weighing her words as her mother froze in the doorway. "We're late again. I'd normally use my extra tips from the diner, but I've got all these college applications coming up . . ." she bit her lip, watching her mother's tense back, waiting for signs of an imminent explosion. "Do you think you'll be able to cover it this month?"

A long moment passed before her mother suddenly spun around, face alight and beatific smile, the picture of calm. "Oh, we'll figure something out. We always do."

Keira hesitated, eyeing her mother warily. "Are you sure? I could also talk to Jack about getting an advance on next month's—"

"Oh, don't you worry, baby." Her mother said, coming to stroke her hair once more. "I know you need the internet for school. We'll find the money. I promise."

Slowly, Keira nodded, searching her mother's face. "If you're sure."

"Oh sweet baby," Tammy said, smoothing the lines that had formed between Keira's knitted brows with one thumb. "You take such good care of me. Now, what would I do without you?"

And Keira smiled back at her then, knowing she'd never have to find out. Because it would always be the two of them against the world.

Keira glanced around the larder as she slowly, and ever so quietly, eased her way down the tightly twisting staircase. Her pulse thudded in her ears, loud enough that it was a miracle Nazor didn't materialize out of thin air, drawn inexplicably to her moment of utmost embarrassment. Keira was sure her gruff swords master would like nothing better. In the several days since the night mission and her failed bind of Marek Larghaen, Keira had had plenty of time to decide what her next steps should be. And there was really nothing else for it. The Legion needed more information about Marek and his associates if they were going to stop whatever dark schemes were brewing in the uplands—made decidedly more difficult thanks to her muddled failure the other night. So it only stood to reason that she should be the one to get that information for them.

Which is why she was creeping out of her home in the dead of night—boots in hand, and careful to avoid the loose floorboard on the last step, poised to give her away. She crept across the cold stone floor in her stockinged feet until she reached the heavy wooden door to the garden. Opening it just a crack, she slid out into the night, gently closing the door behind her. She kneeled to slide the boots over her stockings, already dampened by the early morning dew.

"Bit early for a stroll, don't ye think?"

The voice cut through the dark, and Keira whirled around, spare boot in hand and at the ready. It took a moment for Keira to recognize the warm baritone voice she knew so well, soft-spoken and with just a hint of a half-forgotten lilt. She blew out the breath she hadn't known she'd been holding and glared at the figure, barely visible in the setting moonlight. He was carelessly lounging on the garden wall to her right, mostly unseen in the pre-dawn mist.

"You should know better than to sneak up on people!" she scolded. Irritated—and slightly embarrassed, truth be told—at being caught unawares, Keira's voice came out sharper than intended.

Danny snorted. "Yeah, the thought of my impending demise was absolutely terrifying...and by shoe, no less. What a way to go."

Keira could hear the laughter in his voice and, tempted though she was to return it, reminded herself of the inconvenience that his sudden appearance now posed to her plans. She turned back to finish lacing her boots with a scowl. Standing, she strode decisively toward the stable, avoiding his gaze. Though she knew he'd follow her, she tramped on through the damp grass. If he wanted to stop her, he'd just have to be direct about it.

She could hear his soft footsteps behind her and felt her annoyance grow. Reaching the stable, she whirled around, ready to get on with it.

"What do you want, Danny?"

Her eyes had adjusted to the moonlight and could now make out the fair-haired, green-eyed problem in front of her. He didn't answer, just stood there, a knowing look on his chiseled face, cheekbones perfectly contoured in the hazy light.

"Well, you followed me out here," Keira snapped. She blushed as she glanced away, annoyed with herself for noticing just how good he looked first thing in the morning.

Danny shrugged. "I was awake anyway. I couldn't sleep and came out for some fresh air. When I saw you, I figured you must have some grand scheme in the works." The left side of his mouth twitched up in that roguish half-grin that all the village girls went wild over. For a half second, she imagined him as he must have been in his old life—bright-faced and eager, the young Army private from South Boston, barely out of high school and off to fight the Nazis overseas. Had he left a sweetheart back home? He never talked about the war, or much about his life before it. Keira shook her head to clear it. There wasn't time for silly musings, not this morning.

"Curs'd block-headed roan," she muttered under her breath, slipping quickly into the local dialect she employed almost exclusively for profanity. Danny's grin widened.

"Nazor forbade you from further meddling." Danny spread his

hands wide, being his usual, annoyingly rational self. "I know you want information, but if you start openly asking after Marek and his associates, it's bound to catch the villagers' notice." He paused, then added, "What with him being dead now and all."

She couldn't deny his logic. *Damn him.*

"I know, I just thought—if I could only hear what people are saying, then maybe I could discover something useful. A hint of who he's been working with. After all—" She swallowed and caught hold of herself. "—It's my fault the Legion's got none of the information we needed. I have to fix this, Danny. If not, there's no way they'll let me compete in the rite this year. Which means *both* of us can look forward to another year of lessons, training exercises, and doing absolutely nothing of worth."

Keira implored him with her eyes, and he studied her, clearly torn between wanting to both help her and protect her.

What else is new? She thought.

He pushed his blonde hair up off his forehead for a moment, only to let it flop right back into his eyes—a nervous mannerism she knew he'd picked up from Elliott.

"Besides," Keira continued, seizing the opportunity to wheedle him further. "What harm could listening do? I'll keep my distance, I swear!"

"I don't know, Keira. You know how secretive the Legion is. There's a reason we went after Marek at night. If people get wind that some secret organization of magic-wielding pneumonancers is interfering with their local affairs, you know there'll be hell to pay—and that's before Nazor gets hold of you."

Keira snorted. "And how, pray tell, would they even know the Legion was involved, Danny? We're not even full Legionnaires and I'll hardly be reading anyone their rights." She could see him giving in, losing his conviction, and her tone softened, almost pleading. "This is all my fault, Danny. You know I can't just do nothing."

She watched him expectantly, looking for that familiar spark she knew so well, that look of slightly pained resignation that said, *I know you have to do this. I don't like it, but I understand.* A moment more, and... *There! There it was.*

He grimaced and gave a slight, barely perceptible nod. Heart lifted,

Keira spun around and jogged to the barn, gathering up the tack for the horses before he could change his mind. She felt Danny close behind her and knew, without looking, that he'd be anchoring his longsword to Boyd's saddle. Despite her earlier reservations, she was suddenly very glad to have him at her back. Almost a foot taller and tightly muscled from years spent laboring on Nazor and Elliott's farm, Danny could be scary when he tried, especially with that intimidatingly long blade he carried. And though she could take care of herself, as she was continually reminding everyone, it was still comforting to know he was there, looking out for her.

That was the thing about Danny, she thought, smiling. *With you or against you, but always beside you.*

It wasn't long before the two of them were riding in companionable silence, taking in the early morning beauty of the forest road, before its peace was disrupted by the low rumble of wagons headed to market. It was then that she glanced over to see the glint of dark red on Danny's forearm.

Keira pulled her horse Cerise up short.

"Your arm," she said, remembering the savage cut Danny had sustained at the hands of one of Marek's bodyguards. She didn't bother to hide the note of concern that colored her words.

Danny glanced down at the bandages and shrugged. "It's fine. Pesky thing just doesn't want to heal. I keep changing the bandages, hoping that'll help, but . . ."

Danny shrugged again but Keira was already dismounting. His brows shot up and his eyes immediately darted around them, searching for some unseen threat.

"What's the matter?"

"I want to look at your arm." Keira declared matter-of-factly.

"I already told you—"

"I don't care what you told me. Let me see it."

Danny sighed with the deeply pained expression of the martyred, but dismounted Boyd and settled himself on a nearby rock. Keira rolled her eyes heavenward, but then came to kneel beside him. Carefully, she took his arm in both hands and slowly unwrapped the bandages. Danny sucked air in through his teeth as she pulled the sticky fabric away, revealing a savage slice that cut deep into his forearm, stretching nearly from elbow to wrist.

"*Danny*," Keira hissed, gut clenching at the sight.

"It looks worse than it—"

"Do *not* finish that sentence please." Keira eyed him darkly before turning her attention back to his arm, lips pursed in concentration. "I want to try something, but it—" She locked eyes with him once more. "Do you trust me?"

Something inscrutable flashed across his eyes and to her surprise he nodded solemnly. "With my life, Keira. You know that."

She swallowed, ignoring the thrill his words sent coursing down her spine. She tried and failed to recapture the lighthearted banter they'd had just a few moments before she took his arm with both hands. "Won't hurt a bit," she assured him.

Danny snorted. "I sincerely doubt that." Still, he eyed her warily.

Keira closed her eyes then, anchoring herself to the ground as she inhaled deeply. She'd tried this form of pneumonancy only once before, on a whim, after coming across a young blue jay whose wing was bent at an odd angle. It had seemed to work then, but this was different. This was *Danny*.

She nudged the tense ball of pneuma just behind her stomach and waited, heart pounding, as it uncoiled and flowed through her fingertips. With a low whistle, her mind seemed to go with it and she could see, or rather *sense*, the layers of muscle, sinew, and skin that coursed through Danny's arm. She let her pneuma morph and change to align perfectly with the molecular structure of that tissue and she began nudging it ever so slightly back into its correct place.

"What are you DOING?" Danny cried and yanked his arm away.

Keira's eyes flew open and she blinked dazedly against the light, still only half conscious as she unraveled her pneuma back into her own body. Danny's eyes were wide as they darted between her and his arm.

When she'd regained her sense of balance, she eyed her handiwork, the taste of disappointment tangy in her mouth. The work of her pneuma had brought the edges of the wound closer aligned, but had failed the final step of actually knitting the tissue together. There was something missing, something different compared to the mere setting of a bird's broken bone. Additional energy perhaps? If she could just—

"KEIRA!" Danny's alarmed tone rocked her back to the present and she realized it was now he who gripped her arm tightly. His skin had gone pale and his eyes were wide as they searched hers.

"What?" She demanded, jerking her arm away.

"I said, what *was* that?"

A smile slowly tugged at the corners of her lip until she was grinning up at him, unperturbed by the scowl that had etched itself deep into his features. "I've been practicing, experimenting really. You see, there was this bird—"

"Obviously," Danny shot back, his voice uncharacteristically sharp. It startled her into silence and she felt her brow knit as she stared back at him. "What I mean, Keira, is what on earth possessed you to experiment with unsanctioned forms of pneumonancy? You *know* the Legion has strict rules. Any deviation, any at all, is enough to get you branded a rogue pneumonancer."

She felt the blood drain from her face at his words.

"I didn't think . . . I mean, I knew they had strict rules, but—"

Danny's expression softened and he gripped both her shoulders gently. "I know you meant nothing by it, Keira. But people take this sort of thing really seriously and the Legion's rules are there for a reason. It's just too easy to get corrupted by Séiro and his chaos. Promise me, Keira. Promise me you won't do it again—not ever."

Keira's gaping mouth snapped shut as she felt her own scowl settle into place. "I refuse to believe that we were given this gift merely for fighting and killing, Danny. I've finally found a way to use pneumonancy to help people. And who knows where it could lead?"

Danny dragged a hand across his face and stared at her for another long moment before replying.

"Look, I know I can't stop you, but just . . . please be careful, Keira. I'm serious. No one can know."

Keira felt herself nodding, as her relief to see Danny's softening expression settled around her like a cool breeze.

"Our secret," she said, grinning broadly. Danny could only shake his head as he readied himself to remount his horse. And though she could still see the tension set in his muscles, Keira knew the anger was gone. All the better, because she knew this was not the last of her experiments. But she would be careful, if nothing else because she needed the Legion's approval to qualify for the rites. But this ability spoke to her on a level beyond any of that, to that same part of herself that had decided in an ER long ago that she would become a physician to protect and care for those too weak to do so themselves. And deep inside, she knew that this skill, this new *gift*, could change everything.

THE SUN WAS JUST PEEKING over the horizon as Keira and Danny rode into Abalás. Keira felt the familiar sense of excitement that always accompanied a trip into the picturesque riverside town, its market vendors preparing to hawk the day's wares. She took a deep breath, inhaling the smell of fish, river kelp, and the salted incense that kept the food fresh as it made its way downriver to Port Galaén.

"Perhaps we should drop in at the bakery first?" Danny suggested. "The fishwives are always gossiping in there."

Keira rolled her eyes. She knew precisely why Danny wanted to stop by the bakery, and it wasn't to hear the latest gossip. Still, she followed him, saying nothing.

No sooner had they entered and browsed the morning's offerings when Lacy—the baker's pretty, doe-eyed daughter—was at their side. She oohed and aahed over Danny's sword, *the same sword*, Keira wanted to remind her, *that he's had the past six months*. Danny clearly didn't mind, though, leaning casually against the wall and tousling his hair in that way Keira knew all the village girls loved. Keira just shook her head and sidled over to the display shelves, hovering near a gaggle of gossiping women. Babies bouncing on their hips, they giggled in pseudo-hushed tones, the way you spoke when you wanted everyone around to hear your news, but wanted *them* to think *you* didn't care a bit. Keira listened intently as she pretended to peruse the pastry options.

"You 'ear the news?" asked one woman darkly. "Taxes set to increase by three tenarii next year."

"I swear," replied another, "them dinas'll never be happy, not 'til they've bled us dry, one by one."

"Well, what do you lot think of what happened to old Marek?"

"Why, what's happened?"

Keira braced herself, not knowing what rumors the Legion had spread regarding the old snake's death.

"Dead," spat the first, smugly satisfied by her own piece of foreknowledge.

"He ain't never," exclaimed her companion, clearly delighted by this morbid insight.

"I heard his own 'lawmen' got him, middle of the night-like. Probably wanted more money, I say, greedy lot like that."

The women all nodded, gasping and sighing in agreement.

"Serves him right, I say," declared a third woman. "He's as bad as them dinas, that one. Always overchargin' taxes, takin' more than his fair share. Everyone knew it," she assured the others, a self-fashioned expert on the subject. "Besides, I heard he's had all sorts of actual dinas from the capital, Bellators even, comin' in and out of his home at all hours. Strange riders in the dead of night, that sort of thing. Clearly mixed up in some unsavory business, that one."

Keira frowned. What would downlanders from the capital, or "dinas" as the women called them, want with a low level crook like Marek? There was no telling, but whatever it was meant the Legion might need to rethink some of their calculus for who may ultimately be behind the recent upswing in highway robbery.

Keira listened for a few more moments before feeling satisfied that there was little else to be gained from the conversation. Scanning the room, her mouth twisted into a scowl when her gaze lit on Danny, who'd somehow accrued an entire flock of preening girls, their high-pitched giggles doing nothing to improve Keira's rapidly souring mood. Danny caught her eye and subtly signaled toward the door. Not waiting for him to politely extricate himself from his female admirers, Keira yanked open the door—a bit too roughly, if she was honest— and let herself out into the shining mid-morning sun.

Keira glanced up at the sound of Danny emerging from the bakery.

"'Bout time," she grumbled. "You find out anything?"

Danny only cocked an eyebrow in amusement.

"Y'know, my mam used to tell me to mind my face, lest it stay like that."

Keira's scowl only deepened and Danny chuckled before promptly informed her that one girl's father worked for the local Tiarna as his personal surveyor. He'd heard from his friend—the lord's personal valet—that the Tiarna had called for an investigation into the sudden death of his chief tax collector, Marek. He'd also launched an inquiry into the funding source of Marek's personally procured bodyguards.

"Seems not all of Marek's superiors were aware of his lawmen's activities," Danny said, looking darkly amused.

Keira snorted and answered dryly, "Well, not exactly an eyewitness account there. Couldn't your little friend have been a teensy bit more specific?" Keira quickly regretted the note of bitterness that crept into her voice at the end and glanced quickly at Danny. His eyes fixed on her and she immediately dropped her gaze as she kicked at the dirt beneath her feet, looking anywhere but at him.

"Y'know, Keira, they're not all bad. You don't have to hold them all at a distance." Though his words were gentle, they stung all the same.

"I know that, Danny," she snapped.

"Then why not try to get to know them? Make some friends, Keira. You might find you like it here more than you think."

Keira pursed her lips, biting back the snarky reply on the tip of her tongue. After all, she had all the friends she needed here. "They don't like me, Danny, they never have. Nazor and I both, with our weapons and clothes. We're just too different."

"They just don't know you."

Now it was Keira's turn to stare, her brows raised incredulously. Danny sighed.

"I've known you for a long time, Keira. I know how much you hate depending on anyone, of owing any debts. But you can't live a life that way, even one as strange as ours. It's too lonely."

"Why thank you, Sigmund." Keira muttered, tightening the sword hilt at her belt to avoid his eyes. Danny sighed.

"Look, some girls just went into the dressmakers' over there. Why not follow them? Make small talk. See what you can find out."

Keira blanched as the girls' peals of laughter echoed across the square.

"Look Danny, I really don't think—"

"It has to be you. I can't very well be seen hanging 'round a dress shop now, can I?"

Keira shot him a look but his face was all innocence. She sighed, unable to come up with a good reason not to—other than the roiling in her gut, that was.

"Fine, I'll do it, Danny." She pronounced, but silenced his gleeful grin with a curt, "But don't be expecting any miracles today."

THE INSIDE of the dress shop practically bubbled with feminine delight, as crowds of women and girls oohed and aahed over the latest rich-hued fabrics just arrived from Port Galaén. The giggling alone was enough to make Keira break out in a cold sweat, but she forced her attention to a nearby pile of fabrics in the muted forest greens and browns so much more common in the uplands. As she carefully fingered the smooth fabric, she listened carefully to the conversation of a nearby group of young women who looked about her age.

"My ma insists purple's all the rage 'mongst the dinas," one girl pronounced authoritatively.

"But where could you wear somethin' like that here? Folk *would* talk."

The others murmured in agreement and Keira watched as the first girl straightened, her chin lifting slightly as she declared, "Well, good thing I don't much care for what folk think."

Keira smiled slightly to herself. Maybe she had more in common with some of these girls than she thought.

So lost was she in her own thoughts that she barely noticed that the girls' conversation had lowered to barely audible whispers.

"What is *she* doin' *here*?"

"Certainly not buyin' no dress."

"Don't think I've ever even *seen* her in a dress."

Keira glanced toward the door, curious who the new arrival might be, but there was no one. Then the sickening realization hit.

They're talking about me.

Keira quickly backtracked the handful of steps she'd unknowingly shuffled in their direction, hiding her burning cheeks as she leafed almost frantically through piles of fabric, trying to ignore the giggling from behind her.

"Can I help you with somethin' love?" The matronly seamstress appeared at her side, carefully eyeing Keira's worn trousers and tunic. "'Fraid we don't make men's clothin' here, dear. Best try the tailor down the street."

From behind, the giggling suddenly erupted into peals of laughter that echoed around the small dressmaker's shop. Keira thought she might be sick.

"Now what's so—"

Keira didn't wait to hear the question, instead pushing past the seamstress and barreling out into the street. She gulped down air like a drowning man and blinked the stinging from her eyes. She should have known better. She *did* know better. Curse Danny and his meddling. Screw all of them, for that matter. Why did she even care what those girls thought of her? She didn't need them. She was better than this. She *had* to be better than this. Because she'd learned a long time ago that no one was going to protect her except *her*.

"Everything all right?"

Danny suddenly appeared at her side, brows knit together and voice tight with concern.

"Fine," Keira muttered, wiping the back of her sleeve across her face. "Let's just get out of here."

Danny hesitated, clearly torn, but Keira pushed past him, making for the pair of horses tied up near the bakery. Reaching Cerise, she leaned her head against the horse's flaxen mane. Eyes closed, she inhaled deeply, ignoring the sound of snide laughter that still reverberated in her ears.

"Hey," Danny murmured from behind her. "I got these for you."

Blinking, she glanced down at the small satchel he held in one outstretched palm. As he tugged on the string, the intoxicating scent of rich spices wafted toward her. She sighed, not bothering to fight the wide grin that spread across her face.

"Leky nuts!" She exclaimed, before eyeing Danny suspiciously. "But you hate them."

He snorted, "That's because I have taste. But see, I've pretty much given up on you at this point. So I figured, what the heck?"

She smiled in silent thanks for the welcome distraction from the dress shop fiasco. Then she helped herself, relishing the low burn in the back of her throat. Danny shook his head with a grimace, marveling as she popped a handful of the eye-watering tree nuts into her mouth.

"It's called flavor, Danny," she said between mouthfuls. "You should learn to appreciate it."

"Regular old pine nuts are plenty flavorful for me. Thank you very much."

Keira rolled her eyes. "Such an Irish boy. Next you'll be telling me you prefer good old corned beef and cabbage."

"I take that as a compliment." Danny declared, grinning at her. "And for your information, my mam makes the best stew you ever tasted, cabbage and all . . . and with no fire extinguisher needed."

"Well, Mom and I were takeout queens—Ethiopian, Thai, Indian—nothing was out of bounds."

"So you're basically flame retardant at this point?"

Keira shrugged, flipping her hair as she grinned back at him. "Guess so."

Danny's teasing had served its purpose by sufficiently distracting her from the humiliating episode in the dress shop. But remembering the true purpose for their visit, Keira quickly sobered. Shading her eyes against the sun, she looked up toward Merchant's Hill and the home of the Tiarna, the local lord himself.

"Didn't you say the girls in the bakery mentioned the Tiarna was investigating Marek's death? Well, maybe it's time we paid him a visit."

Danny nodded, quickly untying Boyd. "Suppose we might as well. Though I doubt he'll tell us much, even given Elliott and Nazor's connections around here."

Then he stopped, cursing, as he reached down to inspect one of Boyd's hooves.

"He's thrown a shoe," he declared finally, grimacing. "I'll have to take him by the blacksmith's before he's ok to ride."

"That's fine, I'll wait here with Cerise."

"Nah, it's already getting late. You go on ahead and start asking around the shops on Merchant's Hill. I'll be there shortly and we can confront the Tiarna together."

Keira nodded, and with mouth set in a determined line, she mounted Cerise and headed up the road.

She was just cresting the top of the hill when a low rumbling made Cerise skitter to the side. Keira grappled with the reins, struggling to stay seated as a thunderous roar echoed through the valley below.

Then the screaming started.

Keira nervously stroked Cerise's mane as she searched in vain for the source of the noise. Then she spotted it—the construction site of an enormous home that sat on the edge of Merchant's Hill. She urged Cerise up the street, still patting her neck in reassurance. As they neared the site, she realized with a start that it was the Tiarna's home that was being renovated. Screams filled the air, and a sickening lump settled in her gullet. Her eyes settled on the pile of stonework that had fallen from a scaffold. One corner rope snapped, its cargo tumbling to the ground below, where a crowd of anxious workers had gathered.

Keira's eyes widened.

No, no, no, she thought. *There are kids. Why are there kids here?*

Keira urged Cerise onward, her eyes darting from person to person as her mind tried to deny what they insisted to be true. There had been kids playing at the base of the house walls, directly in the falling stonework's path. She could see them crying, clinging to their mothers. *Who are they? The workers' children? Why were they playing there?*

Not the point, she decided, riding up to the nearest woman.

"Is anyone missing?" Keira called down to her. The woman looked up, tears in her eyes as she clutched a wailing boy to her chest.

"Lil' Anya Cuball, the poor wynnie, haulin' pebbles just below when it fell. They're tryna dig 'er out now, but..." Her lip quivered as she glanced down at the shaking child in her arms; he couldn't have been more than five or six.

Keira didn't wait for her to finish. Spurring Cerise forward again, she galloped up the remaining hill toward where the crowd of laborers desperately shifted through the rubble. A shout rang out as one man stumbled away from the wreckage, arms clutching a girl about ten years old. She lay limp, straw-colored braids obscured by the gray soot that dusted the length of her tiny body—her tattered blue dress stained red with blood.

"Molly," Keira breathed. Could it be? The girl had her hair color, those same braids. But it couldn't be...could it?

Without thinking, she was off her horse and sprinting toward the young girl, who'd now attracted a wailing crowd—the laborers arguing over what to do, who to call for. Keira had just started elbowing her way to the front when she suddenly remembered Danny's warning.

You promised you'd be careful. You cannot *risk unsanctioned pneumonancy.*

She swallowed, indecision warring within her. After all her efforts to make things right with the Legion, would she really risk everything now?

But this was a *kid,* a kid who was *dying.* And a kid who looked an awful lot like Molly, the closest thing she'd ever had to a sister.

I can't lose her. Not again.

She couldn't stand by and do nothing, not when she alone might help. Danny would understand. He *had* to. And the Legion . . . well, she'd deal with whatever fallout came later.

Her breath caught when she spied the crumpled child in the center of the circle. She'd volunteered in the local emergency room in her former life, all part of her grand plan to go to medical school one day. She'd seen her share of gore, but the sight before her made even her stomach turn. The side of the girl's face was swollen, hair matted with blood and dirt from a crushing blow to the side.

Keira kneeled beside her, ignoring the murmurs of the watching crowd. As she inspected the girl's bruised face, she desperately tried to remember her lessons in first aid. She felt for the whisper of breathing as her fingers sought a pulse in the girl's birdlike wrist. *Yes!* She felt both, wispy and thread-like, but definitely present. She did a quick sweep of the girl's body, feeling for hidden wounds or broken bones. The head wound was the most obvious, but Keira was more worried about the instability she felt when she pressed the girl's hip bones together. A broken pelvis could be deadly, she knew, especially in a child this small. She could easily bleed out internally with no sign on the outside. And that wasn't even counting the blood-soaked dress that clung to the girl's legs. Keira quickly located the source—a large gash on the inside of the girl's leg.

She pressed a knee down into her groin, hard, trying to stop the crimson flow, but Keira could already see the effects of the girl's blood loss—her paling skin, the thin line of sweat that beaded her brow and upper lip. She would lose her, and soon, if she didn't do something quickly.

Think, Altman, think, she ordered, racking her brain for something, *anything* she could use to stop what everyone knew was coming. Her pneuma could fix what was broken, that much she knew. But while broken pottery and torn fabric were simple enough, her success with the bird's wing had been limited and she suspected a shattered pelvis was another matter entirely.

Then a thought occurred to her. What about blood vessels? She knew they were tiny, only a few cells thick at the most. Could she mend them with her pneuma? She knew surgeons often cauterized bleeding vessels, burning the ends until they sealed themselves off. Based on the amount of blood, though, she suspected this girl had severed her femoral artery. Even with her basic pre-med biology, Keira knew that cauterizing such a gigantic vessel would merely cut off blood flow to the limb, leading to gangrene and even death.

No, the only chance this girl had was for Keira to try to knit the two ends of the blood vessel together, restoring blood flow to the rest of the leg. How much energy would that take? Certainly more than realigning the edges of Danny's flesh wound had. Keira knew that order—in this case, the bonds to connect cells together—could not be created out of nothing. Order could only be generated from the energy released by progressive disorder. To create, one first had to destroy.

But did she dare? She was talking about trying to harness the energy of chaos, a feat that many had tried and failed to accomplish. She was on the verge of despair when the words from an old lecture of Elliott's came suddenly to mind.

Like flows deftly unto like.

It was a lesson from years ago, one in which Elliott had explained that energy from broken bonds was most easily channeled into the formation of similar ones, even if they belonged to someone else.

It was worth a shot.

Reaching deep into herself, Keira drew upon her pneuma. It quickly sprang to life, following the lead of a hesitant whistle. It twisted and turned, knotting itself into the shape desired. Placing her hand on the girl's blood-soaked leg, Keira sent it deep into the confines of bone and sinew, feeling it wind its way deftly between planes of muscle and fascia until she realized with a start that she'd found what she was looking for. The two ends of the severed artery hung ragged, their shattered walls dark with poorly clotted blood. Eyes closed, she reached quickly for the dagger at her hip, knowing with absolute certainty what she must do.

She acted without hesitation, savagely piercing her own palm, dragging the blade's edge smoothly, deftly, across her skin. Even as blood poured from the wound, in her mind's eye, Keira watched as the ragged edges of the girl's arteries began slowly, surely, knitting themselves together. She felt no fear, even the pain blunted by the thrill that was her creation. She was Pneumos herself, wielding destruction, bending it to her will and forging order out of chaos.

The artery repaired, Keira lifted her knee and felt the crimson tide sprang forth, rushing to fill the vessel's void, perfusing the limb and bringing life to deadness. Again she shifted her mind upward, reaching, searching through muscle and bone for the injury she knew to be there.

And there it was: a branch off of a main artery, sliced by cracked bone and pumping oxygen-rich blood into the cavernous recesses of the girl's cracked pelvis. Deeper still, Keira's knife dug, and she felt her own body protest. But drunk as she was with the power that coursed from her severed flesh and into this girl's tiny body, she could hear nothing over the roaring in her ears.

Brawny hands shook her roughly from her trance, a voice ordering, "Keira! Stop now! It's too much!"

Her eyes flickered open, meeting the terrified olive-green gaze before her. Dazed, she watched more than felt as Danny pulled her up and away from the young girl. Pushing through the crowd with one hand, he kept her firmly pinned to his side with the other. Looking back, Keira saw with a distant sense of satisfaction that Anya's eyes were open. Though crying and clearly in pain, she could answer questions from a woman who smiled in delight even as tears coursed down her own face, her hands clutching the girl as if she might disappear at any moment.

Danny pushed his way through the crowd and as they left, Keira heard the growing whispers, filled with awe, wonder, and a hint of fear. "*They're back*," the whispers declared. "*Spirit binders*," came the echo. "*The spirit binders have returned.*"

By the time they made it to the horses and led them far from prying eyes, Keira was staring at her palm as if it belonged to someone else, watching as it turned slick with blood. Danny sat her gently on the ground, and she watched as blood flowed down her forearm with the absurd sense that she probably should do something to stop it. Then he was rinsing off the cut with the water from his canteen, mouth set in a firm line and eyes shadowed. Keira flinched at the sting of the cold liquid and saw his jaw clench, but still he said nothing. She had the strangest urge to cackle at the absurdity of the situation, but seeing Danny's face, quickly thought better of it. Only when her hand was clean and bandaged did he finally look her straight in the eye, and she had to stop herself from shivering at the look he gave her.

"What," he demanded, grappling with intense emotion, "the hell was that?"

THE RIDE HOME was not exactly a pleasant one. Keira had tried her best to explain to Danny why she'd *had* to save that little girl. She'd sought to paint a picture for him of just how amazing it had felt to be *inside* Anya's body, sending her pneuma through muscle and bone, healing as she went. She tried to articulate the feeling of power and purpose, the certainty that this was what she was *meant* to do—that her ability was the reason they'd stumbled upon Anya in the first place. Danny had not been convinced.

A sense of dread mounted as Keira thought about what awaited them the closer they got to home. Nazor would kill her. She'd disobeyed a direct order, the primary directive that guided their actions in Loren, and the one thing Nazor cared about more than anything: Do not expose the Legion. There would be no talking her way out of this one. And Elliott . . . well, Elliott would be worse. He wouldn't yell or curse, just stand there, looking disappointed, wondering if a mistake really had been made, if Keira wasn't right for the Legion. Maybe Pneumos had been wrong to bring her here.

Keira shifted nervously, chewing on her lip as she tried to think of how she'd break the news to them. *Maybe at dinner*, she decided. She'd wait until all the day's chores were done, and Nazor had had her evening mudlo. That ought to put her in an excellent mood.

She had no more time to think about it as they rounded a corner in the path and came upon the distant, yet unmistakable, figures of Elliott and Nazor. They were arguing vehemently outside the barn. Danny looked at Keira and opened his mouth to say something— probably to ask if they should try to sneak by. He never got the chance.

"What have you done?" The question came from Elliott, deadly in its calm. And though Danny and Keira were still twenty yards or more away, they heard his words clearly. Danny reached up to push his hair off his forehead, obviously as nervous as Keira.

This is bad, Keira thought. *I've really done it this time.*

Deciding to accept the inevitable, the two slowly made their way toward the barn. Keira's mind was racing, trying desperately to find the right words.

"Look, I know you're mad," she said apologetically. "I know we aren't supposed to use unsanctioned pneumonancy. I broke the Legion's rules, and I'm sorry."

Elliott gave her a considering look while Nazor remained unfazed, face hard as ever.

I have to make them see, Keira thought, *to know the value of what I've discovered.*

"But you have to understand—the girl, she was *dying*, like really dying, and I, well, I—I *healed* her."

Nazor's face blanched, and Elliott's brow furrowed. He leaned in slightly. "With herbs and medicines?"

Uh-oh. Keira paused. *Hadn't they heard? What else were they angry about, if not that?*

"I mean . . . I *healed* her. With my pneuma."

Nazor's breath escaped in a low hiss, and Elliott's mouth pressed into a firm line, brows knit tightly together.

"So, let me get this straight." Nazor's voice was low, deadly in its fury. "Not only did you two go into town, *against* orders, on some glory hunt for Marek's associates, but you endangered the entire Legion's operations in Loren?"

Her voice was silky smooth. She could have been talking about the weather for all anyone else could tell, but Keira knew better, knew that edge well, and took its meaning. Danny shifted his weight uneasily. Keira's face was burning, and she searched in vain for the speech she'd meticulously prepared on the ride back, but came up decidedly empty-handed.

"I see." Nazor's dark eyes were hard, shining like obsidian. "Yet again, in search of her own glory, Keira Altman puts her own wants, needs, and desires ahead of *everybody* else."

"Now, wait a second!" Danny protested.

Cold shock had settled in Keira's spine at her words, to be replaced just as quickly by abject rage. "That is *not* what happened!"

Nazor regarded her coldly. "Isn't it? You failed at your binding, a man *died*, and to cover your own shame, you made yourself the hero of the story, as usual. No regard for who else may be hurt."

"Are you kidding me?" Keira sputtered. "A little girl was *dying*, and you wish I'd done . . . nothing? Or no, you just wish I hadn't been there in the first place!" Keira's fingers felt numb, and she knew her hands were shaking. "Not if it breaks Legion rules. Pneumos forbid we actually use our *brains* for a change, rather than letting *them* do all the thinking for us."

Nazor glared at her, matched look for look by Keira's own furious gaze. Nazor started to reply, but Keira beat her to it.

"Just think how useful this will be in the rites? The ability to heal myself? To heal someone else? If I could just practice more—"

Nazor scoffed. "You think you're going anywhere near the rites after this little stunt?" She demanded, eyes narrowed into slits. "Think again."

Her words fell like a blow as their meaning sunk in. No rites meant no way home. No way to find her mother or Molly. Keira could feel the tears welling up and she furiously blinked them away. She would not give Nazor the satisfaction.

"This form of pneumonancy is forbidden, Keira." Elliott said quietly, interrupting the epic stare-down between Keira and Nazor. "You know that."

"I know no such thing!" She insisted, rounding now on Elliott. "All I know is what you two tell me. And . . . and I don't believe it! How do you explain whatever pneumonancy brought us here in the first place?" Her chest was heaving and her hands had balled into fists. "Whatever process brings Legionnaires from one world to another, creating nearly identical bodies out of nothing, it has to involve some-thing similar, doesn't it?"

Her eyes searched Elliott's, pleading, but he was already shaking his head. "It's not the Legion who brings legionnaires across worlds, Keira, but Pneumos herself."

"Guess I should take it up with her then, huh?" Keira muttered.

"Watch that tone," Nazor snarled, leveling Keira with a glare that she readily returned.

She started to reply, but was interrupted by Elliott's quiet, almost imperceptible voice.

"How?"

Keira glanced at him, still squared off against Nazor's towering frame. "How what?"

"How did you do it? How did you harness the energy to heal her?"

His lanky frame looked almost small as he gazed sadly at her. Keira tried and failed to swallow the ball that burned in the back of her throat. She resolutely refused to look at her hand, yet somehow suspected that Elliott already knew the answer to his question. Slowly, she raised her bandaged hand to show him. Keira heard a sharp inhale from Nazor and watched Elliott squeeze his own eyes shut, shaking his head slightly.

"So, to save one human being, you would harm another?"

Keira could feel this all slipping away from her. "It was my choice. I was willing—"

"And what about next time? What happens when it isn't *your* body or *your* choice? Or when the price is far higher than a minor cut?" For the first time that Keira could recall, Elliott actually looked *angry*. "The rules exist for a reason, Keira. When it comes to our pneuma, we do not—I repeat, we *do not*—yield to our more destructive impulses, even when well-intended." He spread his hands helplessly. "We serve Pneumos, Goddess of Order, but her lover, Séiro, the God of Chaos, is just as cunning. You know that. And it is far too easy to let ourselves be seduced by the promise of power, even when we hope to wield it for good. It's too difficult to control."

Keira's face was scarlet now. She didn't know what to say that would somehow make it better, make the truth seem more innocuous. And just like that, her discovery seemed less ingenious and more like the self-righteous masochism her friends obviously saw it as. It had never really been about the little girl; it was about *her*—Keira, who after being callously plucked from one world, one life, and dropped unceremoniously into another, finally felt some measure of control over death itself.

Trying and failing to ease the lead that had settled in her stomach, she mumbled something about seeing to the horses. Grabbing both sets of reins in hand, she jogged them over to the stable. The others let her go. She'd barely made it inside when the waterworks started in full, and she sobbed her way through untacking the horses. She wept for far more than her own embarrassment and ineptitude, but also for the life and family she'd lost and would surely never see again. Not now, not after what she'd done.

~

MEANWHILE, just south of Abalás, a rider spurred his destrier on, gathering speed as he barreled down the southern road toward the port capital of Crîd Eálas. He'd barely believed his ears back in the tavern—the whole town had been buzzing with news of the miraculous survival of little Anya Cuball, and the spirit binder who'd saved her, slicing into her own flesh to save the wynnie. It wasn't until he'd seen the child himself, awake and talking despite her near-death experience, that he'd known what must be done. So south he flew, to convey the news of the spirit binders to Lady Junia—a clear sign the Legion had indeed returned to Loren.

SIX

As the days lengthened and temperatures grew more heated, so too did the murmurings in and around town. Word had quickly spread around the upland river region of Anya Cuball's miraculous recovery and the mysterious spirit binder who'd saved her. Keira was aware of this—she couldn't help but be. The whispers that followed her around town and the hushed silence that greeted her in every store were clear evidence they all knew what she did and precisely who she was.

As much as it pained her to admit it, she couldn't help but concede that perhaps Nazor had been right. She had exposed them, maybe even put them all in danger. She'd threatened the work of the Legion in the area. Old stories about Elliott and Nazor kept cropping up too, tales of the spirit binders who saved Loren from the Cross-Sea invaders and rescued a princess from the dragons of Mt. Ánghen. Nazor scoffed when Keira asked her about these, explaining that legends had a way of getting out of hand.

However, there was one thing all the river folk seemed to agree on: If spirit binders had returned to Loren, they might just as easily be more threat than friend. In time, Keira and Danny took to avoiding Abalás. It wasn't so bad, though Keira missed the sights and sounds of market day, the flood of people traveling upriver from exciting places. But until the rumors quelled, she'd have to settle for the mundanities of home life and her endless training.

"Ouch!" Keira cried, grimacing as she shook out her right hand. She let her sword tip drift toward the ground as she eyed Danny accusingly. "You did that on purpose."

"Did not," he replied, twirling his blade in lazy arcs as an impish grin tugged at his lips.

"Keep your guard up!" Nazor barked, tapping the bottom of Keira's blade.

Keira immediately dropped back into a fighting stance as she and Danny circled each other.

"That's it, keep a distance."

Keira could feel Nazor's eyes on her, ever-probing, always finding her wanting. She glanced toward the older woman nervously, nearly missing Danny's quick center jab. At the last minute, she knocked the blade to the side, its tip coming dangerously close to her left shoulder.

"Eyes on your opponent!" Nazor roared. "You trying to get skewered, Altman?"

Keira bit her lip, feeling a blush coloring her cheeks as she refocused on Danny.

"Oya, look at Danny. See how he keeps his stance? Why can you never remember, girl?"

Keira quickly adjusted her stance as she glanced up at Danny. His eyes were soft and he gave her a slight, encouraging nod.

"Come on, Nazor," he said warmly. "What's that you always said? An Igbo warrior could fight blindfolded if she had to. Seems Keira's halfway there."

Nazor snorted and Keira couldn't help but roll her eyes, even as she smiled at him in thanks.

"Indeed," Nazor replied, smiling at Danny despite herself. Her voice filled was with a warmness that never seem to be leveled in Keira's direction. "Well, the Igbo I knew would also know better than to let their guard down, even for a moment."

With this last, Nazor shot her training staff toward Keira, who just barely blocked it. She flushed as her feet stumbled backward, cheeks burning at Nazor's resulting chuckle.

She eyed her mentor, taking in the heavy chain mail against

Nazor's ebony skin, the deadly blade at her hip, and the carefully arranged crown of braids atop her head. She looked every inch the Igbo warrior. Meanwhile, even after years of training, Keira often still felt like a bumbling colt.

"I didn't know swords were still in use in the sixties," Keira muttered under her breath and was rewarded by Danny's answering grin.

"In the war we used whatever was available to us," Nazor replied thinly, her lilting Nigerian accent gone cold. Her hearing was clearly sharp as ever. "And if you knew what true chaos looked like, you wouldn't be so cavalier about your training."

Keira quickly sobered. Nazor came from a time of civil war back in their old world. And though she rarely spoke of it, Keira knew the horrors she'd seen still weighed heavily on her.

So she forced herself to refocus, exhaling deeply as she shook the tension from her shoulders. She settled again into a fighter's stance as Danny sidestepped around her.

He lunged forward and she danced out of the way, letting him chase her until just the right moment. As he stepped forward, she lunged to meet him, batting his sword out of the way as she swept one leg low, catching the back of his knee and buckling it.

She whooped with joy as he went down, scrambling out of the way . . . but not fast enough. A hand shot out, wrapping around her wrist as she felt herself jerked forward. She collapsed on top of him, a tangled bundle of limbs as their laughs echoed through the nearby trees.

From behind, Keira heard Nazor mutter something darkly under her breath. She didn't understand the words, and wasn't sure she wanted to.

"I can see we're finished for the day," Nazor said dryly. She eyed the two of them still cackling maniacally, their sweaty faces now coated with dirt from the training yard. "I'll leave the cleaning up to you two then, give you something to *really* laugh about."

They lay collapsed in a heap for a moment longer, catching their breath as the sound of Nazor's footsteps receded. It was then that Keira noticed she was rather *on top* of Danny, her hand pressed firmly against his chest—his rather broad chest, she noted. Keira silenced that line of thinking immediately, feeling a slow burn creep up her face as she worked to disentangle their legs. Danny let her go, seemingly unaware of her embarrassment.

"It's good to be back in training," he said suddenly, brushing off his pant legs as he stood. "Y'know, like old times."

Keira snorted. "With me getting my butt whooped, you mean?"

Danny grinned broadly. "Well, I wasn't gonna put it *quite* like that. But since you mention it . . ."

Keira kicked a pile of dirt at him, dirtying his newly cleaned pant legs. Danny froze, eyeing her with one eyebrow raised. She stuck her tongue out at him. Then slowly, Danny reached for a massive dirt clump that lay innocuously nearby. Danny's expression was all innocence as he took a step and then another toward her.

"No, no . . . oh no, you don't, Danny O'Leary!" This last came out as a squeal as Danny lunged for her and Keira jumped back, laughing as he snagged her around the waist. Keira squirmed, covering her face against the rain of dirt that settled in her hair as Danny crumbled his dirt clod above her.

Keira gave him a giant shove, landing them both in a laughing heap. They lay that way for a long moment, catching their breath as they stared up at the thick branches overhead, emerald leaves dancing lazily in the light early summer breeze.

"I've missed this," Danny said suddenly, chest rising and falling in a mesmerizing rhythm beside her. "You and me. The last few weeks have felt . . ." he eyed her carefully, clearly judging her reaction. ". . . a little *off*."

His words immediately made Keira tense and she slowly rolled to one side to sit up, tugging her knees securely into her chest as she traced designs in the dirt with one finger. She felt his eyes heavy on her back.

"I have to be ready, Danny."

"You will be," he said, reaching up to place a warm hand on her shoulder. She shivered despite herself at the contact. "But there's no rush, either. We've basically got eternity, right? Endless lives and all that? I mean, Nazor and Elliott have been going strong for a few hundred years at least."

She glanced at him and he grinned broadly at her. She felt her own smile crack and she glanced away, certain he could see the guilt etched all over her face. Because she wasn't planning on eternity, or anything close to it, in fact.

"Hey," he murmured, forcing her eyes back to his. "I know you're eager to complete the rites, get on with being full Legionnaires and all that. But whadya say we make sure we can hold our own before getting in over our heads, yeah?" His smile was kind but Keira felt herself stiffen.

"And by *we*, I suppose you mean *me*, right?"

"What? No, Keira, I mean *we*." His eyes darkened in confusion as he searched hers. "We both got a good deal to learn still. I'm still hopeless with even basic binds. You know that." He grinned at her, waiting for the teasing response she always had quick at hand. When it never came, his smile slowly faded.

"Keira, talk to me, please. You're my best friend . . ." his words trailed off in a dejected air that made Keira's chest tighten. Her fingers went instinctively to the locket at her neck, tracing its curling design with one thumb as she let the feel of it calm her.

But she couldn't look at him, couldn't try to explain why she couldn't wait, why she needed to complete the rites—and *soon*. Because somewhere in the universe her mother was waiting for her, *needed* her. But Danny, he wouldn't—or rather *couldn't*—understand why she would choose to leave them behind.

Why old habits were so hard to break.

But was she really ready to leave them all behind? Danny was her best friend and Elliott and Nazor had both done so much for her. They were the closest thing she had had to a family in a very long time. Keira blanched, her stomach suddenly feeling very hollow. But she gritted her teeth.

I made it here once, she thought. *I could do it again. It wouldn't be goodbye, not . . . not really. Just temporary. Once I make sure Mom is settled, back on her feet, I . . . I could come back.*

But even as the thought occurred to her, she knew it was nonsense. Elliott, Nazor, Danny—they all came from times and places far different from here. If she somehow managed to leave, to return to her home, the likelihood she saw any of them again was crushingly small. She shoved the thought away before it unravelled what little control she had left and scrambled to her feet.

"Keira! Wait, just—"

But she was already gone. Snagging her gear from the nearest fence post she hurried back toward the house. She could feel Danny's worried gaze but refused to look back, convincing herself it was better for both of them this way.

Keira trudged back to the house after one such training session, leather riding jerkin and chaps swung over one shoulder. She and Danny had been practicing mounted battle maneuvers, and they were both soaked through from exertion. Keira was so exhausted that at first, she barely registered the group of red-cloaked Bellators tending to their horses in the pasture outside the barn. She pulled up short when she saw them, their plated cuirasses glinting in the mid-afternoon light. They would have stood out in a crowd even without their uniforms, the men with their close-cropped hairstyles, and the women in the tight plaits that Lorenan military service required. Keira turned a questioning look toward Danny, whose brow was furrowed in an expression matching her own. Of course, she'd seen the odd Bellatori messenger riding south through Abalás toward the port towns of the fertile inlet, but there were no permanent garrisons in this area, and she'd never seen so many Bellators gathered in one place.

With a sinking feeling, Keira wondered if this was yet another ramification of her actions in Abalás. Suspecting that Elliott and Nazor were their best bet for getting some answers, they hurried toward the house. Keira and Danny barreled through the front door to find Elliott seated at the table with what appeared to be a high-ranking Bellatori officer. The impressive plume of his metal helmet pooled around the earthenware dishes that remained uncollected from the midday meal. Behind Elliott, Nazor stood just outside the fire's light, coolly regarding the seated officer's companion, who stood near the window of the far wall. The air of hospitality only thinly veiled the obvious abnormality of the situation.

What are they doing here?

Keira swallowed hard, fingers inching toward the dagger at her hip.

Something isn't right.

"Ah, here they are!" Elliott exclaimed warmly, every bit the picture of calm. "These are our wards. Danny, Keira, may I present Millus Flavius of the Northern Imperium? He and his Bellators have come all the way from Crîd Eálas and kindly stopped to pay us a visit."

Keira stared at him blankly. His voice gave no hint that anything was amiss. To hear him, you'd think they received soldiers on their doorstep regularly. Looking closer, it was only the tightness about his eyes that signaled all was not as it should be.

Millus Flavius turned stiffly to face them. His face had the grizzled, weather-beaten look of a career soldier, and though he must have been near fifty, his muscles were still tightly coiled. He was cleanly shaven with closely cropped gray hair. Though he seemed less than interested in them personally, he had an air of satisfaction about him that told Keira he'd likely been expecting them.

"Well," he began gruffly, "now that you're all here, we may proceed to business." Keira heard the high-arched syllables of a down-lander in his voice, uncommon in this area except for the visiting merchants who traded their goods upriver, and wondered again at his purpose this far from the major trading routes. She didn't have to wonder long, though, as he quickly produced a rolled scroll complete with a wax seal, which he stoutly displayed on the table before Elliott.

With an air of forced formality, he continued. "We are charged by the Regio of Loren with escorting his son, the Lord Landrianus, to a meeting of the Council of Benadur and then home to Crîd Eálas." Flavius gave Elliott a considering look, clearly weighing his reaction.

Elliott was all wide eyes and feigned admiration. "My, the future Regio himself, how marvelous! I suppose we're just a stop en route then," he chattered. "Of course, you all are welcome to whatever hospitality we can offer."

"That is not why we've come." Flavius's voice was hard, all edge and no give as he stared intently at Elliott's serene face.

"Why have you, then?"

Keira saw the twitch in Elliott's neck, saw Nazor's hand shift to rest on the hilt of her claymore. Eyes darting around the room, Keira calculated how many steps it would take to reach Elliott. Three, she decided, weighing whether to throw her dagger first at Flavius or his silent lieutenant standing by the opposite window.

A dim flicker to her left had Keira snapping her head in that direction. It took her eyes a moment to register the third Bellator in the room. Or was she? Indeed, it was a she, but her clothing was far from the regimented uniformity of the Bellatori masses. *How had she missed her?* This woman was clothed in all black, save for her leather gauntlets and cuirass. Yet the most striking feature was the wrapped headscarf that obscured all but her eyes—the traditional headdress of the Cross-Sea warriors.

Keira inhaled sharply. She'd heard tales of these fighters from travelers abroad—their honor-bound system of chivalry, the beaded head talismans that marked their kills for all to see. The woman carried a long, curved sword, and if she decided to use it, Keira suspected she would have far less than three steps' worth of time to make her move. There was a twinkle in her eyes that Keira suspected the woman was thinking the same thing.

With a start, Keira realized Flavius was still speaking. She turned back to face the room, while simultaneously keeping an eye on the woman in black.

"On our journey, we have also been charged with investigating accounts of pneumonancy in the northern river regions." His tone made it clear what he thought of such a side quest.

"Really?" Elliott's voice sounded uninterested, bored even, and Keira saw Flavius's jaw tighten.

"Indeed, and locals in the town of—" He paused, having clearly forgotten the name, and snapped his fingers at his lieutenant.

"Abalás, sir," the man put in helpfully. His face had an eagerness that Keira thought bordered slightly on worship. This Flavius certainly could inspire loyalty, she decided, or else he was merely far more powerful than she'd realized.

"Yes, Abalás. Your neighbors seemed to think that I should call on you and your, uh—wards." He turned again to eye Keira and Danny, both still standing in the doorway.

"I can't imagine why. We're just humble farmers." Elliott was being flippant now, and Keira saw Flavius's face tighten as his eyes flitted to Nazor in her chain mail tunic, belted claymore at the ready.

"Indeed," he said skeptically. "Well, the Regio seems to think that this return of *spirit binders,* as the locals call them, signals some sort of second coming. A Legion of magical warriors, come to somehow set the world to right." Flavius paused here, his gaze hard and challenging. "Let me be clear. I have been a Bellator for a very long time, and as such, I put little stock in fairy tales and magical interlopers. I didn't see any of them around when the clambacks invaded the Southern Shield, and I don't expect an appearance anytime soon."

Flavius stretched out one leg beneath the table, flinching slightly when the joints cracked and popped. Keira's eyes widened as she spied a savage scar winding down it, stretching from beneath the commander's tunic across the knee and down to the ankle.

"The truth is," Flavius continued, a hint of weariness in his tone, "I have enough to worry about. I'm sure I don't have to tell you that the Regio's failing health brings with it a measure of uncertainty among the ruling class. What with shifting loyalties amongst the Benadur, religious fundamentalists insisting that *no* secular ruler is to be trusted, and individual families hiring bandits and encouraging general lawlessness, we are all of us on the verge of looming chaos."

Flavius gave each of them a hard, square look. "So, if you are telling me," he said pointedly, clearly indicating that this was indeed what he wished to be told, "that I can cross magic-wielding Legionnaires off my list of worries, I will gladly convey that message to the Regio."

No one spoke as his words hung in the air, heavy with implication and, to Keira's mind, opportunity. Try as she might to suppress it, she felt a rising thrill of excitement. *This is it*, she thought. *It's finally time.* The chaos they'd been warned about for so long had finally arrived and they were going to stop it together. *This is why I was brought here. It's not too late. This is the chaos we're meant to fight. And once we do, the job will finally be done.*

Cool relief washed over her and she felt herself straighten, a slow, confident smile forming on her lips. She watched as Elliott and Nazor glanced at each other, having one of their silent conversations. No doubt coming to the same conclusion that she had. Finally, Nazor stepped forward, looking Flavius dead in the eye.

"*That*," she said quietly, daring him to contradict her, "is what we are telling you."

There was a pause.

Had she heard them right? Was Nazor really saying what Keira thought she was?

Keira stepped forward then, legs compelled as if by someone else. Her mouth opened, and words began pouring out, unbidden.

"Wait, what about—"

A vise-like grip tightened on her elbow. Danny's alarmed expression and barely perceptible shake of the head stopped her in her tracks. Keira turned back to find all eyes in the room boring into her. Flavius's gaze was narrowed as he looked slowly between her and Elliott.

Nazor spoke next, her words directed at Flavius. "You have ascertained the truth of it," she said smoothly, ignoring Keira's outburst. "There are no pneumonancers or legionnaires in Abalás. Your Bellators have nothing at all to fear, nothing to distract from your task."

Flavius hesitated a moment longer, eyes darting between the three of them, before finally rising to his feet, some resolution clearly reached. He thumped one arm against his chest in salute, nodded crisply, and then they were gone.

All the energy slipped from Keira's tense muscles as she sagged against the door. There it was—the click of the key in the lock that would keep her trapped here forever, training for a future that was likely never to come. For even the looming chaos wouldn't call the Legion forth from its shadowy shield of anonymity and complacency.

No, Keira thought. *This is it. I'm done waiting for the Legion.*

CHAPTER

SEVEN

Keira didn't want to fight anymore, didn't want yet another explosion and the inevitable guilt and fallout that would result. But as they watched the Bellatori cohort recede down the wooded road, heading for the junction that would take them west, Keira couldn't help herself.

Rounding first on Elliott, the closer and therefore most accessible mark, she exclaimed, "What was *that*?"

He rubbed his eyes and pinched the bridge of his nose. "Now is really not the time, Keira." Turning to Nazor, he added, "Will you write to them? Tell them what's happened?"

Nazor nodded and stiffly ignored Keira as she turned and strode inside.

Keira could feel her ears turning red, and she tried, she really did, to throw sand on her own temper as she waited, expectantly, for some sort—*any* sort—of explanation.

"Well?" she said sharply when none was forthcoming. Elliott looked up from the fire he'd begun stoking, readying it for the coming dinner preparations.

"Well, what?"

"What are we going to do?" Keira asked, exasperated.

Elliott shook his head and continued working. "Nothing."

"*Nothing*?" She couldn't believe what she was hearing, couldn't believe that this was the man who'd stood before her, telling all those

71

stories about the meaning and purpose of the Legion, the dangers of chaos and their duty to subdue it.

"We do nothing without orders from the Legion, Keira. You know that. Nazor's writing to them now."

"And if the Legion's too late? If Loren really is on the cusp of a civil war, then no one will be safe—not us, not the Legion, and certainly not anyone around here. I doubt they have two swords to rub together. People will die, Elliott. Fathers and mothers and . . . and *kids*, Elliott. They need us, they need *help*." Keira's eyes met his and she searched them for some flicker of understanding.

But Elliott's lips merely pursed together, considering her words for a long moment, before repeating, "We wait for the Legion."

Keira gaped at him for a moment for snapping her mouth shut. She needed to leave—needed to get out of there before she actually started throwing things. She had to escape this place where she'd been trapped for the last year. She'd been ripped from the life she'd known and loved and told that it was all for a reason, that she had a higher purpose. Well, that purpose was here. It had walked in, sat down, introduced itself, and then been asked to leave. What was the point of it all, then? The training, the studying, the isolation? What was it for, if not this?

Keira felt her nails digging into her palms as she stalked toward the door. Throwing it open, she paused, unable to resist throwing in one parting blow.

"Screw the Legion, Elliott," she spat, "I'm done."

OVER THE NEXT SEVERAL DAYS, Keira made a concerted effort to avoid each and every one of them. She told herself it was because of her temper, that she couldn't trust herself around them. But the truth was that she couldn't forgive them, couldn't forgive their unwillingness to put the wellbeing of actual real life people over the policies and pointless declarations of some faceless organization. If the chaos Millus Flavius described really was coming, then now was the time for action, not hiding and waiting for orders. Too bad no one else seemed to see that.

So, every day, as soon as chores and training had been finished, she found herself down by the river. She couldn't say why. Maybe a subconscious yearning to go back to the place where everything began, the place she first arrived. It's not like she thought she could get back. She'd tried that already, years ago, when the pain was still fresh and the reality of her current situation far less apparent. No, she suspected it was something else. Something about the river's flow, the sound it made as the water trickled over smoothed rock. There was a peace in feeling it run over her bare feet as she waded up to her knees, a strange catharsis in knowing that every drop of water was here for a moment and gone the next, moving ever forward on its inevitable journey.

Keira snorted and waded deeper into the water. *There it is*, she thought. *I'm finally starting to crack.* Of course, the river didn't have thoughts; it was just water. She envied it though, envied its pure, innocent nature.

The crunch of gravel down the bank made her look up. She sighed at the sight of Danny's sandy blonde hair bobbing in the distance. She supposed she had to give him *some* credit—he'd waited days before coming to tell her to snap out of it—but she certainly wasn't about to give in that easily.

She refused to look at him as he drew near. They stood there in silence for a while, just watching the river running by. Keira kept her eyes locked on the silver glint of minnows nibbling at her feet, searching for something edible, waiting for Danny to speak. But that quickly became boring.

"Did Elliott send you?" she eventually asked.

Danny shrugged and bent down to splash some water on his face. "You missed dinner. He's worried about you. But you know that."

Keira kicked at the riverbed, churning up the dirt, and watched as the gathered minnows fled in terror.

"So, are you here to knock some sense into me, then? Tell me to stop being a baby?"

Danny said nothing, just stood watching the sun glint off the tiny rapids. "I'm sure you have your reasons."

Keira knew he was just waiting for her to spill her guts, knew he wanted her to rant, to get it all out so they could move on. *Well*, she thought firmly, *I'll not be giving him the satisfaction.* Instead, she turned and gathered up her things to begin the trudge back to the wooded path. She waited for him to stop her, for him to turn and start following her. She even paused to fiddle with her bootlaces, but still nothing.

Finally, when she could take it no more, she spun around, glaring at his disinterested back, and said, "You know, you could have backed me up."

At first, he did nothing, and she wondered if he'd even heard her. She was just about to repeat herself when she saw him slowly turn, a mischievous smile on his face and a mild look in his eyes. She realized then that he had baited her, and like an idiot, she'd fallen for it.

Damn him, she thought. *Damn him and his provocative silence.*

Well, it was too late to stop now. "You know, it's hard enough to argue with them one on one," she complained. "When they team up like that, it's basically impossible." Danny chuckled and shook his head. Gritting her teeth, she ignored him and pressed on, "I'm just *saying*, it would have been nice to have some backup."

Danny cocked his head in that annoyingly cute way he had and gave her a considering look. "You realize that's the goal, don't you?" he asked.

She stared at him, not entirely understanding where he was going with this, but growing nervous as he continued. "To have that bond they do, that connection. They fight like a team because they are one, always *together*." He shifted his weight, rubbing at the back of his neck. His Boston accent had thickened so that "together" sounded more like "togethah."

Keira shook her head. "We *are* a team, Danny. I—I mean you're my best friend. We don't have to be *together*—you know, like *that*—to be a team!" She threw the words at him, desperate to keep him at bay. Because she knew deep in her bones that if she didn't, if she let him get close to her, she'd never want him to leave.

Danny stepped toward her, and Keira felt herself instinctively draw back. A flash of hurt crossed his face, and she instantly regretted pulling away from him. It was gone in an instant, though, and he didn't move again. Instead, he said, almost whispering, "Would it really be so bad?"

His words broke something open inside of her and her fingers itched to touch him, to wrap her arms around him, and never let go.

And what then? A voice in the back of her mind asked. *What happens when he leaves? When you leave? How long till it all falls apart and you're left once again completely alone and broken beyond repair . . . just like her.*

She didn't move. And Keira hated herself then, hated herself for the pain she was causing him. But a deeper, darker part of herself hated him, too—hated him for seeing her in a way that no one else could, that no one else had ever been allowed to.

"Look, I know that stuff with your ma really messed with—"

"Stop, Danny. Just . . . stop." She glared at him, all her rage now concentrated on him alone. "You do *not* get to do that—to use your weird pneuma dreams against me like that. I didn't tell you those things! I didn't invite you into my life, and I didn't ask for any of...this!" She gestured wildly around herself. What did you even call something as crazy as what her life had become?

Danny held his hands up in surrender. "Look, I'm sorry. I didn't mean—"

She didn't let him finish, couldn't let him say whatever sweet-natured sentiment she knew was on the tip of his tongue. Couldn't let him tempt her further.

"We've talked about this, Danny," she said through gritted teeth, her excuses like straws for the grasping. But she didn't care. "I need space. Privacy. Can you give me that? One shred of dignity in this whole crappy situation?"

She felt rather than saw him deflate. She yearned to reach out, to apologize and tell him she understood. But something held her back, a bone deep instinct screaming at her to run and hide and protect herself from any further hurt. Still she felt his pain in her own bones and hated herself for it. She knew he hadn't asked for those dreams, these odd scenes from her life back home that came to him completely unbidden. There was no rhyme or reason for them—some strange twist of the pneuma that bound them as cantor and grounder. But the injustice of it rankled her, that he should be privy to the darkest and most intimate moments in her life, while his past remained safely secured behind grounder defenses.

He'd seen the fights with her mom and their inevitable fallout, glimpsed the abusive boyfriends her mother couldn't seem to stay away from. And he'd witnessed Keira's own death on a mountain road during a freak thunderstorm, a memory Keira herself didn't even have. The knowledge made her want to burrow deep in a hole and stay there. But she knew it wasn't his fault, knew he hadn't asked to be her grounder, to be pneuma-bound to someone like her. He didn't deserve to be part of her fallout.

The silence between them was unbearable. Finally, she had to look up, had to meet those eyes. But Danny was not, in fact, looking at her. Instead, he stared at something behind her, brow furrowed and head cocked slightly.

"What is *that*?"

She turned to see where he was looking and saw with a start that a tiny plume of smoke slithered above the tree line.

"Where is it coming from?" Even as the words left her lips, her stomach answered with a wave of nausea.

"The farm," Danny breathed. "It's coming from the farm."

CHAPTER

EIGHT

Branches tore at Keira's face, hair, and clothes as she and Danny sprinted back toward the house. Her breath came heavy, and her lungs burned. She stumbled on an exposed root, but Danny caught and steadied her, urging her to keep going. As they ran, she mentally took stock of the situation, flying through a list of the equipment she carried, just as Nazor had taught her.

Oh, Nazor, she thought desperately. *Are you all right?* She couldn't think about that, not now. Nazor would be the first to reprimand her for wasting precious time and energy on needless sentiment in the middle of a crisis.

Oya, gather your wits about you, she imagined the woman growling. *The enemy will not wait for you to get your bearings.*

The light that shone through the trees before them brightened, signaling the end of the wooded trail. Keira noticed the smell first—*charred flesh.* The bottom of her stomach dropped out, and then the shrieks started.

From this distance, Keira couldn't make out any words or voices. Sweat beaded her hairline, and she had to physically stop her shaking hands from drawing the sword she now thanked Pneumos she'd brought with her to the river. Then came the image of Elliott's crooked smile, his unruly auburn locks flopping into his face, filling her with guilt. She'd barely spoken to him in the last few days.

Please be alright, Elliott. Please.

Just ahead, Danny signaled for her to slow down. They crept toward the edge of the tree line, staying low to the ground and hopefully out of sight.

A smoldering ruin greeted them. At first, all Keira could see was fire, looking positively alive in its torturous, twisting dance. It leaped gracefully from the rooftop of the ruined house, licking ravenously at the base of the barn. Then came the shadows, at first shapeless, formless figures, slowly morphing into people, all clad in black cloaks.

There are so many.

Her panicked thoughts flashed to Elliott and Nazor. Where were they?

Not the house, please, not the house was her next desperate, silent plea.

Then she spotted them. Elliott was squatting in the dirt before the house's cracking frame, head in hands, and though she couldn't see at this distance, she knew that his lips would be pursed in a soundless whistle, notes trilling just beyond her hearing. Before him stood Nazor, chain mail armor shining red with reflected flame. Keira saw her crouch, heard the screamed epithets as she brandished her weapon at the black-cloaked figures surrounding them. She stood precisely poised between them and Elliott, daring them to come near, to step within reach of her cutting blade. Her braids swung as she spun to meet each of them. And all around them, the earth exploded in showers of rock and dirt, jutting upward in protective sheets of root-filled soil, shielding the two of them from assault by stone or flame.

"Elliott," Keira breathed, marveling at his skill, his precise channeling of the energetic chaos around him into protective order. Around the edges of the clearing, she could see his adversaries: hooded figures, similarly crouched, their lips moving in an unseeing chant.

Lifting a trembling finger, Keira pointed to them, murmuring, "Who are they?"

Danny, who'd been busy tightening his sword belt around his waist, looked up quickly, his face darkening.

"Worshippers of Séiro. With this amount of power, it has to be."

Keira blanched. Séiro, the god of chaos. *But how?* She thought, her mind desperately trying to make sense of what her eyes insisted to be true. *How did they find us?* And with a visceral clench not unlike a swift kick to the gut, Keira realized what she'd done.

It's me. I'm the reason they found us, just like the Bellators. I'm what brought them here.

She would have cried then, screamed, or even begged forgiveness, had it not been for the shrill, terrified squeals that emanated from the barn, its side now engulfed in flames.

"Get the horses!" Keira barked at Danny, drawing her sword. "I'll go for the ones on the ridge."

Danny stared at her, brow furrowed and eyes turbulent, before nodding curtly. But just before turning toward the barn, he put a hand briefly to her cheek. She was too shocked to respond, and just stood there dumbly as he said, "Be careful."

Then he was gone.

Shaking off her daze, Keira turned to the ridge above the house. She knew they likely wouldn't have grounders—that would require giving up far too much of their power—which meant they were vulnerable to attack any time they cast their pneuma. Sword drawn and at the ready, Keira crept along, careful to stay just inside the tree line to avoid detection.

As she slowly approached the first hooded figure, Keira could feel his casting—the pneuma clumsy and blundering, drunk on its own power and focused on nothing but destruction, further fuel to its gluttonous hunger. *I have to be able to use this*, she thought desperately, springing frantically from idea to idea, hoping something, anything, would stick.

I'll sneak up on him, she decided, *bind him from a distance.* A lump of uncertainty settled in her mouth. She'd never performed a binding without Danny. She often hesitated to seek his grounding, but it was always there if she needed it. What if she dissociated too much?

A crash and Nazor's roar from below were enough to convince Keira there was no time for hesitancy. Her mouth set in a thin, firm line, she continued forward. If she stuck close to the surface of his consciousness and focused on a muscle bind only, she would be fine. She could do this.

Keira had been ten when she'd broken her arm speeding down the hill on a runaway bicycle. Her mother had predictably been hysterical but she'd barely even cried as the doctors moved and palpated her arm. That was the day she'd decided to become a physician. Through stinging eyes, she remembered them performing the nerve block in her shoulder—a small needle, a squirt of lidocaine, and she felt nothing at all down her arm while they realigned the bones in their proper place. A muscle bind was sort of like that, she decided.

Crouching maybe twenty feet from the other pneumonancer, she touched her left fingertips gently to the earth, anchoring herself as best she could, and cast her pneuma. It moved slowly, slithering along the ground, winding around root and stone, crawling toward the figure who stood as yet unaware. She slid up his foot, inching her way just under the skin, keeping her pneuma light and barely noticeable. She spread out until her pneuma was a thin sheet over his entire body, but far from the stream of consciousness she knew would incite panic if it were touched. In her own mind, she visualized the anatomical charts Elliott had hanging near the herbs in the larder, recalling the bundles of nerves in the shoulders and hips that controlled movement in the extremities. In those areas, she burrowed her pneuma deeper, winding around the nerves, breaking the connection between axon and dendrite until she felt the satisfying *thump* of the figure's body collapsing to the ground.

She released him then, sliding back into herself, and stood shakily from her crouch, legs aching in protest at their sudden use. She ran up to the pneumonancer, who was now swearing loudly, and quickly gagged him with her lunch towel. The muscle bind would only hold for a few hours—nerves were hardy things and would regain connections fairly quickly—but she suspected they'd have some questions for him once this was all over. Still, better to keep him out of sight for now. Reaching under his limp arms, she dragged him into the tree line, then stood and turned to the next figure on the ridge.

A magnificent crash emanated from the valley below her, followed swiftly by the roar of a hungry furnace. Keira looked down to see that the barn roof had collapsed in on itself as the flames within, newly exposed to fresh oxygen, surged greedily toward the sky. Keira's hands shook as she fumbled with tightening her sword belt and her eyes fluttered closed. In that moment, she prayed with everything in her that Danny and the horses had escaped, that they weren't trapped inside that raging inferno.

But knowing there was no time to waste, Keira resumed creeping further up the ridge, sword at the ready and eyes fixed on the next target. She tasted the air around her and felt none of the earlier man's drunken delight. This woman—Keira could sense now that she was female—was casting with the precision of a skilled pneumonancer, revealing only a glimmer of the excitement the other one had been near to bursting with, and none of his drunken foolery.

Keira gritted her teeth in frustration. This one would be much harder to sneak up on. Still, she had little choice. From what she'd seen in the valley below, merely charging them with a sword wasn't exactly doing Nazor much good. Crouching down once more, she again cast her pneuma out, slithering above the ground until it reached the woman. Keira spread her pneuma out just under the woman's skin, probing gently for the spots needed to bind muscle.

Thin, icy claws seized her between one heartbeat and the next. They pulled Keira's pneuma deeper, sucking her into the depths of the woman's own pneuma store. Keira panicked, tried to resist, tried to retreat. But she was losing her grounding, that essential tether to herself. She clung to everything her pneuma touched, ripping and severing as she went, but the claws took no heed, relentless in their piercing retraction.

Then a firm hand gripped her wrist as a strong, rooting presence engulfed her pneuma, absorbing it into itself, unraveling her from the woman's barbed flesh and reeling her back into her own body. Her pneuma balked at this strange presence, unused to its touch and resisting its sway, but Keira suppressed the sensation, desperate for something, *anything*, that would save her from the icy grasp of the woman in black.

With a gasp, Keira's consciousness slammed back into her body. Fresh oxygen filled her lungs, and her head swam as her still-crouched legs crumpled further beneath her. A roaring in her ears threatened vertigo, and she didn't dare try to stand. Just managing a glance up, she met the ebony eyes of Nazor.

"W-where's Danny?" she gasped. "Elliott?"

Something flashed across Nazor's eyes, but was gone in an instant. "Elliott . . . can't help us just now. Danny's with him." Keira's stomach rolled and her head felt light. Nazor's voice sounded very far away as she said, "You must get up, Keira. She's coming."

Nazor moved then, squaring off against someone in the dim light ahead. Keira forced herself to her feet, battling down the waves of nausea that rolled through her body. Hands shaking and clammy with sweat, she grappled for the sword at her belt, drawing it unsteadily. With a roar, Nazor dove forward then, aiming directly for the woman on the ridge. A tree trunk exploded to Nazor's left, and she shielded herself from the falling debris, faltering not one step in her stride. A chasm erupted in the ground before her, and she rolled out of the way of the showering dirt, lithely leaping over the crack that split the path ahead.

Move, Keira ordered, her shaking legs silently. *You've got to move.*

Rock shards hurtled toward her from an exploded boulder up ahead of her, and she finally convinced her rubbery limbs to cooperate, if only through instinctive self-preservation. Capitalizing on the momentum and the helpful dose of adrenaline surging through her veins, Keira ran. She circled around, coming at the two of them from behind. She could see through the trees that Nazor was methodically cutting through the earthworks the woman in black had hastily erected.

I've got to distract her, Keira thought as she stumbled over the pock-marked terrain. Emerging from the trees on the opposite side of Nazor, Keira looked around, desperate for something to use. She didn't dare try another bind, not with Nazor fighting and unable to ground her. And it's not as if she could just follow the Séiro worshippers' lead of indiscriminate destruction and risk losing control—she might kill Nazor in the process. But what was there to use? *Trees, trees, and yes, more trees,* she thought wryly.

She froze. *That's it!*

Crouching, Keira pressed her fingers lightly to the ground. Her pneuma quivered, pushing against her, begging to be released, but still she waited, an old saying of Elliott's once more on her lips.

Like flows deftly unto like.

Then her moment came. She felt the pneuma discharge mere milliseconds before she saw the tree explode, but it was enough. Propelling her own pneuma after it, she wrapped around the falling pieces as they fell through the air and deftly channeled the expelled energy, re-weaving the connections into a semblance of their former whole. As it fell, she knew it wasn't the best-looking branch she'd ever made, but it was solid, hard, and gaining speed.

Just as the woman morphed a ball of fire from her own branch, capitalizing on the discharged energy of her explosive campaign, Keira's branch struck her. She cried out in pain—not a mortal blow, but good enough for Keira's purposes. Nazor, quickly registering what had happened, took advantage of the woman's distraction. Leaping over the earthwork before her with a howl of fury, Nazor sliced downward with her massive claymore. The woman crumpled into a heap, killed instantly, as Nazor sunk to her knees beside her.

Keira stumbled toward them. The house and barn were smoldering quietly now, and there was no sign of Danny or Elliott as she looked below. She pushed that observation away.

One thing at a time, she thought. *Just get to Nazor.*

Tired eyes greeted Keira as she reached her training master.

"Are you all right?" she asked, scanning the older woman for injuries.

Nazor stared at her blankly, saying nothing, before turning to look at the valley below. They stood that way for a moment, both without words.

"He's gone," Nazor said simply. "Elliott's been . . . undone."

Keira recoiled, folding herself against the nearest tree, sinking down it slightly as her eyes filled with tears. She shook her head, violently trying and failing to cast away that dreaded word.

"Nooooo." The moan that the word pulled from her was physically painful and tears filled Keira's eyes, blurring Nazor's face. "That can't be . . . I mean, he . . . he can't."

Yet as Keira sputtered incomprehensible words, Nazor only stared at her, eyes dark and clouded with pain. And her silence was confirmation enough. A sobbed ripped through Keira's chest.

Not Elliott, Keira begged. *Please. Why did it have to be him?*

But Elliott had known the risks. They all had. She thought then of those icy claws, the panic that had filled her as she'd been wrenched away from her own body. She shivered. Thank Pneumos for Nazor's grounding, or she'd likely have met a similar fate.

Keira shook her head, banishing those thoughts. Pressing the heels of her palms hard into her eyes, she straightened and turned back to Nazor. The older woman still looked glassy-eyed and small, slumped in a heap next to the dead Séiro worshipper.

"I bound one, just up there." Keira's voice was raw but surprisingly steady. "We should interrogate him, find out what they wanted. And how they found us."

Nazor said nothing, merely continued to stare at the valley before her. Keira was just wondering if she should go alone to retrieve the man when Nazor suddenly sighed and tried unsteadily to climb to her feet. And for the first time, she seemed her true age to Keira, a woman who had survived poverty and civil war in a country and time far from anything Keira had ever known. Those experiences left their own scars, Keira knew, no matter how hard someone may try to hide them. She offered Nazor a hand then, more surprised than anything, when the older woman actually took it, leaning heavily on her as she staggered to her feet and the two of them turned to the unsavory task at hand.

Keira and Nazor carried the limp pneumonancer down the hill toward the pond behind the house. Nazor had ordered Danny to take Elliott there when he'd finally stumbled from the barn, entrusting Elliott to him while she'd gone to find Keira.

As the two of them staggered toward the water, gagged package in tow, Keira suddenly felt herself engulfed in a crushing hug. She was normally so cautious about touching, hesitant to initiate, and quick to disengage. But these weren't normal times.

Dropping the man's feet, she turned to return Danny's embrace, desperate in that moment for his solidness, the feeling of security he always seemed to have in excess. After a moment, she held him at arm's length, anxiously scanning the length of him. To her relief, she saw only a few minor burns on his hands that he'd already bandaged. When she finally met his gaze, she saw tears in his eyes, and asked raggedly, "Elliott?"

Danny shook his head, swallowing a choked sob as he bent to help carry the limp man over to the shoreline. Dazed, Keira's eyes drifted toward the pond, lingering on a dark figure lying with perfect stillness near the water.

Elliott.

Keira drew closer, stifling a cry of her own, as she could only stare at her mentor. He just looked so *wrong.* His once warm amber eyes were now clouded, opened slightly and yet unseeing under heavy lids. His long, nimble fingers, so often twitching or tugging at some invisible thread of pneuma, now hung limp, seemingly lifeless. She could still see the shallow rise and fall of his chest, but knew in her soul that his pneuma, the energy that made him *Elliott,* was gone.

And he was never coming back.

Danny came to join her then, draping an arm protectively over one shoulder and pulling her tightly against him. From behind a dense curtain of despair, Keira watched as Nazor staggered toward Elliott. She kneeled beside him then and gently pulled his head into her lap with a tenderness Keira could never have imagined coming from the gruff woman. Nazor gently brushed his hair from his forehead and pressed her tear-stained lips against his brow.

"*Obi'm,*" she whispered against his skin. "You promised me, *Obi'm.*"

Then through the silence a piercing wail exploded from her, half sob and half scream. The sound coursed down Keira's spine, making her stomach curl in on itself as she felt insides crumble. Something inside of her was breaking and no matter how much she tried, she couldn't pull the pieces it back together. Luckily, she didn't have to.

Danny's arm pulled her against his chest, and she collapsed into him. She wrapped her arms around him, not caring what it meant as she buried her face against his warm solidness, the *aliveness* of him. Tears coursed down her face, dampening her shirt as she felt Danny's own fall lightly into her hair. She couldn't bring herself to care, to think much else beyond the sobs racking her body as she mourned the only father she'd ever really had, or would likely ever know.

~

WHEN HER TEARS had all been extended and the jerking sobs slowed, it was Danny who drew her attention back to the lone surviving rogue pneumonancer. They needed answers and they needed them now. Determined that this interrogation would go better than her last, she nodded toward Danny as he threw their captive to the ground, eliciting a pain-filled groan from the other pneumonancer.

"Who sent you?" Keira demanded.

The man said nothing, dark eyes narrowing and jaw tightening behind unshaven black stubble. For the first time, Keira noticed a thin, twisting black tattoo that started above his right brow and snaked across his face, stopping just below his left nostril. She'd thought it a scar at first, but could see now that its path was intentional. The man spat, glaring at them both with blatant hatred. Danny stepped forward, but Keira grabbed his arm, deciding on a new tact.

"Tell us what you want," she murmured. "Your friends are dead, but maybe we can come to some sort of…understanding."

The man barked a deep, hacking guffaw. "An understandin', is it?" Keira noted the lilting cadence of an uplander, then grimaced as the man spat again. "There can be no understandin' with the likes of you. Séiro sees all, and chaos is looming. No Marian princeling can stop what's comin'." He started laughing then, a high cackle that sent shivers down all their spines.

Keira saw only a glimmer of movement to her right before the high cackles were cut short by choking gurgles. Keira stared at Nazor's knife, plunging out from beneath the man's chin. She gaped as blood spurted from his open mouth, and his eyes slowly filled with blood. The man swiped weakly at his neck with limp arms before slumping to the side, blood pooling around him Keira watched, mute with shock, as Danny kneeled to feel for a pulse at the man's wrist, before standing stiffly and turning to face Nazor.

There she stood, staring mildly at the man before her, seemingly unconcerned by either his death or the two pairs of eyes fixed on her in horror.

"What was *that*?" Keira demanded. When she said nothing, she persisted, growing angry now. "Why would you do that? We were trying to interrogate him."

Nazor turned her disinterested gaze to Keira and shrugged. "He could tell us nothing, because he knew nothing."

Keira didn't know whether it was shock, exhaustion, Elliott, or some combination of everything, but out of nowhere, her face flamed hot with fury.

"How do you know?" she snapped. "He could have told us *why*, or how they found us—given us some *reason* for all of this!"

Nazor was absolutely still, regarding her coldly through narrowed eyes.

"We have a reason. We know how they found us."

Keira's lips turned numb, her breath catching in a sharp inhale, but Nazor continued, her words coming in a quiet hiss. "The same way the Bellatori cohort did."

The air punched out of her in a sudden whoosh as her eyes darted between Nazor and Elliott's limp form. "I didn't . . . I mean, I never wanted to . . . she was a *little girl*, Nazor. What was I supposed to—"

"You were *supposed* to follow orders," Nazor hissed. "You were supposed to show just a modicum of gratitude, to put your *family* first, just this once."

Her words cut through Keira like knives and more than anything she wanted to scream, at Nazor, at herself—hell, even at Danny, though she couldn't possibly say why. But more than that, she wanted to leave, to get out of there before she said or did anything she'd regret.

But where can I go?

Her eyes fell on the charred remains of the farmhouse, all her belongings, memories carefully hidden away over the last year—all gone in an instant. With a choked sob, she realized she was once again homeless, with no real options, no family to take her in. Not since—

With an explosion of pent-up fury, she rounded on Nazor.

"*Family*?" She demanded. "Is that what we are? Well look, Nazor. I'm sorry this happened. I really am. I'm sorry that everything I touch seems to go to absolute *shit*. But you know something else? This isn't all on me. I didn't choose to come here. I didn't ask to join this fight. I'm not the one that refused the Bellators' offer. But you, Nazor, you were his *grounder*."

Keira saw Nazor flinch at the word, but she didn't care. She was pouring out all of her rage, unloading all her pain, and someone else would have to take it. She'd *make* them take it.

"You were the one person who was supposed to take care of him, to protect him! He's gone because of y—"

Danny jerked her arm hard then and glared between her and Nazor, eyes tight with fury. "Stop it, both of you. Stop it right now. Elliott wouldn't have wanted this, and you both know it."

Keira yanked her arm away and turned back to scream at Nazor some more. But the look on the woman's face...it was an expression of utter despair. Pain etched itself across every line of her face, and her eyes were hollow pits of shame and self-loathing.

In an instant, all of Keira's fury was gone. All the rage, vindictiveness, and spite—it vanished from her in a moment, leaving behind only emptiness and the bitter taste of guilt.

"Nazor, I—"

"Go." Nazor's face was hard in its pain, unyielding in its misery.

"W-what?"

"I said *go*. Go after the cohort. Tell them what happened. Warn them of what pursues them, of the danger facing the prince. Now's your chance. Go be the hero, Keira."

Keira looked from Nazor to Danny, but neither would meet her eyes. She didn't know what to do. *I can't leave them,* she thought. *Not with Elliott like . . . this.* She continued to stare at them, searching desperately for the right answer.

This is what you wanted, the nasty voice inside reminded her. *Go on, get out of here.*

Not like this, she thought miserably. *This isn't what I wanted.*

Yes, but this is what you've got. And this is what you deserve.

After what felt like an eternity, she gave a tiny, barely perceptible nod.

She watched then as Nazor and Danny turned away from her and started back toward the ruined buildings, to search for anything that could be salvaged. She remained behind, alone next to the pond and the person who used to be Elliott.

Finally, curling up in a ball next to him, she sobbed, "Oh, Elliott. I —I don't know. I don't know what to do. Please, just tell me what to do." But of course there was no reply and never would be.

NINE

Crîd Eálas

The man before her smelled of blood and singed fabric. Looking him over from head to foot, Lady Junia realized that this was likely due to him actually *being* scorched. Not that this was any sort of excuse. She wrinkled her nose slightly, regarding his shredded black garments, blistering hands, and the deep gash on his side that still oozed blood through his bandages.

Leaning over to her advisor, she murmured, not altogether quietly, "Tell me again who this person is?"

"A priest, your highness, come before you today with concerns about the rise of pneumonancy in the north."

Junia kept her face perfectly blank, careful to hide the glint of excitement that rose unbidden. *I knew it.*

"I see," she said instead. She turned back to the man, examining him more carefully. He certainly didn't look like any priest of Pneumos she'd ever seen. "Tell me," she began mildly, "From which sect do you hail?"

The man looked up from where he kneeled before her, and she gasped at the sight of a dark tattoo snaking down at an angle across his face. The whole of one side was decorated in twisting spools of black, giving the distinct impression of a mask. What's more, the eye on the tattooed side was clouded and opaque, a point of whiteness in the gaping dark. Junia suppressed a shiver and glanced at the guards stationed around the room for reassurance.

"My brothers and sisters abide amongst the nomadic peoples in the arid lands to the north," he replied in a grating, raspy voice, a product no doubt of the fire that had burned his hands so severely. "We worship the cosmic balance that exists between order and disorder, recognizing the contributions of both Pneumos and Séiro toward the preservation of that order, and we work diligently to see that balance maintained."

Prettily packaged lies, Junia thought. She knew a worshipper of Séiro when she saw one.

"I am told that you come today with concerns of rising pneumonancy in the north," Junia said. "I, too, have heard troubling tales. I sent my Bellators in search of them, but they ultimately proved unsuccessful." She paused, considering her next question carefully. "Tell me, do you think the kingdom has much to fear from them?"

"They are a great threat to you, my lady!" the man exclaimed, stepping forward slightly to the vexation of her guards, who quickly blocked his way. Holding up a hand to them, she bade the man to continue.

"They do not recognize Marian authority, acting only in accordance with their own rules," he said, urgency evident in every syllable. "Our sect has sought them out as well, my lady. They attacked me and my brethren, and as I'm sure you can surmise from my appearance, we were vastly outnumbered. I beg you, my lady, to grant us supplies and men so we may renew the hunt. They must be brought to justice!"

Junia eyed the man, pretending to consider his request, though she already knew her answer. Still, it would not do to betray too much eagerness.

"You shall have anything you require," she said finally, watching as a slow, hungry grin spread across the man's scarred face.

~

Near Abalás

THE NEXT MORNING, Keira awoke to find herself alone and but with a threadbare stable blanket draped over her. A brief search found Danny gathering up everything that might be of use from the wreckage of the ruined farm. Her breath caught as she stared at the charred beams standing at odd angles from the still smoldering remains of her home.

It's really gone.

She'd lived here for over a year, the longest she'd ever lived anywhere. And despite all her efforts to leave, to complete the rites and find a way back to her mother, in that moment she would have given every ounce of pneuma she had for one more supper spent making faces at Danny as Elliott lectured and Nazor glared disapprovingly at them both. A lump caught in her throat, but she forced it down. She didn't deserve to feel sorry for herself.

Glancing at Danny, she asked, "Where's Nazor? I—I wanted to apologize for last night."

Danny, his back to her, replied stiffly, "She's gone."

"Gone?" Keira repeated, aghast. "What do you mean, *gone?*"

"She left. Took Elliott with her. Said she was going to find someone who could help him. I assume she meant the Legion."

When Danny finally turned to look at her, his eyes were blood-shot, the skin beneath shadowed, and Keira wondered if he'd slept at all last night. Tears filled her eyes as she stared at him. It wasn't just her life here that she'd ruined.

"Danny, I'm so sorry." Her words came out barely above a whisper and she wasn't sure if he even heard. "I—I didn't mean for this . . . for any of this to happen. Please, you have to know—"

"Shh," Danny said, at once pulling her into a tight hug. "It's alright," he said even though they both knew it wasn't. "It's going to be all right."

Keira immediately stiffened at the sudden contact but Danny didn't pull away, only lightened his hold as she felt her body slowly uncoil. Then he pulled away, holding her by the shoulders as he searched her eyes. "It's not your fault, Keira. You didn't mean for any of this to happen. You couldn't have known."

Keira tried to nod, but the guilt weighed her down so she couldn't quite meet his gaze. Gently, Danny placed two fingers under her chin and gently raised her eyes to his. "It's not your fault." Each word peeled a bit of weight from her shoulder until she could take one shuddering breath and nod. The small motion somehow broke the spellbound thread that held their gazes and Keira could pull away, trying to ignore the way she instantly missed the warm weight of his hands.

Without another word, they both turned and resumed shoving the few items they'd been able to salvage into small rucksacks. They lashed these behind the saddle of each of the horses, who, thank Pneumos, seemed to be relatively unharmed after the previous night's ordeal. When everything was readied and the two were about to mount up, Keira ventured a cautious question.

"How do we even find them? The Bellatori cohort?"

Danny's mouth tightened, but his tone was mild as he replied, "Elliott told me once that the future Regio always studies with the high priests of Mount Ánghen for several years before reaching the age of maturity. The surest way from here is through Gregür Pass."

Keira nodded, weighing his words. "So, we try to catch them in the pass?"

"They'll probably stop in Raboneís to resupply before heading into the Olpheís Plains. You can go for miles there without seeing a living soul." Danny shrugged. "I say we try to catch them there."

"Roger that, Sergeant O'Leary," Keira said with a tentative smile, hoping for his usual response to the jest.

Danny tried to smile back at her, but there was a darkness in his eyes, an exhaustion that would not be overcome. Keira's smile faltered, then fell entirely as he turned away.

It's okay, she told herself. *He'll be alright. I mean, it's Danny.*

But as they rode out of the valley and along the western road, the ruined farm receding behind them, Keira was not at all confident of that fact. She could only stare at Danny's stiff back ahead of her, wondering if she'd lost not only her home but also her entire family in one fell swoop.

It took several days to make the journey, but as they neared, Keira felt her excitement growing. As they crested the final hill, she caught her breath. Raboneís was like nothing she had ever seen before. Nestled as it was amongst the rolling hills of Gregür Pass, the northern and southern ranges rising sharply on either side, it was the picture of a town in motion. The buildings themselves seemed little more than temporary structures, having sprung up seemingly at random along the main road that led toward the Olpheís Plains, and Keira remembered Elliott explaining that the winter mudslides and summer windstorms left few structures standing for long. Keira tried in vain to keep her hair tied up and out of the way of the fierce winds, but she eventually gave up and contented herself with peering through her long black curls. At least they kept some of the dust out of her eyes, she decided, though the same could not be said for the grit that coated the inside of her mouth.

As they rode their horses through the streets, eyes scanning for signs of the Bellatori cohort, Keira was struck by how many people there were. They were every type and creed, from Tramorian traders with caravans of camels laden with goods to the nomads of the Olpheís Plains, their brightly painted wagons and roaming herds of sheep and goats filling every side road they ventured down.

It was absolute bedlam, and Keira loved every minute. The stern river people, on the other hand, looked on at this mayhem with abject disapproval. The streets were also filled with a surprising number of Bellators, their bright red cloaks standing out even amidst the fracas of sight and sound. Keira knew that there was a Bellatori toll post just beyond the pass—the Marian crown always got its two penarii from all trades in the region, she thought wryly. But the heavy military presence here seemed excessive. Had there been trouble in this area? They'd heard rumblings even in Abalás of the old Regio's failing health, and she wondered if the situation might be even more serious than the rumors had suggested.

They continued on, hoping to find a tavern of some sort to ask after Millus Flavius and his cohort. Keira felt worn to the bone, having made the usual three-day journey with Danny in just under two in a desperate bid to reach the cohort before they passed through to the Olpheís Plains and Mount Ánghen beyond. They stopped briefly to ask for directions to the nearest tavern from an old upland riverman. He clearly resented being this far away from his beloved waters, even if it was to hawk his fish to traders heading to all parts of Loren. Grudgingly, he pointed them in the right direction, and they continued steadily on. Narrowed eyes followed them as they went, giving Keira the distinct impression that their presence was altogether unwelcome.

～

THE TAVERN WAS SITUATED DIRECTLY next to the Lorenan side of the toll post, and Keira could see the lengthy line of traders filing toward the several toll minders, chests open and waiting to receive tribute. The tavern itself was little more than a tent, the door flap nearly blown off with each major gust of the winds through the pass. They tied the horses up outside, careful to bring with them anything of value, and stepped inside the dimly lit tavern.

Keira was struck first by the sweet scent of pandry smoke that filled the air, stinging her eyes slightly but also warding off the mosquitos that buzzed outside. She and Danny scanned the room and quickly found the figures they were looking for, situated leisurely around a table at the far end of the room. Millus Flavius looked as equally unimpressed with his current surroundings as he had in their home.

Had it really been only a few days ago that he had visited? Keira shook her head, unable to believe how much had changed in that time, how very different the world now seemed.

They made their way toward the table and saw first Flavius, then his companions, glance up and stare in recognition. Flavius's eyebrows raised as he studied them, but said nothing as they approached. Keira recognized the man to his right as the lieutenant who had accompanied him back at their farm. She was able to get a better look at him here and could now see that he looked surprisingly...*uplandish*. Though he wore the cropped hairstyle typical of Bellators, his hair had a reddish hue, and his skin was notably paler than that of his bronzed compatriots, who no doubt grew up spending long hours in the coastal sun. There were a few other Bellators with them she didn't recognize, but Keira saw no sign of the female Cross-

Sea warrior, whose distinctive headscarves would make her hard to miss.

Keira shifted uneasily when they reached them, unsure where to begin, how to explain all that had happened. Danny, thankfully, had no such qualms.

"We were attacked," he stated bluntly, "the day after you left."

There was no edge of accusation in his voice, but Keira noted the lieutenant's eyes narrow at the implication.

Flavius continued to regard them with a mild expression. "By whom?"

"Worshippers of Séiro." Danny held his gaze steadily. "They destroyed everything. Elliott is . . . gone."

There was a weighty pause before Flavius responded. "I'm sorry to hear that. He seemed a good man and certainly deserved better."

Keira was surprised to hear a note of sympathy in his voice, and even more surprised to find that she believed it. Flavius gestured to two chairs, and they both took a seat, Keira giving an internal sigh of relief to have something solid and unyielding to sit on. The lieutenant leaned across the table toward them, his face suddenly intent.

"Tell me, though—why would a solitary priesthood from the distant arid lands concern themselves with a small farm of no import?"

Keira and Danny glanced at each other. This was the tricky part. If they revealed who and what they were, they risked exposing the Legion and potentially endangering any ongoing operations. Still, it wasn't as if there was a place for them there anyhow—not anymore. Besides, there was too much at stake. The Legion's goals wouldn't be worth much if the Regio died without an heir and the entire country went up in flames.

"You know why." Keira leveled Flavius a challenging look. "We're a threat to them, to their power. They know that, and so do you." She saw something flicker in his eyes, even as his expression remained unchanged—something she might just be able to convince herself was respect.

Then it was gone, his visage again unyielding. "Why come to us, then?"

Danny took this one. "We think they're coming for you." In

response to his unspoken question, he continued, "Something one of them said, 'Chaos is looming, and no Marian princeling can stop what's coming.'" He glanced at Keira, then added, "We knew you were charged with protecting the prince, so we came to warn you."

Flavius gave them a long, considering look before nodding curtly.

"We thank you for the warning. Now—" His eyes became steely, boring into theirs. "—as I told you all before, my cohort was charged with investigating reports of pneumonancy on our way to retrieve Lord Landrianus. As you have just confirmed that such accounts are true, I will be obliged to convey this information to the Regio." Flavius surveyed the two of them, judging their understanding. "He will, I regret to say, be obliged to question what the return of this *Legion* means for the future peace and security of Loren."

Flavius shifted closer and lowered his voice, eyes piercing in their unyielding gaze. "Therefore, I must ask—do you recognize the Regio's authority as the rightful ruler of Loren?"

Keira and Danny glanced at each other before hurriedly nodding. "Of course," Keira told him.

"And are you willing to submit to that authority and fulfill any just obligations imposed on you as citizens of this realm?"

Their response was slower this time, as they both balked at the implications of the word *any*. Keira realized she was holding her breath, but couldn't quite seem to let all of it out. It was Danny who finally spoke, meeting Flavius's eyes steadily.

"We do."

Flavius leaned back in his chair, apparently satisfied. "That's good to hear."

Keira slowly released the breath she'd been holding, relief swelling her veins.

"But talk is cheap."

Keira froze as Flavius unsheathed his belt-knife, examining the gleam of the sharp blade. "I don't know you, and so cannot say what your word is worth. So, I would . . . *suggest* that is in your best interest to join us in our escort of Lord Landrianus to Crîd Eálas. Once there, you may make your case personally to the Regio. Otherwise, he may be forced to ask how far your loyalty *truly* extends."

Keira and Danny stared at him in shock. Was he actually threatening them?

Flavius gave a bark of laughter at their expressions, making Keira jump. She hadn't imagined this sober man capable of making jokes, and was honestly more surprised by this than the implied threat.

The aging Bellator sheathed his knife with a grin. "Trust me, I don't much like the idea of adding two *unknowns* to my cohort. Yet I am duty-bound to follow orders, and that means honoring my Regio's intent by them. So, take some time and think about it. We leave at first light tomorrow from the toll post. In the meantime, though, get something to eat. You both look like hell."

His companions laughed as Keira and Danny both exchanged glances, still tense from the exchange. The conversation quickly turned to more benign subjects but Keira remained stiffly wary. When the time came to order another round of drinks, she volunteered to fetch them, eager for a brief reprieve. Rising from the table, she couldn't help but wonder at the altogether enigmatic Millus Flavius and his curious sense of *duty*.

As Keira waited at the bar for her food and ale, she marveled at the hodgepodge of humanity that had found its way to Raboneís.

"Excitin', isn't it?" The voice came from behind her, and she turned to see a tavern hand wiping up spilled ale from the bar's surface.

Keira snorted. "I suppose. Although, as far as taverns go, this one seems pretty tame."

He grinned at her, pushing back the mop of brown curls from his forehead. "Oh, I dunno. You seem like someone who hasn't had much excitement in a while."

Now it was her turn to smile. He wasn't handsome in a traditional sense—his eyes were slightly too far apart, and his nose looked like it might have been broken once or twice. Altogether, he had the kind of face you'd be likely to forget, except for a slight twitch of the mouth she thought Elliott might have described as "cheek."

A sharp pang stung her chest at the thought of Elliott and she swallowed hard, feeling her brows knit together. Misinterpreting its meaning, the tavern hand hurriedly said, "Sorry, I meant nothin' by it, only that you seemed to like bein' around people." He shrugged. "Stick around here long enough, and most grow to hate 'em. The name's Neval, by the way." He offered her a hand, and she willingly shook it.

"Keira. And you? Do you hate people?" she asked, adopting a flippant tone. His voice betrayed him as an uplander, and she wondered what had brought him so far from his river home, wherever it might be.

His face darkened at her question. "*Some*, though not all. But, you see," he mused, picking up an earthen cup to dry, "the laughs, the gaiety, the constant need to make merry—all it does is hide what's really underneath."

"And what is that?" Keira was becoming genuinely curious about this rather charming tavern hand. His voice had a lyrical quality to it, and his words made her suspect that he was far more than he appeared.

He leaned closer, regarding her steadily. "A tinderbox."

Before Keira could respond, a commotion outside brought Danny and the rest of the Bellatori cohort to their feet. They headed for the exit, and momentarily forgetting about the tavern hand, Keira ran to follow them. Pulling back the flap, she saw a crowd had gathered around a lanky Bellator.

With a start, Keira realized that the object he held suspended in the air was, in fact, a little boy. He couldn't have been more than seven or eight—and the soldier was systematically smashing the child's face in with his fist.

TEN

Raboneís Tavern

As his customers rushed out of the tavern, intent on determining the source of the commotion, Neval Brennan quickly hung up his apron and slipped out the back. Circling around, he spotted a cocky Bellatori arse beating a little boy —likely caught running tickets, if Neval had to bet. He knew young children were prized for the job, with their uncanny ability to slink unnoticed amongst the tent buildings as they ran up the line. They were paid to bring stamped tickets from the southern end of the line of traders all the way past the toll post to the north.

Unfortunately for this mouse of a boy, he wasn't very good at it. *Dumb kids.* They risked losing a hand, or worse, just to help some fat Tramorian merchant avoid his taxes. This boy was the third one this week to be caught.

Well, thought Neval, *with any luck, he'll be the last.*

The timing was now, he knew. His people were ready. It was certainly a shame, though—he'd been having a lovely chat with that girl, Keira, all wide-eyed and excited-like. Neval chuckled.

Well, we'll see how exciting you find Raboneís now.

Neval felt a familiar wave of excitement wash through him, an eagerness honed to a brutally efficient lethality that he knew he could draw on in times such as these.

Well, there's nothin' like a prison term to hone one's bloodlust, he thought with a giddy grin as he sprinted down the hill away from the tavern. The time had come, he knew, for the Bellators and their Marian overlords to receive a message, loud and clear.

Loren was not theirs to toy with any longer.

~

DANNY LUNGED FORWARD, catching the Bellator's arm just as it began another arc toward the sobbing child.

"Wh-what the hell?"

Enraged, the Bellator rounded on Danny, jerking his arm free, but maintaining his grip on the scruff of the boy's neck. Danny stepped back, arms outstretched, placating in their emptiness.

"Let the boy-o go now," he said the words evenly but Keira could see the glint in his eye. "I think he's learned his lesson well enough."

The Bellator's face twisted into a sneer, looking Danny up and down with disdain. "Has he, now? See, I'm not so sure, little urchin like this. I say he'll just go right back to running those tickets. That would be much harder if he wasn't able to run, you see."

Danny didn't move, but Keira could see the muscles tighten across his back, knew the hard line his mouth would have formed. She started toward them, sliding through the crowd as calmly as she was able, restraining herself from breaking into a run.

The Bellator's fist flashed toward Danny, who tried to jerk out of the way. Too quick, the blow caught him just under the jaw and sent him careening back several steps. His hand jerked to the hilt of his sword, and Keira saw the Bellator drop the child and reach for his own blade. She lunged forward, desperate to intervene before Danny got himself killed.

Keira didn't see where the first stone came from, merely saw it come sailing from the corner of her eye, its graceful arc a stark contrast to its crushing endpoint. Blood poured from the Bellator's nose as he stumbled back, slack-jawed with disbelief. He tried to shield his head as more rocks began flying toward him, shouting for reinforcements. Then a brief stumble, likely over someone's outstretched foot, sent him careening toward the ground. The moment he hit, he was completely obscured from view as a mass of humanity descended upon him. Their shouts echoed around the tent-lined street and were quickly followed by the Bellator's screams of pain. Keira shivered despite herself.

Danny, she thought, trying to keep her footing as a mass of people surged past her, aiming for the fallen Bellator. She looked around wildly, desperate for a glimpse of his sandy blonde hair. *There.*

Taking advantage of the distraction, Danny had dived for the little boy and now had him curled under one arm as he braced himself against the flood of people. Keira called out to him, trying to elbow her way through the crowd. What had started as a targeted attack had morphed into a full-blown mob with men and women alike just struggling to remain upright. The smell of sweat and fear was over-powering, and Keira felt a profound sense of claustrophobia as limbs pressed in on her from every angle. Danny turned then, eyes lighting on her, and began pushing his way in her direction.

Screams erupted from Keira's right. A legion of mounted Bellators had reached the scene and were systematically cutting their way through, batons brandished and armor glinting. Their horses reared, beating back the oncoming rioters. Keira flinched as she saw multiple people trampled beneath flailing hooves, their cries intermingled with equine squeals of warning.

She fought her way toward Danny with renewed vigor. *Don't trip, you* cannot *trip, Altman*, she ordered, knowing that one misstep would send her tumbling beneath unforgiving feet, likely never to rise again.

She reached Danny and nearly collapsed against him in relief. They clung to each other, the small child wedged between them as they fought their way to the edge of the crowd. No sooner had they reached it, then they were met by a mass of armed uplanders racing up the hill. They were brandishing fish spears, torches, nets, and anything else that could be remotely considered a weapon, and their ragged cries of rage sent a chill down Keira's spine.

She realized then that the man leading the charge was none other than Neval, the tavern hand she'd met earlier. Yes, that mousy brown hair and sly smirk were unmistakable. He caught her eye as they neared and winked at her, a look of savage delight on his face as he bellowed a strangled war cry that was quickly taken up by the others.

Danny and Keira jumped out of the way as Neval's uplanders smashed into the rioting mass that had already assembled, heading straight for the mounted Bellators without caring who got caught in the middle. More screams erupted from the terrified crowd, now crushed between the advancing Bellators and the crazed upland mob.

Keira and Danny trudged away, dragging the little boy—who'd long since gone unconscious—between them. Many of the tent buildings had caught fire by this point, hapless victims of the lit torches that rioters and Bellators alike brandished. The fire was spreading; the smoke stinging their eyes and burning their throats as they tried to escape. Still the wind whipped around them, turning the entire valley into a flaming furnace as flames leaped from tent to tent. Terrified occupants poured from them, clutching treasured belongings and crying children to their chests as they fled the fire that consumed all in its path.

Keira and Danny stumbled then across one of the nomad's painted wagon homes. The roof was ablaze, while screams and choked sobs could be heard from the inhabitants within.

"Danny," Keira breathed, whirling to face him. "We have to help them. They'll burn alive otherwise."

He gave her a hard look then, his jaw already beginning to swell and determination clear in his eyes. Without warning, he deposited the young boy in her arms and, pulling the fabric of his tunic up over his nose, sprinted toward the burning wagon. Keira staggered under the unexpected weight and stared after him, horrified.

"Danny!" she screamed, trying to follow him, but she was blocked by a sudden surge of people rushing past. Then she remembered the child. She couldn't leave him alone in this hellish landscape. A crushing weight of helplessness engulfed her as she watched Danny scramble up the steps of the cabin. Throwing his weight against the burning door, he barreled through, a cloud of smoke pouring out behind him.

Pneumos, Keira breathed, *please no, not him, too.* But all she could do was watch and wait and pray. The seconds ticked by and the push of the mob grew ever more insistent. But she only clutched the boy to her, refusing to take her eyes off the wagon, watching as flames advanced around them. *Please.*

Then he emerged, hacking and wheezing as he carried a bundle of blankets in one hand and pulled a woman behind him with the other. His right shirtsleeve was on fire, and Keira shoved her way toward him.

"It's—" A wave of racking coughs overwhelmed him. "I'm fine, Keira."

But she ignored him and proceeded to beat out the flames, burning her own hands in the process but hardly caring at that moment. *He's ok*, she thought, trying to think through her heart hammering in her ears. We're *gonna be ok*. Her hands roamed over him as he sat coughing up black phlegm and wheezing, reassuring herself that he was really there, that he was okay.

The woman Danny had dragged from the burning wagon was crying silently as she unwrapped the bundle of blankets with trembling hands. A baby's cry pierced the air, and the woman doubled over, sobs wracking her frail body. She clutched the baby to her breast, face turned up in wide-eyed gratitude to Danny, who managed even through wracking coughs to give her a weak smile.

The crash of the collapsing wagon roof brought them all back to reality and Keira felt the blood drain from her face. *If he'd been a moment longer . . .* But she forced that thought from her mind. They simply didn't have time.

"We have to go," she said, eying the approaching flames. "We make for higher ground, outside the town."

Danny offered to carry the little boy, but Keira leveled him with a look and he conceded to help her settle the child on her own back, his arms secured around her neck. Onward the three of them trudged, precious cargo in tow, and only collapsing to the ground when they'd finally reached the top of a nearby hill. It was only then that Keira could look back at the ruin that had once been the bustling town of Raboneís. What had begun as a terrible cruelty had now turned into a savage riot that would claim many more lives.

A tinderbox, Neval the tavern hand had called it, this seething resentment that hid just under the surface in Loren ready to ignite at any moment. And he'd been right.

~

Keira and Danny stayed up all night, watching as the town below them burned. Several others had joined them throughout the evening, looking just as charred and exhausted as they did. The little boy had eventually regained consciousness, and once Keira was reassured that he'd sustained no permanent damage from the Bellator's overeager fist, she prepared him a pallet and he quickly fell asleep. The nomad mother and her infant had also fallen into an exhausted slumber.

Venturing out to locate the missing horses, Keira found that they'd escaped to a nearby valley, along with much of the town's livestock. Returned with horses in tow, Keira wandered over to find Danny trying in vain to reach the burns on his upper back with the soothing balm he'd wisely thought to throw in his rucksack. She kneeled and took the jar from him. Using just her fingertips, she gently applied the balm to the blistered skin. But with her eyes, she traced the curve of his back, marveling at the broad planes of muscle. He inhaled sharply at her touch and she blushed, glad he couldn't see her face. She quickly handed the jar back, careful to keep her face averted, and busied herself with repacking items into their rucksacks. She felt his eyes on her and knew he was about to say something she *really* didn't want to hear. Casting her mind about for something else to distract him, she settled on the obvious.

"Well, I suppose we'd better try to get what sleep we can with such a long journey tomorrow." She offered him a grimace.

Danny paused, giving her a curious look. "And by a long journey, you mean . . ."

"North, of course. To Mount Ánghen."

"Have you gone soft?" he demanded, and she felt herself tense defensively. "You actually *want* to go off on some half-brained quest to find that royal hoo-ha? What about Nazor and Elliott?"

Guilt settled like lead in the pit of her stomach as the image of Elliott lying far too still flashed in her memory. She hadn't forgotten. Gritting her teeth, she shoved the feeling away.

"We don't even know where they are," Keira argued reasonably. "Besides, you heard what Flavius said. If we don't go, the Regio will think the Legion's dangerous, that we're a threat to the crown. They'll be after us next."

"Then let them!" Danny cried.

Keira blinked, staring wide-eyed at him in disbelief. She couldn't remember the last time she'd heard Danny yell—*really* yell. She didn't know what to say.

"Listen to me, Keira. I understand you think this is our . . ." He searched desperately for the word. ". . . our *purpose*, that doing this will somehow earn us the Legion's respect. But this fool's errand is *not* our responsibility."

"Look around you, Danny!" Keira's voice broke as she gestured at the carnage below. "This place is falling apart. All that talk of order and chaos over the years, *this* is what Nazor and Elliott were talking about. This *is* our responsibility, because this is our—"

She stopped, catching herself before she uttered the words *home*. She didn't understand Danny's anger, his refusal to accept the mission before him, to do what obviously needed to be done. But even in her frustration, she couldn't lie to him, not to Danny. And she had no intention of making this place her home, not really.

Danny snorted derisively. His Boston accent thickened, as it always did when he was angry. "And you think this Landrianus bloke is the one to fix it? That's garbage, Keira, and you know it. He'll be as corrupt as the rest of 'em, because that's all he's eva' known."

"And if we let those Séiro worshippers kill him before he's even tried? All that gets us is anarchy, Danny, more chaos."

They glared at each other, at an impasse, with neither sure where to go from here. Finally, Danny sighed, rubbing his eyes as he tried to reason with her once more.

"We already have a job—to find our family and rebuild our home."

"They're not our *family*, Danny!"

She regretted the words almost as soon as they left her mouth. Danny stared at her, shock and hurt warring on his face. The sinking rock of guilt settled again in her stomach and she wanted desperately to take the words back, not just for the hurt they'd caused, because at their core they were *untrue*.

"Dan—"

"That's it, isn't it?" His voice was choked with emotion. "We'll never be enough for you, will we, Keira? You will *always* want more, the life you had."

Pain was etched in every line of his face. Keira wanted to run to him them, wrap her arms around him and say she was sorry, but something inside stopped her. She couldn't say what it was, what made her constantly keep him at arm's distance. But in that moment, it was all that was holding her together. He watched her expectantly, and when she didn't respond, shook his head angrily.

"What am I even talking about?" he said in disgust. "Of course it's all about you. It will *always* be about you, what *you* need, *your* path. Screw the rest of us, because Keira Altman is on a mission, and Pneumos help anyone who gets in her way!"

She recoiled from him, having absolutely no idea what to say to fix things, and still not really understanding how it possibly got so broken to begin with.

"Go on then, Keira," he said mockingly. "Go run off with the cohort. But don't for a minute think you're playing the hero here. You may think you're running toward something, still trying to *fix* everything you've screwed up, but the truth is that you're always just running away."

"Running away? From what?!"

"From the legion? From us? From your own fear of failing at the only thing you think you have left? Take. Your. Pick."

He stomped off then, grabbing Boyd's reins as he trudged down the hill. Keira's stomach was leaden as she dug the heels of her palms against her eyes. She couldn't go back, not now, not when she could still *fix* this. She had to make up for her missteps—for Marek, for Anya Cuball, for Elliott, for everything. There was no way she could appeal to the Legion empty-handed, not after everything that had happened, not if she wanted them to accept her. The Legion was her only way out, her only way *home*, and she was not about to let some man—not even Danny—hold her back.

Not like Mom.

She froze, refusing to believe the nasty voice inside her, exposing her own carefully constructed facade. This was *not* about her mom. She wasn't like her and she never would be.

And Danny . . . Danny was different. She knew that, deep in her bones, where her fears couldn't burrow down to. He had always been there for her, always stood by her, even when she was at her worst. He'd defended her choice to heal little Anya Cuball and reminded her that Marek's death wasn't her fault. He pushed her to be better, challenged her to expect more from herself.

On days when she couldn't stand the sight of her own face in the mirror, Danny would smile that crooked grin and she'd know everything would be all right. And while the selfish part of herself was itching to go out on her own, to join this cohort and prove herself to the Legion and earn her ticket home, the better, more noble part knew that Danny deserved better. She couldn't abandon him, not after everything they'd been through.

So, with a determined clench of her jaw, Keira threw her ruck over one shoulder and grabbed Cerise's reins. As she staggered down the ledge toward the cohort's rendezvous point, she racked her brain for the words she'd need to explain why they couldn't join the cohort. She needed to convince Millus Flavius that the Legion wasn't a threat to the realm. And if she failed, and the might of the Marian Empire turned against the Legion, rogue pneumonancers would be the least of their problems.

Keira couldn't quite make out the time, hiding as the sun was behind the smoke that still clung to the valley. Most of the fires had died out the night before, but a few smoldering tents could still be seen on the horizon. As she trudged toward the toll post, Keira could just make out the cohort ahead of her. As she approached, it became clear that she and Danny weren't the only ones who'd had a rough night. Several of the Bellators sported cuts and bruises. Flavius himself looked decidedly gruffer than usual, and his red-headed lieutenant was actively wincing as he changed the bandages on his leg. Keira could just make out a nasty-looking burn in the shape of a beam across one side.

Flavius eyed her as she approached, with no sign of either welcome or reproach. He looked as exhausted as she felt, and she was happy for the silence.

"I take it you'll be joining us, then. Where's your friend?" It was the lieutenant who'd joined them, taking in her sooty appearance.

Keira swallowed the lump in her throat and shook her head. "Actually, that's what I wanted to talk about. You see . . ."

"I'm right here."

Shock froze the breath in her chest and she spun around to see Danny reining Boyd to a hard stop behind them. She gaped as he quickly dismounted and strode toward the narrow-eyed Millus.

"As Keira was saying, we'll be joining you to retrieve the prince from Mount Ánghen. After all, the Legion wants peace and order as much as the Regio."

Flavius said nothing as he scrutinized the two of them, suspicion etched in every line of his weathered face. Keira tried to smooth her own features into an unassuming smile as she nodded in agreement.

"Indeed," Flavius said finally. "I'm sure your particular *skillset* will be of great use to us."

And with that, he turned and led his own mount toward the front of the gathered cohort.

Danny watched Flavius go but Keira couldn't tear her eyes away from his profile.

"You-you came."

Danny's eyes met hers and he regarded her solemnly. "Of course I came."

"I wasn't—I wasn't going to leave with them." Keira blurted. "I just came to explain why, to try to protect the Legion." She swallowed, searching his inscrutable gaze. "I wouldn't leave you, Danny."

He nodded slowly, "I know that, Keira." Then he paused. "I mean, who else could abide your terrible taste in river nuts?"

The corners of his eyes crinkled, and she grinned broadly at him. Then her eyes drifted down to the charred edges of his right shirt sleeve and the hastily applied bandages beneath—an all too vivid reminder of what he was risking by going along with her plan, what they both were. Her smile faded.

"Thank you," she whispered, meeting his soft green eyes. "I couldn't do any of this without you."

He regarded her for a long moment, eyes holding fast to hers.

"You'd do the same for me."

She swallowed and nodded, feeling the truth of his words in her bones—and it absolutely terrified her. Danny wasn't going anywhere, and neither, apparently, was she. And while this thought should have been comforting, she couldn't shake her feeling of unease. Because the closer he got, the more exposed she felt—the more she felt like running.

Keira took a deep breath, trying to clear her head of such dark thoughts. They were just friends, partners even. And while all had certainly not been resolved between them, they were *together*, and that's what mattered.

Keira eyed him from the corner of her eye as the call came for the cohort to move out, still marveling at the unexpected sight of Danny riding quietly beside her.

With you or against you, she thought, *but always beside you.*

And for just a moment, she didn't feel like running at all.

ELEVEN

As the ruins of Raboneís faded into the distance, Keira settled into the rhythm of plodding progress as the cohort made its way North toward Mount Ánghen—fighting as she did, the rising tide of boredom that already frayed at the edges of her nerves. Travel really was extraordinarily dull in this world, she decided. There was no music or podcasts, nothing at all to buffer the senses against the miles and miles of road that stretched before them.

Danny had volunteered to scout out the road ahead and Keira watched nervously as his tiny figure receded into the distance. An ache of worry gnawed at her stomach, but she fought it down. She'd offered to go with him, but he'd waved her off, saying he'd be faster and travel more distance on his own. She'd chaffed at that comment, making him grin, but in the end she couldn't fault his logic. He *was* the better rider.

He'll be fine, she reminded herself. *He's more capable than you with a blade. That's for sure.*

Still, the fear churned in her belly and she closed her eyes, willing the nausea to pass.

"I see you two joined us, after all."

Keira glanced up into the cool amber eyes of the lieutenant they'd first met back in Abalás.

"Figured you all could use the help," Keira replied cooly.

The man's eyebrows shot up, and he grinned broadly. "I see. You sound confident. Sure you can handle yourself on your own? There aren't enough of us to manage any dead weight, you know."

Keira tensed, leveling her trademark scowl at him. "I'll be fine."

The man seemed unperturbed by her sour tone, merely chuckling lowly and lifting his hands in mock surrender. "Hey, don't shoot the messenger. We've all had a rough go of it, so just wanted to warn you. The name's Centus Tiobraide, by the way. But the wynnies call me Aaron."

He winked at her then, and she rolled her eyes in response. She took his hand though, answering, "Keira Altman."

She'd been right, then. Aaron was definitely an uplander—his name and dialect confirmed it. That was intriguing. You didn't see many uplanders fighting with the Bellatorio, and you *definitely* didn't see them reach the rank of Centus. From what she'd heard, it took some major nepotism to reach the higher ranks, which almost always meant deep downlander connections.

Keira studied him curiously as the others readied their horses. *He must be quite the social climber*, she thought. She couldn't help but like him, though. He had a relaxed manner and didn't seem to take himself too seriously. This was in stark contrast to just about every other Bellator she'd ever met—which, to be fair, was only a handful. But to be both an uplander and a Bellator, that must involve some serious split loyalties.

I wonder what he thought of last night's incident?

Before she could ask though, Millus Flavius gave a quick whistle, summoning the Centus to the front of the cohort. Gathering his reins in one hand, Aaron gave her another wink.

"Duty calls. See you around then . . . spirit binder."

Keira watched him go, curiosity tugging at the back of her mind. But after a few moments, her gaze was again pulled back to the horizon, watching and waiting for any sign of Danny's return.

~

THEIR DAYS FELL into a steady rhythm over the following days. Danny made it back from his scouting mission safely and while things with him were still a bit strained, they both went to great lengths to pretend otherwise. The lack of shouting matches and the polite discourse were enough that Keira could almost forget the conflict that lay beneath it all—almost.

Danny, meanwhile, had found a budding friendship in Centus Aaron Tiobraide. On any given night, they could be heard swapping war stories around the fire at all hours. During the day, the two often rode together up front, discussing tactics or Lorenan history. It was on just such a day that Keira found herself riding next to the elusive Cross-Sea warrior, dressed in bright purple scarves that wrapped artfully around her head, obscuring most of her face and neck. A beaded strand wrapped around the crown of her head, holding the scarves in place before dangling to the side of her face, a turquoise seashell fastened to the end.

Keira had often wondered about the other girl, so starkly different from her Bellatori compatriots, even the female ones. When she'd asked, Aaron had explained that the Cross-Sea warrior was part of an exchange program at the Academy Bellatori. It had been part of a peace agreement established years ago with the Cross-Sea states— promoting intercultural dialogue, mutual understanding, and all that jazz. Keira knew that Cross-Sea warriors were renowned for their fighting ability, but she'd never thought they'd be so . . . beautiful. There was something about her lethal elegance that was both intriguing and mysterious.

The girl must have sensed the direction of Keira's thoughts, for she turned and gave her a knowing look.

"Go on then," she said.

Keira started, having never actually heard the woman speak before. She stared at her, not knowing quite how to respond. "What?"

The woman's almond-shaped eyes crinkled at the edges, and Keira heard her give a low chuckle.

"Your stare speaks volumes, Keira, as does your silence. Tell me, what has so occupied your thoughts?" The woman's voice had a soft, clipped intonation, her syllables tumbling one after the other even as the breath between her words expanded.

"Y-your scarves," Keira stammered, settling on the first thing that came to mind. "They're so lovely. Do all the people in your country wear them?"

The warrior inclined her head in thanks and considered her question. "It is considered a very personal choice. Many do, but not all. It is a question of how much of yourself you wish the world to see."

Keira blinked, intrigued. There was something so appealing about that—the ability to control how much of yourself you showed to others.

"Maybe I should follow your lead," she said, a small smile tugging at her lips. "Danny says my face is an open book. But it would be nice to close it every once in a while."

The warrior laughed unexpectedly—a high, feminine sound that made Keira's smile widen. "I just realized I never got your name."

The warrior inclined her head again in that odd way she had and said, "Inaba Sara. But please, just call me Sara. So tell me, have you always lived in Loren?"

"Well," Keira said, hesitating. It had been a while since anyone had asked her about her background. The villagers in Abalás tended to avoid her and the legionnaires who passed through already knew who she was and where she came from. "It's sort of a long story. But no, not always, just the last few years, actually."

"Hmm," Sara said, her eyes suddenly mischievous. "Well, that is the lovely thing about long trips, isn't it? They're perfectly primed for long stories—preferably filled with adventure and just the hint of some romance."

Once again, Keira found herself smiling. It had been a long time since she'd had someone to talk to like this and never someone so similar—a girl around her own age who was a warrior in her own right. Keira's mind flashed back to the girls in the dress shop with their sideways glances and mocking laughter. It had been years since she'd even tried to make friends, other than Danny, of course.

"Ahh, I see what you mean about the open book." Sara said. "I've embarrassed you."

Keira felt her blush deepen and she shook her head. "Not you, just a . . . bad memory. So in the Cross-Sea Lands nobody shows their faces?"

Sara graciously accepted the turn in the conversation and said, "Men and women in my country will often choose to show their faces only to trusted friends and family—preferring to communicate with the wider world through words and gesture rather than expression. And you would be surprised how much may be conveyed through the eyes alone." As if in point, Sara's own kohl-lined eyes crinkled, the purple accents on her eyelids making them appear bold and excited.

Keira nodded slowly, curious about this land and culture so different from anything she'd previously known. But the need for privacy, now that was something she understood. "I feel like that would be very freeing. You're content with yourself and don't need anyone else to see or approve of you."

Sara sent her a curious look, and Keira couldn't help but wonder if she'd said something wrong.

"My scarves give me control over who I allow to see me, but *everyone* needs those they can let in," she said, raising her eyebrows.

Keira squirmed slightly at the emphasis placed on "everyone." She was no longer sure if she liked the direction this conversation was going.

The woman continued. "Everyone needs to be truly known. The key—" Here she paused, giving Keira a considering look. "—is to make sure the people you allow to know you truly deserve it."

Keira avoided those eyes that saw all too much, and they rode quietly for a while, her mind swimming with Sara's words. She thought of Danny then—wondered if maybe, just maybe, he deserved to see more of her. She wasn't sure if she could handle that, and more importantly, wasn't sure if he could, either. With her luck, one peek at her messy inner self would send him running in the opposite direction. And that was a heartbreak she just didn't think she could bear.

She shook her head ruefully. That was the real problem with long trips, she decided—too much time for thinking.

THE DAYS PASSED one after the other with the soul-crushing monotony that only an unchanging landscape could provide. And as the Olpheís Plains stretched long on either side, the only thing that made it bearable was the long conversations Keira struck up with Sara. They talked about everything, from weaponry and preferred training drills to the latest styles of dress and music that were popular in both Loren and the Cross-Sea Lands. The two even broached the subject of their families, though Keira was sure to couch her stories in vagaries that kept the more revealing details to herself. And by the end of the first week, Keira had to admit to herself that maybe, just maybe, she had a budding friendship in front of her. The thought sent a thrill of excitement and absolute terror coursing through her. So of course, her first instinct was to run in the opposite direction. Best not to jinx anything, she told herself.

Which was how on the following day, she found herself riding at the front of the cohort, next to none other but the Millus himself. Gaius Flavius was a man of few words, and while Keira would normally find this incredibly annoying, the more time that passed with Danny subtly avoiding her, the less she actually felt like talking to anybody. Riding next to Flavius at the head of the cohort, Keira was left alone to dwell on her thoughts. Unfortunately, her thoughts weren't exactly the reprieve she was hoping for.

By hour three, the silence was back to driving her nuts. *I mean, come on*, she thought, *who just says nothing at all?* Even when a snake had slithered across the path earlier, startling both their horses, the man had said absolutely nothing! A few pats on his horse's neck, and that was it. It was absolutely infuriating.

By hour five, Keira decided to do something about it.

"So," she said as nonchalantly as one could to the old gargoyle. "Did you always want to be a Bellator?"

Flavius kept his gray eyes fixed straight ahead. Keira waited a few moments and had opened her mouth to repeat the question when he suddenly replied in a low, clipped tone.

"Yes."

That was it. Keira waited for more, but nope, that was all the answer she would get. *Okay*, she thought stubbornly, *now you're just being childish.*

"Well, what drew you to this line of work?" she asked. *Try to answer that in one word or less, Millus.*

Flavius chose less, saying nothing at all. Keira was not about to be so easily thwarted.

"Tell me about your family." she prompted.

He turned to stare at her, his mouth a thin, straight line. "You ask a lot of questions," he said finally.

Not knowing how to respond to that, Keira merely shrugged. "Thank you, but the last one wasn't a question." She raised her eyebrows at him pointedly and was rewarded with what, to her absolute shock, proved to be the tiniest of smirks.

Flavius ran a hand over the bristles of his closely cropped graying hair. "My family have been members of the Bellatorio since before the Marian wars of ascension here in Loren." Keira raised her eyes in surprise but said nothing, not wanting to spook him into silence. "While the first son is duty-bound to manage the family's affairs, the second and third sons have always joined the Bellatorio."

Keira smiled. "I get it. It's like the family business."

"Indeed."

"Do you have any children?"

Flavius glanced at her, startled, before clearing his throat. "I do. A son. His name is Cyrus, and I'm—well, I'm not married to his mother." His ears turned a deep red, and he cleared his throat again roughly. "It wouldn't have been fair to her, you see. But he has my name and my support, and that's what's important."

Keira nodded. She'd become acquainted with Loren's complex inheritance laws only superficially in the few years she'd been there, but she knew legitimacy was always a touchy subject.

"Does he want to join the Bellatorio?" she asked, hoping to steer the conversation towards lighter subjects. Flavius's jaw clenched. *Apparently not that one, then.*

"He is a Bellator, yes. Personal aid to Imperator Servius of the Southern Imperium, in fact."

Keira heard a note of pride in his voice and nodded appreciatively, but the tension in his jaw made her pause. "Does he—well, does he enjoy it?"

Flavius's head snapped toward her, eyes narrowed. "What kind of question is that?"

Taken aback, Keira faltered. "I—I don't know, I just—"

"What does it matter if we *enjoy* our work? We work because it is our duty, nothing more."

Alrighty then, Keira thought. *I'll take that as a no.*

The rest of the day's ride was passed in silence.

LATER THAT NIGHT, as Keira was adding a log to the fire, she passed by Flavius doing his usual pre-bed weapons and armor check. She watched, somewhat nostalgically, as he methodically cleaned each piece with the same sand-and-vinegar concoction that Nazor had been so fond of. Keira knew that Flavius carefully laid each piece out beside his sleeping pallet in the same order every night. Presumably, she thought, so he could grab them at a moment's notice if they were attacked in the dead of night.

So like Nazor, she thought, the memory sending a pang through her. Because along with memories of Nazor came those of Elliott, his nimble fingers binding a satchel of herbs and the laugh that came straight from his belly no matter who was around.

Flavius's eyes jerked up and caught her staring. She blushed and turned away as he went back to cleaning. She turned then to her own sleeping pallet, slipping off her boots before sliding beneath the blankets.

When he'd finished, she heard him climb to his feet and move towards the fire. She guessed he planned to bank it for the night.

She had just burrowed herself in deep beneath the blankets when a sharp cry pierced the night.

She was on her feet in a second, sword at the ready. She calmed slightly as she realized Flavius had only stumbled, but now gripped one leg as he dragged himself back to his pallet. She ran toward him even as he waved her and the other concerned responders off.

"I'm fine," he said through gritted teeth, sweat pouring down his brow.

"You most certainly are not," Keira countered, searching his leg for any external sign of injury or disease. There was nothing. It looked like a perfectly normal leg, but Flavius was clutching at it like it was on fire.

"It's the blood sickness," he said, his normally weatherworn skin paled to a sheet-like white. "It'll pass."

Keira blanched. She'd heard of the blood sickness. Tales of those afflicted—mostly in the tropical islands of the Southern Shield, but sometimes spread north by merchants and traders—had made their way to Abalás over the years. Its unfortunate victims experienced episodes of intense pain in one or more of their extremities with no outward signs of injury. Elliott had talked about studying it once, believing it related to the blood-borne diseases of their old world. Unfortunately, he'd never gotten the chance.

Keira waited by Flavius's side until the pain seemed to pass. He collapsed backward on his pallet, and she quickly grabbed a wet cloth for him as he'd sweated through most of his clothes. He gave her a grateful nod. She waited for a moment, intensely curious, but not wanting to intrude.

"Caught it during the Shield Wars," Flavius eventually said. "My entire unit did. I was a Centus at the time, with a hundred men under my command. Seventy of them died from the damned thing, and the rest of us were left to rot from it."

Flavius gingerly tested his leg, bending and extending it, then slowly rolling his ankle, first one way and then the other.

"When I got back, my family connections were the only thing that kept them from discharging me." Flavius shrugged, but his grim expression belied the gesture. "I was on the fast track back then, expected to make Millus by thirty and Imperator by forty. They gave me Millus, but only in *appreciation* for my family's service." His jaw was tight as he looked around at the rest of the sleeping cohort. "This assignment here—retrieving Landrianus—is symbolic, a way of ushering me out. In their eyes, I'm a man far past my prime who should have been discharged years ago, but refuses to go gracefully."

Keira had no idea what to say, her breath catching on every word of sympathy or pointless reassurance. Anything she could say to this man who'd fought and sacrificed so much would be either a platitude or an insult. But was a quiet retirement really all he had to show for it?

"Millus?" she asked hesitantly. "Why tell me all of this now?"

Flavius paused for a long moment as he considered her question thoughtfully. "Let's just say you remind me of someone I used to know

—a very long time ago. You have her fierceness." A small smile tugged at his lips but he quickly banished it with a shake of his head, as if this might clear it also of unwanted memories.

"Never mind the grumbling of an old man, girl. Off to bed with you. We have an early start tomorrow."

Unsure what else to do, Keira complied, but laid awake for what felt like hours afterward, thinking about the chaos of wars, the people who fought in them, and the shells that returned home at their end. If Loren really descended into a civil war as Flavius suspected, what would become of him and his loyal cohort?

TWELVE

As they neared the end of the first week of travel, Danny, not for the first time, wondered what exactly he'd been thinking. It had been a long time since he'd had spent a full week in a saddle, and he was now acutely reminded of what he'd been missing. He shifted again in his seat, wincing at the combination of raw skin and stiff muscles that greeted the movement. Aaron moved his horse up next to his and shot him a sideways grin.

His voice was all innocence as he asked, "Need a pillow, friend? I'm sure we could scrounge somethin' up for you. The road can be hard for those still a little green."

Danny snorted. "Green is it? Shall we put that theory to the test when we make camp? My blade's been getting a bit dull these days."

"Oh ay, first let's just see how you're walkin' come mornin', O'Leary. The legs never lie, see."

"Pretty sure that's never stopped me before."

"And your girl, what does she think of wobbly legs?"

Danny felt himself stiffen and he forced himself to breathe out slowly. "Her name's *Keira*, and you'd have to ask her yourself, though I'd caution you not to do so unarmed."

Aaron chuckled.

"Ay, she's certainly a fiery one. When she showed up at the toll-house, I thought for sure you two had gone your separate ways—or that you were dead in a ditch somewhere."

Danny snorted, "Seems you were wrong, Unfortunately for you."

"See, back in the tavern I got the sense you weren't much interested in joining us."

"Don't know what you're talking about, Aaron. I've always been one for the cause."

He did, though. He'd actually thought a lot about it over the last few days. Why exactly had he come after her? Yes, it was out of loyalty and worry for whatever scrape she'd get herself into. But there was something else, too.

He'd always had a temper, prone to rash decisions borne more of injured pride than good decision-making. According to his mam it was one of his worst traits. And once his temper had cooled after their argument, he'd realized that she'd been—at least in part—absolutely right.

Danny was an excellent soldier, and excellent soldiers stood down and waited for orders once the mission was accomplished. Sure, in an ideal world, they'd wait for directions from the Legion, moving forward only after those with more experience and knowledge than they finally came to a decision. But this wasn't a war, he reminded himself. In fact, they were trying to prevent one, and there wasn't exactly time to stop and ask directions at every point along the road.

But Keira . . . well, she'd never been much of a soldier. She saw a path ahead, one that promised to fulfill the goals they were striving for, and she took it, trusting in their training that they'd eventually find their way out. He admired that about her, that determination, that confidence—even if it sometimes got her into trouble that *he* inevitably had to bail her out of.

She'd come a long way, he realized, thinking back to the timid girl who'd appeared suddenly by a riverbank, dressed in blue jeans and a Red Hot Chili Peppers hoodie—apparently the name of a band, she'd later explained. She'd grown from a scared girl utterly unaccustomed to rough living or the harsh physical demands of training to the capable woman in front of him. She'd grown strong in the months since she'd arrived, used to the ache of well-worn muscles and the indignities of living off the land. He couldn't help but be impressed. It had taken him years in the army to reach that point, city boy that he'd been.

But that was Keira—always surprising him. And she pushed him too, challenged him to be better. She never just accepted things as they were, even when it would be soooo much easier if she did. Just like this whole venture, he realized. If she were just willing to take the easy path, they'd have returned to the Legion, to Nazor, and await their next assignments. Let someone else decide how their skills were best used. But Keira had never been one to take the easy path.

"Well?"

Danny blinked, realizing with a chagrined smile that Aaron had asked him a question.

"Sorry, what was that?"

"I said, you ever miss it? Puttin' on a uniform? Bein' a part of somethin'?"

Danny inhaled, memories of the war—his war—flashing before his mind unbidden. There'd been chaos, yes, bloodshed and carnage on a scale he'd never thought possible. But there'd been good times too—a fierce camaraderie borne of long hours hunkered down in foxholes and adrenaline-filled sprints across deadly terrain. He'd had brothers back then, blokes from all walks of life who seemingly had nothing in common, suddenly willing to die for each other. That bone deep conviction that you truly belong, body and soul.

"Every day."

Aaron nodded, clearly expecting this answer.

Maybe that was why he felt such loyalty to the Legion, Danny wondered. Was this just a new war for him? A new way of belonging? If so, he was really making a muck out of it. Because as much as he tried to find that same connection within the Legion, something always seemed to stand in the way. Whether it was Elliott and Nazor's odd secrecy or Keira's reluctance to truly trust him, he was always left feeling like he just needed to try a little longer, work a little harder. Then maybe, just maybe, he would be good enough.

"Well, you know how it is," Danny said finally, realizing Aaron was watching him curiously. "It feels good to wake up every day knowing you have a purpose, a mission, that you're doing some good in the world."

Something flashed in Aaron's eyes, and Danny saw a muscle twitch in his jaw.

"You know," Danny said. "Like you have in the Bellatorio."

"Definitely," Aaron said, nodding in agreement, even as his posture remained tense. "The Bellatorio."

They said nothing else then, but sat in companionable silence, watching as the last remnants of the day drifted beyond the horizon.

THE FIRST WEEK slid into the next as the cohort plodded their way through the Olpheís Plains. Danny had taken to playing a game with the surrounding landscape, trying in vain to spot trees or wildlife, *something* that would indicate that it was anything other than the barren scrubland it appeared to be. Periodically they would pass groups of Olpheís nomads, traveling the road in the opposite direction, their brightly colored wagon homes in stark contrast to the hungry, desolate faces of the children peering through their windows. They were clearly traveling in search of a better life, and it broke his heart to see their faces crumple with the news that Raboneís had burned, that they'd have to travel far into the Lorenan heartland to bring their herds of sheep and goats to market.

Danny knew that the Olpheís were not well regarded in most of Loren. Thought of as thieves and vagabonds, they'd been driven into the barren wasteland of these plains because they were unwanted everywhere else. To his surprise, he saw obvious sympathy in Flavius's eyes as he peered into their dejected faces. The cohort would often buy a lamb or two to roast from these desperate travelers, who eagerly accepted their coin with deep bows of gratitude. As he watched them leave, Danny wondered about the woman and baby he'd pulled from the burning wagon. Had they made it? And what kind of life could Loren even offer them?

It was the eighth day after they'd left Raboneís when a scout spotted smoke on the horizon. Aaron immediately volunteered to check it out, and Danny offered to go with him.

To his surprise, Keira spoke up. "I'll go, too. Someone needs to watch your backs."

Danny tried to smile but knew the look came out all pinched. They hadn't really talked since leaving Raboneís and the weight of their last argument still fell heavily between them.

As the three of them rode toward the smoke, Danny thought about what, if anything, he could say to ease the tension. The only problem was Aaron, who seemed content to fill the silence with his own brand of inane chatter. Besides, after his comments about Keira the other day, Danny was reluctant to hand him yet more ammunition. Eventually, though, her silence was too much and he resolved himself to find some neutral topic.

He was about to ask Aaron about his favorite type of upland music (sure to snag Keira's interest) when they rounded the top of the next hill and the words faded from his lips.

The smell hit him first, long before his eyes registered what they were seeing. *Death.*

The corpses lay strewn as he suspected they'd fallen, fleeing a circle of burned-out wagons. There were men, women, and children, and by the state of their swollen bodies, Danny suspected they'd been dead for a few days at least.

They slowly made their way toward the site of the massacre, pulling fabric over their mouths and noses as the stench of rotting flesh assaulted their senses. The world suddenly felt very far away and Danny struggled to breathe.

In through your nose, he reminded himself. *Out through your mouth.*

"Who did this?" he asked, voice faint.

Aaron answered, his voice hard and flat, with barely contained rage. "A raiding party, likely hell-bent on keeping the nomads from settling here. No doubt they were hired and paid for by the local Tiarna."

"How do you know?" Keira breathed.

Danny could only stare as they passed a young woman clutching a baby to her chest. What remained of her olive skin was bloated and blood-stained, and flies settled on her empty eyes and cracked lips.

Aaron dismounted and ripped the clasp from the cloak of a body—a man dressed in the plain leather jerkin of a river land hired sword. He showed the clasp to Keira and Danny—it was silver, with a stag's insignia across the front, evidence of a nearby Tiarna's sponsorship. Aaron spat on it and threw it back onto the rotting corpse.

"But why?" Kiera asked, shock and disgust warring for control of her face. "Why should the Benadur care if the nomads settle in Loren? They're not hurting anyone."

Aaron gave a harsh laugh and turned a derisive look toward her. "Because the nobility is so compassionate? No, these nomads are scum to them, fit only to be wiped from the bottoms of their overly polished shoes."

Danny glanced over at him with some surprise. Not that he was overly fond of the Lorenan nobility—he'd heard plenty of the peasantry in and around Abalás complain about the upper class's hold over Loren. Even Elliott had bemoaned the unfair tax burden on the poorest of the poor. But he'd never heard a Bellator speak this way, and never with so much . . . hatred.

"Doesn't . . . well, doesn't the Bellatorio serve the Council of Benadur?" Keira asked slowly.

Aaron's jaw tightened, and he gave her a piercing look. "We serve the Regio, who is indeed accountable to the Council. And I am, of course, loyal to the Bellatorio." His gaze held hers, eyes searching. "But at the end of the day, I am a Lorenan, and while I do what I must to keep my family fed and clothed, it does not make me blind to the excess and injustice of this world." He said this last part bitterly, staring down at the body of a little girl who couldn't have been over ten, though her disfigured features made it difficult to say for sure.

Danny barely heard the last of the Centus's speech, trying as he was to keep a grip on his stomach. His heart raced and an odd sense of panic settled in his limbs. Every body or burned out caravan they passed jolted him back into his own thoughts—dark and twisted as the scene before them. Every image conjured up an answering memory—fire for fire, death for death. The clothes may be different, the weaponry more crude, but the twisted face of death shined just as brightly from all.

Without thinking, Danny slid from Boyd's back and staggered off the road. Slumped against the side of a burned out caravan, he heaved the contents of his stomach into the dirt. He focused all of his willpower on staying upright as the memories came hard and fast.

Creeping through an open field in the dead of night—wide open, vulnerable—waiting for the attack that would come at any moment.

Curling up as tight as he could in a foxhole, shielding his head against a rain of dirt as the scream of shells obliterated the surrounding forest.

Sunken faces peering through shattered windows in bombed-out buildings, hollow eyes tracking their procession through the streets like frightened prey.

"Danny, Danny *breathe*."

He shook his head, eyes squeezed shut, though the images forced their way through unbidden.

The gurgling noises of a boy even younger than he, the wheeze of breath forced through shattered lungs—his fault, all his fault.

"Danny, look at me. I'm here. I'm right here."

Strong arms wrapped around him, and he buried his face in soft curls. They were shaking—no, *he* was shaking.

Keira.

"Shhhhh. This is here, not there. This is now, not then."

Slowly, he felt himself settling back into his body. The images faded and the sensation slowly returned to his limbs.

Funny, he thought. *And I thought I was supposed to be the grounder.*

And with this thought came the realization that they were both kneeling in the mud. He was still clinging to her. Shame coursed through him and he looked away.

"Hey," Keira whispered. Pulling his face back to hers, she carefully leaned her forehead against his, eyes fixed on him. "You don't have to look away. I'm not."

Danny stared at her, breathing in the soft scent of lavender that always seemed to follow her.

You are here, not there. This is now, not then.

A throat cleared from behind him and he suddenly remembered they weren't alone. Staggering to his feet, he pulled Keira right along with him.

"You, um. You all right then?" Aaron asked, rubbing a hand against the back of his neck.

Danny grunted in acknowledgement as he remounted his horse.

"We should get back to the others, let them know what's happened."

Aaron nodded, turning his horse to lead the way back to camp.

Danny followed, carefully avoiding Keira's worried gaze as they made their way back through the massacre.

You are here, not there. This is now, not then.

CHAPTER

THIRTEEN

The shock of discovering the murdered Olpheís nomads cast a pall over the cohort. They'd made camp for the rest of the day, taking the time to organize a grave-digging detail, but now found themselves back on the road, plodding along in a somber procession.

Keira herself still struggled against the waves of fury and indignation that coursed through her limbs. Until this point, the chaos threatening Loren had been largely an abstraction—some nameless entity that the Legion opposed and Keira needed to defeat if she was to gain their favor. But then it had taken Elliott from her, and now . . . this. *This* was what chaos looked like in the flesh, what they all faced if order wasn't restored . . . and soon. Chaos was lives destroyed—mothers, fathers, and children dead and with no thought given to a decent burial. It was hatred meted out indiscriminately to those too weak to defend themselves. And it rankled Keira to her very core.

In the days that followed, though, her attention and concern focused more and more on Danny. As they passed more nomads headed south, he could barely look at them, these sad sojourners. His panic at the sight of the massacre had caught her wholly off guard and, if truly be told, scared her to her core. Danny was her rock, immovable and constant. But he needed her now, and she'd be damned if she let him struggle alone.

Keira had tried for days to talk to him about what had happened, but each time he hastily changed the subject. She didn't want to force him, Pneumos knew she what that was like. But the night before, she'd woken to find him tangled in his bedroll, drenched in sweat. Unable to decipher his frantic murmuring, Keira had tried to rouse him as gently as she could. He'd come to with a ferocious roar, and she'd jumped back in surprise as he grasped for the sword that, thankfully, he'd kicked away in his sleep. His unseeing eyes looked straight through her at some unseen enemy.

His eyelids then drifted shut nearly as quickly as they'd opened, and he curled back up in his bedroll, movements still jerky but less frantic than they'd been. Keira had stared helplessly at him. He looked so small, curled up like that, like the little boy she could just imagine him being. She was struck by a sudden desire to wrap him in her arms, soothing and holding him until the nightmares passed, but she didn't. She couldn't name the thing that stopped her, but felt its hold all the same. So instead, she returned to her own bedroll and the fitful sleep she knew awaited her.

Watching him the following day, Keira wanted to talk to him the way they used to. She wanted to laugh and joke and tease him. But most of all, she wanted to tell him that everything would be all right. She wanted to assure him that the dreams would pass, that when all of this was done, they could go back and rebuild the farm near Abalás, returning everything to the way it had been. But how could she convince him of something that she didn't even believe herself?

Give him time, Sara had advised when she'd explained their situation, the awkward silences that now descended where only comfortable companionship had lived before. *You're doing what you believe to be right. And he obviously knows that or else he wouldn't be here. He'll come around eventually and the two of you will sort things out.* Keira dearly hoped she was right.

In the meantime, Danny continued to struggle. The nightmares became more frequent, and his mood turned more morose as each day dragged on. Eventually, even Aaron grew tired of his sour moods and left him to ride alone, trailing on the outskirts of their cohort. Keira watched him, heart aching, and wanted nothing more than to give him some comfort, but still he did everything possible to avoid her.

It was three days after the massacre that Keira found her opportunity. One horse had thrown a shoe, and it forced the whole cohort to make camp while it was repaired. After settling Cerise, Keira tracked Danny down. She found him perched on a fallen log near the campsite, silently whittling a point onto a wooden stake. Keira plopped down beside him and watched his careful efforts. She noted the deep shadows beneath his eyes and the way he stared blankly at a point just beyond the horizon. A cold stone of worry settled in the pit of her stomach.

"I know about the nightmares, Danny." She finally said, feeling him stiffen beside her. She pushed on. "I know things between us have been . . . weird, but please, talk to someone at least. Maybe Aaron or Flavius? Surely, if anyone could understand, they would."

He said nothing and they sat in silence for several minutes. Keira desperately wanted to say something, anything, but she resolutely forced herself to shut up for once. This was Danny's time, and she knew he needed to be the first to speak.

Finally, Danny broke the silence. "I used to get them a lot when I first arrived—the nightmares, I mean."

He wasn't looking at her, only staring at something far off in the distance, something she could never see.

"They faded after a while—by the time you got here, they were only once in a blue moon."

"Were they about the war?" Keira asked quietly. "Your war, I mean."

Danny nodded, and she saw his jaw tighten.

"I wish I could see them."

He stared at her in disbelief.

"No, you don't."

"It would only be fair. You have to deal with all my crap." She paused, watching him carefully. "I'm sorry, you know. I know no one wants to have someone else's dark shit in their heads. You didn't choose any of this.

"I'm your grounder. That's just how it works."

She swallowed, heart aching at his defeated tone, the weary set of his shoulders. He was exhausted.

"Well, it sucks."

He nodded, but said nothing further. She didn't press him, but just waited, mentally preparing herself for whatever he might share.

"It was after Normandy," he began, turning the pointed stake over in his hands. "I'd been in the army for a few years, made sergeant by that point. I mean, if you'd survived that long and were willing to keep goin', hell, they'd beg you to take the promotion."

He shook his head, bitterness etched in every line of his face, which suddenly seemed much older. "The landing was hellish enough, but it was the overland invasion that really—" He stopped, swallowing hard, then turned to stare at her, eyes desperate and pleading. "It was the *people*, Keira. Their faces were just hollow. Clearly starvin', and they looked so *beaten*. We're walkin' through these tiny villages, and they're just—they were *gone*, Keira, whole villages, just flattened. And the graves, well, the graves were everywhere."

He grabbed her hand then, startling her out of her reverie. "And I'd like to think it was just the Germans, Keira, but—" He shook his head vigorously. "I know, it had to have been us, too."

He was stammering now—the words tripping over themselves in their rush to escape. "Our boys had made bombing runs ahead of the landing. They were trying to disrupt communications and transportation, but—" he stopped then, squeezing his eyes closed, "the looks on their faces...some of those looks were because of us, and I—well, I've never known how to live with that."

His eyes were glassy as they looked deep into hers. She wanted to cry, but she didn't. Instead, she wrapped her arms around Danny and just held him as he shook. In that moment, despite all she'd fought for and pursued, she wished for all the world that they were back on their little farm near Abalás, back when it seemed nothing terrible could ever reach them.

Finally, the shaking stopped and the two of them just sat there, holding each other.

"I don't mind, you know." Danny said finally, glancing up at her.

"Don't mind what?"

"The dreams, your memories, I mean. They help actually, help me understand."

"Understand what?"

"Well . . . you."

She inhaled sharply through her nose, fighting down the familiar sense of panic that came with the thought of being so utterly exposed. He'd shared so much with her, she could let her guard down, just this once. So steadying her nerves, she slowly ventured forward.

"She wasn't all bad, you know, my Mom." Her eyes shot to his, searching for any sign of disbelief. But his face was carefully neutral.

"I'm sure she wasn't."

"Some of that stuff, with her boyfriends, well she didn't know how bad it was."

Danny was quiet for a long moment.

"She didn't belief you, even when you told her."

And when Keira glanced at him, she saw the clenched angle of his jaw. A familiar shame washed through her and she tightened her fingers on the edge of the log until her knuckles turned white—physically restraining herself from leaping to her feet and running as far away as she could.

But he needed her. Danny was hurting and she couldn't leave him now.

"Mom had . . . Mom had her own issues, Danny. She needed me."

She still needs me.

She didn't say the thought aloud. After all, they'd had this argument before. How many times had she tried to run away in the first few months in Loren? How many days had she spent by the riverbank where she'd first arrived, before she even really knew how to channel her pneuma, trying to craft some sort of bind that would send her home?

Danny had told her repeatedly that it was hopeless, that it did no one any good if she got herself killed or undone trying to find a way back. Eventually, she'd stopped trying, and she knew he'd assumed she'd given up. But she'd never stopped hoping. Elliott had taught them about what service to the Legion meant, of the eventual discharge that could send you home, back to your own time. And one way or another, she would find her way back.

"Looks like the others are about ready to get going," Danny said suddenly, shocking her out of her own thoughts. She nodded, trying and failing at a smile. He paused, eyeing her before squeezing her hand gently. "Thanks, Keira."

She blinked up at him in surprise.

"For what?"

"For being here. For . . . understanding."

She tried and failed to swallow the knot in her throat.

"Always, Danny."

THE SHADOWS that weighed on the cohort seemed to grow lighter as they continued on in their travels, the sprawling bulk of Mount Ánghen growing larger by the day. They each found comfort where they could. Danny and Keira resumed their daily training sessions, the ice between them finally showing signs of thaw. In time, their new friends, Sara and Aaron, joined them. But still a tension remained, a knowledge of the true stakes at play in this game they played.

For their part, Danny and Aaron seemed to deal with the pressure by taking obscene pleasure in trying to kill each other day in and day out, each seeing how far they could push the other before he yielded.

And while each bout ended in laughter and handshakes, Keira sensed that both had been more bothered by the murder of the Olpheís nomads than they wanted to let on.

Keira and Sara tended to roll their eyes at such nonsense. Training was one thing, risking injury on silly one upmanship was quite another.

So when Danny and Aaron were both assigned the night watch one day, Keira and Sara decided it would be wise for the two not to go unchaperoned. They'd made camp on the edge of a thickly wooded grove that offered some protection from the fierce winds that whipped across the plains. And so the four of them found themselves alone well after midnight, sitting around the banked remains of the evening fire on the edge of camp, swapping stories of Legion missions, Bellatori raids, and the warring clans of the Cross-Sea Lands.

Eventually, the four settled into companionable silence, watching as the last embers faded from the banked fire.

"Well, I'm hungry," Sara declared suddenly, stretching languidly as she rose to her feet. After a brief rummaging through her gear, she unearthed a small metal tin and brought it back into the small circle of light cast from the glowing embers.

She cracked open the lid, unleashing a smoky, spiced aroma that made Keira's mouth water.

"They're called Ana-Hoshi, sun-dried delicacy meats from my homeland. My sister sent them to me."

The three of them gathered around to take in the delicious smelling snack foods.

Aaron nodded. "My brother used to do the same. Care packages do wonders for the homesickness when you're off on campaign."

A tiny spark of irrational jealousy pricked at Keira. "You have a sister? Are you two really close, then?"

Something flickered in Sara's eyes but was gone in an instant. "As girls, we were inseparable. As we got older, well . . . you know sisters."

Keira smiled and nodded, though of course, she really had no idea.

"But we keep in touch and she sends me these little reminders of home."

Sara passed the tin to Keira then, who took a piece before passing it along to Aaron. Rich spices assaulted her mouth as she chewed the smoked meat, relishing the low burn in her throat as she swallowed.

"Ooooh, Sara, that's so good!"

Sara's eyes crinkled at the edges as she smiled, nodding her head in thanks.

Aaron sniffed the contents of the tin, nose wrinkling with suspicion as he withdrew the tiniest sliver of dried meat.

"Don't bother giving any to that one," Keira said, nodding toward Danny. "He's never been able to handle his spice."

Danny's eyes narrowed at her, and she offered a beatific smile in return.

"You know it's true."

Danny snagged the tin from Aaron's still suspicious inspection and plucked his own piece from within.

"Just because I don't share your masochistic tendencies, Keira, doesn't mean I'm not perfectly capable of—"

His eyes bugged as the taste finally registered and he enacted a comic fish gulping motion as he tried to chew while simultaneously swallowing the very air to cool his throat.

"You all right there, friend?" Aaron laughed, clapping Danny on the back, which appeared to only make the swallowing process harder.

Keira about fell over in cackling delight and even Sara's tinkling laugh echoed around the fire pit.

"Not . . ." Danny heaved, "Funny." His face was red by the time he finally swallowed and a thin sheen of sweat dotted his brow.

"Here, take some water," Aaron said, offering Danny the filled ladle from a nearby bucket just as Danny lurched himself to his feet, resulting in spilled water all down his front.

The group erupted in yet more laughter and Danny's eyes sparked.

"You should see your face," Keira laughed, wiping a tear from the corner of her eye.

"Oh, should I?" Danny asked, reaching nonchalantly for the handle of the nearby bucket.

"Ooooh, no. No, you don't, Danny O'Leary!" Keira cried, jumping to her feet just as Danny lunged for her. She darted around the fire pit, squealing as first one arm and then another encircled her waist. She tried to wiggle away, bracing one arm against his as the full bucket he held tilted perilously toward her.

"Do you yield, Legionnaire?" Danny growled. A low laugh rumbled through his chest and reverberated through her own body, making her tremble from more than just exertion.

"Never!"

The bucket inched ever closer.

"Shhhh," Aaron warned, still laughing himself. "You trying to wake up the entire camp?"

Taking his point, Danny slowly released her. "Next time," he promised, eyes twinkling.

"You wish," Keira shot back, breath catching at the sight of Danny's still heaving chest. She pivoted away from him, busying herself with re-arranging her blankets and praying she wasn't turning red.

"*You* two seem on better terms," Sara whispered, sidling up next to her with brows raised suggestively.

Keira shoved her lightly, feeling her face flush.

"Does this mean—"

"What's that?" Aaron asked suddenly, and the tone of his voice drew them all up short. In an instant, they were all suddenly reminded of the dangers of the road, the massacre they'd just witnessed, and the reason they were standing guard in the first place. Aaron's hand flew to his hilt as he gestured out toward the darkness. "There's something out there!"

He started forward and, not to be outdone, Danny was by his side in an instant. Keira and Sara gripped their own weapons, tensing as the two boys creeped forward. Keira felt her pulse hammer in her ears as Danny drew closer to the dark, impenetrable woods. Aaron signaled to Danny and the two of them split up, each coming to one side of the nearest crop of bushes.

Danny counted them down—one . . . two . . . three. The two of them lunged forward into the bushes from either side. Keira tensed as the attack was met by a loud screech and shouted epithets from the boys.

Aaron staggered back, swiping blindly with one hand as he clutched his other hand to a bleeding gouge across one cheek.

"What in the BLOODY—"

A blur raced across the ground toward Aaron and Keira gave a shout of warning as she staggered forward. Danny was quicker though and raced after it, swinging his sword in an arch that just missed the creature. A hiss echoed around the outcropping and Keira blinked in surprise as the large feline snarled at the four of them, holding its ground as it slowly retreated into the woods.

They all stared after it in silence for a long moment.

"It appears our foe is, in fact . . . a cat." Sara said, amusement coloring her innocent words.

"Pretty big cat," Aaron muttered, cursing as he touched his fingers to his cut cheek once more. Danny snorted and they all join in a loud chorus of laughter. Aaron glanced back at the woods, looking sheepish.

"Thought it might have been one of those damn Tiarna, or their men." Aaron muttered, ignoring their sniggering. "Too bad. I'd have liked to teach them a lesson or two."

The tone of his words brought the laughter to a swift halt and they all looked over at Aaron, his knuckles white as he clutched his sword and stared out into the darkness.

"I too would see justice done, for the fate of the Olpheís nomads," Sara said slowly, head cocked to the side as she surveyed Aaron carefully. "But surely that means an investigation and a trial before punishment is issued."

Aaron leveled her with an icy stare.

"There is right and wrong. And those who prey on the weak forfeit all my sympathies."

No one said anything to that, but the weight of his burning anger simmered around them, a live wire that none dared touch.

"What exactly is going on here?"

They all spun to meet the cool gray eyes of one Millus Flavius, who definitely did not share their amusement.

"I ordered a night watch, not a carousing. And you, Tiobraide, I expected more from you."

Aaron stiffened, and Keira saw a flush course across his face as he dropped his gaze.

"I-I'm sorry Millus. It won't happen again."

Keira felt for him, knowing how much Aaron looked up to Millus Flavius—'worshipped' was probably more accurate, actually.

"Indeed," Flavius said finally, eying the four of them with an inscrutable expression. "Well, I rest assured knowing that the camp is at least well-guarded against our enemies—feline or otherwise."

And with that, Flavius turned away, but not before Keira caught the twinkle of laughter in his eye. She stared after him, surprise and amusement warring within her. And it made her wonder what Gaius Flavius must have been like at their age, before the years of war and hardship had carved sharp corners into him. Had he been like Aaron? A young hothead, quick to laugh but full of righteous indignation and itching to prove himself?

She supposed she'd never know.

CHAPTER

FOURTEEN

It was day eleven when they finally reached the base of the towering Mount Ánghen. Gazing up at the snaking stairs that wound their way up over the harsh crags of the slate-gray mountainside, Keira fiercely stomped on her looming fear of heights. After all, this was the only path to the famed monastery in the sky, where the great sages of Pneumos tutored and cared for the lone Lorenan prince and future Regio.

There were few things Keira hated more than terrible jokes and talking about her feelings, but dizzying heights were most definitely among them. As they climbed the ancient stone steps, Keira clung absurdly to the cliff wall, fighting the waves of nausea that threatened to drown her whenever she ventured too near the stair edge. Seeing the trouble straight off, Danny had at first teased her about short people and not liking it so far from the ground, much to the raucous appreciation of the rest of the cohort. Nevertheless, he'd settled in behind her as they climbed, placing an encouraging hand on her shoulder whenever she paused to steady her nerves. Things weren't entirely back to normal between them, but their cooled tempers and Danny's confession about his nightmares and the war had helped. It was a start, at least.

The higher they got, the more Keira struggled to breathe, which was absurd, of course. They weren't high enough for the air to have thinned *that* much. Aaron urged her to slow her breathing so she

139

wouldn't pass out, and she did her best, but her rising panic wasn't exactly the easiest to suppress. When the gates of the mountain monastery loomed before her, its towers and parapets carved from the cliff itself, she breathed a sigh of relief and picked up her pace, despite her aching quads.

When they finally reached the landing in front of the massive gate, they were greeted by a rake-thin man in blood-red robes that fell gracefully around him. The sun glinted off his hairless head, and his black eyes looked out from under eyelids that lacked even the smallest of lashes.

Do they pluck them one by one? Keira wondered, morbidly fascinated. *Or wax them all at once?* Probably not the best time to ask, she decided.

Flavius approached the monk first and saluted him with a hard thump of his forearm across his chest. The monk bowed languidly in response.

"I am Millus Gaius Flavius," he declared formally. "My cohort and I have journeyed from Crîd Eálas on behalf of Regio Claudius and do humbly request an audience with his highness, Lord Landrianus."

The monk regarded him, his hairless eyes large and unblinking.

"Yes," he replied in a high, wraithlike voice. "We received your message. Lord Landrianus is expecting you." And with that, he turned and glided through the imposing gates, leaving the cohort to follow him.

He led them into the receiving hall and commanded them to wait while he informed the young prince of their arrival. Keira shifted uneasily, staring around at the charcoal black pillars evenly spaced on either side of the magnificent hall. Spider-like red veins snaked up their length towards the clerestory, where ancient windows allowed clouded light to filter into the chamber below.

"They worship Pneumos, you said?" she murmured quietly. "I don't know—this place gives me the creeps."

Danny grunted in quiet agreement, eyes darting to the shadowed corners of the grand hall. Keira noticed several Bellators had rested their hands on their sword hilts, which didn't exactly put her at ease. She was just wondering if she ought to loosen her own sword when the door at the opposite end of the hall flew open with a crash, startling everyone as the sound reverberated throughout the hall.

In strode a rangy youth, only nineteen or twenty, his age betrayed by the sparse beard that grew just along his jawline. His carefully coiffed chestnut hair fell in waves to his shoulders, and his sapphire-blue eyes roamed lazily around the room until they settled on the cohort. He strode over to the ornate chair perched on the dais at the front of the hall and collapsed into it, one leg flung lazily across an armrest as he sprawled his long limbs across the piece of furniture. The two Bellators that followed him in—apparently the only protection needed in this desolate place—took their places on either side of the chair, faces carefully expressionless.

The prince made a half-hearted gesture with two fingers toward the cohort, evidently beckoning them forward. Keira gritted her teeth but approached him with the others. She didn't care if this guy was the future Regio—he was obviously a pampered arse.

"Since when do monasteries have throne rooms?" she muttered out the side of her mouth.

Danny snorted quietly. "Apparently since they acquired spoiled princelings."

Flavius kneeled before Landrianus, thumping his fist in salute. "Your highness, we bring word from your father, Regio Claudius. Your presence has been requested by the Council of Benadur, who from the holy lands of Ulgáris do ensure order in the name of Pneumos, protection to the sovereign realm of Loren, and peace to its citizens therein."

Flavius rattled off the traditional script with aplomb and, at the prince's apathetic gesture, rose to his feet, standing at attention before him.

Landrianus let out an exaggerated groan. "Sour old bastards. As if it wasn't enough to banish me to this Pneumos-forsaken place! And now I'm to heed their every beck and call like some page boy."

Flavius was perfectly still, but Keira saw Aaron stiffen at the prince's words while the other Bellators shifted uncomfortably. No one spoke of the Council that way, least of all a Marian. The Council was the last connection the people of Loren had to their pre-Marian sovereignty. Sure, Elliott had always said their power was minimal, but they were an important symbol, a vital concession that kept the people contented.

Landrianus barely seemed to notice his misstep, looking around as if suddenly bored by their appearance before him, and clearly resentful that they had brought him actual work to do. Keira pursed her lips. *Either he's so privileged that he doesn't realize what he's implied,* she thought, *or he's an idiot and just doesn't care.*

"Send word to the Council and to my father..." Landrianus paused, a smirk twitching at the corners of his mouth, ".... giving them my *deepest* regrets that I'll be unable to accept the invitation, being *most* busy with my studies here."

At his words, a chorus of giggles erupted from the far door where he'd entered from, and Keira spotted three pairs of eyes peering out from the other room. At the notice of the cohort, the three immediately fled, their delighted shrieks echoing down the hall, but not before Keira glimpsed loose hair and scantily clad shoulders disappearing around the corner.

I'll bet you're busy, Kiera thought, her frustration with his flippant tone growing by the minute. *Doesn't he know what's at stake here?* An image of burned wagons and the dead Olpheís nomads flashed in her mind and she felt her temper flare.

Landrianus, obviously unruffled by the interruption, stood then to go, and Keira saw Flavius shift in discomfort, clearly unsure what to do. He glanced at Aaron, who looked equally flustered and more than slightly annoyed. However, to Keira's shock, neither of them seemed ready to stop him.

Oh no, you don't, she fumed, striding toward him without consciously deciding to do so.

The two Bellators who flanked him immediately stepped forward to block her way. Keira felt movement behind her as well, her companions of the last two weeks no doubt perfectly willing to tackle her at the first sign of royal inclination.

"Excuse me," she called. The silence behind her was deafening in its disapproval. "That is, your highness?"

Landrianus paused and glanced curiously over his shoulder. "Yes?"

She cleared her throat, finding it suddenly and inconveniently dry.

"Your highness, we've traveled a long way and seen much of your realm. And it—" She hesitated, gritting her teeth, before barreling on. "Well, it's falling apart, your highness."

An audible gasp behind her made Keira's stomach somersault. Still, she persisted. "There is discontent, your highness, among the peasantry who cannot pay their taxes and resent the brutality of some of your Bellators. There are attacks on the Olpheís nomads. And Raboneís—I mean, for Pneumos's sake, Raboneís was destroyed by an angry mob."

Her words were tripping over themselves by the end, and when she finally finished, she was met with absolute silence, the entire room waiting for what the future Regio would do to punish such insolence.

Landrianus turned to face her fully, his head cocked at an angle as he stared at her in confusion. It would have been hilarious if she wasn't so nervous.

"And who are you?" he asked finally, crossing his arms in obvious disapproval.

"Keira Altman, your highness."

"Well, you're certainly not a Bellator. You'd be flogged for such insolence."

"She absolutely would," came a steely voice behind her, which she recognized as belonging to Flavius. "However, she is a pneumonancer with the Legion of Pneumos—not yet a full Legionnaire, but she has been of some assistance to us."

Landrianus suddenly regarded her with more interest. "Really? An actual pneumonancer? I assumed they were just stories." He looked her up and down with a small smile. "This one is certainly plucky."

Keira glared at him. She *really* hated being talked about like she wasn't there.

"I would have thought you'd have learned of us in your *studies*," she shot back at him. She watched as his expression darkened and cursed her own temper. Well, it was too late now.

"How dare you," he began, voice low and deadly. "I am the future Regio and head of the Marian dynasty. I will not be spoken to in such a way."

"Well, someone has to!" Keira exclaimed in exasperation. "People, *your* people, are dying! And you're—what? Going to stay here screwing around instead of actually doing your *job*?"

For a moment, Keira thought he might throw something at her. But just then, she couldn't care less. The scent of charred wood and death still curled in her nostrils and she sure as hell wasn't backing down for the boy king with a complex. She watched as Landrianus's hands clenched and unclenched, and his teeth ground together almost audibly. Finally, seething, he said, "Get her out of my sight."

A vise-like hand gripped her arm, and she looked up into the thunderous face of Flavius, who looked as if he'd like to strangle her himself. She met his gaze with far more defiance than she felt and wondered absently if her pneuma could get her out of whatever jail cell they were about to throw her in.

"Please excuse her impertinence, your highness." The voice came from her other side, and she looked over to see that Danny had stepped forward to kneel before the prince. "We've had a lengthy trip, and our Legionnaires speak with more *directness* than is acceptable when addressing royalty. I ask that you please forgive her."

Keira's eyes shot daggers into the back of Danny's head. She didn't want that rat's *forgiveness*. He was fully prepared to stand idly by while Loren fell into chaos. What kind of leader was that? But, yielding to the crushing squeeze of Flavius' hand, she conceded to stand in silence.

Landrianus took a moment, glancing between her and Danny, weighing his options. Finally, with a quick flick of his hand, as if bored by the entire fiasco, he gestured for them to leave. "Just take her away."

She felt Flavius's hand loosen. His grip was immediately replaced by Danny's, tugging at her sharply. She moved to follow him and caught sight of Sara—eyes glinting with amusement. Bolstered by her friend's support, Keira dared to shoot one more backward glare at Landrianus, the spoiled fool content to fiddle while Loren burned. Well, she would *not* allow that.

Danny dragged her out to the courtyard at a pace that forced her to jog to keep up with his long stride. Finally, when they had reached a secluded section near a tree in the far corner, Danny let her go and promptly sat down on a rock, stretching his long legs in front of him and leaning back against the tree. He gazed at her expectantly.

"Go on, then."

Keira stared at him, dumbfounded.

"Get it *all* out, out here, where you're less likely to get arrested."

Not needing to be told a third time, Keira launched into the furious tirade that had been on repeat in her head since first entering the monastery.

"What a pompous, no-good, ignorant, infuriating asshole!"

Danny nodded, eyebrows raised, but said nothing.

"*He's* the one who's supposed to stop the looming chaos? He can't even be bothered to leave his little harem and speak to the council! He's supposed to lead the *country?*"

Danny shrugged. "Fate's a fickle mistress."

Keira threw her hands up in exasperation. "There's no way he'll be able to do it. He can*not* be the reason we're here, the one to keep chaos at bay."

Danny cocked his head, studying her. "Maybe he's not. Maybe the Legion should turn its attention elsewhere. He's the future Regio, the one the cohort was sent to retrieve. That doesn't mean he's the answer to what's coming. Does there have to be something more than that?"

Keira groaned. "Come on, Danny. We were brought to Loren for a reason—*here, now*. If not to secure the succession, then what?"

He smirked at her. "You know, for someone who wanted to be a scientist in another life, you place a lot of stock by reasons and callings. Who knows? Maybe the universe's just one big Charlie Foxtrot, without rhyme or reason, and we're all meant to just keep on gettin' on."

Keira fluttered a hand at him, dismissing that choice tidbit. "We have to find someone better," she insisted. "The Legion can't allow that pampered princeling to assume the throne. I mean, give him *more* power? He'd be better off choking on it. Hell, we all would."

Danny's mouth twitched. "That might be a little difficult, seeing as he's the heir. Or are you proposing regicide to boot?"

Keira sighed and rubbed her eyes, stinging with exhaustion from the days on the road.

"Of course not," she said, plopping herself down next to him. "But we're running out of options here. Landrianus is terrible, but maybe he's better than the alternative. Maybe the Legion can still use him." Keira groaned then, throwing her head back against the tree as she stared up at an annoyingly perfect sky.

"Is that really all this is about, Keira?" Danny asked quietly. "Saving Loren, stopping chaos from descending? Because you were pretty hell bent on proving yourself to the Legion long before we realized how bad things really were."

Keira felt her face heat and glanced away, unable to meet his eyes. Her mother's face suddenly came to mind, laughing and rumpling Keira's hair after she'd absentmindedly left the stove on or forgotten to pay the electric bill. "It'll all work out, baby. You know it always does." And she'd been right, usually because Keira found some way to take care of it. But suddenly, the way forward didn't seem so clear.

Everything she'd told Danny was true. Loren really did hover on a knife's edge. They'd both seen that. But it was also true that she had her own reasons as well, something Danny could see all too clearly, even if he didn't fully understand them. Even if he didn't know about her mom.

But one thing was for sure. This boy king would not keep her from finding a way home.

She stared up at the sky and wondered how on earth things had gone this badly. Setting out on this fool's errand, yelling at the future Regio, and now hiding things from her best friend. This was definitely a new low.

Just then, the rest of the cohort emerged from the great hall. Most headed for the stairs, presumably to make camp with the horses at the base of the mountain. But the two peeled off and began heading toward Keira and Danny.

Flavius and Aaron said nothing when they first reached them, making Danny and Keira glance nervously at each other. Then Flavius began, stiffly, "His highness, the future Regio Landrianus, has decided that he will, in fact, be making the journey to speak with the Council of Benadur. We leave at first light."

Keira stared at him. Finally registering what he was saying, she fought valiantly to keep a grin from her face. Based on Flavius's poisonous glare, she suspected her efforts were not appreciated.

It was Danny who spoke, asking, "Shall we make for the base with the rest of the cohort?"

Keira's stomach flip-flopped at the thought of all those stairs, which would surely be even more terrifying on the way down. But Flavius shook his head.

"No, the four of us will stay in the monks' dormitories tonight. His highness would like to see *you*—" He shot Keira another glare. "—first thing in the morning. And I will most certainly be accompanying you, rest assured."

With that, he spun on his heels and headed for a door at the far end of the courtyard. Keira guessed it led to the dormitories. Aaron paused before following him, giving Keira a wink and whispering, "You only said what needed sayin', to be sure." His eyes darkened, and an edge came into his voice. "You're right—the people deserve better."

Keira smiled gratefully at him, and he patted her arm before following Flavius into the dormitories. She turned back to Danny, who was giving Aaron a considering look as he walked away. Keira saw the slight crease between his brows that meant he was confused about something.

She punched him lightly on the arm. "All right then, Sarge. What do we do now?"

Danny shrugged. "Well, I suppose we follow them to Ulgáris. Once Landrianus is safely under the Council of Benadur's protection, we can break off, find the Legion, and tell them all we've learned. If there's a choice to be made about whom to back, they'll be the ones to make it."

Keira nodded. It was a good plan, she decided. The succession would be secured and the Legion would no doubt be grateful, maybe enough to let them complete the rites this year. If they became full legionnaires, that would bring her one step closer to her goals, one step closer to home. Maybe, just maybe, some good could be salvaged from this otherwise awful situation.

KEIRA DREAMED of her mother that night. In the dream, she wandered through the dark hallways of the mountain monastery, always just glimpsing dark curls as they whipped around the far corner. She never saw her face in full, but Keira somehow *knew* that it was her.

"Find me, Keira." Her mother's voice whispered. "I need you."

"Mom?" She called into the void of the mountain. "Mom, where are you?"

There was no reply.

As Keira's feet sped to a run, the hallways seemed only to lengthen. She cried out after her, but Keira's mother didn't seem to hear her, or at least never slowed. Keira felt like she was running through molasses. A voice came from behind her, and she looked back to see Danny in close pursuit and gaining by the second. She tried to run faster, convinced somehow that he'd try to stop her if he caught up. But her feet only slowed further and further until she felt icy fingers wrap around her wrist.

Keira awoke with a start, dripping sweat, and sheets tangled about her legs. She laid there staring at the ceiling of the tiny cloister cell and willed her racing heart to slow. Thoughts of her mother and

Danny bubbled to the surface but she shoved them down with savageness born of years of practice. She had just about resolved to get up for some water when the *click* of a nearby door pricked her ears. She listened as soft footsteps led away from the cell block.

Surely someone's just up for water or a bathroom break, she thought. But there was something about it that bothered her.

On a sudden whim, Keira rolled out of bed and clipped her sword over the tunic she'd worn to sleep. She grabbed her shoes in one hand as she reached for the door. Slowly, ever so quietly, she nudged the door open a sliver and then a bit more. Thankfully, it didn't creak.

Leave it to monks to ensure silence in all things, she thought, smiling to herself.

At the end of the hallway to her right, she could just make out the receding light of a candle around a corner. She left her door ajar, not wanting to risk waking anyone with the click of the latch, and began creeping down the hall after the disappearing light. She kept one hand on the hilt of her sword, though she couldn't have said why. As she passed a window that overlooked the courtyard, she could see by the light that it was still well before dawn, with clouds obscuring all but a sliver of the moon.

When she reached the corner, Keira carefully peered around its edge to make sure the candle had passed around the far turn. Seeing that it had, she sprinted down the hall to reach that corner before its glow had disappeared around the next. She continued this way as the candle and its mysterious conveyor made their way from the cloistered dormitories back toward the main keep. She had almost reached the juncture where the hallway joined the keep when movement from outside drew her eye. Slowing her pace, she slid to one side of a window overlooking the courtyard and carefully peered around the sill.

Two figures could just barely be seen sneaking around the far edge of the courtyard, nearly obscured by the shadows cast from the wall. Keira looked more closely and as they slipped through the gate that led to the mountain stairs, she saw the flutter of crimson cloaks.

A stone dropped in her stomach, and she turned and began sprinting toward the main keep, no longer caring who heard her at this point. She didn't know exactly where she was going, but as she emerged into the great hall, Keira paused only to hastily tug on her shoes before making straight for the back-corner door.

Come on, Altman. Move.

Her feet slapped the hard flagstone floor as she burst through the door. She turned to see a grand staircase at the end of the hallway. Taking the steps two at a time, she reached the top landing within seconds, finding herself smack in front of an ornately decorated door, flanked on either side by lit torches.

No guards.

Setting her teeth, she barreled through the unlocked door.

Once inside, she froze, her mind trying desperately to register the fire-lit image before her. For there was Landrianus, fast asleep, as expected. Yet above him glinted the unsheathed blade of Centus Aaron Tiobraide.

Keira and Aaron's eyes met across the dimly lit room, both gaping in shock at the sudden appearance of the other. He recovered first, his eyes narrowing to regard her with the same coldness she'd seen when they found the murdered Olpheís. Keira saw his grip tighten on the sword and did the only thing her mind could process in that instant.

"Stop!" She screamed. Her voice echoed through the stone keep, and she saw Aaron grit his jaw and glare at her as he swung the sword.

Keira didn't think, didn't plan out the contingencies. There was no Plan B. She dove deep inside of herself and sent her pneuma coursing out of her fingertips on the back of a high-pitched whistle. She threw it toward him and felt her knees buckle. *Clumsy*, she cursed herself. *You forgot to ground yourself.* It was too late now, though, and Danny had no idea she was here. He couldn't save her this time.

She pressed on, feeling her pneuma surge toward the startled Aaron. She wrapped him in it, thin as a sheet, diving in at the pressure points needed to manage the muscle bind. This time, though, surprise was not on her side. Aaron writhed and twisted, trying desperately to throw her off. He let out a strangled cry as he raked his fingers over his skin, clawing at the unseen energy that washed over him. Keira tried to keep her focus, tried to hold the bind, but felt herself loosening, her pneuma unraveling from its hold on her body and his.

From somewhere outside of her body, she saw Landrianus jolt awake and stare in wide-eyed horror at the soldier screaming and writhing above him, his naked blade slashing at an unseen assailant. The prince scrambled from the bed and began calling for help, even as his eyes flashed desperately around the room, presumably in search of some weapon.

Keira could feel herself fading, knew that she had to release the bind if she hoped to return to her body. She tried to fight off the gravity that sought to draw her deeper inside Aaron, toward the stream of consciousness that even now yielded glimpses of his younger self.

A child living amongst the river people of Idarín.

Aaron as a youth, running off to join the Bellatorio.

Promises of a life without poverty and want glinting before his eyes.

Aaron rising through the ranks, fighting the Tramors during the uprising in the arid lands to the north.

And the violence, so much violence. The pain and oppression, witnessed and partaken of.

The heart-wrenching knowledge of his own culpability.

But most of all, the hatred.

With a wrenching jerk, Keira pulled her pneuma loose and begin reeling herself back in. She settled to the floor with a *thump*, body and spirit quivering in one exhausted heap. Gasping for breath, she stared up through sweaty strands of hair at Landrianus. His panicked face jerked back and forth between her and Aaron, who was already rising to his feet, free from Keira's bind. The Bellator trembled as he stood, but the hand gripping the hilt of his sword held steady with a resolution that spoke of years of determined struggle.

"You just had to get involved, didn't you?" he hissed at her, eyes narrowed into slits of fury. "You just had to defend this maggot, though you know as well as I do that he's a pampered arse. A filthy princeling who doesn't care one shit's worth what happens to any of us, much less the country, not as long as he can keep whorin' and lazin' about. He's better off dead than the shit of a Regio he'd become —better for all our sakes."

Landrianus sputtered wordlessly, and for the first time, Keira saw genuine fear in his eyes, rather than just indignant outrage.

"That's not the point, Aaron," she said breathlessly. "And you know it. We have a duty."

Aaron let out a harsh, derisive guffaw. "*Duty*, is it? Was it my duty to slaughter hapless Tramorians during the war, too undisciplined to properly outfit themselves and too prideful to give up when they ought? Is it my duty to stand by now as *my* people get trampled underfoot by their Marian overlords and the cockless Council we're meant to feel *grateful* to even have?" He spat on the floor in front of Landrianus, looking him up and down in disgust. "All because some stupid boy was born the latest wretched member of a failed dynasty that didn't have the sense to die out a hundred years ago when it ought to 'ave."

He took a step toward Landrianus, and Keira stumbled to her feet, leaning heavily on the doorframe as she drew her sword shakily from its scabbard, utter exhaustion warring against sheer willpower.

Aaron laughed in her face. "You can barely stand, Keira. Do yourself a favor and stay out of my way."

It was then that Landrianus bolted for the door. Keira stumbled forward, but was too slow to stop Aaron as he lunged for the boy's collar and dragged him backward, throwing him in a twist of flailing limbs against the wall. Landrianus crumpled to the floor, still conscious, but dazed from the impact. Keira staggered toward them, but knew she wouldn't make it in time to stop Aaron.

Then a whirl of red rushed past her, and Aaron spun to meet the new threat with the metallic clang of crossed swords. The impact of their clash forced the two men apart from one another, and Keira stared in shock at the weatherworn Flavius, sword raised in determined guard, circling warily around his protégé.

"Yield or die, Centus," the old soldier growled.

Aaron howled derisively, easily parrying Flavius's arching strike with a flick of his wrist. "Try again, old man." Then, growing severe, his brow furrowed as the two of them continued to circle like spitting cats. "He's not worth it, Flavius. He's a spineless brat who doesn't know the first thing about real leadership. You really want to die, all to make *him* the next Regio?"

"You swore an oath, Tiobraide," Flavius replied solemnly, "as did I. He *is* the future Regio, and nothing you say can change that."

Aaron shook his head and grimaced, bitter disappointment etched in every line of his face. They continued to circle, toying with each other, while Keira edged around the room toward the slumped prince. Holding her own breath, she felt tentatively for a pulse in the boy's wrist, gasping with relief when she found it. She touched the back of his head, and her fingers came away sticky with blood.

He'll have a lousy headache tomorrow, she thought grimly, *if he makes it that long.*

Another clash of steel jerked her head up, and she saw Flavius grunt in pain as he barely blocked a crushing overhead swing. Aaron's blade bounced off the older man's sluggish parry, and he whipped his sword around for a two-handed crosscut. Flavius danced backward, just beyond the blade's reach. He would have been fine, too, were it not for the slight stumble that left him a hair off-balance.

That was all Aaron needed. Lunging forward, he wielded a savage uppercut, slicing into Flavius's side just above the hip bone. Flavius grunted as he tried to sidestep the bulk of the younger man's strike, but the effort cost him in stability. He grabbed wildly at the bedpost to steady himself and, with an upward glance at the heavy canopy, ripped it from its hangings, letting it tumble to the ground between the two men. Aaron dodged most of the weight, but struggled to untangle himself from the roped tassels. Flavius took his chance then, diving across the bed and ripping a decorative plate shield off the wall.

He beat his sword against it, hilt to plated edge in a riling, thumping beat that echoed down the halls of the keep. Aaron's jaw tensed as he glared at his mentor and began squaring off as the older man stepped slowly around the bed.

A muttered groan from the young prince to her left suddenly turned both men's gazes to them, and Keira watched in horror as Landrianus's eyes fluttered open. He groaned again, reaching a hand to the back of his head. Aaron's eyes brightened, seeming to remember for the first time his actual task in all of this. Keira stumbled to her feet to face him, arms shaking as she gripped her sword two-handed and assumed the guard stance. Aaron started toward them, but the thumping beat of sword on shield intensified, and

Flavius came sprinting around the end of the bed. His sword swung up in an overhead arch, parried with a clang by Aaron. The shield whipped out of nowhere then, slamming edge-first into Aaron's neck, just above the shoulder. He stumbled back, dragging ragged breaths into his lungs. The blunt strike on his neck was already swelling.

Keira realized then that it was probably as good a time as any to get the hell out of there. She glanced down at Landrianus and quickly surmised that he would be zero help. He was conscious, but stared around himself with incomprehension. Shaking her head, she grabbed one of his arms, hauling it across her shoulders and securing it with her sword hand. With her other hand, she grabbed a fistful of his breeches at the waistband and heaved him up to a standing position, staggering slightly under his weight. He was, after all, nearly a foot taller than her.

Slowly, excruciatingly slowly, she drag-walked him toward the door, casting fearful glances at the two Bellators as she went. The two men still grappled in combat, but she thought she saw Aaron weakening. His breathing had become more ragged. Meanwhile, Flavius's tunic was soaked with blood, its rusty hue deepening the already crimson fabric. Sweat dripped from both their faces as they circled each other. Aaron lunged toward Flavius with a lightning thrust, knocked to the side by Flavius's decorative shield as he sidestepped around him, bringing the hilt of his sword down hard on the back of Aaron's head. The younger man careened forward, barely bracing himself on the edge of the bed before whipping around to receive Flavius's own sword thrust straight into his gut.

Shock filled Aaron's face as he slid down the side of the bed, limbs buckling beneath him. His sword clanged to the ground even as his hand desperately grasped for it, his other pressed feebly to the gaping wound in his stomach, the fabric there already soaked through. With a groan of pain, Flavius kneeled beside the younger man, knocking the fallen sword out of reach.

Keira plopped the barely awake prince unceremoniously back onto the floor and ran to kneel beside Flavius. The waves of nausea from her binding mishap had mostly cleared, but reemerged as soon as she saw the loops of bowel poking through Aaron's blood-soaked fingers.

He was shivering, his face gray and lips already turning blue. She didn't know what to say, didn't know how to comprehend the reality of Aaron's betrayal.

Instead she asked, "Why? After all the chaos we've seen, Aaron, how could you try to destroy our one chance of peace?"

Aaron's eyes blinked at her, as if trying to focus on something far away, and his voice came in a harsh rasp as he chuckled, wholly without mirth.

"Peace? I used to believe in that—used to believe that's what I was doing, preserving the peace for future generations." His eyes cleared momentarily, and he fixed Keira with a hard, piercing look. "That was a lie. I've seen what the downlanders are really about. They care for nothing but their own wealth and comfort. My people—" A choked sob escaped his crushed throat as he shook his head. "My entire life has been a betrayal of them. The Bellatorio cares nothing for us...only mud beneath its feet." His next breath was lengthy and wavering. Keira heard a low gurgle in the back of his throat. "...thought I could... make amends. He said...not too late."

Flavius gripped the front of Aaron's tunic. "Who said? Who told you to do this, Tiobraide?"

Aaron's breaths had become shallow, and Keira had to lean in close to hear his next faltering words.

"...said he would lead us...end of the Marians at last."

Aaron fell silent then, and Keira gaped in shock as she felt for a pulse in his neck. It was there, but faint. He'd not be waking up again. Beside her, Flavius rose unsteadily to his feet and Keira noticed with alarm the pallor of his own skin. Cutting a strip of fabric from the tangled sheets, he wrapped it around his own waist, attempting to quench the stream of blood from his side. Keira looked back at Aaron's ashen face, wondering how she could have been so wrong about him.

The sound of footsteps sprinting down the hall made them both whip around, swords at the ready. Danny crashed through the doors, staring in horror at the scene before him. Relief washed through Keira, and she sheathed her sword with a sigh. Danny crossed the room in a moment and wrapped her in his arms. She inhaled the scent of his skin as her face pressed against his shoulder, reveling in his solidness as her own legs threatened to give way.

After a moment, Danny pulled back and looked her dead in the face.

"What the hell happened?"

CHAPTER

SEVENTEEN

The four of them stumbled out into the courtyard, Landrianus walking now, but braced between Keira and Danny. Flavius scouted ahead, but Keira noted the way he leaned heavily on every doorframe and wall they passed. She pursed her lips, watching him worriedly. She'd offered to try to heal him earlier, pointedly ignoring Danny's clenched jaw, but the old soldier had mulishly refused, insisting he was too old to have pneumonancers poking around his insides. He'd also insisted on leaving immediately, wanting to get the prince out of the monastery before daybreak.

"No telling who else in this wretched place has been compromised," he'd growled. Keira had somehow resisted the urge to point out that the traitor had come from *their* party, rather than the monastery. That fact alone still left her numb with shock. Aaron had seemed every inch the dutiful soldier. If even *he* could be turned against the Marians, then the danger was even more significant than she'd imagined and the threat of civil war loomed larger by the hour.

They'd made it to the twisting staircase when Landrianus finally said, "I thank you all for your timely intervention."

Keira glanced at him. Well, at least he'd escaped brain damage—she'd been starting to wonder. She shrugged as she took the wall side of the stairs, throwing a grateful look at Danny, who'd said nothing before taking the edge side of the open cliff stairs.

"Of course, your highness." Flavius gasped. "It's our duty."

"Yes, yes," Landrianus continued, still leaning on them slightly as they began their descent. "Still, it is all rather shocking, don't you think? I mean, a Centus in the Bellatorio turned traitor?" He shook his head in amazement. "It's enough to make you wonder about the discipline of the entire organization."

Keira tried to suppress her irritation, seeing Flavius stiffen as he leaned against the cliff wall ahead of them, sword still held at the ready. It wasn't as if she hadn't been surprised herself, but something about the princeling's tone, his cluelessness as to the state of his own country, was absolutely apparent. He had, after all, initially refused to even go before the Council, as his father had requested.

She gritted her teeth and willed herself to reply mildly, saying, "Certainly, your highness, though I think it had more to do with Aaron's upbringing than his vocation."

Danny shot her a look, eyebrows raised, obviously willing her to shut up. She knew he was right—they were exhausted and injured. This wasn't the time to get into a verbal sparring match with the future Regio.

Landrianus looked at her curiously, though. "I don't think I take your meaning, pneumonancer. His upbringing . . .?"

Keira fought the hard tone that entered her voice as they stepped carefully down the ancient stairs. "He's an uplander. He grew up among the peasants most affected by your father's taxes and Bellatori abuses. His people are still fighting your family's right to rule."

Landrianus seemed confused. "But we've been ruling for centuries. Surely they can't blame me for something I had no role in."

For once, Keira chose her words carefully. "It's not that *you* are to blame for what your ancestors did," she began, "but you enjoy enormous privilege in the system they set up, while others do not. And many people—Aaron's people, in fact—are actively suffering under that system."

Landrianus was quiet for a moment, and Keira wondered if what she was saying might actually get through to him. Then he shook his head and said confidently, "That's ridiculous. My family brought order to these lands. Before us, there was only chaos, the Benadur squabbling amongst themselves while their Tiarna got away with literal murder."

Keira opened her mouth to argue back, but he continued. "And it isn't as though we didn't make enormous concessions to the Lorenans—this bloody Council, for one thing. Not to mention the five years I've spent in this horrible place, studying the ways of *Pneumos*." He said this last bit with an air of ridicule that made Keira grit her teeth.

"Oh, yes, the Council with no power . . . that you publicly insult. And as for your suffering here . . ." She rolled her eyes, thinking about his giggling companions from the day before. "It appears you were managing quite well with your . . . friends."

Landrianus had the decency to flush, but otherwise ignored the implication.

"Well, you have some nerve, pneumonancer," he noted, "lecturing me on my obligations to right this supposed great wrong committed by my family. After all, your precious Legion was among our greatest supporters in the wars of ascension. They helped make 'order out of chaos,' as you all like to say."

Keira gaped at him. She had never heard such a story, and a glance at Danny confirmed he was as oblivious as she was. Could it be true? Could Elliott and especially Nazor, with her hatred of all things colonial, really have taken part in setting up such an oppressive political system, empowering the people who would inevitably abuse it?

Maybe it wasn't so oppressive at the time?

She grit her teeth, realizing this was yet another thing she'd need to discuss with Nazor, should they ever find her again. She barely noticed that Landrianus was still talking.

"—nothing but respect, as I would expect, being their future Regio and all. I have to believe you must be mistaken. My people would never want to hurt me."

Keira's ears burned, and her nose tingled as fury filled her entire body. She knew it wasn't all to do with this petulant man-child—there was anger enough at Nazor, the Legion, the Bellatorio, and most of all the local Tiarna who stooped to murdering children. However, Landrianus was close at hand. So despite Danny's warning look, Keira charged ahead, consequences be damned.

"Yes, I'm sure that's why a career Bellator gave it all up just for the chance of murdering you in your sleep," she said drawled. "I'm sure that's why that same Bellator could somehow convince the guards who've been with you for *five years* to turn on you in a single night. No doubt that's why, even as we speak, worshippers of Séiro are headed this way, also intent on murdering you." Keira scoffed in disgust. "Face it, your *highness*. You and your family are not popular. Maybe not *all* the problems in this country are your fault, but you and your family are the most visible enemy. So you *will* take the blame if you don't step up and start getting your crap together."

She was breathing heavily now, from both exhaustion and anger. Landrianus just stared at her, shock etched in every line of his face.

"N-no one's ever spoken to me like that," he murmured.

Keira glanced at him, a tad nervous despite herself. He didn't look angry, precisely, just surprised. She waited for him to say more, but he didn't. He only continued down the stairs in silence, apparently mulling over her impetuous words.

WHEN THEY FINALLY REACHED THE bottom, Keira could see that Flavius's condition was rapidly worsening. While Landrianus bemoaned the splitting headache she'd predicted, Flavius was now leaning heavily on Danny and she saw him stumble more than once under the man's weight. His face had turned the color of sheet metal, and even the sweat had dried, leaving his skin cold and clammy.

They reached the cohort's campsite just as the others had begun to stir, fetching water for the horses and stoking the embers of the previous night's fire. Sara, the Cross-Sea warrior, was the first to spot them. She waved a hand at Keira in greeting but as she grew closer her brow furrowed. When she Flavius, she rushed forward, shouting for the others as she helped Danny bring him to the fire. By the time Flavius was settled, a crowd had gathered around them, murmured whispers flying between the assembled Bellators. Flavius took a small sip of water before speaking in a voice like sandpaper.

"We've been betrayed," he said bluntly. No emotion tinged his voice, but its effect on the cohort was electric. "An attempt was made on the life of the future Regio Landrianus," he continued, unperturbed, even as his eyes seemed to sink further into his skull, "by Centus Tiobraide."

Absolute silence fell among the cohort as its members stared at their leader in shock. Keira glanced at Landrianus, half expecting the prince to step forward to accept their condolences. However, he remained firmly rooted beside them, as transfixed as the rest by the dying Millus.

"This betrayal strikes us all deeply, I know," Flavius said hoarsely, "but our mission remains unchanged. The prince's life is still in danger, as the worshippers of Séiro are no doubt not far behind us. To avoid them, we will take another path through the Olpheís Plains."

Flavius's eyes met each one of theirs. Keira wondered if he'd finally acknowledge his injuries and the looming elephant in the room. She knew in her heart that he would not be joining them.

"Ready the camp," he ordered. "We leave in ten minutes."

There was a moment's pause, and then the cohort erupted into a flurry of activity. Embers were doused, tents collapsed, and rucksacks loaded onto shoulders or lashed to the backs of horses. Keira ignored all of this as she moved to kneel beside Flavius. Slowly, afraid he might stop her, she lifted the makeshift bandage from his wound.

The older man barely flinched, but Keira felt her heart sink as she saw the wide gash still actively oozing, small loops of bowel visible. Judging from the rising smell, she strongly suspected that at least some had been perforated by Aaron's strike. She looked up to find Flavius's eyes holding hers steadily, unflinching in the surety of what he knew was to come. Keira blinked away tears as she quickly rinsed and re-bandaged the wound, careful to keep the lowest layer moist. The grizzled warrior was quiet, seemingly content to watch the flurry of activity around him. Finally, he turned to her, voice calm but direct.

"Take the western road through the plains," he mumbled. "It's longer, so they won't expect it. You'll have to travel through Gregür Pass—no getting around that—but then head directly south to Crîd Eálas. I don't trust that pit of vipers in Ulgáris for a second. He'll be safer with his sister, the Lady Junia, in the capital."

Keira nodded, not bothering to insist that he'd be able to lead them. She sensed innately that he was not one for empty reassurances. Instead, she looked off toward the western road and wondered if the worshippers of Séiro would be so easily fooled. She turned back to Flavius, realizing with a clenched feeling in her chest that this might be her last chance to ask.

"Did you suspect?" she asked hesitantly. "About Aaron, I mean?"

It was Flavius who looked away then, fixing his eyes on the fire's doused embers.

"I knew he was angry. Hell, I've been angry." Perhaps sensing her surprise, he gave her a challenging look. "You think just because I'm a downlander, that I don't see what goes on, that I don't care?" He shook his head ruefully, jaw clenched in frustration. "But I'm a Bellator, first and foremost. My family has served the Bellatorio for hundreds of years now. It isn't perfect, far from it, but it is mine. I thought Aaron felt the same, but I was wrong." He looked into her eyes, searching for what she didn't know, but definitely looking for *something*. "Do not make the same mistake I did," he warned. "Duty alone cannot cover all wrongs."

Keira looked over to see Danny helping Sara collapse a tent. What was their duty? To Loren? To the Legion? To each other? The sound of Flavius's shallow breathing pulled Keira's attention back to him, and she noticed that his pulse had sped up significantly. Not for the first time, Keira cursed this place and its lack of antibiotics and surgeons. She also cursed herself for getting killed before she'd even made it to college, let alone medical school. She briefly considered trying to heal him with her pneuma, like she had little Anya Cuball, but short of eviscerating her own bowel—which even she wasn't dumb enough to try—she had no idea how she'd manage it. Besides, Flavius had insisted that he had no desire for anyone to meddle around with his insides.

Instead, she merely asked, "Should we try to get you back up to the monastery before we leave?"

He opened his eyes and shook his head. Keira could see the sheen of sweat across his brow, but resisted the urge to offer him a cloth.

"No time. I'll wait by the stairs. They come down this way to tend their horses each day. They'll ensure I have a proper burial."

Keira flinched at the word, tears again stinging her eyes. She furiously wiped them away and glared at the old Bellator.

"We can't leave you alone to die."

He gave her a long, steady look, his rapid breathing making it harder to speak. "Duty, remember? It may not cover all, but sometimes, it is enough. You...must protect the future Regio. That's all that matters. Only—"

With difficulty, Flavius pulled the red signet ring from his hand and placed it unsteadily in hers.

"Give this to my son, Cyrus. T-tell him—well, tell him whatever you want about me. Only make sure he leaves the Bellatorio. He has no interest in fighting. He...he'd much rather be a painter." Flavius smiled weakly at her. "C-can you imagine that? My s-son, a p-painter."

Keira floundered for the words she wanted, something to convey her sorrow and gratitude and panic at the task before her. She wasn't ready for this—she knew that as well as anybody. She was just a girl, plucked out of her own world and time and placed in one that barely understood. Landrianus, pig-headed though he was, deserved someone like Flavius, deserved someone who knew what they were doing—someone unquestioningly loyal. Not someone who couldn't even protect the people she loved.

Not knowing any concise way to convey these thoughts to a dying man, she settled instead for the generic.

"I will," she promised. "And thank you. With Aaron, I thought... well, if you hadn't come, I definitely wouldn't be here, and neither would Landrianus."

She anxiously watched the older man, whose eyes had widened in fear as his breath came in ever-shallower rasps. He looked somehow like a little boy just then, she thought. This grizzled war veteran, who'd sent untold men to their graves, was as scared as anybody when it came to meeting his own end. Nearly choking with emotion, Keira put a hand on top of the man's head, solely out of impulse. She leaned in close and whispered, "You have fulfilled your duty, and your tour is ended. Rest easy, Bellator."

As his eyes fluttered closed, she felt tears again fill hers. He was still breathing, but as she watched, the lines smoothed from his hard face, granting him peace in a way that even sleep had never offered. She felt Danny beside her then, and with the help of a few others, they lifted Flavius and carried him toward the stairs. They tried to make him as comfortable as they could. Landrianus, no doubt feeling obligated, spoke a few words about honor and sacrifice. Keira hardly noticed, her throat tight and stomach aching as the waves of emotion undid her entirely.

There was an awkward silence as the cohort shifted on their feet, clearly waiting for something to happen, for someone to tell them what to do. Who would tell them what to do? The weight of their expectation settled on Keira, making her pulse thrum and her breath come in shallow waves. But just when the panic reached its height, she *felt* them. Like a cool breeze brushing against her cheek, she somehow knew the words that needed saying.

"Millus Gaius Flavius was a true Bellator," she began, "duty-bound and honorable to the end. He died protecting the future Regio, and his final request was that we do the same. We will follow the western road through the plains and travel south to Crîd Eálas." She surveyed the gathered cohort, seeing uncertainty etched across their faces, and not a paltry amount of hostility directed toward said princeling. Gritting her teeth, she continued, "I don't know where you all come from, or what your lives have been like. I don't doubt that some among you may even sympathize with Centus Tiobraide's efforts." She paused again, looking each of them directly in the face. "I'm asking you to put that aside. Like Millus Flavius, I'm asking you to place duty and honor above whatever political opinions or affiliations you may hold."

She let her words sink in before continuing, voice breaking slightly. "Gaius Flavius was a man I admired, and one I considered as a friend. I, for one, will protect Lord Landrianus Marian, not only because it's my duty, but because to fail to do so would make his sacrifice meaningless. If you cannot do that, if your conscience prohibits it, then I ask that you leave now."

There was absolute silence amongst the cohort. Keira held her breath, waiting for someone to call her out, to tell her she didn't know what she was talking about, or ask what gave her the right to command them to do anything. But they didn't. They just stood there, waiting. With a start, she realized they were waiting for *her*. And for the first time since arriving in Loren, she felt the true weight of others' trust settling on her. These men and women, warriors all, were counting on her, trusting in her judgement and willing to follow her leadership. All because one man decided she was worthy. The responsibility was equal parts thrilling and terrifying.

Letting out her breath slowly, she glanced at Danny and Sara, who nodded encouragingly, eyes shining with pride. Buoyed, if only for a moment, she turned back to the cohort and gave the order.

"Move out!"

EIGHTEEN

Crîd Eálas

Lady Junia studied the small square of parchment, regarding the tiny slanted script again. She pursed her lips, rereading its lines before reaching out and dropping it into the hearth. She watched as it danced lazily in the flames, the tang of disappointment sharp on her tongue.

So, she thought, *you really were a traitor, Aaron Tiobraide*. She'd suspected as much. She'd made inquiries into his supposed contact with known terrorists and rebel sympathizers, that devil Neval Brennan from Raboneís, for one. Junia shook her head in disgust. Still, she couldn't help but wish Tiobraide had at least succeeded in this one job.

A knock on the door interrupted her thoughts, and she quickly smoothed the lines of frustration from her face, assembling a visage of perfect serenity, marked only by wide-eyed sororal concern.

"Enter," she called mildly, folding her hands meekly in her lap. In stepped Oswald, looking even scruffier than usual. He bowed deeply to her.

"My lady, you summoned me?"

She resisted the urge to wrinkle her nose in disgust. The man smelled as common as he looked. She knew this persona of his was necessary—valuable, even—in one who spent his life lurking in alleyways with unsavory characters, but she resented its presence on her priceless carpets.

"It seems the Bellatori cohort has retrieved my brother from Mount Ánghen and means to return by the western road through the plains. An attempt was made on his life, and they fear further reprisals." Junia paused, tapping her fingers in a rolling motion on her armrest. "I fear he has come under the influence of two pneumonancers that fell in with the cohort. As such, I'd like you to send word to our *friends* in the north, alerting them to their planned route. I fear for my dear brother's safety."

She kept her face perfectly still, but watched as Oswald's head cocked and a slow, knowing grin spread across his face. Junia said nothing, but inclined her head almost imperceptibly in response to his curt nod.

"I will see it done, my lady."

Oswald exited, and Junia turned back to the fire. She knew it was dangerous, playing with the likes of Séiro worshippers, but the risk seemed worth it in this case. If Landry had diverted from his path to Ulgáris and the vipers lying in wait there, then this would be her last opportunity to see him dead before he reached the capital.

So much cleaner that way, she decided, walking toward her desk and the parchment waiting there. She still had her own allies to summon.

～

Olpheís Plains

TO THE SURPRISE of absolutely no one, the future Regio was possibly the most aggravating travel companion in the whole of Loren. Keira had to continuously remind him that stealthy travel meant limiting their use of fires and keeping up a steady speed. Predictably, he complained about both. He was tired and sore, or he wanted something hot to eat. At one point, he even requested heated water for a bath. She'd laughed in his face at that one, much to his chagrin.

He was also annoyingly talkative, even for Keira, who'd long since made a habit of driving Danny to distraction with her chatter. With Landry, though—who'd insisted she use his preferred nickname, rather than the more formal Landrianus—the trouble was more so that his inane blather devoted itself almost solely to his own bravado. Danny had a knack for listening kindly and nodding with feigned interest, but Keira was not so patient. She had long since tried to nip this tendency in the bud, telling Landry flat out that no one cared one whit for his supposed accomplishments, but this only encouraged him. Whether it was feats of strength or intelligence, he seemed determined to prove her wrong.

On this particular morning, Keira had been roped into riding next to him yet again, Sara having slipped away at the last possible moment. Keira gritted her teeth as he regaled her with tales of his victories at some fencing competition and the wooing of some court lady in Crîd Eálas. She usually just ignored him, but she was in a particularly foul mood and couldn't help poking jibes at the stories. Whether by commenting on the likelihood that his competitors threw the fencing competitions or how any lady who allowed herself to be fought over clearly needed more excitement in her life, Keira took ignoble pleasure in reminding him exactly how unimpressive she found him. Eventually, he gave up and settled into a satisfyingly sullen silence.

For the life of her, Keira couldn't pinpoint why he felt the need to continually brag. Her only conclusion was that he'd clearly been starved for stimulating company all these years and had lost all sense of social grace, poor bastard. That, or he really was as pompous as she'd once thought. Yet despite all evidence to the contrary, there was something about him that made her doubt his assumed confidence—an earnestness that spoke of deep-rooted insecurity, a yearning for friendship that she suspected had been mostly absent in his young life.

They rode in blessed quiet for a while, both absorbed in their own thoughts. Then, out of the blue, Landry blurted out, "Do they really suffer? The peasants, I mean. Are they really that unhappy?"

Keira stared at him, fighting the nearly overwhelming urge to roll her eyes. His concern actually seemed genuine, so she considered his question carefully before responding.

"They're resilient," she said finally. "They find joy where they can, but it's not the bucolic country life you may have been taught. They labor day in and day out to pay their rents to the local Tiarna and taxes to the Benadur and Regio."

Landry seemed to weigh this. "I was always told their labor keeps them occupied, and that without it, they would become idle and rebellious."

Keira rolled her eyes at this, but resisted the urge to point out that such an idea was precisely what the wealthy *would* say, as a justification for their own excesses. He was just being honest, after all.

"Every year, they seem to earn less and see a larger chunk taken out for corrupt rulers to grow fat on," Keira explained. "They die young from hard work, unsanitary conditions, and a lack of healers. And so resentment grows."

Landry said nothing this time, looking thoughtful. Seeing an opportunity, she hastened to add, "The Tiarna and Benadur have noticed, you know." This made him glance up at her in surprise, and she barreled onward. "They know the resentment their policies have caused, but instead of taking responsibility, they try to channel the uplanders' resentment elsewhere. They blame outsiders, like the Olpheís nomads, for letting their flocks graze on the hillside, or call them thieves stealing the uplanders' livelihood. Then they lead raids into the plains and murder whole caravans of nomads. The people are appeased, but only temporarily, so the raids continue, people die, and nothing *ever* changes."

Keira couldn't keep the bitterness out of her voice. Worried she'd said too much, she glanced at Landry. He eyed her dubiously.

"I've heard nothing about this."

Keira snorted and cast a rueful glance at the surrounding plains. "Don't believe me? We came across six or seven burned-out wagons just on our way to fetch you. Men, women, children, even dogs—all murdered and left to rot in the sun. You want to know what kind of chaos you're facing when you become Regio? That's only a taste of what's coming."

Keira rubbed her eyes then, suddenly exhausted, not only from the days on the road, but from the enormity of what lay before them. It all seemed so impossible just then. Landry's face was white, etched with a look of shock and possibly nausea. Keira suddenly felt a wave of sympathy for the young prince, so entirely unprepared for what lay before him.

Struck with a sudden urge, she lightly punched his shoulder and tried to give him what she hoped was a reassuring look. "You're not alone, you know. We want to help you."

He glanced at her, eyes wide and hopeful. "Really? You'll stay then? Help me fix things?"

Keira swallowed, guilt gnawing at her. "For . . . for a time. We have our own duties, you know, our own . . . responsibilities." She glanced sideways at Danny, wondering if he'd heard. Luckily, he was deep in an animated conversation with Sara about some aspect of Cross-Sea fighting tactics.

Keira's gaze returned then to Landry as a flash of disappointment came and went across his face. She couldn't help a small smile at his earnestness and tried to adopt a lighter tone. "First, though, you seriously need to be a little less annoying. I know you've been locked up in a monastery for years, but none of us wants to hear about the time you beat so-and-so at a foot race, blah, blah, blah."

He grinned back at her and even chuckled slightly. "Agreed."

The sound of hoofbeats drew Keira's gaze forward, and Danny cantered past to meet the arriving scout. His face was grim when he returned.

"The gorge is dead ahead," he said, jaw clenched. "And it doesn't look good. The cliffs are too steep to take the horses up from this side, but there's room for archers at the top if they approach from the south. It's perfect for an ambush."

Keira looked at him helplessly. "Well, we can't go around—cutting to the north would cost us time and bring us too close to Raboneís. Something tells me whoever's in control of it now will be none too friendly toward our future Regio here."

Landry looked like he wanted to say something, but Danny interrupted. "I'm telling you, Keira, once we go in there, there's no turning back. It's a straight shot north to south with hardly any cover."

Keira gnawed on her lip. Glancing around, she saw that the rest of the cohort had gathered close by. To her surprise, she realized they were all looking expectantly at *her*. Not Danny, and certainly not Landry—*her*. She quickly swallowed the nervous lump that had risen in her throat and tried to figure out how she could get them through this.

Think, Altman, she ordered. *What would Nazor do?*

Then it hit her, and she looked sharply up at Danny. "We'll take the gorge, but first we have some preparations to make."

Danny arched an eyebrow at her, but nodded, the hint of a smile on his lips.

"What's the plan?"

CHAPTER

NINETEEN

Gregür Gorge was typically avoided for the perfectly good reason that it had a nasty habit of killing people. Stretching over a mile long, there was no water source, and it lacked trees or even the smallest bush, making it blazing hot in the summer and freezing cold in the winter. Rocky gray crags stretched up above it to the dizzying height of nearly eighty feet. Even looking up at them was enough to make Keira's stomach flip-flop. All of this made it a prime setting for bandits to prey upon foolish travelers wishing to avoid the tolls in Raboneís. The local villages had been asking the Bellatorio to clear it out for years, but their motivation to eliminate such a useful deterrent to tax evasion had been somewhat lacking.

The gorge was eerily silent as they approached, lacking even the smallest bird whistle or rustle of leaves. It was enough to make Keira's skin crawl. She'd had most of the cohort adopt a staggered formation, spreading out far enough to make each person harder to hit at range, but close enough to circle quickly if they were to be ambushed. That's *the idea, anyway*, she thought, gnawing on her lip. She glanced at Danny, who gave her a reassuring nod. They were the one exception to the staggering policy. She'd argued fiercely with him when he'd insisted on playing the decoy, making her instantly regret proposing this plan in the first place. But his insistence that he was closest in height and build to Landry and would therefore fit his clothes best was hard to argue with. Besides, it was *her* plan. She couldn't very well

173

change her mind just because Danny would play the most dangerous part. How would that look to the others?

Still, it made her nervous, and her fingers tapped reflexively against her thigh as she scanned the cliffs above them, looking for the slightest movement that would suggest what she knew in her bones was coming. For his part, Danny was every inch the ambivalent nobleman, riding regally in Landry's royal pajamas. Not that anyone else would know that, he'd rightly pointed out. They were far too fine a fabric for anyone to suspect they were merely for sleeping in. Keira snorted as she watched Danny flick away a fly with a flutter of his fingers, nose wrinkled comically. He was playing it up, she knew, trying to make her feel better about the whole thing, and it was working—sort of.

She had to admit that the highlight of the entire plan had been getting to smear Landry's face with dirt. She knew that the prince in question was riding sullenly in back, dirty and dressed in a red Bellatori tunic. Now *that* was a satisfying thought.

Looking up, she guessed they'd made it about halfway through the gorge. With a surge of relief, she realized she could just make out the opening at the far end of the canyon. *We're going to make it!*

A moment later, she saw movement from the corner of her eye— just the slight sound of pebbles skittering down the side of a cliff— but it was enough. She dove for Danny just as the arrow came whistling over Boyd's head. The gelding reared in panic, sending Keira and Danny tumbling to the ground in a ball of limbs and fancy clothes as a cry of alarm rang out from the assembled cohort. Immediately the Bellators converged on them, jumping from their own horses and sprinting with shields overhead as the arrows began flying.

Miraculously, no one was hit as the Bellators slammed their square shields into the ground. They joined them together to make a moving tortoise-shell barricade with Keira, Danny, and Landry in the center, doing their best to brace the shield roof of the movable structure. Slowly, the cohort marched forward, the sound of arrows thumping deep into the wood or pinging off metal. The roar was deafening, especially when rocks joined the deadly rain of arrows. The Bellators were determined, though, marching to their steady chant of "Arouff, arouff."

Keira looked up through a small slit in the shield wall to see a black-cloaked man come careening down the eastern cliff. He turned end over end until he landed with a satisfying crunch on the ground ahead of them.

Well done, Sara, Keira thought fiercely. She'd known it was a risk to separate the cohort, but she was intensely grateful just then that she'd thought to send scouts to climb the ridge and provide them with some cover. Sara and a female Bellator named Lu had volunteered, as they were excellent climbers and best suited for this stealth mission.

As the cohort continued its death-defying march, they stepped directly over the fallen attacker. With a start, Keira realized where she'd seen those black robes before. The man's face bore the angled tattoos of the worshippers of Séiro. Keira shot a glance at Danny, whose eyes were also wide with alarm. *How did they find us?* She thought fiercely. She'd been expecting a bandit attack, but these rogue pneumonancers had no reason to believe they'd come this way.

Someone has betrayed you, an icy voice warned. She shoved it aside —there'd be time enough to think about that later. For now, she needed a new plan. If there were pneumonancers amongst their attackers, they were about to have more than arrows and rocks to contend with.

No sooner had she thought this than a roar above them made her look up just in time to see a shower of boulders raining down on them like some avenging avalanche. She froze. Blood rushed in her ears, and her heart pounded, but her feet remained leaden, refusing to obey the commands her brain furiously screamed at them. Strong hands reached from behind to yank her back just as the roof of the tortoise shell caved inward under the weight of a very human-sized boulder, right where she'd been standing. She felt the back of her head slam to the ground as a giant weight pinned her down.

Keira wasn't sure how long she laid there, but when she regained some sense of herself, ears ringing and nausea rising, the first thing she saw was a pair of green eyes swimming above her. Firm hands shook her shoulders roughly, and his mouth was moving, but it took a moment to realize the word he was mouthing was her name. No sooner did she realize this, though, than a cacophony suddenly assaulted her senses.

"Keira! We have to move!"

She somehow nodded, though it sent daggers through her skull, and was rewarded with the look of utter relief that crossed Danny's face. He dragged her to her feet, and together they staggered toward the Bellators that had circled around Landry. The usually hapless prince actually looked somewhat competent, brandishing his sword with ferocity at an enemy that was, unfortunately, very much out of range. His Bellatori guards, meanwhile, had wisely turned to more ranged weaponry and were bravely trying to pick off the archers on the cliffs above. The onslaught of arrows had slowed by this point, thanks no doubt to Sara's and Lu's efforts.

Keira scanned the cliffs on either side, looking for the black cloaks of the pneumonancers, though she had no idea what she'd do if she spotted one. Belatedly, she sensed a wave of energy and threw up a shielding arm as a boulder not five feet in front of them exploded. She and Danny were both knocked off their feet, but by some miracle, the flying rubble did no significant damage. Stumbling to one knee, she glared up into the vindictive face of a black-cloaked pneumonancer perched on the cliff edge.

At the sight of his maniacal grin, Keira felt only rage. It burned through every inch of her, a roiling fury at these bastards who had already taken so much from her. She punched rather than nudged the pneuma in her center and felt her body stagger back as it flew from her on a whistle that echoed painfully off the recesses of her own brain. Her pneuma struck like a viper, fusing effortlessly with the rocky ledge as it contorted to match its shape. A slight squeeze, and she watched from above as the cliff edge melted away in a sliding mass of molten rock. The pneumonancer shrieked, out of pain or fear she didn't know, but she watched from outside herself as he was sucked beneath its rolling wave. The icy taste of satisfaction filled her, and she searched eagerly for her next target.

Keira felt a tug and realized with a surge of frustration that something, or someone, sought to pull her back, to reel in her pneuma like a thing to be controlled. Absently, she ripped her arm from the grasp of that grounding hand and reveled in the freedom her pneuma had found. Her mind's eye settled then on another black figure, kneeling on the eastern cliff edge, lips moving in a silent chant, seemingly unaware of the creeping figure that loomed behind, knife unsheathed and gleaming. Sara was a heartbeat away when the pneumonancer's eyes snapped open. Keira tried to call out, but her spirit's breath was voiceless, and her body was too distant to be heard. A crack echoed through the gorge, and Keira watched helplessly as a massive tree along the cliff edge teetered and then fell.

Sara saw it a split second too late. She dove back, avoiding the bulk of the trunk, but Keira silently gasped in horror as a branch struck and pinned her to the ground, unable to move beneath its weight.

Then came fury—hotter, wilder than before. Keira felt herself losing control, but couldn't find the will to care. She exploded toward the pneumonancer, hating him and wanting nothing more than to rip that cruel smile from his face. Keira struck him with full force, not bothering to hide or sneak. She wanted him to know she had him, wanted him to feel her squeezing the life out of him. He tried to resist, but he'd been caught unawares, and her pneuma wrapped itself around him entirely before he could cast out his own. She didn't bother with a nerve block, instead going straight for his neck.

The human body was more challenging to amalgamate than any rock. Comprised not merely of bone and sinew, but by their own pneuma as well, leaking from their very pores. To twist your pneuma into a matching shape required an intimacy with their very being, becoming almost one with them as you destroyed them. It was something Keira had never thought she'd do, but at that moment, she wanted nothing more than to melt this man's spinal column and feel his pain as she did it. She sensed him resisting, knew she would beat him. From somewhere in the distance, she heard his screams as the molecules that comprised his bones began to shift. It was a slow process, but just then, she wasn't at all sure she wanted it to be fast. These people had taken Elliott from her—Nazor, too, in a way. She had lost Flavius and Aaron to the chaos they perpetuated.

Now they had taken Sara. They had to pay.

Keira felt her grip on the man falter as powerful arms wrapped around her body in a crushing embrace from behind. Danny's pneuma flooded through her, overpowering her will and reeling her back from her own murderous intent. She fought him off, hating him for seeking to save this scum who deserved no mercy. She heard herself scream at him, demanding that he let her go, but he persisted. Eventually, she felt the pneumonancer wriggle from her grasp, stumbling away down the path he'd come from, desperate for the temporary reprieve he'd neither earned nor deserved. With a mental sigh of angry frustration, Keira allowed herself to be snapped back into her own body and felt her knees buckle beneath her.

Keira felt Danny's grip loosen as he came around to look at her. She glared up at him, rage warring with the conscience she could feel only now that she was firmly back in her body. She trembled slightly, angry not only with Danny for binding her against her will, but also with herself. As she met his eyes, she was surprised to see genuine horror there. He was looking at her like he barely knew her.

"You were going to kill him," he breathed. "You *wanted* to kill him, wanted him to suffer."

"You've killed people," she shot back, desperately fighting the rising wave of nausea that threatened to overwhelm her. "We both have."

"You wanted to *feel* it." He continued to stare at her as if seeing her for the first time, and Keira felt the absurd urge to hide, to look away and never let him see her again. "You wanted to feel his suffering."

A familiar sense of self-loathing flooded through her. It had been temporarily overshadowed by the past weeks' excitement and the role she'd found for herself among the cohort, but it was back now with a vengeance.

You're no leader, the voice sneered at her. *You're just a little girl, selfish and out for revenge.*

Keira swallowed hard, clambering up on wobbly legs to look around, desperate to escape the voice ringing in her ears. It seemed like most of their attackers had gone. The ground was littered with bodies, and the surviving members of the cohort stumbled around, clearly worn to the bone.

You put them all in danger, the voice continued. *They're dead because of you.*

She barely noticed that Landry had run up to her. He spoke eagerly, but she paid no attention, just stared at the surrounding carnage. She didn't look up until she felt him shove a letter into her hands. Keira absently noted the purple seal, but there was something else about it, something familiar. She quickly put that thought to the back of her mind in favor of far more pressing concerns. She ripped the letter open and scanned its contents, even as Landry verbally recounted the entirety, nearly verbatim.

"It details our exact route from Mount Ánghen to Crîd Eálas!" he exclaimed. "How could this have happened?"

This question she recognized as her own, and she stared back at Landry blankly. Did he not understand by now? Did he not realize that she had failed them, that this was her fault?

No, another voice said, *we were betrayed*. The worshippers of Séiro should never have found them. This should never have happened.

She clung to that thought, a life preserver that buoyed her up amongst the waves of self-loathing. This wasn't her fault.

Then whose was it?

TWENTY

She's alive. Keira focused on this one thought, a point of hope amidst all the uncertainty as they prepared to leave. She scanned her friend's injuries as Sara mercifully slept—multiple fractures and a clear concussion. It was far too much for Keira to heal on her own, even if Danny would ground her. But Sara was alive, and Keira was determined to keep her that way.

Keira turned toward Danny and Landry. "We have to divert. There's no way she'll make it all the way to Crîd Eálas."

Danny shook his head. He'd been oddly quiet since she'd tried to kill Sara's attacker, so she was surprised to hear him speak up now.

"Too risky. Flavius warned us not to trust the Council. If we go through the hill country, we're practically bringing Landry to them."

"Ulgáris is the closest major city," Keira argued stubbornly. "We can't just leave her in some village we stumble across. She needs a proper healer."

They glared at each other before Danny finally turned to Landry. "It's your call, your highness. You're the one at most risk here."

"Not counting Sara," Keira muttered. But she also turned to Landry for his opinion. Landry glanced nervously from Danny to Keira, uncertainty etched in his face. His eyes finally settled on hers, something she couldn't quite make out churning in their depths.

"We go to Ulgáris," he said firmly.

Keira grinned brightly at him, giving him a warm punch to the shoulder. *Maybe he isn't such a selfish turd,* she thought. Danny's eyes darted back and forth between them, jaw clenched, before turning on his heel and stalking away toward Boyd. Landry watched him go, looking tense.

"Don't worry about him," Keira said, though the fluttering in her heart as she stared after Danny was physically painful. "He'll come around." Now, if only she could make herself believe that. The weight of it all settled on her as she stared after him—all of her failures, everyone she had lost. And for what? For some last ditch shot at peace that was likely doomed from the start?

"It's not your fault, you know," Landry said suddenly.

Keira turned to stare at him, blinking in surprise.

"Sara, I mean. You couldn't have known."

Keira smiled sadly at the young prince. "It is, though, Landry. I made the call, so it will always be my fault, the good and the bad. That's what leadership is." She hesitated, watching his brow furrow with concern. "Honestly, the sooner you learn that, the better."

She left him standing there alone to tell the rest of the cohort about the change in plans. In short order, the cohort was on its way, heading due east toward the hill country and Ulgáris.

THE TRIP to Ulgáris took several days under normal conditions, and they were forced to move more slowly given the difficulty of bearing Sara's litter. Danny still sullenly avoided Keira, much to her frustration. It seemed like as soon as they were in a good place, something had to come and ruin it. Whether they were fighting over the Legion or now Landry, they just couldn't seem to get on the same page for long. She watched his back as he rode ahead of her and thought sadly that she missed the easy companionship they'd used to have.

Her brooding thoughts were interrupted by Landry, who'd spurred his horse to ride up beside her. She braced herself for another of his long-winded anecdotes about exploit or another of his, and so was quite surprised by his question.

"Danny seems not himself. Is he feeling all right?"

Keira shrugged. "You'd have to ask him. I'm not sure if you've noticed, but he hasn't exactly been speaking to me lately."

"Well, he hasn't really been talking to anyone," Landry pointed out. "I'd thought it was because I overruled him, but now . . . I'm not so sure."

Keira was impressed that he'd actually cared enough to notice someone *other* than himself for a change. She sighed, rubbing at her eyes absently.

"No, it's me. Danny is . . . protective." She glanced at Landry, trying to decide exactly how much to tell him. "He's upset that I almost lost control back in the gorge." Landry waited expectantly, no sign of surprise on his face. He'd clearly suspected something along these lines, and she gave him a quizzical look. "Do you know how pneumonancy works?"

"Only what's written in the old texts," he admitted. "I know it involves channeling the pneuma to make order out of disorder. Definitely nothing practical, though."

Keira nodded. "Well, *practically* speaking, casting out your pneuma makes you vulnerable to dissociating from yourself, which is why pneumonancers like Danny act as grounders." She shrugged again. "It just comes more naturally to them, I suppose."

"So, Danny is your grounder?"

Keira smiled thinly, without warmth. "When I allow him to be."

Landry didn't ask her to elaborate on this point, for which she was grateful.

"When you delve too far, though, it also leaves you vulnerable to getting sucked into chaos-making. It's hard to explain, really." She shook her head, remembering the rush she'd felt squeezing the life out of Sara's attacker. "I suppose it's addictive in a way, and the freedom it offers is so tempting. But going down that path . . . that's how you end up like those worshippers of Séiro. I guess . . . well, I *know* I trod a little too close for Danny's comfort."

"So what would happen if you tried to cast without a grounder around?"

Keira swallowed and her thoughts immediately flew to Elliott, of his horribly limp body and blank eyes. "It technically can be done. But you risk losing yourself entirely, fully dissociating, and being unable to return to your body. We . . . we call it the *Undoing*."

Landry's brows furrowed, but he asked no more questions as they rode on in silence.

~

As the ancient hill city of Ulgáris came into view, Keira finally understood its reputation as the jewel of the hill country. Perched atop the tallest hill in the area, Ulgáris's towering stone walls crept out to the very edge of the rocky outcroppings, overlooking the ravines that dipped sharply on all sides. As they began the steep ascent along the lone, twisting road that led toward the city, Keira thought it was little surprise that Ulgáris had never been conquered by the Marians all those years before. She shuddered to think of charging up this hill against an onslaught of arrows and molten tar. Far easier to wait them out via siege after subduing the rest of Loren, though she supposed it had allowed the Council to ensure their own survival.

Passing beneath the city gates, Keira gaped at the pre-Marian influence evident in everything from the clothing to the architecture. As they climbed the cobblestone streets that wound through each level of the city, Keira stared up at the external staircases of intricately twisting wrought iron that wrapped around every edifice. Brightly painted nooks and crannies were carved out of walls to hold the ancient statuary dedicated to the elemental spirits long revered in these parts, before any mention of Pneumos or Séiro had graced the peoples' ears. At the feet of these statues, worshippers had placed flowers and coin, offerings to the spirits in hopes of good business, bountiful harvests, and healthy families.

The cohort's presence did not go unnoticed, either. Everywhere they passed, eyes followed them, tight with suspicion and detest as they took in the bright red capes of the Bellators. As they approached the center of the city, the impressive form of the Cruín could be seen before them. Several stories tall and perfectly round with a domed roof, Keira remembered from her lessons with Elliott that this was the ancient seat of power in Loren and the place where the Council of Benadur now ruled in proxy.

After a lengthy discussion over the preceding days, it had been decided that they'd go straight there, rather than try to creep around the city unawares. Keira was glad for that decision, as they had clearly already been identified by the guards at the gate. They were greeted at the bottom of the steps leading up to the Cruín by a white-robed sage, who looked altogether too pleased to see them.

"Welcome to Ulgáris, your highness," he intoned, extending a deep bow to Landry. "I send greetings from the Council of Benadur, who from the holy lands of Ulgáris do ensure order in the name of Pneumos, protection to the sovereign realm of Loren, and peace—"

"Yes, yes," Landry interrupted, unconcerned with formality. "We have wounded among us. I will gladly appear before the Council, but first, I will see my cohort tended to. Where is the nearest healer?"

The sage stared at him, obviously startled, then sputtered, "O-of course. I will send for the court physician. Benadur Mualath has offered your highness lodgings in his family home."

"Yes, yes, but where will my cohort be lodged?" Landry asked impatiently. "They need rest and medical treatment."

Things were obviously not going according to plan, and the sage looked flustered as he waved a hand for his servants to join them. "Your Bellators are welcome to stay in the city guard's barracks. My people will show them there now."

Keira quickly dismounted to assist them in untying Sara's litter so it could be brought to the barracks. The sage clearly meant for Landry to follow him to the Council member's lodgings, but Landry hesitated, torn.

"I mean to keep my personal guard with me," he suddenly asserted, gesturing for Keira and Danny to follow him. "I'm sure Benadur Mualath would not begrudge me my personal protection."

The sage didn't pause for more than a moment, but it was enough to arouse Keira's suspicions. While she would have preferred to remain with the cohort and make sure Sara received the necessary medical care, that hesitation was enough to change her mind. She did *not* trust these people.

"Of course, your highness. If you'll follow me this way?" the sage intoned, bowing again.

With a final glance back at the cohort to assure herself that they were, in fact, being tended to, Keira trailed behind Landry, not at all reassured by the Council's supposed show of generosity.

TWENTY-ONE

Benadur Mualath's family home was, in fact, a towering, elaborately decorated mansion mere blocks from the Cruín. As Keira and Danny were shown down the hallway to their rooms—inconveniently in the far wing from Landry's—she couldn't help but marvel at the ornate tapestries portraying scenes from Lorenan history. She knew Mualath was the Benadur of the hill country, but she still hadn't been expecting anything so...elaborate.

Their rooms were next to each other, and she paused before entering, turning to Danny.

"Hey, about before . . . I feel like we should talk. I'm sorry, you know—about back in the gorge. I shouldn't have lost control like that. If I'd let you ground me, I know I wouldn't have. I just—" Her words trailed off, and she shrugged, grimacing slightly at him, knowing he would understand.

He didn't look at her, just stood gripping the handle of his door. He closed his eyes briefly before turning slightly to meet her gaze, his olive-green eyes intent on hers.

"I can't, Keira. I just can't."

It was like a swift kick to the gut, and she blinked at him in shock as he opened the door and strode into his room.

He *can't*? What the heck did that mean? Can't what? The *click* of his closing door jolted her from her thoughts but her mind was still a jumble. This was *Danny*—what did he mean, he can't? For as long as she'd known him, Danny had always been there for her. Sure, they fought and argued, but at the end of the day, he had her back—always. Without him . . . Keira swallowed, decidedly *not* wanting to think about what a future without Danny meant. Elliott was gone. Nazor might as well be gone too. Without Danny, who did she have left? Keira shoved down the rising panic within her. They were all tired. They just needed some rest and everything would be back to normal.

Shutting the door to her own room behind her, she stared at her surroundings, barely taking in the luxurious four-poster bed and beautiful wall tapestries. She wandered over to the bed and threw herself back onto it, staring up at the plush canopy in despair, her gaze tracing the curling gold embroidery twisting itself into spirals on the maroon fabric. She felt her eyes become heavy and watched the lines grow and twist and change as she drifted off to sleep.

KEIRA'S EYES FLEW OPEN. She was still in a strange half-dream, half-awake state when she stumbled from the bed, spinning in circles as she tried to bring the surrounding room into focus. She watched through the window as the sun raced toward the horizon, altogether too fast. The shadows within the room rapidly lengthened, stretching up the far wall and painting the tapestry scenes in shades of darkness. The scenes themselves seemed to shift uncontrollably, the running stags' legs beating in rhythmic unity as they fled the looming hunting party. From somewhere in the distance, Keira heard the howl of a hunting horn and the barking of dogs. She stumbled backward, turning wildly away from the stags' feverish eyes. She was met instead with the scene of a battle, the clang of swords audible to her ears as she watched the tapestry ripple and leap to life. Screams of the dying echoed all around her as the threads of fabric morphed into anguished faces.

Then, amid it all, she saw herself.

Dark curls ripped loose from their bindings, sword outstretched, she slashed through the surrounding people. She saw a majestic city burning, its streets littered with bodies. The Legion was there—she could tell by their gray cloaks and masked faces, the kneeling cantors and the guarding grounders. She watched as, one by one, they each fell to the bite of blades or the searing flame of chaos-wielding pneumonancers. At last, she stood alone, the sole remaining pneumonancer in an advancing sea of enemies. There was nothing to be done, and she was soon overtaken.

I've failed them, failed them all.

Keira's breathing came fast, heart beating out of her chest as the tapestry continued to expand, overtaking the rest of the room, sucking her into its depths.

It's not real, a distant voice murmured. *You know it's not real.* But despite herself, Keira's body was reacting viscerally. Adrenaline coursed through her veins, panic overpowering her, all the while a deep, gnawing sense of failure dug its fingers into her and dragged her down toward its own unknowable depths.

You haven't failed, the voice continued, pleading now. *The Legion lives, you still have time. Loren can be saved! Remember what I taught you, Keira.*

Elliott?

It couldn't be, Keira reminded herself. Elliott is gone. And yet his voice rang clear in her mind, as if he stood just beside her. And that thought was enough to free her feet. Keira stumbled away from the moving tapestry, searching desperately for a way out of this nightmare. She tripped over something, and the sharp pain of her knee hitting the floor was enough to shake her slightly loose from the illusion. She could see the door and lurched toward it, hand outstretched. The distance stretched before her, and her legs felt as if they were wading through mud as the echoes of battle and screams pounded in her head. Finally, her hand gripped the cold metal of the door handle, and with trembling fingers, she lifted it and threw herself through the open doorway.

The floor of the hallway was gloriously solid, and its walls miraculously still. Keira breathed heavily on her hands and knees, wondering what the hell kind of dream that was. She waited to hear Elliott's voice again, but there was nothing. A crash and the sound of screaming jerked her head up as she lurched to her feet, stumbling toward Danny's room.

This was no dream.

She threw open his door to find Danny held deep in the grip of his own illusion bind. His fists pounded against a tapestry of a bucolic picnic scene, moaning as tears streamed from his eyes. Keira ran toward him.

"Danny! Danny, stop! It's not real!"

Keira grabbed for his arm, but staggered back out of his reach as his fist swung around, missing her jaw by mere inches. He lurched toward her, eyes wide and looking straight through her.

"Danny, please!" She continued backing away, looking around desperately for something she could use. Still, he advanced.

"You killed her," he groaned. "She's dead!"

Finally, her back pressed against the door that had swung shut behind her, Keira fell upon the only thing she had left. Nudging her pneuma gently, she whistled and sent it flying at Danny, wrapping around him tightly, struggling to replace whatever this illusion was with her own bind.

He stopped advancing and stood still, trembling and whimpering. "Keira? Keira..."

"I'm here," she called, but he didn't seem to hear her. On an impulse, she stepped toward him hesitantly, then with more confidence. She reached him in a few steps and flung her arms around him, clinging to him body and soul as she sought desperately to release him from whatever spell held him captive. It was at that moment that she felt his fear, his own sense of failure.

He thinks I'm dead.

She could have cried just then—for Danny, for herself, for Loren, for the whole horrible situation that they had found themselves in. Instead, she looked up into Danny's eyes and found them clear. With a shuddering sigh, he wrapped his arms around her and pulled her tighter. They stood that way for a long moment until both of their shaking had stilled. Keira breathed in deeply the smell of him, reveling in the feel of his powerful arms around her. It felt . . . good. Far better than she had any right to. She pulled back and reluctantly, Danny let her go.

"It's okay," she said finally, unable to think of anything else. "We're okay. We're both here."

Danny nodded, breathing heavily before finally saying, in a raw, cracked voice, "But Landry isn't. We have to find him."

MUCH LIKE KEIRA'S VISION, the halls seemed to stretch before them as they sprinted through the corridors, heaving the rucksacks they'd thought to grab and desperate to find the wing that held Landry's rooms. They rounded a corner just in time to see a shadow disappear through a doorway. Keira's breath came fast and sharp as she barreled into the room, nearly running straight into two crouching children.

They hovered curiously over a very sweaty Landry, but jumped back in surprise at Keira and Danny's entrance. The girl was maybe seven or eight, while the boy couldn't have been older than five. Both were pristinely clean and dressed in the fine robes of hill country nobility. *Probably Mualath's kids*, she thought.

Danny immediately ran to Landry, who was curled up on the ground and wrestling with what looked like his bedsheets, muttering threats and epithets all the while. Keira quickly sheathed her sword and kneeled beside the two children. They looked ready to flee at the first loud noise, so she tried to adopt as light a tone as possible.

"Hello, you two. What are your names?"

The little boy had inched slowly behind his sister, only two blue eyes visible from around her skirts. But the little girl puffed up her chest and adopted her most regal manner as she addressed Keira solemnly.

"My name is Iona Mualath, and this is my brother, Desmond. Who are *you*?"

Keira felt the absurd urge to laugh at the tiny girl's carefully arched eyebrow, but adopted an equally formal tone. "My name is Keira Altman, and this is Danny O'Leary. We wanted to thank you for helping our friend here. It looks like he had some terrible dreams."

Iona's lips pressed together in a thin, disapproving line. "We heard him yelling bad words. Mama says it isn't polite to say such things."

Deciding that Keira wasn't about to skewer them, little Desmond suddenly poked his head all the way from around his sister, adding eagerly, "Father says this room makes your brain go catawally. We're not supposed to be in here, but we wanted to see the funny man." Desmond's smile suddenly fell, and his little brows knit together. "You won't tell, will you?"

Keira shook her head and tried to smile reassuringly, even as she mentally cursed the duplicitous Benadur. "Your secret is safe with me," she promised. "Now, my friends, we need to get the funny man here some help, but we mustn't be seen. He would be so embarrassed, you see, if people knew he'd been yelling such catawally things. Can you two help us?"

Their faces lit up eagerly, and Keira felt a twinge of guilt for taking advantage of them. But after a glance at Landry's ashen face, still dazed but having finally opened his eyes, she quickly pushed the thought aside. *We need all the help we can get.*

The children proved to be a godsend. After Danny had managed to rouse Landry from the illusion bind, the children sneaked them through a passage hidden behind an innocuous-appearing wall tapestry, showing them to the family well. This hidden circular staircase wrapped around a well shaft that must have dropped over a hundred feet into the water below. Apparently, wealthy families in the hill country often used them to escape the cities in times of siege. As they half-walked, half-carried Landry down the stairs, Keira glanced down into the shaft through one of the inward-looking window holes and quickly regretted it.

The children took them down as far as the street level and then exited into a courtyard to the side of their family home. They waved and scampered off as Keira and Danny prepared to continue their descent.

"We cannot leave."

They both started, looking at Landry in surprise.

"Your highness, we can't stay here," Danny protested. "The Benadur want to have you killed."

Landry glared at him. "You don't think I *know* that?" he hissed. "You don't think I realize that a member of my Council has turned on me? Of course, I do. But the fact remains that we cannot leave without my Bellators."

Keira's stomach rolled with sudden guilt. In all the excitement, she'd nearly forgotten about Sara and the rest of the cohort, who would wait for them in the city barracks. But did they really dare to sneak across town with the Council after them? She shook her head, looking desperately at Danny, who she could tell was struggling with the same thoughts.

"Landry," she began, "we can't risk it. If they find you, all of this—Flavius, Aaron, *everything*—will have been for nothing. We have to go."

"I will not leave them," he insisted stubbornly. "A leader does not abandon those who follow him. When the Council discovers we're gone, the others will be in danger. They must be warned."

Keira glared at him. Now was a hell of a time for him to start acting all kingly. She turned a pleading gaze toward Danny, hoping he at least could get through to him. But he only cocked his head, considering.

"I'll do it."

Keira stared at him, uncomprehending. "You'll do what?"

"I'll warn the cohort," Danny said wearily.

"Like hell, you will!" She couldn't believe he would suggest something so ridiculous.

"I can also get the horses this way. We won't make it very far on foot, especially if the Council comes after us."

"He has a point," Landry said, turning to Keira. She could tell he was fully in favor of the plan, which she found absolutely infuriating.

"But they know what you look like," Keira sputtered. "Either they'll kill you, or hold you for ransom and *then* kill you."

"I don't think so," Danny said slowly. "Look, there's a reason they tried to hold us in illusion binds instead of killing us outright. They're stalling, waiting for something—maybe even for worshippers of Séiro to arrive, so they can get information on the Legion."

"So...what? You're just gonna help them out by sticking around?"

"No, I'm going to make sure we have a fighting chance." He stepped toward her then, fingers skimming her arm. She knew he probably meant this to be reassuring, but the spider-like veins of electricity that went shooting over her skin made her want to pull away. She resisted the urge, only staring at him, pleading for him to understand what she couldn't bring herself to say.

I can't lose him, she thought. *Not him, not Danny.*

After all that had happened, she thought she could survive anything. But not that, not Danny.

She opened her mouth, wanting to tell him how much he meant to her, how much needed him

He'll leave you eventually, a voice in the back of her mind sneered. *They all do, remember? And then you really will be broken—even more shattered than you already are. Have I taught you nothing?*

Keira closed her eyes, willing the thoughts away. But the more she tried, the more they wound their way around her, tightening their grip until they were all she could hear.

"Fine," she said instead, forcing her mouth into a grim line as she yanked her arm back.

As she turned away, she caught the flash of pain that crossed his face and hated herself for causing it once again. She was too angry to turn around, though, so instead picked up their packs and began the long descent to the water below. She didn't look to see if either of them was following her, but eventually heard the patter of a single pair of feet following her down the stairs—Landry.

Danny had gone.

CHAPTER

TWENTY-TWO

The sun was altogether too high when Danny emerged from the street-level exit of the dive well—not ideal for sneaking through a busy city undetected. He tried to put aside the churning in his gut, the warring emotions of frustration and hurt that refused to leave him be. After all they had been through, and perhaps because of it, Keira's words could cut him to the core, and that knowledge hurt worse than anything. They were supposed to be partners, in this thing together, for eternity. They used to be a team. But now she had Sara and . . . Landry. He tried to put aside the vicious surge of jealousy that arose at the thought of the young prince. It was irrational, he knew. But he couldn't help but see that she was lighter somehow around him, less coiled in on herself.

But if he was being honest, he knew the real reason for his jealousy ran far deeper, emotions that had been simmering for years. He'd tried to move on, tried to forget about them when it became infinitely clear that Keira's past pain and betrayal would never allow her to return his feelings. Even so, he'd hoped. And that was the most painful of all.

He tried to push the fight with Keira from his mind, and was mostly successful, knowing as he did that dwelling on it would only make what he had to do now even harder.

Danny waited breathlessly behind the wall of the small courtyard for a crowd to pass before slipping smoothly into their ranks. He did

193

his best to keep his head down and slouch slightly to hide his height, but he knew he stuck out all the same. He headed west, slipping through the crowd with as much urgency as he dared, peering desperately ahead for the soaring dome of the Cruín. Without the red robes of Bellators flanking him, the people he passed seemed more at ease, laughing and teasing each other in the market stalls that lined the road. He kept his head down, hoping none would peer too closely.

When Danny finally reached the central square that lay before the Cruín, he headed straight for the city barracks on the southernmost end, feet pattering with what seemed like excruciating volume on the terracotta stones. The front gate was manned by two city guardsmen, and he assiduously skirted around its edges, looking for another way in—there was no telling what orders those guardsmen had been given, after all. He immediately recognized what must be the stable, and a quick look through an open window assured him that their horses were still there.

Danny made a quick survey of the barracks, and his heart sank with the realization that there was no way in, at least not on the first floor. But multiple unshuttered windows lined the second floor, so he began scanning the ground around him, looking for something he might use to climb. His eyes fell again on the stable he'd passed earlier. There was a narrow alleyway between the two buildings—if he could reach the thatched stable roof, he might be able to jump the distance to the open second-floor barracks window. Danny gnawed at his lower lip, eyeing the gap. It was truly a terrible plan, but just then, it seemed his only option.

Danny's heart pounded as he made his way back to the stable, pausing at the corner of the barracks to peer into the alleyway. Empty. He kept low to the ground as he crossed the alley, hiding amongst the tangle of weeds below the open stable window. Peering just over the ledge, he scanned the animal-filled interior.

There was no one.

So placing a foot on the sill, he used it to propel himself upward with open hands, just managing to grab the edge of the thatched roof. With a giant heave, he pulled himself up and over. His arms burned, the sinews of his fingertips threatening to snap as his breath came in sharp gasps.

Just when he thought he'd collapse from the effort, he got first an elbow and then a knee onto the roof. Rolling onto it, he lay in an exhausted heap, staring up at the perfectly cloudless sky and trying desperately to remind his lungs how to work. The urgency of his task shook him from his collapsed stupor, and he rolled over onto his hands and knees and made his way back toward the edge.

"What the hell is goin' on?!"

Danny froze, his breath catching in the back of his throat as his brain raced desperately between various courses of action. A mumbling voice answered the first, and Danny let out his breath in an audible sigh of relief.

They were still inside the stable.

They continued arguing about something he couldn't quite make out, and he crouched on the roof for what seemed an eternity, waiting for them to leave. His pulse pounded, anxiety level rising, as every second meant Keira and Landry were slipping farther and farther away. Eventually, the voices faded, and he dared to continue toward the edge of the roof.

The alleyway was easily five or six feet across, and he steeled himself to jump, eyeing the second-floor windowsill with distrust. He was high enough that a fall would definitely sprain—if not break—something. He closed his eyes, shook out his hands, and before he could second-guess himself, took a running leap across the alleyway.

His knees hit the stone wall with a bone-rattling crack as his hands and feet scrambled for holds in its smooth surface. Panic filled him in the split second it took to find a grip on the windowsill, and he hung there, sucking in a giant breath of air before heaving himself up onto his elbows and rolling headfirst into the room.

He landed in something soft and wet.

Scrambling to his feet, he wiped his hands on his pants in disgust as his eyes adjusted to the room's darkened interior. Fear and shock flooded him when he realized he was staring into the unmistakable face of Inaba Sara. Her eyes were wide and fearful as she lay in a pool of her own blood, her slit throat long since ceasing its steady flow.

Danny staggered back and turned in an ungainly circle, taking in the massacre that surrounded him. Each of the Bellators lay where they'd fallen—some on the floor, weapons in hand, and others still in bed, silenced in their sleep as they rested from their long journey.

Danny felt a wave of nausea mixed with fury overwhelm him, and he placed a trembling arm against the wall. The world around him seemed to blur and melt, the faces of Bellators morphing into those of GIs. Their red cloaks turned to green cammies as lacerations became bullet holes. He fought the vision off with everything he had, feeling himself teeter on the edge of a black abyss.

This is not then, he thought fiercely. *This is now, and Keira needs you.*

The trance was finally broken by the sound of footsteps quickly approaching. He spun around, searching desperately for something with which to defend himself, and coming up empty. The footsteps drew closer, and he thought back to Keira, fiercely glad that he'd sent her and Landry on ahead, and praying desperately that they didn't wait for him. They could make it to Crîd Eálas if they hurried, he decided. They had to.

Then the door swung open.

TWENTY-THREE

With every step they took away from Ulgáris, Keira's worry and regret grew. Danny was back there, risking his life to find the cohort. Anything could have happened to him by now and she'd never know. He could have been captured, injured, or . . . or killed. Keira felt sick at the thought, her knuckles blanching against the rucksack she carried. Why in Pneumos' name had she agreed to this plan?

She glanced at Landry, who'd been surprisingly stoic as they waded through the waste-high sewer water of the underground catacombs. She carried her rucksack overhead as the water lapped at her torso and tried not to imagine the myriad of creatures that were likely swimming around her at that very moment. Landry seemed resigned to the situation, even as his tunic became waterlogged and his boots mud-soaked. Keira had to admit she was impressed.

"Probably not how you thought your first trip to the holy city would go," she joked, trying and failing to quell her inner panic.

Landry snorted. "Not quite the triumphal return I was promised when I left for schooling in Mount Ánghen, to be sure."

Something brushed past Keira's ankle, and she swore, staggering backward in alarm—straight into Landry, who had to brace himself against the wall.

His low chuckle quickly bloomed into guffaws that bordered on hysteria, and Landry leaned further into the wall as he gasped. "My fearless protector!"

Keira tried to glare at him, but smiled slightly despite herself.

"Come on, then. The sooner we get out of here, the sooner we get you back to your royal bedchambers, your highness."

Landry rolled his eyes but followed her, still grinning. They continued on in silence for a while, until he asked, "They'll be fine, won't they?"

Keira's jaw clenched at the question, her terrified thoughts expressed aloud and had to force herself to breathe normally. She was surprised to hear what sounded like genuine concern in his voice and squelched the sarcastic remark she'd been about to make. Before she could respond, he added, "I mean, they'll make it out of the city all right, with the horses. They have to."

She desperately wanted to reassure him, to confidently tell him that everything *would* be all right, if only to convince herself. But the words caught in her throat, and she swallowed them. Instead, she looked Landry straight in his pleading, still too-innocent eyes, and told him the truth.

"I don't know."

She watched as his face crumpled. At that moment, he might have been seven years old for all he'd never known the pain of having put others' lives at risk. Keira pitied him. After all, that had been her a few short weeks ago, before her world had inverted. She kept her face blank, though, knowing this had to be done.

"Landry," she said, allowing her voice to soften minutely. "If you're going to be Regio, then this will not be the last tough decision you'll have to make. A civil war is coming, and if we can't avoid it, then you *will* have to ask people to risk their lives for you."

"I can't," he protested. "It's too much. I . . . I . . ."

"I know it's hard," she said, watching him pale and shake his head slightly. "It *should* bother you—in fact, I'd be more worried if it didn't." She offered him a cautious smile, which he didn't return, so she continued. "The fact that this power bothers you so much means that *maybe* you'll actually deserve it someday."

Landry let out a barking laugh and shook his head. She felt something squeeze her chest, realizing as she did that he really cared.

Underneath all the pampering and privilege, he actually *cared,* actually wanted to be a good ruler. So even though she was wholly unsure of just about everyone and everything in her life, Keira realized maybe she could trust that. Perhaps she could trust *him.*

"Don't go flattering me now," Landry said, blushing a bit.

"Who, me?" Keira, shaken from her own thoughts, gave him a playful punch on the arm. "Never. You'll always be a pompous asshat to me, princeling."

EVENTUALLY, the catacomb waters grew clearer as they pushed through them, and they could just make out a light visible in the darkness ahead. Keira unsheathed her sword, not sure exactly what they'd find when they reached it. As they approached, though, she quickly realized that the light was coming from the ceiling, where a grated hatch could be reached from a rusted metal ladder below.

She sheathed her blade and, signaling for Landry to wait at the bottom, hauled herself up the ladder and toward the hatch. It was heavy and difficult to budge, given its years of rusted seclusion. She braced her shoulders against it and fixed her feet in the corners of a slick ladder wrung. Using her legs to propel herself upward, she slowly wedged it open. The squeal of rusted metal sent gooseflesh rippling down her arms, and she quickly scampered up and out of the opening, hand on the hilt of her sword lest anyone be drawn by the noise.

Keira found herself in a small, wooded glade covered with shrubbery. All the better to hide an escape route, she thought, grateful just then for the noble families' finely tuned sense of self-preservation. She stood quietly, listening for the approach of footsteps and wanting very much to silence the thump of her heartbeat in her ears. All she heard was the gentle ripple of a far-off stream—no doubt the source of the dive well's water. She returned to the open grate and gestured for Landry to join her.

Landry heaved himself up into the clearing, making an echoing clang as he climbed that made her cringe. He laid there, panting, staring up at the sky as she carefully scoured the surrounding landscape. She found the southern road just on the other side of the glen and returned to find Landry standing up and attempting to wring the liquid from his water-logged britches.

"We should wait here for Danny and the others," Keira said, carefully averting her gaze from Landry's bare legs as she spoke and fighting to keep the burning from her cheeks. "If they got the horses, they'll be coming down the road just over there. I left a cairn alongside that Danny will recognize, in case we somehow don't hear them coming."

Landry nodded as he laid his britches out to dry on a nearby bush and settled down against a tree to wait.

"You'll want to dry those out before the sun sets," Landry noted, nodding at her own clothes and glancing at the quickly setting sun.

"I'll be fine," Keira said stiffly, knowing her ears were very much scarlet at this point.

Landry shrugged. "Suit yourself."

He let his eyes flutter shut then, the nerve of him. Leaving Keira to stand watch, alert for any sign of the cohort, of Danny.

~

He didn't come.

As dusk settled into darkness, Keira struggled desperately against the rising sense of panic that threatened to suck her under. Landry had put his clothes back on by this point, and the two of them sat huddled together against the cold, the tree at their back providing only minimal shelter from the wind. They dared not start a fire for fear someone coming from the city might see it. Keira shivered beneath her still-soaked clothing, even after they'd pulled an old ratty blanket from the rucksack to huddle under.

And so, the night passed in fitful bouts of sleeping and shivering, Keira trying and failing to hear the approaching sound of hoofbeats on the road below. At one point, she felt Landry's head nod onto her shoulder, and awoke briefly near dawn to find her own leaning against his. Too exhausted to move it, she instead yielded to the impulse and fell fitfully back to sleep.

She couldn't say exactly how much time passed, but based on the leaden feel of her limbs when she woke to the rustle of shrubbery, it had to have been several hours.

"Nice to see you two as well."

Keira's eyes flew open, and she stumbled clumsily to her feet, sword half-drawn as she spun to peer directly into the weary, olive-green eyes she knew so well.

"Danny," she breathed, a broad smile threatening to break her face in two. She flung herself toward him, throwing her arms around his neck, her body flooded with relief, excitement, and a host of other emotions that she couldn't even name.

He's back. He's okay.

The thoughts banged around in her head in a cacophony bordering on mental hysteria. Delirious as she was with happiness, it took her a moment to realize that Danny's body was stiff and unrelenting against hers. She drew backward slightly, confusion warring with the relief that coursed through her. Then she knew—something had gone terribly wrong.

Exhaustion was etched in every line of Danny's face, and a deep sadness warred with hostility as he looked from her to Landry. Keira felt her ears burn and knew her face had turned a deep crimson. She suddenly realized how this must look.

"Dan—" she started, but he held up a hand, stopping her. She could have cried for the look of pain she saw on his face.

Landry took zero notice.

"Danny! Good to see you!" He clapped a hand on Danny's shoulder, oblivious to the stony look Danny gave him. "Where are the others, then?"

Danny's face shattered, anger giving way entirely to desolation. His Adam's apple bobbed slightly as he swallowed, and a sense of dread seeded itself deeply in the pit of Keira's stomach.

"What is it, Danny?" she asked quietly.

He glanced at her, but spoke only to Landry. "They're gone, your highness," he said hoarsely. "All of them. I made it inside the barracks, but I was too late. They were all dead."

Numbness spread from Keira's fingertips, closely followed by a slowly dawning horror.

"No," she whispered. Danny only stared back at her. "N-no they can't . . . all of them?" She searched his face and saw a spark of sympathy flash in his eyes. Danny slowly nodded.

"I'm sorry, Keira."

She reached a trembling hand out to brace herself as she slumped heavily against a nearby tree. *Sara—oh, Sara.* She remembered Sara's laugh like the jingle of bells, the way her eyes crinkled at the edges when she smiled, conveying more with a single look than Keira could in an entire conversation. She'd been Keira's first real female friend. The first one not to look at her like some sort of freak. She'd had a family and a home and now she was gone.

What have I done? Keira thought, eyes squeezing shut as if to keep out reality. *Why did I have to bring us here?*

Landry just stared at him blankly, incomprehension clear on his face. Finally, he shook his head, as if clearing it of unwanted visitors.

"T-that's impossible. What reason could the Council possibly have—they were just soldiers. They only did as they were ordered." His voice had gained an octave and begun to shake.

Keira, roughly wiping a sleeve across her own face, stepped toward him, ignoring Danny's hard look of reproach. She grabbed his shoulders with both hands and jostled him, forcing him to look at her.

"This isn't your fault," she said fiercely. "I'm the one who brought us here. This is on me. My fault for thinking I could be some kind of leader. That I had any right to—"

Her voice broke and she turned away to blink furiously at the tears that sprung to her eyes. A warm hand squeezed her arm that and she glanced toward it, hoping and expecting to see Danny's reassuring smile. But it was Landry, eyes filled with understanding and an echo of the despair that pulled at her.

Her heart lurched. He looked so small then, like a tiny bird thrust ill-equipped and unprepared from its nest. None of them had started this war, yet they were the ones being dragged headfirst into it.

"You made the best decision you could, Keira. If we hadn't stopped, she would have died for sure. And I agreed with it," he said, his face wretched with shame and sadness. "That makes it my responsibility as well."

At that moment, she wanted nothing more than to take his pain away, to shield him from the nasty realities of this world. She would have shielded them both, for that matter. But she knew she couldn't. This was their lot and this pain was theirs to bear. The best they could do was to ensure the loss wasn't in vain. So she nodded, straightening up as she looked between Danny and Landry, both drowning in their own misery.

"We have to keep moving," she said, filling her voice with a steely resolve she didn't quite feel. "We'll only be safe when we reach the capital, and until then, no one must know who you are, Landry."

Landry had been forced to leave his more expensive tunics behind when they'd fled the monastery, and after the failed attack at Benadur Mualath's home, he wore only a plain white shirt and breeches. After borrowing one of Danny's worn leather jerkins, he looked no more a princeling than your average stable hand.

As they made their way down to the roadside where Danny had tied the horses, Keira asked him hesitantly how he'd escaped the barracks.

"A young squire of the city guard," he replied stiffly, still not looking at her directly. "I got the jump on him when he came to dispose of the bodies. I snuck out wearing his clothes." He shrugged. "No one asked twice when I said Benadur Mualath had ordered the cohort's three best horses be brought to him."

Keira was warmly greeted by Cerise's insistent nuzzle and shot Danny a grateful look that he ignored as the three of them mounted the horses.

"Look Danny, about back there—"

"Forget it." He ordered shortly, his voice leaving no room for argument. She blinked in surprise.

"But I just wanted you to know—"

"I said," Danny bit off, "leave it. I don't want to get into this, Keira. Not here, not now."

Keira's mouth fell open as she stared at him but she quickly closed it, looking away as she bit down on her lower lip. Burying her wounded feelings, she set her mouth in a straight line and turned Cerise's head south, toward Crîd Eálas.

CHAPTER

TWENTY-FOUR

It rained almost continuously for three days as the trio made their way south. If Keira had found long-distance riding painful before, it was nothing compared to riding all day in soaked britches. They rode at a brisk, unyielding pace, convinced that someone from the Council was never far behind. They slept in shifts off the main road, always leaving one person to keep watch and never daring to start a fire. Not that a fire would have done them much good —the rain would have doused anything they tried to light, anyway.

They reached the hill above the fishing village of Ceffí just as the limited supply of food they'd brought with them finally ran out. *Thank goodness*, Keira thought wearily. She would have given anything just then for a warm bed and a hot meal. As the road wound its way down the hill, she noted with an absent curiosity that the trees seemed to thin out as they went until, finally, they emerged from the forest onto an overlook above the village itself.

Landry gasped, startling the horses. Keira reined in Cerise's head as she worked through her own shock, unable to tear her eyes from the sight before them.

The entire village was underwater. As they guided the horses through what had once been the main street, they watched as villagers waded through nearly knee-deep floodwaters, skirts and pant legs tied high as they carried loads and packages on their heads to avoid the damp splashes of the other passersby. Their faces were weary masks of exhaustion that betrayed a deep note of resignation. Keira realized suddenly that these people were thoroughly unsurprised by the situation in which they found themselves. She could see that many of the newer-looking buildings had been elevated onto stilts, while the less fortunate were forced to run their businesses and live in homes with a perpetual foot of water underfoot.

They eventually made their way to the local tavern, having been forced to dismount and lead the horses through the deeper stretches of the river-filled road. Handing the horses off to a stable boy to lead up the ramp to the lifted stable, the three of them climbed the steps of the tavern and ventured into its smoky interior.

It took Keira's eyes a moment to adjust to the dank light as they weaved through tables. A man who appeared to be the owner stood talking with a younger man near the fire. Keira watched as he quickly poured a handful of coins into the younger man's fists, which were immediately whisked away into a leather side pouch. As Danny moved to ask the owner for rooms for the night, Keira caught the face of the younger man as he turned. Something tugged at the back of her mind as she watched him slide past her toward the door.

"I know you!" The words escaped her mouth before she had time to think about their wisdom, especially as they were trying to reach Crîd Eálas unnoticed.

The man turned his wide-spaced brown eyes toward her and pushed a few curls off his forehead absently, revealing an oft-broken nose.

"Neval, right?" she asked. *Too late to backtrack now,* she thought, cursing her own stupidity. His eyes had already sparked in recognition as he looked at her, so she pressed on. "I'm glad to see you made it out of Raboneís."

He cocked his head at her, teeth somehow glinting even in the low light. "You as well, lovely Keira. Quite the tinderbox, did I not say, that Raboneís?"

A shiver ran through her as she suddenly recalled her last memory: Neval leading the charge of villagers against the Bellators, a strangled war cry coming from his throat. Fear gripped her, and she stopped herself from jerking her head around to look for Landry just in time. He wasn't safe here—none of them were.

As if drawn by her thoughts, Landry suddenly appeared at her elbow. She cursed him silently as Neval looked between the two of them questioningly.

"This is, uh...Arlan," she blurted, hoping Neval hadn't noticed the pause and willing Landry to play along.

"How do you do?" Landry extended a hand formally, which Neval eyed suspiciously before taking.

"An uplander's name with a downlander's words," he commented wryly.

"We moved south when I was a child," Landry replied smoothly. "Became household servants to a noble family."

Neval made an indiscernible noise in the back of his throat. Keira nodded weakly at him, trying to think of a way to excuse themselves from this conversation. Landry, however, was clearly oblivious to the imminent danger he was in.

"Tell me, is flooding like this typical of the region?"

Neval cocked his head at him, eyes narrowing slightly. "Every year during the wet season, at least since the dam."

Don't ask, don't ask, Keira mentally pleaded.

"The dam?"

Keira wanted to smack him.

"The Karthaíla dam?" Neval's whole body stilled and he arched one eyebrow at Landry. "You really aren't from these parts, are you? It was built four years ago for the supposed improvement of irrigation for the downlander farms, not to mention luxurious stone water ducts for Port Karthaíla. Only left the minor problem of flooding the entire Ceffí Valley every year."

"That's terrible," Keira breathed, drawn in despite herself as she surveyed the handful of soul-shattered people in the tavern. Most slumped over drink as eyes drifted closed in exhaustion. Her heart ached to see them and the injustice of it all rankled her.

"It is," Neval agreed mildly, his jaw tightening at the words. "This is all that's left. Everyone else has moved on or is . . . dead." Something flashed across his face at the words and Keira briefly wondered who all he'd lost, the souls that haunted this angry rebel.

"I'm so sorry," Keira murmured, meaning every word. Beside her,

Landry nodded furiously. Neval inclined his head briefly in acknowledgement before continuing.

"Your sympathy is rare, I'll admit. After all, who can be bothered about a lowly upland fishing village?"

His voice had turned harsh, and he spat on the ground to punctuate his point. A low rumbling met his words from the gathered pub patrons who, by this point, had halted their own conversations to listen in on theirs. Keira felt the slowly dawning sensation of a rabbit caught between crosshairs and wanted nothing more at that moment than for them to be on their way. Landry looked altogether too shocked to realistically be an uplander, who would have grown up inculcated with tales of downlander excesses and oppression.

They needed to leave—*now*.

"Well, the time is soon comin' when we won't be so easily ignored." Neval's voice had continued to rise in volume, and this statement was met with raucous cheers of agreement from his makeshift audience. Keira met Danny's eyes from across the room and shot him her best pleading glance, silently begging for an excuse to leave. His brow furrowed, and with an apologetic word, he quickly gripped the tavern owner's hand and began making his way back toward where Keira and Landry were standing.

"Tell me again," Neval continued, "where you said you're from originally?" He aimed a withering look at Landry, who, to his credit, managed not to shrivel completely.

"Abalás," he blurted, throwing out the name he'd surely heard Keira and Danny mention frequently. Neval's eyes tightened in disbelief, and he had just opened his mouth to say something when Danny finally reached them.

"Afraid we must be moving on," he began. "Room prices here are far too high for the likes of us."

Latching onto this excuse, Keira smiled apologetically at Neval. "Good to see you, but you must excuse us."

She grabbed Landry's arm and half-dragged him out of the tavern, leaving Neval's all-too-perceptive eyes to watch them go with undisguised interest.

~

BY THE TIME they had re-saddled the horses and replenished their dwindling supplies, the rain had resumed in full, and Keira peered with disappointment at the warm lights of the tavern receding behind them as they continued on their way down the southern road. Landry hadn't uttered a word since the confrontation with Neval, and he seemed to be mentally chewing on something as they picked up their pace, trying to put distance between themselves and Ceffí before they had to stop to make camp.

"You want to tell me what that was about back there?" Danny asked, pulling Boyd up next to her and leveling her with a curious look.

Keira raised an eyebrow at him. "I guess you're speaking to me now?"

He shrugged. "Well, my options are a bit limited at the moment."

"Gee, thanks." She rolled her eyes at him and noted the slight dimpling at the corner of his mouth.

It's a start, at least, she thought. She explained who Neval was and how she'd met him in the Raboneís tavern, then how she'd seen him again leading armed men in the riot. Danny shook his head in disapproval, giving her a somber look.

"He's trouble, that one."

"What *I* want to know," Keira began, verbalizing a thought she'd been mulling over since leaving the village, "is why he's in Ceffí."

"Maybe he's from there?"

Keira wasn't so sure about that. "Maybe, but wherever he goes, trouble seems to follow. I don't like that he's this close to the capital. It may not be as safe there as we think."

Danny made a noncommittal sound in the back of his throat, but otherwise said nothing.

"That was awful, though," she said, thinking about the gaunt faces of the Ceffí villagers. "The way people have to live there. I mean, that's why we're doing this, right? To prevent this kind of chaos."

Danny gave her a long, inscrutable look before replying. "There's a difference between order and justice, Keira. All this work we're doing to put Landry on the throne, to prevent chaos. Do you really think it will make things better for these people?"

Keira looked at Landry, unusually quiet, as he rode ahead of them.

"He has a good heart, Danny." She said, raising her brows at his dubious look. "He does. And you can tell that this is all affecting him. If we can help him see what his people are really suffering, that may be the most good that can come out of this whole mess."

Danny paused for a moment, considering her words.

"Then I suppose we'd better get him there in one piece," he said grudgingly. "Even if he is a pompous princeling."

Keira grinned at him and he gave her a small smile in return. They were partners again, even as the weight of all that lay unspoken still settled heavily between them.

FINALLY DARING a fire for the first time since leaving Ulgáris, Keira and Landry set to making rabbit stew from the supplies they'd purchased in Ceffí, while Danny went in search of more wood to bank the fire for the night.

"You've been quiet since Ceffí," Keira commented mildly, adding diced potatoes to the pot as Landry stirred. He didn't meet her eyes. "Do you want to talk about it?" She tried to keep the hope from her voice, betraying no sign of concern.

Landry said nothing, his wrist moving in rhythmic time over the pot. "Not really."

Keira nodded, restraining herself from pressing further. Luckily, Landry was as bad at silence as she was.

"It's just . . ." He paused, searching for the right words. "I don't know how this happened, how things became so . . . so *wrong*." Keira opened her mouth to say something, but he pressed on. "My father is a kind man, you know," he said, almost defensively. His eyes searched hers, and she tried to make her gaze as unassuming as she could. "He wouldn't have permitted such a thing if he'd known what would happen."

Keira paused, turning over the words she wanted to say in her mind for a moment. "It can be easy for those who have a lot to pick and choose the things they find *convenient* to know," she said gently. "It doesn't make your father a terrible person. The real question is whether you will let the knowledge you have now change how *you* govern."

Landry still looked troubled. "It just seems like every day, being Regio becomes more and more impossible. How am I supposed to lead these people? Why would they follow someone they blame for making their lives so terrible?"

His eyes pleaded with her for an answer, and she searched desperately for the right words, for the right balance of honesty and encouragement that he needed. She didn't get the chance.

"Good luck with *that*. They'll never follow you." Danny's voice was icy and had a snide edge that seemed wholly unlike him. Keira glanced back to see him standing behind them, having walked up as they spoke.

Landry turned to face Danny now, hands upturned and eyes pleading. "But . . . if I prove I can be a fit leader, that I can make their lives better, surely they'll come to accept me as Regio."

Danny snorted. "You think a nice tax break and the promise of more say in what happens to them will be enough to settle them? The uplanders will never trust you."

"What if I reconcile with the Council, show them I can be reasoned with? Maybe then the people will—"

"The Council?" Danny laughed mirthlessly. "You and your family will always be invaders to them. They may tolerate you for the advantages in land and wealth that it may bring them, but all it takes is one sign of weakness. They get one whiff of blood in the water, and they *will* turn on you. And when that happens, no amount of money or power will be enough to save you."

Landry turned back to the pot, anger and fear warring on his face. Keira gritted her teeth, shooting Danny a glare.

"Alright, that's enough." She put a hand on Landry's shoulder, and he met her eyes. "You'll find a way. And we'll be there to help you."

Danny made a strangled sound somewhere between anger and disgust. She looked back just in time to see him turn on his heel and stalk back toward the forest. Keira massaged the bridge of her nose between thumb and forefinger, feeling utter exhaustion overcome her.

Pneumos save me from the absurdities of men, she thought. *Just when I think I've got one sorted, the other has a meltdown. And they say women are the emotional ones.*

Patting Landry gently on the arm, she turned and followed Danny.

She found him in a clearing a few yards away, methodically snapping the thinner branches from a fallen tree. He didn't look at her as she approached, but judging by the hard, thin line of his mouth, he definitely knew she was there.

"What was that about?" Keira demanded. "I thought we agreed we were going to help him, not kick him when he's down."

"I *am* helping him," Danny muttered. "He should know the truth."

"Yeah, but you could give him a break," Keira said, keeping her voice light. "He's been through a lot."

"We've all been through a lot," Danny said darkly, a shadow crossing his face even as he turned away from her to reach the far side of the tree. "And frankly, I think he's been given far too many *breaks* in his life. Pompous arseling was your nickname for him, if I recall."

Keira shrugged. "He's come a long way. Which you'd see if you gave him half a chance."

Danny snorted, still not looking up from his vigorous branch-snapping.

"Look, Danny, I know the last few days have been awful for you. Finding the cohort like that—" Keira swallowed hard, willing her voice not to break and only barely succeeding. "I can't imagine what that must have been like."

Danny said nothing, so she pressed on.

"But Landry needs us. If he's going to assume the throne, he needs to start off in the best position possible. He needs our help and advice, especially—"

"Don't you get it?" Danny spun around, raking his hands through his hair and glaring at her. "Landry will *never* become Regio. He and his family—they're on their own. There is no more Marian Empire, no armies coming to help them. The empire died a hundred years ago, and to be honest, maybe they should have died with it."

"How can you say that?" she exclaimed. "It's Landry. He's our friend."

"Is he? Maybe to you . . . or maybe he's more than that."

"Come on, Danny. He's like a brother to me. I feel responsible for him. I have to take care of him because, frankly, he needs all the help he can get." Keira rolled her eyes and shot him a grin, hoping to lighten the mood.

Danny didn't return it, so she walked over and grabbed him roughly by the shoulders, forcing him to look at her.

"Danny," she breathed. "I need you—I *rely* on you. You're the person I go to when I need help, the one I want to talk to when things get tough. You have to know that *no one* can replace you, least of all Landry."

Danny finally met her eyes, and it was all she could do not to look away from the emotion she saw there.

"Then why is it so easy for you to let him in, huh?" Danny asked hoarsely. "Every time I try to reach you, you do nothing but shut me out."

Keira flinched. She searched for the words she needed, the ones that could explain...whatever it was she felt so deeply, but couldn't quite articulate.

"Landry...he sees me only as I want to be seen," Keira said hesitantly. "As a warrior, a mentor—a leader, even. But you, Danny...you know *me*. You see me as I am, warts and all. I can't hide, well, *anything* from you, and that is pretty damn terrifying."

Danny stared at her, long and hard. She saw the yearning in his eyes, knew what he wanted from her. She also knew there was a part of her that wanted it, too.

Two steps. Two steps were all it would take to reach him, to throw her arms around him and let him hold her, let him chase away all of her fears and doubts. Her fingers itched to touch him but her feet remained stubbornly in place. She couldn't do it, and it nearly broke her heart.

"Promise me, then," he said. "Promise me that after we see him safely to Crîd Eálas, we'll leave." He paused, searching her eyes. "We'll escape whatever's coming—and you *know* something is coming. We'll find Nazor and the Legion, and we'll get back to *our* life."

Keira shook her head reluctantly. "You know it won't be that simple."

"But it could be." His gaze was intense, eyes pleading. "Promise me."

Keira hesitated, torn. She wanted to say yes, wanted to give him whatever he wanted. It was *Danny*. He deserved the life that he'd signed up for, not this crazy vigilante quest she'd gotten them caught up in. But could she really leave Landry to his own devices?

He has a family, an inner voice reminded her, *and an army with generals he actually pays to take care of him. This is not your responsibility and you have your mother to think of. Or did you forget why you started this in the first place? Surely you've done enough to get back in the Legion's good graces.*

But Landry needed her help. He couldn't do this on his own. And she'd seen what was coming, seen how the uplands were being brutalized and the Olpheís nomads killed. How could she just leave and let all that continue?

Stop trying to play the hero, a still-darker voice murmured. *You can't do this. You know you'll fail eventually. Get out now, before you get even more people killed—just like Elliott and Sara.*

The thought sent an icy shard of pain through her chest and Keira had to remind herself to keep breathing, to keep standing.

Danny was still staring at her, hopeful eyes boring into hers. She couldn't disappoint him, not again, so Keira nodded weakly. They would leave as soon as Landry was safe in Crîd Eálas. She was rewarded with Danny's broad smile and the look of relief on his face.

She desperately wished that she shared the sentiment.

TWENTY-FIVE

No one spoke as they neared the shining city of Crîd Eálas. The weight of recent events and the shadow of the previous night's argument cast a long pall over the trio. But despite everything that had happened, as they gazed out over the city, Keira was struck with awe and a small kernel of excitement. The city's terracotta roofs and ivory walls reminded her so much of the Mediterranean style she remembered and loved from her own world. And with its massive encircling limestone wall, perfectly reflecting the turquoise waves, Crîd Eálas was a marvel of Marian architecture and ingenuity. Built from nothing, a humble seaside village that became the capital of the newest branch of the empire, Crîd Eálas was a symbol as much as a city.

Above it all sat the Vindolum, the ancient fortress that overlooked both Crîd Harbor and the city itself. Built in the earliest days of the Marian invasion, its rounded turrets were the most apparent sign in Loren of Marian strength and majesty. As such, it had become home to the royal family itself. As they rode across the bridge leading to Crîd Eálas's famous landward gate, the Porta Lorena, Keira felt a shiver run down her spine and gooseflesh ripple across her arms. For even after all they'd gone through, something told her that getting out of this city would be far more complicated than getting in.

~

Crossing the great hall in the Vindolum toward the waiting Regio and his daughter, Keira's first thought was an absurd curiosity about how the Marians had invented such excellent indoor temperature regulation. Despite the sweltering early summer's day, the inside of the fortress was cold, due no doubt to the light-colored limestone and the carefully placed windows in the uppermost reaches of the walls, which permitted both light and a fresh sea breeze to offer relief to the grateful people below.

Danny pointedly clearing his throat brought her back to reality, and she realized with a start that they'd nearly reached the end of the great hall and were even then approaching the Regio's throne. When Landry sank to one knee before his father, Keira and Danny quickly followed suit, careful to cock their heads slightly lower than his, as was custom.

"Lord Father," Landry began, using a formal, stiff tone Keira hadn't heard since Mount Ánghen, "I am returned from my years of study at Mount Ánghen. Pray find me prepared in body, mind, and spirit, and worthy of the duties set before me."

Keira glanced at Landry from the corner of her eye, surprised to see beads of sweat on his brow. *Not exactly the homecoming I expected for him*, she thought wryly. She shifted nervously, trying to ease some of the pressure off her knees as she glanced upward through the veil of hair that hung down before her face. She could see the old Regio seated on his throne. The too-big robes hung off of him, even as he struggled to maintain his upright posture. His hair had long since gone gray, and his beard, neatly trimmed though it was, betrayed thinning spots that evidenced his age and advancing illness. He opened his mouth as though to say something, but was swiftly interrupted by a wracking round of coughing that left him wheezing and doubled over. Keira struggled internally with whether she should go to the struggling man herself, since no one else seemed about to intervene.

Then a figure emerged from the shadows on the king's right. The woman was tall and slender, moving with a grace that set her apart instantly as a person of significance in the room. The other courtiers bowed low as she passed them, surreptitiously avoiding her gaze. She was dressed very much in the downlander style, the vibrant sea blue of her dress falling in airy folds around her, a sheer scarf winding up her arm but leaving bare her olive-skinned shoulders. Her rich, lustrous hair fell in black curls around her head, pulled back from her face by the gold circlet she wore perched on her head like a crown. She was the picture of elegance and grace, her dark brows arched regally over espresso eyes.

She swept toward the aged king, unfolding a handkerchief from an unseen pouch, which she offered to him with a flourish. Once he'd accepted, she sailed down the steps toward them, drawing Landry to his feet and wrapping him in a warm embrace.

"Dearest brother," she breathed, the honeyed words flowing smoothly. "I am so glad to see you home. We've heard tell of the hardships you faced on the road. It is a blessing to find you whole and unharmed."

Landry's eyes lit up, and he squeezed his sister warmly in return. "It's wonderful to see you, too, Junia. And good to be home, truly. I'd also like to introduce Keira Altman and Danny O'Leary, Legionnaires whom I've come to regard as loyal friends."

He gestured for them to rise, and Keira gladly complied, unbending her knee from the hard flagstone. She stepped forward just as Junia turned her dark eyes on her. Though her face remained fixed in a welcoming smile, Keira saw something tighten in the woman's eyes. She looked closer, but a moment later, it was gone, smoothed over by an innocent gaze that left tingles racing down Keira's spine.

"Truly, there is nothing I desire more just now than a warm meal and a dry bed." Landry laughed jocularly, turning to Keira and quickly growing more somber at her expression. "This evening, though, we must speak with my father. I've learned much on my journey, and there is much to discuss."

Junia smiled indulgently at him, though Keira saw a tightness in her eyes. "We?" she asked sweetly.

"Yes—the Legionnaires and I. There is much to be said."

Junia didn't look at either her or Danny, but Keira saw her stiffen and felt a corresponding wave of personal satisfaction.

"Of course, I'm sure they were quite *helpful* to you on your journey," Junia replied, smooth as silk. "But I'm afraid our father will be far too weary this evening. I, however, will happily meet with you. I've taken over many of the day-to-day tasks, you see."

Keira felt her jaw clench, but tried to keep her face smooth.

Landry, on the other hand, seemed to see nothing wrong with this arrangement. "Oh, wonderful! Yes, why don't we meet after dinner then, in the library?"

"No, no, in father's study. That's where I've been working, you see. Best to keep everything in order."

Interesting.

A murmur came from behind Junia, and they all looked to see the old Regio trying to say something as he straightened himself on his throne. With a swirl of skirts, Junia was by his side in an instant, crooning and patting his arm reassuringly.

"Yes, yes, Lord Father, of course."

With a flick of her fingers, she summoned two valets from the corner, who brought with them a wheeled chair that they gently guided the sick man into.

"You must excuse our father," she said. The words were directed at Landry, but clearly meant for the entire room. "He's had a tiring day. We will reconvene with royal audiences in the morning."

Her words carried with them an authority that surprised Keira. All around them, courtiers snapped to attention, bowing to the retreating Regio as they quickly dispersed. Junia met her curious gaze with one of serene confidence, and Keira couldn't help but see a challenge etched in the angle of her jaw and the stiffness of her neck.

Let it go, the voice in the back of her mind insisted. *This is not your problem anymore.*

She shook her head, still uncomfortable with the situation, but conceded to follow Landry and Danny as they were shown to their rooms. She resisted the urge to look back at Junia, even as she felt the other woman's eyes on her.

～

UPON REACHING THEIR ROOMS, the three of them paused outside.

"I've already asked for food to be brought to our rooms and water for baths." Landry laughed, sounding near delirium in his excitement.

"I can't believe we really made it. Everything will finally work out. We'll speak with Junia tonight and come up with a plan."

Keira cocked her head at him, considering. Part of her wanted to share in his excitement—Pneumos knew she wanted a bath and a hot meal as well. But she couldn't quite lose the bitter taste in her mouth after their meeting with Junia. She didn't trust her, that much she knew, and frankly, she doubted very much that Junia was at all pleased about her and Danny's arrival with her brother.

"Are you sure..." Keira paused, weighing her words and ignoring the warning glance that Danny had shot her. "Are you sure your sister is the best one for us to be dealing with, Landry?"

He looked at her with no small amount of confusion. "What do you mean? You heard what she said. My father's too ill."

"Yes, I know," Keira said impatiently. "But you don't think it's just a little odd that she suddenly takes over ruling the country, and everyone just goes along with it?"

"No," Landry insisted, chin jutting out at a stubborn angle as his arms folded in front of him. "She's the Regio's daughter, and the only other member of the royal family living in Crîd Eálas. I know you're not from the capital, but that's just how things are done here. She would have been expected to step in when my father was too tired or unable to fulfill all his duties."

Landry's insinuation stung, and Keira tried not to flinch visibly. But her embarrassment only fueled her frustration.

"Still," Keira pressed, "she admitted she heard about you nearly being assassinated by a Bellator—in a cohort *she* put together, by the way—and then attacked by your own Council member. And yet she decided not to actually *do* anything to help?"

"What was she supposed to do? March an army northward, leaving the capital undefended amid local unrest?"

"Convenient excuse is what I say," Keira muttered. She looked to Danny, hoping for some support, but found him scrutinizing his shoe and studiously avoiding her gaze.

Landry threw his hands in the air. "Look," he began, frustration clear in his voice, "My sister practically raised me after my mother died. Pneumos knows my father was too busy to be bothered." He shook his head, bitterness etched in every line of his face. "She loves me and would see me on my father's throne. She is *not* the one we need to be worried about, or have you forgotten about Neval Brennan and his imminent rebellion? If anyone's a threat to me, it's him."

Seeing that the conversation was leading nowhere, Keira finally threw her hands up in defeat, but couldn't help rolling her eyes. Shooting her a look of exasperation, Landry threw open his door and stomped through.

"We'll discuss this later," she heard him mutter before being cut off by the slam of his bedroom door.

Keira groaned audibly, pinching the bridge of her nose between thumb and forefinger.

"What are we going to do with him?" she asked Danny.

"I don't know Keira," he said tiredly, "but honestly, I just want a bath and some food. Can we talk about this later?"

Keira sighed. In truth, the promise of warmth and sustenance was too tempting to pass up just then. Nevertheless, she could have used his support.

"Fine," she said curtly, striding purposefully into her own room and closing the door with a satisfying *thud*.

TWENTY-SIX

Baths really are undervalued in this world, Keira decided, trailing her fingers lazily through the soapy swirls of the now-lukewarm water. She could have stayed that way for hours, just basking in the glow of cleanliness and warmth. But her stomach was rumbling, and the carefully fluffed pillows of the canopied bed beckoned to her. So, somewhat reluctantly, she toweled herself off and gratefully slipped into the gloriously soft robe that had been left for her. It had been quite a to-do when she'd found the room only stocked with dresses and gowns—Junia's work, no doubt. But after a quick argument with the assisting steward, her own clothes were hurried away to be washed and readied for her to reclaim after her well-deserved nap.

Keira was just about to settle down for said indulgence when a quick knock echoed on the hard wooden door. With a deep sigh of annoyance, Keira pulled her robe tighter around her and poked her head out into the hallway. A nervous-looking page met her gaze with a frightened look of his own as he quickly bowed, holding out one of the two wax-sealed parchments in his hands as he did so.

"Letters for Keira Altman and Danny O'Leary, ma'am."

Keira reached out and took her letter, watching as the page went next to Danny's room, but quickly closed her door before his could open. With a deft slice of her knife, she cracked the wax seal and unfolded the letter.

Keira and Danny,

I pray this letter finds you well in Crūd Éalas and you were successful in your mission to retrieve the prince. I send you welcome news from Port Galaén, where I came to seek the help of our fellow pneumonancers. Thanks to the skilled work of Legion healers, your mentor and our dear friend, Elliott, has mercifully returned to us. Praise be to Pneumos.

I now ask that the two of you join us with all haste. These are dangerous times, and as I'm sure you are both aware, chaos is looming. The Legion will decide its course of action over the next few days, and given the events of recent weeks, your input would be highly valued.

Pneumos guide you and bring you safely home.

Yours Truly,
Chinazor Onodugo

Keira's breath caught as she read and reread Nazor's letter. Could it really be true? Elliott was alive and returned to himself? Keira's vision blurred even as a broad grin spread across her face. Clearing her throat, she roughly swiped at her eyes, but her ecstatic thoughts were quickly replaced by ones of self-reproach.

What are you doing here? A voice inside asked. *You really think Landry needs you? He doesn't even want your advice. He has a host of advisors and an entire army at his disposal. If he wanted your help, he'd ask for it.*

Keira imagined herself rejoining the Legion, officially assuming the title of Legionnaire. They'd all be there to celebrate—Nazor, Elliott, and, most importantly, Danny. She'd have secured a place, earned the respect of the entire Legion. And Elliott . . . Pneumos, but she missed him. He knew her so well, always seemed to see the hurt she couldn't quite put into words. The thought of seeing him again and finally being able to talk through the swirling fog of thoughts that littered the inside of her head . . . well, that would be worth anything. Wouldn't it?

But what about Junia? the voice reminded her. *You don't trust her. Could you really just leave Landry to whatever she's planning?*

I tried to warn him, she argued. *He wouldn't listen.*

She was going in circles now and felt like banging her head against a wall to knock some thoughts loose. Instead, Keira rubbed her eyes. She glanced at the bed with yearning, but knew there was no way she'd be able to sleep now. She needed to talk to someone, and much as she didn't want to, she knew it had to be Danny.

"WHAT EXACTLY ARE YOU SAYING?" Danny asked, brow furrowed and arms crossed in front of his chest.

Keira swallowed the lump that had formed in her throat the moment she'd barged her way into Danny's rooms. "I'm saying that I think we should write to Nazor. We can tell her everything that's happened, so she can share it with the Legion, but it would also let us explain why we need more time."

"More time? Keira, you can't be serious! We did what we were asked. Landry is here, he's safe, and he's got an entire army at his beck and call. There is nothing more we can do."

Keira gave him a pleading look. "Danny, I *know* his sister is planning something, but he won't listen to me. If we leave before I find proof, then he'll be going in blind to face who knows what!"

"That is not our problem." Danny glared at her as he punctuated each syllable of his words. "Or at least, it shouldn't be. And rejoining the Legion is the best thing we can do for him now."

Keira stared at him, disbelieving. "What's going on with you, Danny? This isn't you."

"Really? And how would you know? Maybe I'm just tired of always having your back and you never giving a shit about me."

Keira winced. His words stung, not the least because she did care, more deeply than he could know.

"That's not true." She whispered, but his expression didn't soften.

"I'm sorry that I dragged you into this mess, Danny," Keira said quietly. "I know that this isn't what you signed up for. But now that we're here, I can't just quit. If we were to leave and something happened, I'd never forgive myself."

She squeezed her eyes shut and massaged her temples with one hand. She was stressed and exhausted and desperately in need of the now lukewarm beef stew sitting by her bed, but there was no way in hell she was going to cry in the middle of her argument.

She opened her eyes to find him staring at her, surprise and hurt evident on his face.

"You really care about him, don't you?"

Not this again. Keira rolled her eyes.

"I told you, I think of him like a brother. But yes—a brother I promised to protect. Why can't you let me do that?"

He'd taken a step toward her while she'd been speaking. She'd tried not to notice, tried to ignore the tingle that raced up her fingers and down her back. She pressed on, ignoring the warmth of his fingers on her wrist.

"Danny, you're my best friend. I care about what happens to Landry, but that doesn't mean—" She paused, realizing he was mere inches away from her. Keira closed her eyes, breathing in the woody scent of him, feeling the flutter of his breath on her face.

"Is that all we are?" Danny whispered. "Friends?"

She shivered as one of his fingers traced a path up the back of her arm. The want of him was palpable, a deep ache in the pit of her stomach that made her breath catch and her legs quiver. She wanted his arms around her, pressing her against him. But still that old fear held her back, that panicky feeling of being lost, out of control, threatened to overwhelm her. Then she opened her eyes and met his pale olive green ones and everything else seemed to fade away. She was here; she was safe; she was . . . wanted.

So she leaned into him, and his lips skimmed hers lightly, kissing her gently, sweetly. Keira's head swam, and her lips followed his, seeking, yearning, folding herself into his warmth and pressing herself fully against him. He drew back, smiling, and then his lips found hers again—firmer, more insistent this time, filled with a desire to match her own. Every inch of her wanted him, relished the feel of him. His fingers trailed the backs of her arms, settling firmly on her hips as he pulled her against him. She went more than willingly, ears buzzing as she wrapped her arms around his neck, letting her fingers lace through his sandy blonde hair. This was perfect. This was magical.

Until the voice stopped her.

You can't trust him, it said. *He'll hurt you, he'll abandon you, he'll leave you less than you are*. It was the same voice she always heard, the one that always seemed to echo her deepest fears. *And you'll hurt him too. Do you really want to do this? Don't you care about him?*

It was her mother's voice.

Present in death in a way she had never been in life, Tammy's voice was with Keira always. She reminded her every day of her failings, of the broken life that awaited her if she repeated Tammy's mistakes. The voice insisted that Keira could only rely on herself, that to depend on anyone else would be to ask for pain and suffering and brokenness. Her mother's voice had followed Keira to an unfamiliar world, a different time, and yet somehow, that distance only strengthened its pull.

Keira froze, stiffening in Danny's embrace as her own arms dropped to her sides. She didn't pull back, only stood there, but it was enough. Sensing her discomfort, Danny pulled away, holding her at arm's length and searching her face, his breathing heavy.

"What is it?"

She shook her head, fighting the tears she knew were inevitable.

"I can't do this, Danny. I thought I wanted this. I thought I wanted —" She couldn't look at him, couldn't meet those beautiful olive-green eyes as she lied. "But I don't."

"Wh—what are you talking about?" His voice was tight and Keira felt his pain in her own body, a wrenching of her stomach that made her want to vomit.

"I can't do this to you, Danny. I just—"

"Do what?" He demanded, eyes searching hers. "I promise you, I want this as much as you do, probably more." His lips tugged into a small half-smile and Keira felt something crack in her chest.

"Because I'll only hurt you!" She cried, the emotion bursting forth in a tidal wave. "I can't stay here, Danny, don't you see that? And when I leave," her voice caught as she wrestled down her own despair.

"When I leave, you shouldn't wait for me. It wouldn't be fair and I don't even know for sure that I can come back, so—"

"Leave? Leave where? Keira, what are you—"

"I told you, Danny," Keira moaned, misery coating every syllable as she stared into Danny's face, his brow furrowed in confusion and disbelief. "I told you when I first got here, when I first agreed to stay, that some day, once I completed the rites, I'd make the Legion send me home."

Danny stared at her, mouth agape and utterly without words.

"Keira, that was *years* ago. I thought you'd . . . I thought *we'd* moved past that."

Keira could only shake her head miserably. "She needs me, Danny."

"*I* need you," he cried, gripping her shoulders again and shaking her gently. "Don't you see that?" His eyes burned as they searched her face, but she could barely see him through the blur of tears that now fell freely.

"But that's not enough, is it?" He whispered, pulling away. He turned as if to leave.

"Danny, wait—"

He spun back around, leveling her with a glare. "She was terrible to you, Keira. You know that, right? She could barely take care of herself, let alone you."

Keira gaped at him, surprise warring with hurt and quickly giving way to anger. "You don't know what you're talking about, Danny."

"Oh, I don't, do I?"

"No you don't."

"I'm your grounder, Keira. How many times have I seen glimpses of your life before Loren? Growing up, you basically raised yourself. After everything she put you through, you don't owe her anything."

Keira winced, closing her eyes as she shook her head.

"Oh yes, I do."

"Please explain," Danny demanded. "How are you in any way responsible for the mess your mother's life turned out to be?"

"Because it was my fault!" She cried. Danny's eyes widened as she continued. "Every asshole that saw her as an easy mark, every abuser that knew she couldn't fight back. I couldn't protect her then. But I sure as hell won't abandon her now, not when there's a chance, *any* chance, that I can make it back."

Danny only stared back at her and she knew he couldn't understand—couldn't relate to that feeling of helplessness that comes from watching your loved ones suffer. That desperate desire to do something, anything, to make it right.

"Keira," Danny said, his suddenly softened tone drawing her attention back to him. "You know I have the dreams, right? About you, about your life before all this."

Keira nodded slowly—no idea where he was going with this.

"Well, I've seen the crash, the one that brought you here, the one where you died." He swallowed thickly and furrowed his brows as he stared at her. "And—and the car went off a cliff, Keira. There's no way anyone survived that fall. Even if you made it back to your world somehow, there'd be no one left."

The buzzing in Keira's ears grew louder until it muffled all other sounds, ricocheting off the insides of her brain until she wanted to clamp her hands over her ears and scream.

"—would have told you sooner. I didn't think you'd—I'd understand if you wanted—"

"Stop!" Keira cried, noting with relief as the buzzing receded. "We don't know anything for sure," she said more quietly, watching as Danny's expression hardened once more.

She shook her head, willing the free flowing tears to stop. Because this changed nothing. After all, this entire campaign wasn't just about Landry or the Legion or even her mom. If fighting chaos meant helping the broken people they'd met along their journey, then she couldn't say no. After all the times she'd pleaded silently for help from strangers that went wholly unanswered, she'd be damned if she abandoned these people when they needed help the most.

"I'm staying in the capital, Danny. I'm sorry."

She watched him as he backed away from her, jaw tight and eyes hooded. He placed a hand against a post of the bed, leaning heavily against it. She wanted him to yell, to scream or curse, or do something —*anything*. Just not this.

"Then I think you should leave," he said finally, refusing to look at her.

She stared at him for a moment before nodding stiffly. Then she practically fled the room, eyes still blurring with tears as the door shut with a snap behind her. She sagged against it, yielding to the sobs that ripped from her chest as she buried her face in her hands. She clutched at her mother's locket, rubbing a trembling finger against its cool metal as tears flowed down her cheeks.

Now you've done it, her mother's voice derided. *You've gone and ruined everything. I hope you're happy with yourself.*

Keira felt her knees buckle as she slid to the floor, wishing for all the world that she could sink right through it, even as it remained pitifully solid.

CHAPTER
TWENTY-SEVEN

Lady Junia had set to pacing. She could feel her anxiety lurking in the corner, threatening to overwhelm her if she let it. Against all odds, her damn brother had made it to the capital. And not only that, but he had recruited actual pneumonancers to join him. Junia wrinkled her nose at the thought of the two of them. The female in particular would prove difficult, she suspected.

She'd seen it first in the great hall meeting—the flash of suspicion in the girl's eyes, the dislike clear in the angle of her head. Junia had made a career out of reading people, all while keeping her own face utterly blank. Yet somehow, this girl had seen through her at their very first meeting. How was that even possible? Most people were easily fooled by Junia's overt sisterly kindness, or at least intimidated by the cloak of regality she wrapped around herself. Was the girl's pneumonancy really that strong? Was she able to read thoughts?

Junia shook her head, ordering herself to stop being ridiculous. If the girl could read thoughts, then Landry would surely know of Junia's plans by now, and he was certainly *not* skilled at hiding his feelings. *Perhaps she just sees me as a personal threat*, Junia mused. She had noted the deference with which Landry had sought the girl's opinion during their meeting that first evening. He certainly held her in high esteem, so perhaps she was merely afraid to lose her influence over him.

All the more reason for Junia to act quickly. If he truly respected the girl's opinion, then it wouldn't be long before she turned him against Junia herself.

Junia reached for a bell that lay on her desk and rang it sharply as she bent to finish the letters she'd started. The door opened not long after, and the rat Oswald entered, looking unscrupulous as ever. She quickly sealed the first letter with wax and handed it over.

"One letter to Ulgáris," she said, then bent to finish sealing the second.

"Summoning the Council to Crîd Eálas, my lady?" Oswald asked, his voice high-pitched and nasally. She shot him an annoyed look, but nodded curtly, handing him the other letter.

"This one to Port Galaén." She moved back behind her desk and rearranged her skirts, glancing at the man expectantly.

"What's in Port Galaén, my lady?"

Her jaw tightened, mouth fixed in a firm line.

"A threat, Oswald, and one I plan to see neutralized."

His eyes turned sly, and he bowed low before turning on his heel. Junia continued staring into the fire, thinking about what needed to be done and what she knew would follow.

As was so often the case, the days Keira thought she'd need quickly turned into weeks. She'd been trying in vain to find evidence of Junia's plotting, all while the city around her slowly descended into chaos. Protests over a hike in bread prices the day before had quickly turned violent. This latest tax increase was no doubt meant to pay down the crown's crushing debt, one of the lovely factoids Keira had learned since arriving in the capital. Yet despite Keira's advice that he try to find a middle ground with the protestors, Landry had overruled her. He'd sided instead with his sister and had agreed to place the entire city under martial law. Curfews had been implemented, and the violence had gradually settled, leading Junia and Landry to claim victory over the situation. But only a fool would fail to see the resentment simmering under the surface. And Keira was starting to wonder if that's exactly what Landry was: a fool.

Keira yawned, placing a bookmark on the same page she'd been reading for the past half hour, and stood to leave the Vindolum's grand library. She and Landry had many a debate that had quickly devolved into arguments and even flat-out yelling at one point. Keira tried to appeal to his better instincts, reminding him of all the suffering he'd seen on their journey to the capital. But then there was Junia, with her sweet crooning and tidbits of advice flowing like honey in one ear and burrowing knee-deep in his dazed brain. No matter what Keira said, she couldn't get Landry to see that his sister was manipulating him.

Keira pinched the bridge of her nose between thumb and forefinger. None of this would be resolved tonight, she decided, resigning herself to yet another night of restless sleep.

As she made her way upstairs, Keira passed Gwen Walsh, a scullery maid who'd taken a liking to her. She offered Gwen a wave that the young girl didn't return. Instead, she hurried on down to the kitchens, carrying an overflowing basket of what looked like laundry. Keira's eyes followed her, a slight frown on her face, before she continued up the stairs. In the few weeks she'd been here, Keira had made a habit of sneaking down to the kitchens at night when she couldn't sleep. It was Gwen's job to ensure that the fire stayed lit at all hours, and she had always welcomed Keira's visits with a snack and warm drink. The two of them had gotten to chatting about Gwen's life growing up in the capital with her family—upland migrants who'd come to the city for work, and who lived with other uplanders on the south end near the fish market. Keira had been grateful for the company, especially since Danny had managed to avoid being alone with her since the night of their arrival. Not that she blamed him.

Keira tried to squash the rising swirl of hurt and anger she felt at the thought of Danny, who had, for some unknown reason, stayed in the capital. He'd stuck around, even as he doggedly avoided her. She was grateful for this, even as his absence made her ache with longing. It was better this way, easier. She'd written to Nazor to explain everything that had happened—the assassination attempts, the revolts, Landry's conniving sister—but had received no response. So yeah, Nazor probably hated her, too.

How did everything end up so sideways?

She'd just resigned herself to never knowing the answer when she heard quiet voices emanating from a dimly lit hallway. Keira couldn't say why she stopped—maybe it was the urgent tone or the hushed nature, or maybe her hackles were just permanently up by this point. Regardless, instead of continuing on to her bedchamber, Keira crept down the hall toward a door at the far end. She could see a sliver of light peeking through beneath it. Pressing her ear to the door, she could just make out the voices coming from within.

"I understand he's just a child," an angry male voice said, "but he's still the rightful future Regio. Or do you mean to undermine our traditions here as well?"

A crooning female voice murmured something in reply that Keira couldn't quite make out.

"We're already facing a total revolt from the upland peasantry—"

He was interrupted by the female voice again, and Keira strained to hear her words, but couldn't quite make out their quiet murmur.

"Well, if that were, in fact, the case, we would need certain... *assurances.*"

Keira heard the scrape of a chair leg against the hard flagstone as someone stood up and began walking toward the door. Keira panicked, on the verge of yanking her ear away and making a run for it, when she heard the woman speaking more clearly.

"I am sure, Benadur Mualath, that we can come to some agreement."

Keira froze, breath catching in her throat. It was Junia. What was she up to?

But the footsteps continued to advance, and Keira wrenched herself away from the door, just keeping herself from breaking into a run as she strode back down the hall as quickly as she dared.

She had to find Landry.

CHAPTER

TWENTY-EIGHT

Keira's mind raced as she half-walked, half-jogged toward Landry's private chambers. She wasn't sure if what she'd overhead was enough to convince him—Junia hadn't exactly confessed to orchestrating their nightmare journey to the capital. Yet scheming with Mualath, who they knew *had* tried to kill them, was more coincidence than Keira was prepared to accept.

Landry just had to see reason on this. His sister was trying to convince the Council to make her Regio, so by necessity, all of her advice must have been meant to undermine him. Keira gnawed savagely on her lip. It was all a little too circumstantial for her liking, but she didn't know what choice she had other than to bring it to him. She desperately wished she could talk to Danny. He would have known what to do. Not for the first time that day, Keira cursed her own poor judgment, and the way she'd allowed herself to be pulled into a situation she'd *known* would threaten her relationship with her best friend. And for what? The chance to be hurt even more?

Keira wanted to wring her own neck. But seeing as that wasn't possible, she would settle for Junia's.

Two swift knocks on Landry's door found her being ushered into his private study by a waiting guard. She'd been playing and replaying in her head exactly how she'd tell him the news, but she stopped short when she saw him, head cradled in hands as he sat hunched over his desk.

232

"Landry?" she asked hesitantly, wondering if she should knock a second time before entering. He looked up to meet her gaze, eyes bloodshot and shadowed.

"How many this time?" he asked, voice scratchy and gruff.

"Sorry?"

"How many dead?" he asked, voice filled with a resignation she didn't think helpful given the situation. "From the protests."

"Oh," she said. "I'm not sure. The city hospital hasn't given me updated numbers yet."

Landry nodded, turning to a goblet of amber liquid she'd only just noticed. Keira shifted her weight, uncertain now how to proceed.

"What brings you here, then?"

Keira took a deep breath. *Here goes nothing.* "It's your sister, Junia."

Landry groaned and rubbed his eyes with one hand, the other still clutching the crystal glass. "Look, Keira, I really don't have time for this."

"Landry, listen—"

"You've been at each other's throats for weeks!" he exclaimed, standing abruptly and turning toward the fire. "Do you not think I have enough to deal with without my advisors bickering amongst themselves? I mean, really—"

"Mualath is *here*," Keira interjected. He didn't turn back to look at her, but he didn't say anything, either. She took this as an encouraging sign and barreled on. "At the invitation of your sister, it sounds like. I heard them talking in the East Wing. Landry, she—"

Keira paused, searching for the right words. Landry turned to fix her with one sharp eye.

"What exactly did they say?"

Keira repeated the conversation as accurately as possible, but tried to emphasize the parts she deemed most damning. In the end, Landry merely shook his head.

"This proves nothing."

"But she—"

"Yes, it is troubling that Junia invited the man who tried to have me killed to the Vindolum. I will have to speak to her about it. But the fact is, he remains a Benadur, one of the Council, and someone we can't afford to alienate entirely, not with everything else that's going on."

Keira gaped at him. "He killed Sara and the rest of the cohort."

"We don't know that for sure. It could have been one of the others."

Landry drained the rest of his drink and immediately poured himself another. Keira watched him skeptically, shaking her head as she fought down the fury that bubbled inside her.

"She wants to be Regio, Landry. She said as much."

"She did not. You just told me what she said, and all it proves is that she's made some kind of agreement with him—which could very well be advantageous to us."

Keira felt her cheeks flush red with anger as she glared at him. "Open your eyes, Landry. Before she shuts them for you permanently."

Landry slammed a fist against the desk, making her jump. He glared at her, and she stared back at him in shock.

"I will *not* condemn my own sister without first hearing her side of the story, Keira. I will be Regio, and I refuse to be manipulated, even by you."

Keira gaped at him, aghast. Was this what he would be like as Regio? Ruled by pride and lured by drink into making foolish decisions?

Danny had been right. She never should have stayed in this viper's nest. She was about to turn on her heel, leaving without a word, when a sound from behind drew her attention.

Marching briskly with an air of self-importance, Imperator Servius, commander of the Southern Imperium, strode into the room to stand at attention before Landry. Keira quickly moved to the side of the desk as Landry took his seat behind it, nodding at the commander.

With a brisk thump of forearm to chest, the man gave his briefing. "Your highness, masses of upland peasantry have been seen congregating on both the eastern and western roads. They are mere hours from the city and appear to be armed."

Landry's face was gaunt, shock etched in every line. Keira felt a lot of things—fear, frustration, and exhaustion, to name a few—but surprise was most definitely not one of them. It had only been a matter of time.

"Alert the city garrison," Landry announced, jaw clenched and fingers tapping wildly on his desk, "and shut the gates. No one comes in or goes out of the city without my direct order."

Servius gave Landry a grim look before shaking his head. "Your highness, I'm afraid that riots have broken out in the city again. Some groups seem to be targeting the gates specifically via sabotage. It—" Servius paused, glancing at Keira as if for corroboration. "Well, it appears to be a coordinated attack, sir."

Landry sat frozen and unmoving for several minutes. Finally, setting her mouth in a thin line, Keira turned to him. They were nowhere near an agreement about Junia, but that would simply have to wait. He needed her now, and that was all that mattered.

"I may know someone who can help."

CHAPTER
TWENTY-NINE

Gwen Walsh whimpered quietly in the middle of the room, half a dozen pairs of eyes fixed on her tiny form. Keira kneeled by her side, reaching for the girl's trembling hands.

"Gwen," Keira murmured, "it's all right. No one here wants to hurt you."

"Speak for yourself," Servius growled. "If I find out the little mouse is involved in all this somehow—"

"Imperator," Keira interjected, glaring at him over Gwen's shaking shoulders, "that is *enough*."

Gwen turned swollen eyes toward her. "I-I don't know, ma'am, I swear it. I-I'm loyal to the Regio, present and future." Her eyes pleaded with Keira for understanding. "P-please don't hurt my family."

Keira squeezed both the girl's hands in her own, trying her best to reassure her.

"I know that, Gwen," she said. "Of course I do. It's just that we have to find out who's behind this. I know your family lives in the South End—have they heard anything? Seen anyone trying to rile the people up?"

Gwen's lip trembled. "P-please, ma'am, I couldn't say—"

"Gwen." Keira allowed a note of firmness to enter her voice, steeling herself against the terrified look she knew would result. "The city is in open revolt, and we know they've been organized. If we can't find this person and convince them to negotiate, then..." Keira shook her head. "More people will die. *Good* people—like your family, Gwen."

A sob ripped through the girl, and she yanked her hands away to cover her face as her shoulders heaved. Keira felt like a monster. She wanted nothing more than to wrap her arms around the other girl and tell her that everything would be all right, but she knew she couldn't do that.

After a few agonizing moments, a murmur came from behind her hands. Keira leaned closer to hear her whisper.

"There's a tavern in the South End. The Miller's Plow." Her eyes peeked through her fingers at Keira. "I've never been, but I know that's where the rowdy folk go at night."

Keira smiled gratefully. "Thank you, Gwen. Now, do you know who's stirring up trouble there?"

The girl didn't return the smile, looking instead like she wished she could sink through the floor. She closed her eyes.

"His name's Neval. He's not from these parts. An uplander he is, but he says—" Here Gwen glanced nervously at Landry's still face. "H-he says the Marians got no right to our money, th-that they don't care about us. But I know that's not true!" Gwen sputtered, glancing around fearfully at the others, as if one of them might slit her throat at any moment. "The Regio's been good to me, Pneumos save him, and I got no complaints."

"So much for the girl never having been there," an icy voice said sharply from the far end of the room.

Keira's head jerked up to meet Junia's level expression and felt her jaw tighten. She chose to pointedly ignore her. *There'll be time enough to deal with you*, she thought acerbically. She turned instead back to Gwen, her own stomach having plummeted at the mention of Neval's name.

"Is it . . . Neval Brennan?" Keira asked cautiously, seeing Landry stiffen from the corner of her eye. Gwen nodded. Keira heard a hiss emanate from the far corner and turned to see Junia's sharp gaze fixed on her brother.

"Not that terrorist again," Junia complained. "You know he's the one responsible for the Karthaíla floods, don't you? Just a few years ago? Responsible for the deaths of an entire Centurium."

Landry nodded, arms folded firmly across his chest. "A crime for which he had ample motivation, as I understand it," he replied tightly.

"A convict!" Junia exclaimed. "Out of prison mere months ago, and already fomenting chaos and insurrection." She shook her head in disgust. "You really must do something about him, brother."

Before Landry could reply, Keira stood up stiffly, giving the girl's shoulder one final quick squeeze as she interrupted the bickering siblings.

"Thank you, Gwen. You've been very helpful to us. There's just one more thing, and then you're free to go." Keira paused, bracing herself for Gwen's reaction. "I need you to take me there—to the tavern."

The girl winced, clearly wishing that she could be anywhere but there, but finally nodded.

Keira motioned to a guard who stood at the far end of the room. "Please take Mistress Walsh to the stable and ready horses for us. We need to move quickly." The man nodded, striding forward to escort Gwen toward the door. Just as they were leaving, Gwen looked over her shoulder, giving Keira an openly reproachful look.

It was Keira's turn to wince. *So much for having a new friend here,* she thought.

Keira turned back to find Landry studying a piece of parchment, Servius peering over one shoulder. She opened her mouth to say something, but Landry interjected.

"A Bellatori cohort will follow you at a distance. When you've located the tavern, you'll signal to them, and they'll quickly storm the place."

Keira stared at him in disbelief and was about to protest when Junia's icy, smooth voice crooned in approbation.

"Excellent idea, brother. Cut off the head of the insurrection at its source. The rest will surely succumb."

Keira glared at her before turning back to Landry in exasperation. "Are you crazy?"

Her words shocked everyone out of their flurry of activity, and they all stopped to stare at her in horror. Landry blinked at her slowly, and Junia's eyes lit with triumph.

"Excuse me?" His voice had a dangerous edge that Keira knew she'd do well to defuse.

"I apologize for my bluntness, your highness, but there's no way killing one man will convince an entire mob to just settle down," Keira reasoned. "They're not an army—they're a group of angry people who believe they have nothing left to lose. Why else would they risk certain death by attacking a well-armed Bellatori force? *You* have to be the one to convince them otherwise."

Junia's face tightened in fury, her mouth opening to object, but Landry waved her off, giving Keira a considering, albeit still hostile, look.

"And how, might I ask, do you suggest I do that?" he asked.

Keira took a deep breath. "By negotiating with them."

Junia actually laughed aloud, causing Keira's ears to burn with embarrassment, much to her own frustration.

"Why not?" Keira shot back.

"Why *not*?" Junia repeated, smirking. "Because my brother is the future Regio of the great nation of Loren and heir to the Marian Empire. He does not bow to common street thugs."

"The Marian Empire is dead, and you and your family will be dead alongside it if you don't change with the times." Keira turned away from Junia's gaping face and addressed Landry directly. "You want to be a great ruler, Landry? This is how you do it."

Landry rolled his fingertips against the desk in a crisp staccato.

"I'll look weak," he said, looking up at her from beneath a furrowed brow.

Keira shook her head. "No, you won't," she insisted. "You've seen what they've gone through, Landry—what they're still going through. Show them you care. Show them that there's a way out of this that doesn't end in bloodshed and yet more suffering."

Keira took a few hesitant steps toward him, eyes pleading as she murmured, "Be better than your father, Landry."

Landry met her eyes, and she could tell he was weighing her words, even as the air hissed through Junia's teeth at Keira's insolence. Finally, Landry nodded, leveling a firm gaze at her.

"We should try."

"And what if you fail?"

The question was Junia's, but Keira directed her answer to Landry. "Then you'll do what must be done, knowing that you explored every option available to you." She held his gaze for a moment, then continued with as much conviction as she could muster. "But if we succeed, Landry, then not only will we have saved hundreds of lives from the bloodshed that's coming, but we will be one step closer to securing your reign and a peaceful transition of power after your father passes."

Landry returned her gaze, and she thought she saw the flicker of something that just might have been hope. Not so easily dissuaded, Junia also turned to her brother, tone shrewd and demanding.

"There must be a deadline. We cannot allow these *negotiations*—" Junia's mouth twisted in contempt at the word. "—to proceed indefinitely, allowing our enemies to further rally against us."

Landry rubbed his eyes wearily, then nodded. Meeting Keira's gaze, he said, "You have until dawn. Make no assurances, but find out what Neval wants and see if he'd even be willing to meet."

Keira sighed with relief. "Thank you, your highness. I won't let you down."

He indicated that she was excused, and she turned on her heel to exit.

"But Keira?"

She paused, half-turning to face him.

"Take Danny with you."

He must have seen her grimace, because he added, "These people are dangerous, and while I don't doubt your abilities, even you could use some backup once in a while."

CHAPTER

THIRTY

Keira's fist pounded roughly on Danny's door until he jerked it open, hair askew and eyes thick with sleep. They widened at the sight of her, instantly awake.

"Keira, wha—"

"Listen, I get that you hate me, and frankly, I wouldn't blame you if you did. But I need your help."

Quickly, Keira told him everything that had happened in the last few hours, from Junia's plotting to the downlander riots and the news that Neval Brennan had returned to Crîd Eálas. Danny listened to it all, gesturing for her to follow him into his room as he pulled on his boots and cloak.

"Landry is giving us time to negotiate with Neval, but we only have until dawn before all hell breaks loose," Keira finished.

Danny nodded thoughtfully, considering everything she'd told him. A familiar sensation of comfort and safety flowed through Keira, and for the first time that night, she actually started to believe that everything really might be okay. After all, she had Danny.

"Look, Danny, about the other night—"

He put up a hand to stop her, shaking his head. "Keira, it's really not necessary."

There was a stiffness to his words that Keira hated—that she absolutely despised with every fiber of her being.

"I just want to explain. It's not that—"

241

"Keira, stop," he said firmly. "I appreciate it. I really do, but we don't have time. I promise, when all of this is over, we can sit down and talk through everything. All right?"

Keira studied him, searching his eyes for some hint of what he was thinking. But those eyes, usually so transparent and open to her, were veiled, and she saw nothing in them but her own pleading expression. Reluctantly, she nodded.

"We'd better get going, then," he said finally, and the two of them made for the stables.

WHILE THE ECHOES of screams and the glint of fire could be seen and heard almost everywhere else in the city, the South End was oddly silent. As Keira, Danny, and Gwen rode through the dark, shuttered streets, Keira's chest was tight and her breathing shallow. She waited for the inevitable spark that would set their world ablaze, but nothing came.

Gwen was true to her word and knew the South End intuitively, leading them through winding alleyways and empty side streets with ease. Despite this, Keira felt antsy, her skin prickling with tension as the hair rose on the nape of her neck. Something wasn't right and she knew it. She wanted to apologize to Gwen for scaring her, but try as she might to engage her in conversation, the usually lighthearted scullery maid adamantly refused to cooperate. She preferred instead to ride in silence before them. And Danny, well—she couldn't very well tell *him* what she desperately wanted to, not in the middle of the street with an angry ex-friend nearby. So Keira, too, rode grudgingly in silence, trying very hard not to think of the myriad of hostile strangers who could be watching them pass at that very moment.

They had come to the end of a dark alleyway when Gwen suddenly pulled up ahead of them, holding up a hand to halt their progress. Keira and Danny quickly reined in the horses, peering through the gloom ahead to see where the girl was pointing. Light spilled from cracks in the building's shuttered windows and the quiet night air was broken by the low rumble of voices and the occasional raucous laugh.

"The Millers' Plow," Gwen murmured, giving Keira a reproachful side-eye. "As promised."

Keira urged Cerise up next to the girl, smiling apologetically. "You have our thanks, Gwen. Now, go see to your family. We'll take it from here."

Gwen paused, seeming suddenly uncertain. Keira cocked her head at her.

"Are you all right, Gwen?"

The girl said nothing, but still looked somehow dissatisfied. Then she nodded curtly and spun her horse around to head back the way they'd come. Danny turned in his saddle to watch her go before giving Keira a grim look.

"That was odd," he commented mildly before turning back toward the tavern. "Shall we?"

Keira nodded and nudged Cerise to follow him as they rode slowly out of the alleyway into the small square before the tavern.

A sudden shout echoed off the buildings, and Keira felt something blunt strike her across the back. She cried out and felt herself dragged roughly from her saddle as Cerise reared up, eyes rolling. Keira struggled against the hands that tightened on her and gasped as someone twisted her arm back and up between her shoulder blades.

"Gag them, please," a voice instructed lazily, sounding for all the world like he was ordering off a restaurant menu.

Keira choked as a ball of fabric was shoved in her mouth and a strip of cloth tied in place over it. Her stomach heaved as her gag reflex activated, and she fought against the bile that rose to her throat. A few feet away, she heard shouts and the sound of a struggle. *Danny*, she thought desperately, struggling in vain to regain her footing even as rough hands forced her to her knees. A shock of pain raced through her body as her kneecaps crunched against the cobblestone. Her hands were wrenched about and tied behind her back, rendering her helpless.

Keira blinked the moisture from her eyes and saw a familiar face float dreamily in and out of focus above her. The wide-spaced brown eyes and Cheshire Cat grin were impossible to mistake. *Neval*, she thought, shooting him a glare that clearly articulated her own murderous intent.

"It's good to see you again, Keira," he said mildly, raising her chin to look him in the eye.

She whipped her face away, but a vise-like hand at the back of her neck forced her head forward and up to meet Neval's downward gaze. A few feet away, a furious Danny struggled against the three men holding him down. One of them cocked back a fist and sent it flying toward Danny's jaw, where it connected with a sickening crunch. Keira felt a wave of nausea roll over her at the sound.

Neval was wholly unperturbed by the violence before him—in fact, he seemed absolutely delighted at their sudden appearance. His smile widened further as he regarded the two of them.

"I'm glad you could both be a part of this." Then his face changed, twisting in disgust as he ordered, "Get them inside."

As Keira was roughly hauled to her feet, she craned her neck around, trying to get another glimpse of Danny. With horror, she spotted his slumped figure being dragged behind her as they were both hauled through the doors of The Miller's Plow.

THIRTY-ONE

Junia's pacing had picked up speed, her skirts swirling around her as she moved back and forth across the room. As she paced, she raised a hand to her forehead, attempting to smooth away the lines that had formed between her delicate brows over the past few hours.

Things were unraveling, and far more quickly than she could have expected. Junia leaned against the desk, eyes closed, as her fingertips tapped its surface in a crisp staccato. After a moment, her eyes snapped open again, mouth set in a grim line, and she rang the bell that sat perched on her desk.

From where she stood, she could see through the double-wide doors that led from the study into her father's chambers. The old Regio was barely visible amongst the heaps of pillows and blankets. His sallow skin betrayed the deep concavities that had carved themselves out from his temples and cheeks. His neck was arched back, and the high-pitched death rattle of his breathing through the secretions that gathered there could be heard even from where she stood.

Junia shivered, looking at the old man with a strange mix of fear, pity, and disgust. *He's not long for this world.* She shook her head to clear it, refocusing on the task at hand. Landry could not be allowed to make terms with the peasantry—he could *not* receive credit for stopping a mob without bloodshed. That would undoubtedly secure his ascension to the throne upon their father's death.

No. I will not let him ruin everything—not again.

A brisk knock came from the door, and she bid them enter, smoothing her skirts with a hand as she did so. Oswald bowed deeply, dripping with deference as usual.

"My lady, how can I be of service?"

Junia gave him a long, considering look. She was taking a risk, she knew, in trusting this man. But she had little choice.

"Notify Imperator Servius and the city guard that the Regio has died and that the assault has been moved up to midnight. The cannons will give the signal, and we will catch these rebels unawares."

Oswald stared at her, looking slightly taken aback. The rasping breath of her father still echoed through the room, but Junia didn't blink.

Finally, Oswald bowed his head. "Of course, my lady."

Junia handed him the written order, stamped with the Regio's purple wax seal, and watched as Oswald swiftly exited. She turned in her seat to stare at the shrunken figure of her father, his face flickering in the light of the dying fire. Closing her eyes, Junia drew in a shaking breath and exhaled through pursed lips, preparing herself for the task ahead.

You know what must be done, she thought.

Standing, she drifted into the king's chambers, a seat cushion gripped tightly in one hand. Gently, and ever so quietly, she closed the doors behind her.

Keira stared up into the unrelenting eyes of Neval and wondered, not for the first time, how everything she touched seemed to go so wrong. They only had until dawn to convince him to agree to negotiate with Landry and this sack of shit seemed far more interested in finishing his dinner. So there they sat, bound and gagged, watching as their captor slowly finished the final serving of mutton. Keira had already tried yelling through the gag to get his attention, but all that had earned her was a swift jab to the ribs from a man she'd nicknamed Bulging Eyes. She didn't care to repeat the experiment after that.

Only when Neval had sucked the last drop of savory stew from each of his fingertips did he turn his attention to his unwilling guests.

"Now, what could possibly bring the future Regio's own advisors to a lowly South End tavern such as this? And what's more, a birdie told me you two are high-level spirit binders to boot." Neval's eyes shifted teasingly between Keira and Danny, a slight grin tugging at the corners of his mouth. "Now, my dear old mother did tell me stories about spirit binders when I was nothin' more than a li'l one, but never did I think they might be real, or that I'd be meetin' one in person." He bowed low and mocking. "So, truly, the pleasure is all mine."

Keira gave an exaggerated roll of her eyes, and Neval chuckled. "Truly, you are a surprisin' one," he told her. "I'd have never thought the pretty wynnie I was chattin' up in a Rabone͑s tavern might be a true fighter, yet here you are."

"Now," he said, rubbing his hands together, "I know you've been wantin' to say somethin' since you got here, so here's how we're goin' to do this. My men will ungag you, so you can answer our questions, but if we get one whiff of spirit bindin', then we slit your friend here's throat."

As if for emphasis, a man to her right wrenched back Danny's head by the hair, eliciting a muffled yelp as he drew his knife and pressed it to Danny's bobbing Adam's apple.

"Sound good, then?"

Keira nodded quickly, making her eyes wide and disarming. Neval nodded to the man behind her, and Keira felt her gag being untied as the ball of fabric was pulled roughly from her mouth. She drew in a full, glorious breath, lungs expanding in grateful freedom at the lack of obstruction.

"Tell me, what did the good princeling Landrianus send you here for? Or do you deny bein' his messengers?" Neval lifted an eyebrow in unveiled skepticism.

"We don't deny it," Keira croaked, her voice sounding raspy even to her own ears. "He did send us. He wants to make terms—find common ground between the two of you."

Neval blinked at her, his surprise clear. Then he laughed, a raucous sound that the men surrounding them quickly matched.

"Does he now?" Neval asked, holding up a hand to silence the others. "And why, pray tell, does he think *I'm* the one he needs to make terms with?"

It was now Keira's turn to be surprised. "Aren't you the leader? Of the rebellion, I mean?"

Neval gave her a narrow-eyed look before shaking his head, a contemptuous smile tugging at his lips.

"Ye think the passion of an oppressed people can be harnessed by one man?" Neval scoffed. "You really are Landrianus's lackey."

Keira shook her head. "I only meant that I was told of the time you spent imprisoned for standing up for your ideals, and I thought—"

Neval's booming laugh interrupted her, and she felt her cheeks flush crimson.

"Ideals, eh? I can't imagine the future Regio Landrianus referring to them as *ideals*. Did he tell you what we did?"

Keira paused. "He did not. I merely assumed—"

"We destroyed the Karthaíla dam," Neval said quietly, "to stop the flooding of lands in and around Ceffí, and only because the good authorities in Crîd Eálas refused to get involved in what they considered Port Karthaíla's concern. Only problem was, the rerouted river ended up flooding fields downriver and ruining some rich downlander's crop." Neval gave her a smile with no humor in it. "Crîd Eálas did feel the need to involve themselves with *that*."

Neval searched her face for a reaction, and she tried to suppress the shock that rose to the surface, unbidden and wholly unwanted. He must have seen something, though, because Neval grinned in triumph. "Not the terrorist you expected, then?"

"Neval, I truly am sorry for what happened to you," she said earnestly. "But...well, I just can't figure out what you hope to gain from this."

Neval's jaw clenched, and his black eyes pierced hers like daggers. "I will see every curs'd downlander subjected to true Lorenan rule, or else exiled from our lands," he snapped. "They're nothin' more than invaders and oppressors."

"The invasion was over two hundred years ago, Neval!" Keira said, exasperated. "Downlander families have lived here for generations. You can't just expect them to *leave*." Neval opened his mouth to object, but she cut him off. "And do you *truly* think the Council of Benadur has the upland peasantry's best interests at heart? If you remove the Marians, the Council will merely pick up the pieces, and the people will be no better off in the long run."

"And what, might I ask, do you suggest?"

"Negotiate," Keira said immediately. "Argue for a say in your own government, councils or a congress."

Neval snorted. "Like the Council of Benadur, you mean? They've got power in name only. Everybody knows that."

"Then ask for more," Keira exclaimed, latching desperately onto something, *anything*, that he might agree to. "The details can be worked out later, but you have to agree to the negotiations first."

Neval looked truly suspicious now. "Why the rush?"

Keira took a shaky breath before continuing.

"You have until dawn before the city guard and the Bellatori garrison march on your positions throughout the city," Keira revealed. "It'll be a bloodbath, but it can be *prevented*."

Neval's jaw hardened, and he said icily, "You expect us to negotiate with a blade hangin' over our necks?"

"I know you don't want to, but neither do the Marians or the Benadur. Look around you! People are rioting, and there are barricades in the streets. What is that, if not a threat to the very heart of Loren?"

"We have a right to—"

"I understand your position, but make no mistake," Keira warned. "The Regio *will* respond to it, one way or another. Come to the negotiating table instead. Find common ground, and ask for a say in the government that rules you. You know it's in everyone's best interest."

Keira paused, watching as Neval spun on his heel and stood before the fireplace, bracing himself against the mantel with both hands. Most of the eyes in the room were fixed firmly on his back, waiting breathlessly for his decision. Keira glanced to the side to meet Danny's eyes. They were warm and encouraging, and she felt the invisible band that had tightened around her chest loosen slightly.

Then three cannons boomed in the distance.

THIRTY-TWO

Keira's face jerked toward the window. The world outside was still pitch black, with no signs of dawn creeping up on the horizon.

"No," she breathed. "It's too early."

From outside, the sounds of screams and thundering hoofbeats could be heard, and the reflections of torchlight bounced off the inner walls of the tavern. Neval's eyes were burning black coals as he advanced on Keira, and she felt her own panic rise.

"Liar," Neval snarled. "Is that why he sent you here? As a distraction, delayin' our response to his attack?"

"N-no," Keira stammered. "He said dawn. He *agreed* to wait until dawn."

"Then seems he's made fools of us both."

Neval spun around, barking orders at his men, rallying weapons, and delineating positions. The room was a flurry of chaos, and Keira glanced over to find Danny inching slowly towards a serrated bread knife that lay unnoticed atop a sideboard. She turned away, hoping she hadn't drawn attention to him, and found herself staring straight into the furrowed brow of a furious Neval.

"Spies or traitors—it doesn't much matter. Deal with 'em," he ordered, sweeping out of the room without a backward glance. "I don't much care how."

"No!" Keira shouted, seeing a man tackle Danny just as he'd been about to reach the knife. Danny head-butted him, cracking the back of his skull against the man's nose. Blood spewed everywhere as a pair of rough hands grabbed onto Keira. She let her knees collapse beneath her, and the man cursed as he found himself supporting all her weight.

Time seemed to slow as she reached inside to grab hold of her pneuma, squeezing it gently so it flowed from her hands. She let out a long, high whistle and felt the pneuma amalgamate to the molecular consistency of the ropes that bound her hands, buzzing slightly as the material morphed and changed, melting away from her and falling in a puddle to the floor.

Hands freed, Keira grabbed for the dagger she'd felt at Bulging Eyes's belt when he'd caught her and slashed backward with it. She jumped to her feet, spinning just out of his grasp as she did so. The man howled as he pressed a hand to the bloodstain on his chest.

Meanwhile, Danny had kicked his assailant away and rolled toward her. She ran to meet him, quickly cutting through his bonds so he could ungag himself. She spun around just in time to see Bulging Eyes bearing down on her, brandishing a meat cleaver he'd grabbed from a nearby table.

Keira danced backward as the swinging blade passed within an inch of her nose. His momentum swung him to the side, and she seized the opportunity, cutting a jagged slice through his shoulder with her own blade. She'd been aiming for his neck, but his rotation had blocked her angle, sparing him the finishing blow. Her cut was still deep, and blood flowed steadily from his arm as the man shrieked in frustration. She backed away, looking around desperately for more weapons—anything other than the puny dagger she clutched in one sweaty hand.

Nothing. There was absolutely nothing.

Bulging Eyes, lumbered toward her again, his face red with rage, though his movements had slowed slightly. Behind him, she could see Danny gesticulating wildly with a pig skewer as the other guard lunged at him with the serrated bread knife. Not daring to cast her pneuma and leave her body open to attack, Keira hurled dishes instead. Bulging Eyes grunted as he dodged a plate she sent speeding toward him, but hollered in agony when a ceramic pitcher nailed him straight in the face. He staggered against a table, staring in a pained stupor at the blood that poured from his face as he touched his nose gingerly with one hand.

Keira lunged.

With a single thrust upward, she stabbed through the man's ribs and into his kidney. He howled and slumped forward, giving her just enough time to grasp the shard of plate that had fallen to the table and rake it savagely across his neck. He was unconscious in ten seconds, dead in twenty.

As she stood staring at Bulging Eyes' lifeless face, she felt someone come up behind her. She spun around in time to nearly stab Danny, who jumped back in surprise.

"Easy there," he exclaimed, wincing as he touched a hand gingerly to his swollen jaw.

Keira grimaced in apology before blurting, "I'll kill him. I'll absolutely kill that sorry arseling."

"Neval, or Landry?"

Keira shot him a wry look. "Both."

Danny grinned at her, and the two of them quickly made for the door. The sounds from outside had turned ominous, the screams and shouts now mingling with the clang of swords and the squeals of terrified horses. They found their equipment stashed in the corner of the main hall and took a moment to arm themselves before running outside.

It was absolute bedlam. The mounted Bellators were cutting through the South Enders in droves, even while taking fire from the hastily erected barricade Keira had seen as she was dragged in. The city folk still out in the courtyard were making the horses bolt with flame and noise. She watched as they dragged one young Bellator from his horse, and he disappeared into the sea of people and weaponry. It was only when the mass shifted that Keira saw his beaten and bloodied head, his limbs twisted in unnatural angles as he lay on the cobblestones.

"Come on." The voice was Danny's. With a firm set to his mouth, he took her by the hand and dragged her bodily down the steps of the tavern and away from the rioting masses.

They almost made it, too.

Across the street, Keira saw a familiar blonde head bobbing as she ran with three small children in tow. Gwen, the girl who had probably betrayed them, was inadvertently shepherding those children straight into the path of the thundering cavalry riders, who barreled toward their unsuspecting victims at full speed.

"Gwen!" Keira shrieked, running toward them.

She wasn't fast enough.

Gwen had seen the danger just in time and was desperately screaming for the children to move back. But behind her, a little red-headed girl had kneeled to retrieve a dropped item.

It was Danny who reached her first. Scooping her up in one arm, he tried to dive out of the way.

Keira watched in what seemed like slow motion as the first horse struck him, sending the tiny girl flying out of his arms. His head crunched against the ground first, followed by his arm, twisting at an odd angle beneath him. Then the flailing hooves of the rearing second horse came crashing down on top of him.

Keira screamed.

CHAPTER

THIRTY-THREE

Please, no! Please, Pneumos, no!

Keira ran toward the broken figure lying at the edge of the cavalry charge, struck every few moments by a misplaced hoof. She could see the blood from here.

So much blood.

When she finally reached him, Keira grabbed fistfuls of his tunic on either side of his collar and, with every ounce of strength she had left, dragged him away from the pounding hooves. She surveyed his body, trying to assess the damage, but made the mistake of glancing at his face first.

Keira snapped her eyes shut, trying as she did to slow her own heartbeat. *You're no use to him if you panic,* she reminded herself. Taking a deep breath, she opened them once again.

His face was swollen, partly from the earlier blow to his jaw, but he also had a black eye, and she could see blood beginning to mat his hair. *First thing's first,* she reminded herself. He was breathing, at least. Keira could see the slow rise and fall of his chest, but she didn't like the gurgling sound that came from the back of his throat. She tried tipping his head back, and that helped slightly.

She felt for the pulses at his neck and wrist, just as Elliott had taught her. They were both there, though the one in his wrist was definitely faint. Then she began sweeping his body for injuries, starting with his head. Her hands came away bloody, and she felt her stomach flip-flop. Breath unsteady, she reached trembling hands back toward his head to probe the area around the wound. She let out a sigh of relief—the gash was bleeding freely, but the bones seemed to be intact. There was no proper way for her to assess any internal damage, though, not in the dark, and especially not while he was unconscious.

Instead, she quickly cut some makeshift bandages from the traveling cloak she was still wearing and tied one around his head to stem the flow of blood. She moved on to his limbs then, which, despite bruises and some fairly deep cuts, seemed thankfully intact.

It was then that she noticed that there was an asymmetry to his chest's rise and fall. When she lifted his tunic, she gasped at the blue and purple splotches that had bloomed across his skin. She watched in horror as, with every breath, part of his chest seemed to move discordantly, sucking in on the inhale and flailing out on the exhale. Swallowing the ball of panic that had risen to her gullet, Keira quickly wadded up the remains of her traveling cloak and tied it around his chest. She tried to cinch it tight enough that the chest wall was held together, but not so tight that he'd stop breathing. For a moment, she considered trying to heal him with pneumonancy, but immediately thought better of it. Knitting together arteries was one thing, but bones were another thing entirely, and she doubted she'd be much help to him if she broke her own bones to try and help.

Keira wiped the sweat from her brow before it could drip into her eyes. She looked around and saw that the fighting had moved away from this neighborhood, into other parts of the city. *This will have to do for now*, she decided, knowing that Danny needed more help than she could possibly provide.

Nearby, Gwen was clutching the little girl to her, smoothing her hair as the girl sobbed into her shoulder. "I need your help," Keira said, turning toward her. "We need to find a wagon and get him to the Royal Hospital." Gwen glanced down at her with wide eyes and shook her head fiercely.

"Look, I'm sorry, but I have to get 'em out of here. I can't just go off on some—"

"You *owe* us," Keira snarled.

Gwen's face darkened, and she opened her mouth to protest.

"Fine," Keira snapped, before Gwen could speak. "I'm sure you had an excellent reason for betraying us, but at the very least, you owe *him*. For saving her."

Gwen closed her eyes, letting out a deep sigh. "You're right. But there's only one person near here with a wagon."

Keira's eyes narrowed. "Who's that?"

"Neval Brennan."

THEY FOUND Neval behind one of the barricades, barking orders to his men even as he offered water to another man with a deep laceration just above his navel. Keira winced, knowing the man's chances of survival were low.

After seeing her safely there, Gwen immediately fled with the children in tow. Keira wished them luck before turning to the task at hand. Steeling herself, she strode forward purposefully, hand twitching toward the hilt of her sword, ready to grab it if Neval or his men made a wrong move.

Neval glanced up as she approached. Despite the confidence of his demeanor, Keira could see the deep lines of weariness carved into his face.

"Well, you seem surprisingly alive," he said mildly, not bothering to face her fully. "To what do I owe the pleasure?"

"The incompetence of your men, for one," Keira said sharply, then quickly mellowed, realizing it was better to keep him in a good mood. "And I need your help."

Neval's eyebrows rose slightly. "Well, I must say, I am a tad busy just now. So, if you'll excuse me—"

He turned away, but Keira interjected quickly.

"Look, there are wounded here. They need help, and I need a wagon to get them to it."

Neval paused, looking her fully in the face for the first time. "Out of the kindness of your heart, I presume," he said warily. Then, glancing over her shoulder, he asked, "Where's your friend?"

"He's hurt," Keira said bluntly, fighting back the terror she was keeping at bay by a hair's breadth.

"I see." He pulled a cloak up and over the face of the man with the gut wound, whose eyes were now staring blankly out into space. Neval sighed before giving her a hard look.

"Fine, come with me."

Keira didn't bother to hide the gratitude that spread across her face. She followed him around the corner of the tavern to find a mostly empty wagon, horses already hitched.

Neval shrugged at her questioning look. "Supplies from earlier. I hadn't a chance to unhook 'em before all hell broke loose."

Keira honestly didn't really care how the wagon had gotten there, only that it had. They quickly brought it around to the front, and Neval gestured for some of his men to help them load the casualties. Keira made a beeline for Danny, relief flooding her as she saw that his condition was unchanged. His breathing was still shallow, but he was alive, and that was enough for now. One of Neval's men helped her load him in the cart, and Keira turned to find two other men arguing over what to do with an injured Bellator.

"Don't want no Marian scum mixed in with our people," one of them growled.

Keira stomped toward them, fury rippling through her.

"That man," she snarled, "is a human being. A human being who was doing his duty as he believed it to be, as surely as you are doing yours. But frankly, at the moment, he's just an injured man asking for help. Are you really willing to let him die?"

The two of them looked like they were about to argue when she heard a stern voice behind her.

"Put him in the wagon."

Keira spun to find the grim-faced Neval at her shoulder.

"We don't execute the injured and unarmed," he explained. "We're not *them*."

Keira felt a reluctant twinge of respect for this man who'd tried to have her killed only an hour before. She nodded gratefully at him, and he returned the gesture. She was about to say something more when the sound of screams and hoofbeats interrupted their brief interlude.

Mouth fixed in a grim line, Neval gestured at the wagon. "You'd better be goin'. It seems we have more friends on the way. We'll try to hold them off, but you don't want to be here when they arrive. Take

Brosnan with you." He pointed out a flat-faced man with a giant bruise spreading across one cheekbone.

"Thank you," she said, briefly wondering if she'd ever see him again. He waved away her thanks and turned to head back to the barricade. "And good luck!" she called after him, purely on impulse.

At that, he shot her an impish grin. "I'm touched, but best save the luck for your laddy boy . . . both of them."

Keira rolled her eyes but smiled despite herself. She quickly clambered up into the wagon beside Brosnan as he clicked for the horses to get on their way. Keira cast one last look back toward Neval, but he was already gone, disappeared behind the barricade with the rest of his motley crew.

AFTER MUCH BUMPING and grinding along the city roads, carefully trying to avoid the hotspots of unrest by sound alone, the wagon and its occupants finally made their way to the Royal Hospital. Not far from the Vindolum, it was one of the oldest buildings in Crîd Eálas and bore the regal columns of an earlier age. Elliott had once called it the most beautiful building in Loren.

At that moment, Keira couldn't care less.

On hearing Keira's cry for help, a flock of Philosian nuns descended upon them, their bright red habits visible even in the moonlight. There was a flurry of activity as the wounded were unloaded from the wagon. Numb with the fatigue that was finally hitting her, Keira refused to leave Danny's side. When it was finally his turn, she murmured a few words about his injuries to the nun taking notes, but mostly focused on keeping one foot placed firmly in front of the other.

Realizing that she was of little use to their efforts, the nuns kindly found her a chair to perch on next to Danny's bed. She watched through a hazy unreality as the efficient nuns changed his bandages, applied strong-smelling poultices, and performed various other ministrations that Keira was far too exhausted to understand.

Instead, she looked only at Danny, her stomach tightening at the sight of his bruised, swollen, and heavily bandaged face. Even when they'd moved him, he'd never regained consciousness. If she lost him . . .

No, she thought. *That will not happen. It can't.*

Keira knew she could survive a lot. She had survived a lot. But not that. Never that.

She knew now, as surely as she'd ever known anything, that she could not survive in a world without Danny. She needed him, needed him like she needed air, and that thought petrified her. Because she knew, more so than the average person, how needing people inevitably led to losing them.

But that battle had been lost and she was done running from it—her own need. She was done running from him. For better or worse, she was in this, even if that only meant for the next few hours.

She must have drifted off in the night, because the next thing she knew, she was waking to find light streaming through the tall cathedral-like windows of the hospital ward.

"Keira?"

Her back ached from having slept slumped in the chair, head pillowed by her arms at the head of Danny's bed. Her mouth tasted like sand, and it took a moment to blink the sleep from her eyes enough to realize that someone was talking to her.

"Keira, what are you doing here?"

Her mind went first to Danny, but after reassuring herself that he was, in fact, still breathing—and still unconscious—she immediately steeled herself against the rising flood of rage. She turned then toward the all-too-familiar voice, meeting Landry's curious gaze with her own far less forgiving one.

"How dare you?"

THIRTY-FOUR

Landry blinked in surprise. "I'm sorry?"

Keira was done. She was tired and bruised, her heart was likely broken irreparably, and the last thing she wanted to deal with just then was a lying piece of shit.

"You swore, Landry!" she snarled. "You promised me you would wait until dawn. Neval had *agreed*, he was going to negotiate! We could have stopped this—"

"Keira please," Landry interrupted through clenched teeth, looking around nervously. "Not here."

Keira knew she sounded hysterical, shrieking in the middle of a hospital ward. She could feel the shocked and curious eyes on her.

She also couldn't care less.

"I will not. Look at Danny. *Look* at him, Landry! This is all your fault." Keira shook her head, lip curled. "I can't believe I trusted you."

Landry seemed to deflate before her very eyes, and she noticed for the first time the lines of weariness on his face that had seemed to multiply overnight.

"You're right," he said finally. "You couldn't trust my word, but neither could I."

This took her by surprise, and her brows furrowed as she looked at him questioningly. "You mean . . . you didn't order the attack on the rebel positions last night?"

Landry shook his head miserably, looking around at the hundreds of wounded that filled the hospital ward, their moans and sobs making up an inaudible murmur that filled the background.

"*I* did this, Keira. It's my fault. If I'd had better control, the confidence of the people—"

Keira's anger dissipated as quickly as it had flared. "Landry, stop," she said. "This isn't your fault. You were trying to prevent this very thing from happening by sending Danny and me to negotiate."

"But I failed," he said, voice cracking. "I failed, and people died. I can't possibly be fit to be Regio."

"That's not true, Landry! The people—" Keira paused, a thought suddenly occurring to her. "So, if you didn't order this, then that means . . ."

Landry nodded miserably at her unspoken question.

Keira gasped. "Landry—"

"I know," he said, eyes wide and begging forgiveness. "You tried to tell me, but I didn't listen, didn't want to think that—"

"Junia," Keira said. Not a question now, but still needing confirmation.

Landry bowed his head. "She's the only person with that kind of clout," he said miserably. "The only person the Bellatorio would listen to, the only one who could overrule me like that. Now that my father —" Landry paused, swallowing hard. "He's dead, Keira. He died in the middle of the night. He—"

Keira could see the sheen in Landry's eyes, heard the catch in his voice. She knew what that meant better than anyone and quickly took him by the elbow, steering him out to the nearby courtyard. Once they were away from prying eyes and ears, he let it all out.

"I've lost everything, Keira. First my father, and now my sister. The peasantry hates me, the Council of Benadur wants to kill me, and now even the Bellatorio has turned against me."

His shoulders slumped, and Keira felt he'd aged ten years from the young man, barely more than a teenager, that she'd met back on Mount Ánghen.

"I have no one left in my corner, Keira," he said hoarsely. "It's over."

"It can't be over," she protested, hating herself for the doubt that crept into her voice.

Landry smiled sadly at her before shaking his head. "You've been a wonderful friend to me, Keira—you and Danny both. And you've stuck by me far longer than anyone would expect of you. But it's over, and not even you can stop what's coming."

Keira opened her mouth to deny what he was saying, but knew in her heart that it would likely be a lie. She closed her mouth and watched as the last spark of hope left Landry's eyes.

"I've spoken with a friend down at the docks," he continued. "We sail at dawn tomorrow morning."

Keira stared at him, aghast. "You're leaving?"

Landry nodded sadly. "I have to. There's no way Junia can afford to keep me alive, not if she wants the Council to declare her Regio. I'm too big a threat to be allowed to live. My only chance is to make a run for it before she's able to have me killed. I was hoping—" He paused, looking almost bashful as he glanced at her. "Well, I was going to offer you and Danny passage to join me if you wanted."

Keira was touched, but too surprised to respond, and he hurriedly continued, "I know you have commitments here in Loren, so it wouldn't be forever. But I could take you wherever you needed to go, even north to Port Galaén, if that's where the Legion is based."

Recovering slightly from her shock, Keira glanced toward Danny's hospital ward.

"Danny—" she began, but Landry quickly interrupted her.

"I'll be bringing a healer with me—just in case, you see. And, well —" Landry looked around nervously. "He's not safe here, Keira. Some of the rioting has been quelled, but barricades still stand in much of the city. If my sister succeeds, there will only be more bloodshed."

Keira chewed on her lip, indecision tearing at her. She imagined them both reunited with Nazor and Elliott, safe and happy, away from all the chaos and bloodshed. But could she really just turn her back on everything they'd worked for over the last few months, abandoning the strides they'd made, small though they might be?

Keira glanced at the hospital ward where Danny lay, still very much not out of the woods, and shook her head. *Yes, I can*, she realized. She was done playing the hero. This was her failure as much as Landry's, and she knew it, even if he was too polite to say so. It was time to leave, to start over, and get back on track. The rest would just have to sort itself out.

She turned back to Landry. "You're right," Keira said. "He would be safest with the Legion. So if your men can get Danny to the ship, I'll go fetch our things from the Vindolum and meet you there."

Landry lit up with the first genuine smile she'd seen from him in weeks, his joy and relief evident. "Yes, I can arrange that," he assured Keira. "Just . . . be careful. Junia has her spies everywhere."

"I will. You too," Keira told him. Then a sudden thought occurred to her, and she asked, "Wait, where will you go?"

He smiled at her again, this time with a hint of sadness. "I think I'll journey to the Cross-Sea lands," he said. "Sara was always talking about how beautiful they are this time of year."

Keira swallowed hard at the memory. "I think she'd like that," she told him. "And you deserve some beauty in your life, Landry."

"We all do," was his only reply before turning and continuing inside.

CHAPTER

THIRTY-FIVE

Keira made it back to the Vindolum without further incident, somehow avoiding the worst areas of violence in the city. She'd planned to sneak in the side entrance by the kitchens and make her way up to the west wing and their rooms. This plan started out well enough, but fell by the wayside when she found the place crawling with Bellators and recently arrived Benadur for the Council meeting.

Don't they know there's a rebellion? Keira thought acerbically.

Because of this, Keira had to stick to the servants' quarters and the side stairs that wound their way up to the higher floors. Finally, she reached the fifth floor, and she made her way to the west wing.

Get in and get out, she reminded herself, mentally calculating exactly how much she could carry and still make good time to the dockyard.

Her thoughts were interrupted by the low murmurings of two maids as they came out of the room in front of her, arms burdened with dirty linens. Keira froze, sliding into the shadows that hugged the wall and holding her breath as they passed. She watched as the second one used her hip to bounce the door closed, listened for the latch that didn't quite click.

Then Keira realized where she was, and exactly which room the maids had just vacated.

Those are the Regio's quarters.

Indecision warred within her. She'd all but resolved herself to their current course of action. They would leave on a ship at first light and rejoin the Legion in Port Galaén. And then what? If her mother was really gone, as Danny had said, then she had no other home to return to. This might be it, *Loren* might be it. And right now her home was burning to the ground.

But what if . . . ?

She hadn't questioned it when Landry said his father had passed away in his sleep. The former Regio had been old and sick, and everyone knew he wasn't long for this world.

But the timing . . .

Well, the timing couldn't have been worse. What if someone had sped up the process? What if Junia . . . could Junia really have killed her own father?

Keira shook her head, doubting she'd find any evidence, even if Junia really had killed him. It's not like it would have taken much effort. But what about proof of her other crimes? Could there be letters or some other documentation of her apparent conspiracy with the Council of Benadur? Hell, for all Keira knew, Junia could have been behind Aaron's assassination attempt, too.

Keira didn't move from her spot in the shadows, even after the maids disappeared around the far corner. Was she really about to open up this can of worms? This was the last chance she'd ever get to stop Junia, sure, but what could she even do with the information if she found it?

Then again, could she really live with herself if she chose not to?

No. The answer was no.

Decision made, Keira crept toward the door. Slowly easing it open, she slipped inside. The room was dreary, with just the embers of a half-banked fire remaining through the door of the study and into the Regio's personal bedchamber. The linen-stripped four-poster gave the otherwise luxurious room a strangely barren appearance.

Keira immediately headed for the desk in the study and began rifling through drawers, looking for anything that might lend her the evidence she sought. She was greeted instead by tax reports, shipping inventory, and grain forecasts, all very dull and equally useless.

What are you doing, Altman? the voice in the back of her mind admonished. *You really think she would leave incriminating documents in the Regio's own desk?*

Keira was just about to close everything and hurry on to the west wing when a seemingly insignificant piece of parchment in the far corner of the drawer caught her eye. The letter itself was signed by Junia, merely a request for an increase to be made to the royal grain stores. Convenient, Keira thought, considering the current situation, but far from incriminating.

No, what caught Keira's eye was the wax seal that had been cut open to read it. It was a deep, royal shade of purple, and the seal itself was just the generic Marian signatory. But what Keira couldn't stop staring at were the three purple drops of wax that had been arranged in a perfect triangle in the upper righthand corner of the seal itself, evidence of authenticity, she supposed.

Where have I seen that design before? she wondered, struck by the sensation of something tickling the back of her mind, but remaining just out of reach.

Then it hit her.

Marek's letter. During her failed binding—what seemed like years ago now—she'd seen in Marek's mind a purple wax seal on the message that he'd received. She'd seen that same seal in the pocket of the dead worshipper of Séiro at Gregür Gorge. She'd barely noticed the dripped dots before—she'd assumed they were merely the mistake of a hastily withdrawn wax ladle. Seeing it again now, though...

Keira shook her head. No, it was far too precise a replica. This was no mistake, and it suggested that Junia was not only inciting low-level Tiarna and their lackeys to insurrection, but that she'd also conveyed their exact location to people who then tried to assassinate her brother. And though the evidence was circumstantial, it just might be enough to cast some doubt in the minds of the people about who was really calling the shots in Loren.

Keira shoved the letter in her pocket and hastily made for the door. She had to get up to her rooms to retrieve the letter's cousin, the one detailing Landry's exact location to his would-be assassins. Her hand was inches from the latch when she heard voices from outside.

It was Junia.

Keira spun around, looking desperately for somewhere to hide.

She spied the armoire just inside the Regio's bedchamber and lunged toward it, pulling its door shut behind her just as the entrance to the study opened, and Junia entered.

"—positioned around the city. I've been assured we'll have control by the end of the day tomorrow."

Keira heard her companion mumble something low and indistinct.

"Yes, yes," Junia replied impatiently. "It's just in here."

Keira heard a drawer being opened and felt her chest tighten.

"Ah, yes, he—" Junia paused, and Keira held her breath.

"Someone's been in here."

Her voice was hard, accusing, and Keira tried to squelch the rise of panic as she heard a blade being drawn. She listened as drawers and cabinets were opened and then blanched at the approach of footsteps. Too cramped to risk unsheathing her own sword, Keira instead went for her dagger. Her hand trembled, and her breath became shallow as she braced herself for what she knew was coming.

The door to the armoire flew open, and Keira lunged, slashing savagely at whoever might be on the other side.

There was no one.

Instead, she felt a hand clamp onto the back of her neck as she was propelled bodily to her knees. A swift kick to her side sent her sprawling onto her back, the air punched out of her lungs like bellows.

When the stars cleared from her eyes, she found herself staring directly into the stern gaze of Nazor.

THIRTY-SIX

"I see you haven't exactly been keeping up on your drills," Nazor intoned dryly.

Keira just stared at her, brain trying desperately to register the fact that Nazor was really *there*, in front of her. After everything that had happened, everyone she'd lost—first Elliott, then Flavius, Sara, and now Danny . . .

Keira choked down a sob. On an impulse, she jumped to her feet and threw her arms around the much taller woman. Nazor staggered back, surprised, as Keira clung to her stiff form, not caring that tears were now flowing freely down her face. Eventually, she felt Nazor loosen, and her arms come around to return the embrace. She felt Nazor pat her awkwardly on her back and even heard what were surely meant to be soothing noises. Keira chuckled slightly and pulled away, raking the heels of her palms against her eyes.

"Sorry," she murmured, smiling in apology at Nazor's embarrassed fidgeting. "It's been a rough few months, and—" She drew in an unsteady breath, trying to smile, but with a tad too much lip quiver. "Well, I'm just so glad to see you, Nazor."

Nazor nodded, smiling kindly at her, but Keira couldn't help but notice a strange shadow in her eyes. *Odd.* She shook off the sensation and, looking around, tried to find something other than this awkwardly emotional reunion to focus on.

That's when she remembered who else was in the room.

Peeking in through the door from the study, Keira could see Junia eyeing her shrewdly.

Wait . . . why was Nazor with Junia?

"Did you, uh . . . did you get my letter?" Keira tried to imbue the look she gave Nazor with meaning and barely resisted looking pointedly at Junia, thinking that might be a bit *too* obvious. Nazor nodded, though, seeming to take her meaning.

"I did. It's why I'm here, actually."

The clipped words, spoken in her usual lilting Nigerian accent, seemed oddly hesitant. This took Keira by surprise, and she shifted her weight nervously.

"You mean, to secure Landry's transition of power as Regio?" Keira felt a glimmer of hope at this thought. *If Landry had the open support of the Legion, that might be enough!*

The look Nazor gave her quickly squelched that thought. Either way, though, if the Legion was getting involved, Keira knew everything would ultimately work out. The three of them didn't need to flee the city and Nazor would know how to help Danny. Everything would be okay.

"No," Nazor said finally. "I'm here to secure Junia's."

The floor dropped out from beneath Keira. She stared at Nazor, sure she must have misheard. But one glance at Junia's smug expression told her she'd heard precisely right.

"W-what are you talking about?"

Nazor took a deep breath, fixing Keira with her notorious *Now, don't do anything foolish* face, and continued. "In the name of preserving order and fighting the looming chaos, the Legion has decided that it is in the best interest of Loren that Junia should assume the throne as Regio."

"Are you kidding me?" Keira sputtered almost incoherently as she looked from an indignant Nazor to the utterly triumphant Junia. "Danny and I nearly got ourselves killed bringing Landry from Mount Ánghen to the capital, saving his butt who knows how often. And now . . . what? You just want to replace him?"

Nazor's mouth was a firm line, and she was giving Keira the same disapproving look she'd used that time Keira had forgotten to lock the hen coop. Keira smarted against the obvious condescension.

"It's for the best, Keira dear," Junia crooned from the corner. "You can't truly believe that my dear little brother is actually capable of running this country. Just look around you."

Keira rounded on Junia and her smug little pursed lips.

"Don't you dare," she snarled, advancing on Junia. She was rewarded for her efforts by Nazor's firm hand on her shoulder, which she promptly shook off.

"Don't you know what she's done?" Keira asked, turning to Nazor instead. "Don't you understand how she's been plotting, manipulating, and twisting her way into power this whole time?"

"Yes," Nazor said. "We're aware. We do not approve, but such is the way of things sometimes."

Indignant, Junia opened her mouth as if to say something, but the look Keira shot her made her close it again.

"Why don't you give us a moment?" Nazor suggested, a bit icily. It wasn't really a question, but Junia treated it as if it was.

"Yes, I think I will. Perhaps when next we meet, you'll have thought more seriously about the correct manner in which to address your *sovereign*." With a swirl of skirts, Junia spun on her heel and exited the room.

Keira gritted her teeth, and even Nazor had to close her eyes in exasperation, pinching the bridge of her nose like Keira had seen Elliott do a thousand times.

"Really, Nazor?" Keira asked. "Her? Why in the name of Pneumos would you pick *her*?"

"First," Nazor replied, "*I* didn't pick her. The Legion did. I presented the facts and the High Council decided. I merely followed orders, as do you." She said this last part pointedly, and Keira grimaced. She opened her mouth to argue, but Nazor wasn't finished.

"Second, she is by far the only politically expedient option. Rightly or wrongly, the people blame Landry for his father's policies. Junia, on the other hand, will be viewed as an unknown entity, and public perception can be shaped around the fact that the uplanders, in particular, expect very little from women in power. Sneer all you like," she said, exasperated, most likely because of Keira's pinched expression, "but it's true, and you know it."

Keira had to admit, the uplanders *were* known for their tendency toward chauvinistic assumptions. But she refused to feel sympathy for the likes of Junia.

"Nazor, what if I told you I had proof that she tried to have her brother killed?"

Her interest slightly piqued, Nazor allowed Keira to rehash her discovery and realization concerning the letters Marek and the rogue pneumonancer had received. Yet when she finished, Nazor looked far from impressed.

"It's not enough, Keira," the older woman said. "You know it isn't. Circumstantial association is not the same as proof."

"But it might be enough to create doubt," Keira insisted stubbornly, arms folded across her chest.

"*Doubt*," Nazor snapped, folding her own arms in exact mimicry, "is the last thing we need right now. This country is in chaos, Keira, ready to rip itself apart. I've seen what that looks like, and I will *not* stand by and watch it happen again."

Nazor's eyes darkened, and Keira knew she was thinking about her daughter. She'd lived through her own civil war several lifetimes ago, though Keira doubted the memories had ever faded. She felt her resolve weaken and firmed up her jaw in response.

"It's wrong, Nazor. The Legion is *wrong* on this, wrong to trust Junia."

"Maybe," Nazor conceded, "but right now, she's the lesser of two evils. When we seek to make order out of chaos, our only mandate is that we build more than we break. And, in this case, it's unfortunately *Landry* that must be broken."

"Well, maybe that mandate is wrong," Keira said, voice low and tight. "Maybe there are some things more important than *order*."

"Like what?" Nazor asked, eyes narrowed.

"Like justice. Or fairness, maybe."

Nazor stepped forward until she was only a few inches away from Keira.

"And who do you think decides what 'justice' means?" Nazor hissed through clenched teeth. "The Ones. Left. Standing."

Keira opened her mouth to say something, but quickly closed it at the look on Nazor's face. This was a side of her Keira had only ever glimpsed, the part torn ragged and raw by a world far crueler than she could ever imagine.

Sensing her resolve weakening, Nazor pressed her advantage. "Help me, Keira. Help me secure a peaceful succession. Prove yourself to the Legion, once and for all. I told them of all you've accomplished here and they're very impressed. I—I'm proud of you, Keira and I think you're ready now—for the rites."

Keira stared at her, mouth falling open in a silent "oh." How long had she waited to hear these very words from Nazor? For all her complaining about her sword master's gruff demeanor, all she'd ever really wanted was her approval and the chance to prove herself. And here she was, offering her the one thing she'd wanted more than anything since stepping foot in Loren—the chance to go home.

Her chest ached at the thought of seeing her mother again, of playing with little Molly. But Danny's words echoed in her ears. *There is a difference between order and justice.* What would he think if he could see her now? Willing to throw away everything they'd worked for, give up on all her noble words and professed ideals for a chance at the life she'd lost. She couldn't do it. She couldn't make that trade. Because no matter what Nazor said, might did not make right.

She didn't know if her mother really was dead or if completing the rites would give her a chance to see her. But there were other people that needed her now. Danny needed her now.

I'm sorry, Mom.

She stiffened, meeting Nazor's gaze with her own unblinking stare.

"I don't think so, Nazor. I can't side with you and the Legion here, not on this. I know what the mandate is and about the Legion's sworn purpose. But I think sometimes a little chaos is necessary to fight a greater injustice."

Nazor's lips pressed into a thin line, and her eyes narrowed. "I taught you better than this, Keira. You know better than to pick a fight you have no hopes of winning."

Keira knew she was right. Junia held all the cards: the Council, the Bellatorio, and now, even the Legion. It didn't matter that she was a terrible person; that she'd stoked civil unrest, tried to murder her own brother, and unleashed the forces of chaos to accomplish her will. The fact was, there was no one left to stand against her, least of all a pesky younger brother.

"Maybe we will lose this fight," Keira said quietly, meeting Nazor's eye and daring her to contradict. "But there will be another, and another, and another after that. We'll keep coming, keep trying until Loren becomes the place I know it can be. And I know you know it too."

Something glinted in Nazor's eye that Keira thought might just be respect, but it was gone in an instant and her mentor chuckled without warmth.

"I'm afraid it's too late for that."

Keira eyed her warily. "What's that supposed to mean?"

For the first time in this entire conversation, Nazor looked genuinely uncomfortable. She shifted her weight awkwardly before fixing Keira with a stern, no-nonsense look.

"You know exactly what it means." When Keira continued to stare blankly at her, she sighed, sounding almost annoyed over having to spell everything out. "You cannot believe that Loren can be allowed to have two heirs to the Regio's throne. That would just be asking for chaos to resurface in five, ten, even fifteen years' time, when Landrianus is fully grown and resentful of his stolen inheritance."

"Y-you can't mean—" Keira gaped at Nazor in horror. At that moment, she couldn't believe that this woman had been her teacher, her mentor, the one she'd turned to for help or advice. Could this really be the same Nazor? Keira felt her earlier nausea rise in her throat, and she stood up to pace, fighting off the growing sense of panic with every ounce of strength she could muster. Then a thought occurred to her, and she spun around to face Nazor directly.

"He's leaving—chartered a ship to leave first thing tomorrow." Keira could have laughed in delight. "They won't get to him in time."

She expected to see surprise, frustration, even a look of defeat on Nazor's face. Instead, the older woman only grimaced, nodding in consolation.

"Yes, we will. That *friend* of his betrayed him. We know what ship he's taking and what time it sets sail. And, well . . . it won't."

She said this last sentence with an air of rigid formality. To hear her, you'd think they were merely discussing some unfortunate but necessary business that no one really wanted to deal with. Keira thought she might be sick, but most of all, she wanted to cry. She wanted to cry for the brave boy who thought he could be Regio, even when all the cards were stacked against him. And when the end seemed inevitable, he'd been willing to exit stage left, to go off in pursuit of a simpler life in a beautiful country far away.

If only he could.

Then Keira froze, the slowly dawning thought bringing with it a fresh wave of unadulterated horror.

"Did you say it *won't?*"

Nazor cocked her head slightly, looking confused. Keira stared at her, breath coming faster with every moment as she asked, "*It*, as in the ship?"

"Yes," Nazor intoned, clearly not sure where Keira was going with this. "It'll be made to look like an act of sabotage by the city rioters. Tragically, the crew will be lost, but it must be done to ensure—"

"Nazor!" Keira nearly shouted, not bothering to hide the choked sound of sobs crushing her chest on their way out. "*Danny* is on that ship!"

Nazor's dark skin turned ashen.

"W-what?" For the first time, a note of genuine fear prickled beneath the calm exterior of Nazor's voice. "What are you talking about?"

"He was hurt," Keira cried, dropping to the floor as she scrambled to see through her blurred vision where she'd dropped her dagger.

This can't be happening, she thought. *I can't lose him again, not to this.*

"Landry brought him onto the ship," she explained. "They're waiting for me there. I have to warn them."

Fingers suddenly lighting on the hilt of the small dagger, Keira jumped to her feet and ran toward the door. Firm hands caught her by the shoulders and spun her around. Keira was openly crying again as she dragged painful breaths through her tightened lungs. She looked up into Nazor's face to see that the older woman had tears in her own eyes.

That was when she knew.

"I-I'm sorry, Keira. It's too late."

THIRTY-SEVEN

"No," Keira said, trying to pull away from Nazor. "It can't be."

"The order went out over an hour ago. If it hasn't happened yet, it will at any minute. There's no time."

Keira shook her head, the heady adrenaline of resolve flooding her veins. *Danny*. This was Danny they were talking about. They were meant to be together. *Pneumos-bound*. She knew that now, had probably always known, but refused to see it for the sake of her foolish pride and fear. She couldn't lose him, not now, not after everything they'd been through.

"This is *not* over," she said fiercely, fixing Nazor with one of her patented glares. "*You* did this. Now you're going to help me fix it."

To her credit, Nazor hesitated for only a moment. Keira waited with bated breath as Nazor completed the brief mental calculus weighing her loyalty to the Legion against her love for Danny. He'd always been like a son to her, and Keira knew that math came out staggeringly asymmetric. Nazor finally nodded.

"We'll take the access path that runs along the city walls toward the dockyard. It's faster, and we'll run into fewer *friends* along the way."

Nazor immediately turned on her heel and made for the door.

And just like that, Keira thought, *she's back.*

She ran to catch up.

THE NIGHT AIR was unusually quiet as she and Nazor ran through the alleyway that hugged the city wall. The oppressive darkness of night was further burdened by the smog of fear and the metallic scent of blood.

Nazor had told her that the original plan had called for a fire to be started in the ship's hayloft as it sat in the harbor, sped hastily on by a flammable, turpentine-like material. But as the two of them scanned the horizon near the dockyard, they saw no light along its length. A glimmer of hope sparked in Keira's chest, and she fiercely resisted the urge to fan it fully into life.

When they neared the dockyard, Keira and Nazor slowed to a jog, unsheathed weapons at the ready as they approached Landry's ship. The shadowed hull of the *Lorakrista* loomed before them, and they carefully scanned it for any sign of habitation.

Nothing.

Reaching the gangplank, Keira volunteered to go first, leaving Nazor to guard the pier, preventing anyone from sneaking up on them. Keira's heart hammered in her chest as she carefully peered over the deck's ledge. The place was deserted—no guards, no ship's crew, no nothing. Keira didn't like it one bit.

Then she saw it.

A flash of movement, and Keira's eyes darted toward the aftcastle, where she could have sworn someone had disappeared through a darkened doorway. Swiftly clambering onto the desk, Keira stayed low as she crept toward the overhang that led, she assumed, to the captain's quarters. Hugging the wall, she paused just outside the doorway, ears perked, trying desperately to listen for any sound of movement as the blood pounded in her ears.

And there it was—the faint scuffle of shoes on plank flooring. Suddenly, a shadow appeared at her shoulder. Keira reacted in an instant, grabbing a fistful of someone's collar as she heaved them bodily to the floor of the main deck. She heard the breath whoosh out of them as they landed, and her blade was at their throat in a moment. She listened to their sputtering and protests as she waited for her eyes to adjust to the lighting.

It was Landry.

She could have laughed with relief at the sight of his red, coughing face. She immediately bent to help him up.

"Glad you made it," Landry said, rubbing his neck where the blunt edge of her blade had pressed. "That was quite the greeting, though."

Keira grinned sheepishly at him, then instantly remembered the actual reason she was there. "Landry, where are your guards?" She frowned, continuing to look around. "And the ship's crew?"

Landry shook his head as he shrugged. "I'm not sure. That's why I came up here. It seemed too . . . quiet."

Keira glanced around uneasily. She tensed as she saw a shadow vault over the deck's railing, but relaxed when she realized it was Nazor, coming to investigate the noise, no doubt.

"I don't like it," she said as soon as she reached Keira's shoulder, eyeing Landry dubiously. Keira turned toward him and quickly explained why they'd come.

"You and Danny are both in danger," she concluded. "Your sister —she's sent her people to destroy the ship and make it look like sabotage by the rioters."

Landry blanched at this. "She really hates me that much?" he asked quietly. "Enough to kill me?"

Keira opened her mouth to reply, but it was Nazor who said, "She wants power and to become Regio. That can never happen while you still live."

"There'll be time enough to hash this out later," Keira said, "but first, we need to get Danny."

Nazor nodded in agreement, and Keira eyed her suspiciously before gesturing for Landry to follow her. She'd need help to carry Danny, and she was not about to leave Landry alone with Nazor. She may have agreed to rescue Danny, but there was no way Keira would risk Nazor reverting to the original plan and offing Landry the first chance she got.

Landry was leading them toward the captain's quarters when Keira saw movement out of the corner of her eye. She spun on her heel, hand jerking toward the hilt of her sword as she spotted seven or eight cloaked figures in black simultaneously clambering over the ship's railing. Keira cried out just as the middle one threw back his hood to reveal the tattooed countenance of a worshipper of Séiro.

An arm shot out in front of her to block her way, and she looked up into Nazor's grim face. "Get Danny," she murmured, cold as ice. "I'll hold them off."

Keira hesitated, knowing there was no way Nazor could do this on her own. There were too many of them.

But Danny, she thought. *What about Danny?*

"*Go*," Nazor snarled. "For once in your life, Keira, do as you're ordered."

Still, Keira wavered, indecision warring within her.

"Go!" Nazor shouted now, shoving her roughly backward. "I said, *go!*"

And suddenly Keira was back in the glade, outside the destroyed house near Abalás, with Elliott undone and Nazor ordering her to leave and go be the hero.

No, Keira thought. *Not this time.*

She shook her head, squaring off to confront the rogue pneumonancers as she shouted for Landry to go on without her and get Danny to safety. Nazor glared at her, and Keira glared right back. Whatever Nazor saw in her eyes, it made her pause, and Keira seized on her chance. She grabbed hold of Nazor's hand as she kneeled to place her other lightly against the ship's main deck. Nudging the pneuma in her stomach, she sent it out on the back of a high-pitched whistle. Realizing instantly what she was doing, Nazor sent her own pneuma toward her, wrapping Keira's body in a firm tether that rooted her securely to the ship's deck, now rolling slightly as the wind picked up around them.

And then she was no longer Keira. With her spirit intertwined with Nazor's, she felt the older woman's essence, her hopes and dreams, her love, and her pain. Keira was no longer *her*, but rather *them*. And while that thought had always scared her in the past—sent her running in the opposite direction, in fact—this time, she'd chosen it. She'd run headlong toward it, and the joining wasn't all that terrifying. Being known so entirely by someone else was disarming, but at that moment, Keira could feel nothing other than safety, security, and the loyalty of a person she knew would die before she let her come to harm.

Is this really what you've been running from this entire time? The voice inside her tsked. But Keira didn't have long to focus on this novel realization, because things were progressing, with or without her.

The tether firmly secured, Keira felt Nazor release her hand and watched from outside her body as Nazor stepped in front of her to assume the guard position. The advancing pneumonancers spread out in a large half-circle as they advanced on Nazor and the crouched Keira.

Keira felt herself starting to panic. *There are too many of them,* she thought, *too many to bind at once.* She looked around, desperate to find something she could use. She watched as two of them approached the mainmast, where a pile of ropes lay forgotten on the deck. Quickly, Keira mentally traced their path to the topsail and down to the lowest yardarm. Then a genuinely terrible idea occurred to her.

Locating the mainbrace, Keira quickly sent her pneuma flying toward it, letting it meld into the layers of twine until, one by one, she felt them snap. Then everything was chaos. The primary yardarm collapsed downward, crushing two of the advancing figures against the mainmast. This lengthened the rope running from the mainmast to the topsail, and the figure whose foot was primed inside the unfurled rope shrieked in pain as he was yanked upward by the ankle to dangle helplessly in the air.

Seizing the momentum, Nazor lunged at the nearest figure in black, meeting them blade for blade as they spun in a whirling duel that ended only with Nazor piercing the woman's side, inducing a gurgling shriek as the figure collapsed to the ground. While she was preoccupied, Keira focused on the two remaining people on the port side. She'd never tried a double bind before, but figured now was as good a time as any to make the attempt.

She spread her pneuma out as wide as it would go, a net that she cast deftly around the figures as they lunged toward her. They froze in their tracks, and she felt them fighting her as she needled her way through their defenses and toward the trigger points she needed to make the muscle bind stick. She felt herself push up against the very outermost edges of her own mental defenses and move past the point of true detachment. She wasn't sure how she did it, or what gave her the courage to risk never being able to return to her own body. But there was something about that tether, the invisible bond holding her tightly to the ship's deck, that gave her the hold she needed. Despite everything—the fights, the betrayal—she remained convinced that Nazor, her mentor, would reel her in. Such was the power of the grounder's tether.

So Keira took the leap, stepping off the mental ledge and feeling herself fall into oblivion, wrapping herself firmly and unbreakably into her targets. She felt their muscles weaken and then collapse, their bodies caving in on themselves as her bind fully took hold. And when she pulled away, breathing in the scent of victory, there was Nazor's tether, right there to reel her back in.

She opened her eyes, giddy with delight, and saw a ball of fire hurtling toward her.

She opened her mouth in a wordless scream, willing her heavy limbs to regain function, only to find they'd failed her once more. Still, the fire advanced, the remaining pneumonancer kneeling to keep his balance on the now-careening deck.

It was Nazor who stepped in front of her. Nazor, who tried to deflect the flames to the side; Nazor, who doubled over in pain against the railing, clutching at her singed face.

Keira clambered to her wobbly feet and staggered toward her. It was then that she saw the fraying dock line just behind her, threads popping as the rope smoldered. Keira called out to Nazor, but the rogue pneumonancer had seen it, too. Keira barreled toward him, watching as he formed another ball of flames from the breakdown of wood piling nearby. He released it mere seconds before she struck him, sending him flying over the railing, crushed between hull and dock as the ship bounced off its moorings. Keira winced, but couldn't bring herself to regret his death.

Then she spun around to find Nazor, badly burned and slumped against the railings. Keira opened her mouth and, in horror, watched as the last threads of the smoldering dock line snapped, and the live wire that was the rope under tension whipped around, slicing through Nazor's side in an otherwise graceful arc.

THIRTY-EIGHT

Keira knew her legs were moving, but couldn't shake the feeling that she was wading through molasses, desperate as she was to reach Nazor's side. When she finally made it to her, Nazor had crumpled against the ship's railing. Her breath came in ragged gasps, and Keira stared at the cracked skin around her mentor's singed lips. Scanning her, Keira could see that the snapped line had sliced deep into the side of Nazor's chest wall. The older woman tried to say something, but its meaning dissolved in a fit of wet-sounding coughs.

"You're going to be fine," Keira said anyway. Panicked, she looked around for something to stop the bleeding and quickly pressed the black cloak of a nearby dead pneumonancer into the wound. Keira called for Landry, telling him to go get help, but she wasn't entirely sure if he could hear her.

Desperate, she closed her eyes, grasping for her pneuma. She had no idea how to do it, but Keira was determined to save her.

Nazor stopped her with a firm hand, lifting her own hands gently off the bleeding wound.

"Stop! What are you—" Keira began, her throat catching, but she halted when she saw Nazor trying to murmur something. Blinking tears out of her eyes, Keira leaned closer to hear Nazor's words, just barely audible.

"Don't—it is time. Tell Elliott . . . tell him I love him, in this life—"

Nazor gasped, clutching her hand into a fist and continued through gritted teeth. "—and our next."

Keira shook her head, fanning the smoldering fuse of anger even as she tried to squelch the rising tide of sorrow.

"Why, Nazor?" she finally said. "Why couldn't you have trusted us, helped us, even? Maybe then—"

A choked sob cut off her words, and she swiped angrily at the tears that overflowed her eyes, rolling down her cheeks. Nazor gave her a tiny smile, even as her eyes widened and turn glassy.

"We all have our fights, to win or lose," she breathed, little more than a whisper. Keira took her hand, unable to look away. For even after everything, despite everything, Nazor had saved her life and Danny's. They may have had their differences, but they were family. And that was more important than the Legion or any higher purpose like order or justice. Nazor had known that, had chosen family when the choice needed to be made. And now Keira knew that, too.

"I forgive you," Keira told her, now sobbing outright as she searched the face of her mentor for something, anything that might show regret or apology. She found nothing. Nazor's eyes were wide and dilated, staring out into space. Her mouth was slightly open, but her breath had stilled. Choking down another sob, Keira felt for a pulse.

Nothing.

Nazor was gone and Keira sat alone in the darkness once more.

KEIRA FOUND LANDRY BELOW DECK, weapon at the ready, as he kneeled beside Danny's stretcher. She stared blankly at him, shaking her head when he asked about Nazor. His brow furrowed in apology, but thankfully, he said nothing.

"What do we do now? Set sail?" he asked.

Keira pinched the bridge of her nose between thumb and forefinger, fighting off the waves of exhaustion that overpowered her. "No—the ship took too much damage in the fight. Besides, we don't exactly have a crew, and there's no guarantee they'd be loyal, anyway. Plus, we need to get Danny somewhere safe." She paused, a thought suddenly occurring to her. "I know where we can take him."

After carefully securing Danny to the stretcher, and with much maneuvering and cursing, they got him above deck and down the gangplank to the pier. It wasn't until they reached the principal dockyard that Keira smelled smoke and looked back to see the *Lorakrista* firmly engulfed in flames. There must have been smoldering embers from the fight left on the aftcastle, Keira realized, gazing back to where Nazor's body lay.

Well, she thought, it's *a pyre fit for a Legionnaire.*

Keira turned away. If there was anything Nazor hated, it was sentimentality. With that final thought, they set off at as quick a pace as they dared away from the burning ship. Keira shot nervous glances toward the horizon and the rapidly approaching sunrise that beckoned the day. She led them toward the fish market that bordered the dockyards, carefully avoiding the curious eyes that peeked from behind tightly shuttered buildings.

When they reached the building that had been described to her in so many fireside chats, Keira knocked briskly on the door and waited nervously. No one answered. She knocked again, louder this time, and shifted uneasily as multiple neighbors poked their heads from nearby windows to see what all the commotion was about. Keira pressed her ear to the door and listened as small feet shuffled inside. She banged again, now just pissed off.

"Come on, Gwen, I know you're inside!" she shouted as loudly as she dared. "You owe us—"

The door in front of her was wrenched open, and Gwen's furious red face appeared.

"I owe you nothing," she hissed. "You can't be here! I swear—"

Keira had just opened her mouth to reply when a voice from inside called out.

"It's all right, Gwen. No need to be rude to your guests on our account. Show 'em in."

Lips pursed in a thin line, Gwen moved to the side and opened the door a fraction of an inch further. Assuming she had little choice in the matter, Keira stepped uneasily through, palms sweaty as they clutched the handles of the stretcher. Landry followed behind her, looking even more nervous, and they both took a moment to adjust to the dim light.

When she did, Keira looked toward the fire to find the owner of the voice—and found herself looking straight into the wide-spaced eyes of Neval Brennan.

THIRTY-NINE

"Hello, Keira," Neval said mildly, gesturing toward the table he sat at and standing to make room for Danny's stretcher. Keira hesitated, thinking seriously for a moment about turning right around and leaving, dragging Danny and Landry in tow.

No, it's too late. He'd just come after them, and Neval might not even recognize Landry. So Keira nodded, and the two of them moved to place Danny gently on the table. She opened her mouth to say something, but Neval beat her to the punch.

"Ah, and it seems you've brought the future Regio with you. How nice now."

Keira saw Landry blanch, and Neval's toothy smile widened. She swore silently. *So much for that plan,* she thought. She glanced around. There were a few of Neval's men with them in the room. They were all sporting their own injuries, many of them heavily bandaged. Even Neval was wearing an arm sling, and from what she could make of the damage, Keira guessed the arm was probably broken. But if his men had even heard Neval's words, they seemed too exhausted to be interested. Still, Keira's fingers itched to grab onto the hilt of her sword.

"Hello, Neval," she said mildly, helping herself to a long swallow of water from the pitcher on the table and then passing it to Landry. Landry glanced nervously from her to Neval, but eventually accepted it and sipped from the rim.

Get it together, she told him silently, hoping he could read her expression. *This won't work if he thinks you're a complete nincompoop.*

"So, what brings you here, your royal highness? Is it not enough to levy taxes or oppress townspeople from the comfort of your grand Vindolum? You must now come to see the effects in person?"

Keira was about to shoot back an equally snarky reply, but Landry beat her to it.

"I think you mistake me for my sister, Mr. Brennan," he said smoothly. "Easy to do, I know—I'm sure we Marians all look alike without the benefit of gowns and crowns."

Neval stared at him for a moment, stunned, then guffawed. Keira grinned internally. *Well done, Landry,* she thought. *There may be hope for you yet.*

She turned back to Neval as he spoke. "Aww, did the two of you have a fight, then?"

"You could say that," Landry replied mildly. "She just tried to have me killed."

On this last word, he fixed Neval with a steady, unwavering gaze. Neval's eyes widened slightly, but his face otherwise remained unchanged.

"Now, why would your sister do somethin' like that, eh?"

Quickly, Keira told Neval everything. She explained about the cohort, their mission to retrieve Landry, and the failed assassination attempt in Ulgáris. She told him about Junia's growing control over not only the Council but also the Bellatorio, and how she had used this power to overrule Landry's order that the attack on the rebels' barricades be held off until dawn. Keira ended with Junia's most recent attempt to kill Landry on his ship, even as he was prepared to leave Loren forever.

By the time she'd finished, Neval had moved to stand before the fire, and Keira had a sudden flashback of their conversation only the night before, when he'd considered negotiating with Landry and forging peace.

This could work, Keira thought. *This could actually work!*

But Neval turned around then, and the grim look on his face banished all hope from hers.

"This is not my fight," he said, mouth a thin line as he shook his head in disgust. "I have no interest in the squabblin' of siblings or the petty intrigues of the nobility. I only care for the people of Loren, and as far as I'm concerned, you're no better than your sister."

Keira didn't know how to respond to that. She should have known this would be hopeless. There had been too much bloodshed, too much chaos. The common ground between them had shrunk to a fraction of whatever sliver there had been to start with.

"You're right to be angry," Landry said simply, palms open in a humble gesture. "You've been wronged too many times over the years to have any reason to trust me now. So, why don't we try something new? Why don't you tell me what you and the rest of the people of Loren need, and I'll just listen."

Neval's eyes narrowed suspiciously, and he glanced from Landry to Keira, obviously expecting some catch here. Keira shrugged and scooted her seat closer to Danny as Landry and Neval talked. At first, both were hesitant, obviously unsure of the other's intentions. Yet the more they talked, the more relaxed they became. Neval told Landry about the country's desperate need for land-use reform, so that the upland river people weren't always playing second fiddle to the downland cities. Meanwhile, Landry shared the difficulties that he and other downlanders had had assimilating into Lorenan culture over the years, explaining how they often felt put off by upland traditions, their thoughts on the role of women, or the nature of Pneumos.

The hours passed, and Keira felt herself nodding off, even as the light outside brightened to full morning.

After one particular interlude, she woke up to find Neval and Landry chatting it up like old friends about the prospects of the local Harpastum team in Crîd Eálas, and Keira shook her head in amazement. *Leave it to men*, she thought, snorting. *On the brink of civil war, and there's nothing more fascinating than sports.*

They both glanced curiously toward her at the sound, and Keira sat up straighter, stretching out her arms as she asked, "So, what have we decided?"

Landry and Neval glanced at each other, slightly embarrassed.

"Well, nothing's been decided per se, but I have a proposition," Landry said. Neval cocked his head slightly at him, but said nothing. "I ask that Neval and his people support me in assuming the throne as

Regio. In return, I promise I will create a People's Council equal to, if not more powerful than, the Council of Benadur, with direct oversight and checks over them and over the Regio. As collateral," he continued, seeing Neval open his mouth to say something, "Neval and his people will maintain their barricades and control over the periphery of the city until I'm able to make good on my end of the bargain."

There was a brief pause as Landry looked from Neval to Keira. Slowly, a broad smile crept over Neval's face, and he held out a hand to Landry, who gladly took it.

Keira squelched her own rising excitement. "That sounds like a promising agreement," she said encouragingly. "The only problem is that we still don't have control over either the existing Council or the Bellatorio. How exactly are we going to make you Regio in the first place?"

This time, it was Neval who spoke up. "What if we forced Junia's hand?"

"How so?" Keira asked, genuinely curious now.

"She's called a public gatherin' outside the Vindolum this very afternoon." Neval shrugged. "It's as good a place as any."

"No," Keira murmured quietly, looking up at them and smiling slowly. "It's better."

Quickly, she explained her plan to them both. It was risky, but at that moment, it was the only plan they had. When she'd finished, they both just stared at her.

"Even if all goes to plan, that still leaves you confronting Junia on your own," Landry said slowly, brow furrowing in concern. "But you'll have no grounder. Won't that be dangerous?"

"For her," Keira said, feeling a savage rush of rage at the thought of confronting the woman responsible for the deaths of so many loved ones. She'd make sure Junia lived to regret each and every one.

Landry frowned at her with concern.

"At least let us help you."

"I don't know," Keira wavered. "If things go wrong . . ."

"Keira," Landry said, laying a hand on her arm. "Since the first day I met you, you've tried to go it alone. And where has that gotten you?"

Keira swallowed, a stab of guilt and pain coursing through her chest. She fought to suppress the rising panic at the thought of risking maybe the last friends she had left.

Friends? Is that what they were? She glanced between Landry and Neval, then to the heavily bandaged uplanders half asleep in the corner. A more motley crew she'd never come across. She shook her head.

"I don't want to . . . Landry, I can't lose anyone else. I don't think I could bear it."

Her voice broke on this last bit, and Neval smiled sadly at her.

"Loss is a part of life, Keira dear. You can't stop it. And the more you try, the more of yourself you stand to lose. Take it from someone who knows."

Keira stared back at him, wondering who he'd lost—the ghost that still haunted his eyes.

"Let us help you," Landry said again. "We're stronger together."

Keira inhaled deeply and then nodded, this newfound trust like a hesitant flame that flickered deep in her chest, all too easily put out.

They agreed Danny would be safest here with Gwen, and then the three of them split up the tasks between them. Each headed off, agreeing to meet in the Vindolum's plaza with the gathering crowds that very evening.

She did her best to go unnoticed as she made her way toward the city garrison. As she went, Keira felt a rising buoyancy that she realized could be only one thing.

Hope.

CHAPTER

FORTY

The day had been a hot one, and the gathered crowds shifted uncomfortably. Heat radiated off the cobblestones even as the sun sank lower in the sky. Keira passed quickly through the mass of people, looking for any sign of Landry or Neval. She found a suitable spot on the edge of the crowd, clambering up onto the low wall beside several children to better see what was about to happen. From there, she spied the mounted Bellators positioned strategically around the square, poised to respond if things turned violent.

The clock tower struck five, and bells rang out, echoing around the square as the crowd fell silent. Keira watched as the high doors to the Vindolum were opened, and the twelve members of the Council of Benadur filed out. Dressed in their long, sage green robes, they formed a half-circle on the stairs leading down to the plaza below. Awed murmurs rippled through the crowd at their appearance, and many touched the tops of their heads in reverence before the twelve.

Keira felt like snorting, but stopped herself. *If only you knew,* she thought ruefully. *You'd have a bit less reverence for your precious Council.*

Then Junia appeared. A disgruntled murmur echoed through the crowd, all semblance of awe or respect gone.

"Good people of Loren," she called out, and the crowd fell silent again. "I come to you today with heavy tidings. I know that many of you have had your lives uprooted by the violence that has descended

290

on our beloved city. Unfortunately, I'm here to bring you the tragic news that my brother, your future Regio, has been killed."

A gasp echoed across the gathered crowd, and the murmurs built to a crescendo before Junia finally raised a hand into the air, and silence fell once more.

"No one is more devastated by the loss of my brother than I, and to have come so quickly after losing my father, our dear Regio Claudius —" Junia paused, dabbing theatrically at her eye, though they were all at far too great a distance to see real tears.

Convenient, Keira thought.

Gathering herself with a ragged breath, Junia continued her speech, assuming an air of authority and inevitability that made Keira's teeth clench.

"Regrettably, in these dangerous times, the usual period of mourning cannot possibly be observed," Junia declared. "A firm hand is needed, lest our beloved land descend into turmoil. I therefore call upon the Council of Benadur, who from the holy lands of Ulgáris do ensure order in the name of Pneumos, protection to the sovereign realm of Loren, and peace to its citizens therein. I ask then, fine people of Loren, that you declare me Regio in my brother's stead, so I might carry on the exemplary work my father started so many years ago."

The buzzing of the crowd grew to a roar as shouting and arguments erupted from the watching mass of people.

"A woman Regio?" Keira heard one man exclaim. "It's never been done."

"But who else?" a young woman with a small herd of children protested. "Or would you rather leave us to the likes of Neval and his horde?"

The cacophony quickly became too difficult to discern. Keira looked instead to the dais where Junia stood, a look of determination on her face. She gestured toward the tallest of the twelve council members, a man with an impressive mustache that Keira assumed could only be Benadur Mualath. The man looked uncomfortable as he shifted his weight back and forth, quickly scanning the crowd before slowly stepping forward. He took a breath, steeling himself against whatever came next.

Keira's eyes jumped from face to face, panic rising in her stomach. *Come on, Landry*, she thought. *Where are you? It's now or never.*

A hush suddenly swept over the plaza, and the mass of people parted straight down the middle. Keira stood on her tiptoes on the small wall and could just see over the heads of the crowd.

It was Landry. He was dressed formally, though wisely eschewing the usual pomp and finery of the royal family. Beside him strode Neval, head held high and arm proudly slung before him, a visible badge of blood loyalty to the cause. Behind them, Neval's men bore the surviving pneumonancers before them. They all sported burns, and their charred clothes, chains, and tattooed faces made them look oddly pathetic in the light of day.

Landry reached the foot of the stairs and turned to face the gathered assembly.

"People of Loren," he began. "My name is Landrianus Marian, son of the former Regio Claudius Marian, and I am very much alive."

The only sound was the languid summer breeze through the square as wide eyes looked from Landry to Junia in silent question.

Landry pointed to the worshippers of Séiro. "These assassins were hired to kill me by the forces at work just below the surface in Loren," he said, turning then to face his sister, who stiffened at his words. Keira held her breath as she watched Junia's ashen face, waiting for him to say the words, to condemn his sister for the twisted snake she was.

This is our chance, Landry, she thought. *We have to undermine Junia's authority. This is how we make you Regio.*

But still, Landry said nothing. Keira watched him, confused, and saw that his face, rather than reflecting her own fury and righteous indignation, was marked by something else entirely. *Sympathy*, she decided. She realized then that Landry would never turn on his sister, the girl who'd all but raised him when his mother had died. She had betrayed him, just as Nazor had betrayed Keira. But no matter what she'd done to him, she was still family. Keira let out the breath she'd been holding and watched as Landry turned back to the waiting crowd. She understood. She wasn't satisfied, but she understood.

"It has been customary, in centuries past, that the future Regio seeks the ordination of the Council of Benadur to confer the power and authority vested in that title. And while I assure you I am most grateful for their *support*, it is you, the people of Loren, that I truly come before today."

There were a handful of murmurs, but the bulk of the crowd remained silent, regarding Landry with uneasy eyes.

"Times have not been good for many in Loren these past few years," Landry continued. "Taxes have been high, laws unfair, and a decent livelihood difficult to come by. I am lucky enough to have been gifted with many talented friends, friends free to tell me the truth about what life is truly like outside the Vindolum's walls. One of those friends joins me here today." He turned then to Neval and said aloud, "I would like to introduce you to a man who needs no introduction. This is Neval Brennan, and he has long been an advocate for the everyday man, woman, and child in Loren. He is here to share his thoughts with you."

Keira's heart hammered in her chest, and she held her breath as she waited to hear what Neval might say. Without Junia's guilt, everything rested with him.

Neval cleared his throat, shifting slightly, and then began his speech.

"Many of you've heard my name, though few have heard me speak. Well, there may be a reason for that." The crowd laughed obligingly, and Neval smiled his wide, toothy grin. "I may not be a man of words, but I am a man of action. Promises go only so far, 'specially without the work needed to back them up. Now, I've had a good long conversation with his highness here, and he has listened carefully to our concerns. But more than that, he's assured me that his first act as Regio will be to institute a People's Council, to give every person in Loren a say in the laws that govern them. And to that, I said, 'Well, that's all well and good, your highness, but how do I *know* that this promise will be kept?'"

A louder murmur of agreement ran through the crowd, and Keira hear numerous voices shouting, "That's right!" and "To be sure!"

She grinned. Neval had them eating it up. *Not a man of words indeed,* she thought, amused.

"Well, do you know what he said to me?" Neval paused, letting a half dozen voices interject before continuing. "He said, 'Mr. Brennan, my word is my bond, but I swear to you that as surely as Pneumos reigns, not a single barricade will be touched, nor a single plaza reclaimed for the crown, until you have your People's Council!'"

This was met with shouts of surprise and a smattering of applause.

"So I ask you, people of Loren," Neval continued. "Will you support Landrianus Marian as Regio, so long as he abides by these promises he has made you before the world and Pneumos this day?"

The crowd roared in approval, and Keira felt a billowing of excitement in her own chest. She glanced toward the half-circle of council members shifting awkwardly before the cheering crowd and saw Junia's stony face regarding the jubilant people.

She knows, Keira thought triumphantly. *She knows it's over.*

Keira looked across the courtyard and made eye contact with the familiar gray eyes of a mounted Bellator riding beside Imperator Servius himself. She nodded at him, and he leaned toward Servius to murmur something in his ear. Keira watched as Servius's mouth twisted into a thin line and the muscles of his jaw tightened. In the end, though, he kneed his horse forward and unsheathed his sword, thrusting it into the sky.

"Regio Landrianus," he bellowed over the crowd. Confident he had everyone's attention, Servius thumped his fist, hilt and all, across his chest in salute. "The Bellatorio is yours, sire."

Further cheering erupted from the crowd, and Landry nodded in acknowledgment. He turned then to address the Council of Benadur, asking loudly,

"Benadur Mualath, chairman of the Council of Benadur, who from the holy lands of Ulgáris do ensure order in the name of Pneumos, protection to the sovereign realm of Loren, and peace to its citizens therein—can I count on your support?"

Keira watched as Mualath squirmed and endeavored to avoid Junia's furious gaze.

Go on then, you old cad, she thought. *You're lucky we're not outing you and your blasted Council for the corrupt snakes you are.*

Finally, Mualath stepped forward, arms out in supplication as he replied simply (and slightly begrudgingly, Keira thought), "You do so have our support, Regio Landrianus."

Further cheers erupted, and Keira watched as Landry shook the hands of the gathered people and then ascended the stairs himself. About to let out a few cheers of her own, Keira pulled up short, realizing that something was missing. Scanning the dais, she suddenly realized exactly what it was.

Junia was gone.

Oh no, you don't, Keira thought. They'd planned to confront her together. She'd promised Landry as much. Well, plans changed. Jumping down from the wall, she weaved her way through the roaring crowd toward the servants' side entrance around the back. *You're not getting off that easily.*

FORTY-ONE

Keira found Junia in her chambers, shouting orders as her maids haphazardly shoved clothing into bags. She didn't bother knocking, but simply strode in, arms folded as she watched the scene unfurl.

"What, leaving so soon?"

Junia spun on her heel to face her, fury and fear warring on her face. The two maids immediately dropped the clothing and unsheathed the deadly blades hidden within their skirts. Keira raised her brows at them, impressed despite herself.

"You," Junia spat. "What are you doing here? You have no right—"

"I have *every* right," Keira said, eyes narrowed, as she moved to stand near the desk in Junia's study.

"I should have known you were behind this. That ridiculous brother of mine never was much for strategy."

Keira ignored her and absently picked up a geometric gold paperweight, fingering its sharp edges lovingly. She felt Junia's eyes on her, sensed her nervousness even as the maids flanked her on either side.

Good, Keira thought, *Let her squirm.*

"So where's your friend, the tall woman?" Junia asked crisply. "I was promised her support, and the Legion's."

Keira's jaw tightened. She knew Junia was trying to rile her.

Well, good luck with that, Keira thought coldly. *I've waited far too long for this moment to have it rushed by the likes of you.*

"She's dead," Keira said flatly.

Junia's eyebrows rose. "I suppose not much of a friend then," she said with a sneer.

"*I* didn't kill her," Keira spat, marveling yet again at the darkness that seemed to inhabit this woman's soul. "She was killed by *your* assassins."

Junia's nostrils flared. "Well," she said tightly, "at least they were good for something."

Keira wanted to kill her then—to tear apart this woman who had killed so many of the people she loved. She wanted her to suffer, like Nazor, Flavius, and Sara all had. Keira wanted it so much it felt like a physical need, a hunger at the end of a famine that even the basest of pleasures wouldn't satiate. And Danny . . .

Keira nearly choked on the fury that rose to her throat at the thought of Danny. She leaned against the desk, gripping the ledge with her fingertips until it threatened permanent indents. She breathed in through her nose and tried to regain control.

"What's the matter, Keira? Lost your nerve?"

Keira glared at her. She wanted revenge so badly she could taste it and pneuma churned in her belly, begging to be unleashed. But Keira knew she would need her pneuma to beat all three of them, and ungrounded pneumonancy carried with it its own dire risks. She would be willing to take those risks for the chance to end Junia's miserable life. Even so, something held her back. Landry's words fluttered in her mind. *We're stronger together.*

They needed her. Her friends needed her. And as much as she would like to give Junia exactly what she deserved, she couldn't take the risk of ungrounded pneumonancy. She couldn't give in to her baser instincts. Because this really was her home. She'd thought the words before, but never truly felt them. Not like this. But seeing Landry and Neval stand side by side before downlanders and uplander alike—seeing the people embrace them both—that had been the final key. The Legion was corrupt and clearly had no plans to send her back to the world she came from. All that was left was here, now. She had friends here, people who needed her. And she'd be damned if she let them down by getting herself killed or undone. Even Junia wasn't worth that.

"How did you get like this?" Keira asked when she'd regained control, genuinely puzzled over how someone could go about losing this much of their soul. Junia looked taken aback by the question, and she stiffened, lifting her chin into the air in a way Keira was sure was supposed to make her feel inferior.

It didn't.

"I am the rightful Regio, the firstborn. It is my birthright. If we were still part of the Marian Empire, my rights would have been *assumed*. It is only here, in this forsaken country, that women are deemed no more competent than chattel or children."

There was a bitterness to her words that tugged at Keira's sympathy. In Junia's voice, she heard the echo of her own lifelong desire to prove herself and the fear of being held down, abandoned by the ones who claimed to love you. Keira knew that fear, had lived with it for far too long. Still, it was too late for that now.

"Maybe you were," Keira answered, "but I think you gave up that right when you turned on the people of Loren and conspired to have your own brother assassinated." She shook her head, giving Junia an ominous look. "No, you gave up any birthright a long time ago."

"Is that why you're here?" Junia spat. "To tie up loose ends?"

For the first time, Keira thought she saw a twinge of fear in those haughty eyes. She paused, savoring that look for just a moment, and then she sighed.

"No," she said finally. "I should—you would deserve it after the number of people you've killed and left to suffer. I hope you realize you are personally responsible for the deaths of people I cared deeply about."

Junia's face tightened further. "Then why not kill me?"

Keira paused again, for her sake this time more than Junia's. She thought of Nazor, of the chaos she'd escaped in her first life, and the turmoil she'd tried to prevent in this one.

"Sometimes order, keeping the peace, is more important than justice," Keira said finally. "At least in the short-term."

She slid back to sit fully on the desk, tilting the hilt of her sword back to accommodate the movement as she did so. She saw Junia's eyes follow the motion of the blade, and her brows knit tightly together. Keira sighed, feeling a flicker of annoyance.

"If I kill you, or if we expose all the treacherous things you've done in Loren, it would only reopen old wounds, stoke further unrest, and possibly upset the fragile peace we've got going here. You, Junia, are not worth that. So, you'll gather your things. You'll take any servants who wish to accompany you, and you will leave. You will leave and never come back, because there is no longer a place for the likes of you here."

Keira held Junia's gaze for a long time, watching the flurry of emotions she saw there: relief, sadness, but most of all, anger. Finally, Junia nodded. With a firm set of her jaw, she gestured impatiently to her maids. Then she gathered her things and was promptly escorted to her waiting ship.

A voice in the back of Keira's head screamed at her: *This is a mistake. She will never be satisfied. She will never let this go.*

Keira shoved the thoughts aside. She knew she'd probably regret this, knew she was taking a risk. But most of all, she knew what Danny would say.

This was the right thing to do. And just then, after everything they'd been through, that thought surprisingly proved to be enough.

CHAPTER

FORTY-TWO

Keira stared in awe at the stories'-high pillars that lined the great hall of the Vindolum, streamed in ribbons of luxurious purple silk. The white petals of Lady's Lace, the Marian family's signet flower, dotted the ground as nobility and invited commoners alike were outfitted in their very best. Keira herself had been convinced to don a pale blue summer gown for the occasion. It left her shoulders bare, as was the custom among the downlanders, and she tugged at it uncomfortably as she waited amongst the others' chittering excitement for the impending coronation.

From across the hall, Keira could see Neval Brennan, his mousy brown mop of hair pulled back for once in a tight queue. He met her gaze and raised a small hand in greeting, grinning from ear to ear.

"He looks like the fox who was just invited into the henhouse," a smooth voice murmured into her ear. Keira spun around in surprise to meet the smiling gray eyes of Cyrus Flavius. She laughed with delight as she looked him up and down.

"I barely recognized you outside your Bellator's uniform!" she exclaimed. They'd shared several meetings in the weeks leading up to the coronation, focused either on negotiating with Neval's men or planning security for the event. She'd come to appreciate his keen insight and mild manner, so like his father.

Cyrus returned her grin and shrugged. "All thanks to you, I suppose. Pneumos knows I've been trying to get out of the Bellatorio for years. It's a noble institution, mind you, but it was never really for me."

"That's exactly what your father said. I'm just glad it worked out as well as it did." Keira squeezed his shoulder affectionately. "You'll make a fine advisor for Landry."

Cyrus shrugged, running a hand through the black hair that was just beginning to grow out from its Bellatori styling. "It's not exactly painting, but it is a position at court. In truth, I like and respect our new Regio. It's an honor to help secure his position."

Keira nodded, noticing with a glow of satisfaction that he wore his father's red signet ring.

"I still can't believe you really made it happen," Cyrus continued. "When you showed up in the barracks mess hall asking for Millus Flavius's son, I thought for sure someone was having a laugh at my expense."

"Well, you really came through for us," Keira said, lowering her voice and pulling him to the side so as not to attract notice. "Without your help, there's no way Servius would have supported Landry that easily."

Cyrus shrugged, grinning. "That old buffoon? He wasn't about to let word of his *dalliances* be spread around the city. I just had to let him know exactly how much attention his visits to Mrs. Galloway's and his 'loans' from the city treasury had attracted."

Keira shook her head. The nerve of some people. "I'm just glad it all worked out."

Well, not everything, she reminded herself.

Cyrus must have seen the flicker of sadness on her face. "Still no improvement in your friend?" he asked, eyes soft and kind.

Keira shook her head, putting on a brave smile as she murmured her reply. "Nothing. It's been weeks, and, well—they tell me the idea of him just waking up gets less likely by the day."

How many days had she spent by his bedside? How many times had she tried to spin some healing pneumonancy to piece the broken pieces back together? If they were just physical, that would have been one thing. But Danny's injuries went far deeper than that.

Cyrus put a hand on her shoulder and squeezed gently. "You'll let me know if there's anything I can do, won't you?"

Keira nodded in thanks, trying to smile, but feeling her nose begin to burn as she did so.

"Your father was an incredible man, Cyrus, and so are you. He would have been so proud of you."

Cyrus rubbed the back of his neck with a shy smile. He looked as if he was about to say something else when horns suddenly blared and the crowd fell to a hushed murmur. The far doors of the great hall creaked open, and the coronation procession began.

The ceremony was one of pomp and circumstance steeped in centuries' worth of tradition. Having obviously never attended one previously, Keira was surprised to find that both nostril-burning incense and the odd goat seemed to play inordinately significant roles. She grinned knowingly at Landry's embarrassed grimace when he stood to make his vow, swaying slightly under the weight of the bejeweled crown. Otherwise, he was the picture of regal grace and Keira felt a swell of pride in her chest.

We really did it.

Pride aside, by the end of the ceremony, Keira was thoroughly exhausted from the kneeling, the standing, the huzzahs, and each and every "Long live the Regio!" She briefly considered joining the receiving line to wish Landry congratulations and a bountiful reign, but thought better of it. In truth, she could think of little else beyond the giant four-poster bed that awaited her merely three floors up.

Unfortunately, she had another far less exciting engagement still to attend that day.

NAZOR'S FUNERAL was to be held on a deserted beach, close to the dockyard where she'd died. Since there was no body to commemorate, the Legionnaires who reached out to Keira had suggested they meet here, to share their memories of Nazor and bid her a speedy journey on to her next life. Sure, Keira would have preferred they do this another time, so that maybe she might actually have a single day to be purely happy. But she understood that many were only in the city for the coronation and needed to leave soon after.

Keira arrived early, and she stood alone for a while, letting the sea lap at her bare feet as she stared out at the horizon. The wind whipped her hair across her face and stung her eyes as she blinked away tears.

"This wasn't the deal, Danny," she murmured into the air, squeezing her eyelids shut to fight the emotions that threatened to overwhelm her. "You're supposed to be here. You promised I didn't have to do this alone."

"You aren't alone," a voice said behind her.

She froze, then slowly turned around. Kind, amber eyes met hers.

"Elliott," she breathed. Keira launched herself at him, throwing her arms around his neck. He hugged her back fiercely as she sobbed into his chest.

"I'm sorry," she bawled. "I'm so sorry, Elliott. It's my fault. It's all my fault."

And then she was incomprehensible, the racking sound of the sobs ripping from her chest obscuring anything that might have been construed as words. In her tears, Keira poured out all the pain, the indecision, and the shame of the last few months. And through it all, Elliott just held her, smoothing the hair on the back of her head and making soothing sounds.

Eventually, her heaving shoulders stilled, and Elliott guided her over to sit next to him on a fallen piece of driftwood. Keira pressed the heels of her palms against her eyelids. When she was moderately sure she wouldn't lose it again, she began fiddling with the hem of her blue dress, embarrassed, and not knowing where to even start. Elliott didn't rush her, merely tilted his head back, and smiled as the breeze off the ocean tickled his face.

"Feels strange not to be wearing black," Keira murmured, still at a loss for words, but unable to take the silence any longer.

Elliott chuckled, tugging lightly at his own pale green tunic. "It is not our way. In the Legion, the end of one life is never 'goodbye,' but only 'until next we meet.'" He smiled sadly down at Keira, who resolutely refused to meet his gaze.

"No one blames you, you know," he said mildly. "Quite the contrary. They're all quite in awe of all you accomplished here." He shrugged. "To be honest, none of us thought it could be done."

Keira made a sound in the back of her throat, halfway between a snort and a sob. Even she wasn't sure which.

"Well, that much was clear," she said, shooting Elliott a sidelong look before immediately regretting it and looking away.

You're hardly one to talk, she told herself.

Elliott considered her briefly before explaining, slowly.

"The decision was ultimately Nazor's. She was the Legionnaire most involved with the case at that point and she presented a persuasive argument to the High Council. But yes, we all backed her up on it. We bet against Landry and it was the wrong call." He spoke this last bit simply, without pretense or excuse. It was a fact that just needed to be said aloud.

"But you bet against me," she said accusingly. "And Danny."

Elliott's brow furrowed. "We were never against you, Keira, or Danny. Neither was Nazor. You know that." There was a note of reproach in his tone, and Keira felt tears fill her eyes again. She squeezed them shut, willing them to retreat.

"Keira," Elliott said gently, and she opened her eyes to meet his, kind and forgiving as ever. "The Legion has requested that you come to Port Galaén, that you undertake the rites and become a full Legionnaire."

Keira froze, mouth falling open in a speechless gape. *The rites?* After everything that had happened, they still wanted her to be a Legionnaire? Keira scrambled to force her racing thoughts in order. This was everything she'd been working toward since she'd arrived in Loren, everything she'd dreamed about. Beyond the recognition or achievement, this had been her ticket home—or so she'd thought.

As if reading her mind, Elliott added, "This doesn't mean you'd be going home, Keira. You'd likely have to serve the Legion faithfully for many years before you broached the idea of a discharge home. But . . . it would be the first step."

Keira swallowed and bit her lower lip. A month ago she would have leaped at the opportunity, the culmination of so many years of training. But now, she'd all but decided where her loyalties lay . . . and they weren't with the Legion.

"I'm sorry, but I can't," she murmured, shaking her head slightly. "Not after what they tried to do. I don't trust them, and without Danny—" Her voice choked off, and Elliott put an arm around her shoulder, pulling her close. She leaned into him, not caring just then that she was getting his lovely tunic all wet and snotty.

"Keira, we made the wrong call," he repeated, voice strained. "And the thing you have to understand is that we will do it again, and again, and again. Because as much as we'd like to think otherwise, we really are only human. And as flawed humans, we will naturally create flawed systems. Now, you can join us, knowing all of that. But the question you have to ask yourself is whether you think you can serve the good that lies even within flawed institutions."

"I don't know, Elliott," she said miserably. "How am I supposed to know if I can do that, or if it's even possible?"

"I'm not sure if I can answer that for you, Keira," Elliott admitted. "All I can tell you is that I think you have to ask yourself whether it's an institution willing to adapt, to learn from its mistakes, just as every one of us grows within it."

He sighed, rubbing the bridge of his nose.

"I can't tell you what you should do, Keira, but the Legion has seen how much you could do here, and how you instinctively knew the leader that Landry could become. They want to hear your perspective. Personally, Keira, I'm asking you to give us another chance. Help make us better." Elliott paused, smiling slightly. "Don't give me an answer now, though. I really do want you to think about it, to think about where Pneumos is calling you. After all, she brought you here for a reason."

It was a lot to think about on a day when Keira was already feeling absolutely overwhelmed. So she merely nodded, and Elliott gave her shoulders a quick squeeze. Raising his other hand, he waved at the approaching figures of the Legionnaires who'd come to pay their respects.

Hastily, Keira dried her tears as best she could and stood to greet them, knowing the hardest part of the day still lay ahead.

THE MEMORIAL SERVICE WAS BRIEF, but beautiful in its own way. They sang the ancient songs of Pneumos that had been passed through the Legion for generations. They took turns swapping stories about

Nazor, known for her steely temper, incredible strength, and unassuming kindness. In the end, the small group of them joined hands as they wove their pneuma together, creating a circlet of braided flame that carved its way deep into the sand at their feet. They released their hands, and as the flames faded, the wind picked up, blowing sand across the burned design until it, too, had disappeared from view.

"Unseen, but never forgotten," one woman murmured. They all echoed the words, touching a hand briefly to the tops of their heads.

The ceremony complete, the group dispersed. Elliott invited Keira to join him at a local tavern where he was meeting old friends. She politely declined, explaining that she wanted to walk on the beach for a while. Keira assured him they'd catch up at dinner, though. He nodded, smiling sadly as she turned to walk farther down the beach.

Keira dug her toes into the cool sand as she walked, shoes in one hand. As she let the smooth ocean waves wash up to her ankles, she felt really and truly free for the first time in days. Away from the oppressive heat of the city and the confinement of its narrow streets, the world felt full and open again.

She breathed deeply of the salty sea air, blinking fiercely at the thought of how much Danny would have loved this view, the freedom of the open sky and the endless sea. Keira had spent the last few weeks watching and waiting in a state of limbo as she'd felt Danny slip further and further away from her. She knew that any day now, a messenger would arrive with word that he was really and truly gone, slipped away in the few moments she'd dared to leave him alone. The thought was a sharp stab to her chest, but it lacked the crushing anvil weight she'd borne these last few weeks.

She would always love him. He had helped make her into the person she was now. His love for her had helped banish the ever-present voice of suspicion and shame. It had freed her from the incessant doubting of not only herself, but everyone and everything around her. The guilt she carried for never fully returning that love, at least not openly, would haunt her for the rest of her days. But she'd told herself she'd never survive losing him, and yet here she was. Maybe not whole, and certainly not healed, but alive.

And she knew then that she could go on living, one day after the next—never easy, but worth it all the same. Too many people needed her still. Landry's throne was new, as yet unchallenged, and therefore vulnerable. Only yesterday she'd heard about the rising discontent of the Tramors to the North and the raiders pillaging along the Southern Shield. As for the Legion . . . well, Pneumos alone knew how that would end up.

Keira took another deep breath before opening her palm to release the small white petals of Lady's Lace she'd saved from the coronation, watching as the wind caught them and sent them cartwheeling above the waves, dancing down to lightly kiss the water before being picked up again and swirled away on winds of chance.

Keira hugged herself against the chill of the fresh sea breeze, brushing lightly at her neck to nudge the strands of hair that laid as yet untouched.

"It's not goodbye, Danny," she whispered, "just until next we meet."

EPILOGUE

Danny ran. Crashing through the forest, branches raked against his face, tearing at his clothes. He stumbled into the clearing, arm raised to shield his face from the blinding sun. In the distance, he saw a blurred figure and tried to call out, but found his mouth dry and tasteless. His knees buckled, and he slumped to the ground, catching himself by his arms as his stomach heaved. Nothing came up. Danny closed his eyes against the swiftly tilting planet and felt himself roll over until he was flat on his back. He felt himself moving in and out of consciousness, and as he did so, he dreamed of her.

Keira.

A head with curly dark hair danced before his vision. He tried to whisper her name, but was fairly sure his tongue wasn't working. He fell gladly back into dreamland until he finally awoke under a canvas-like roof. The curly-haired woman appeared again, and Danny realized with leaden disappointment that it was not, in fact, Keira. But then, where was she? Where was *he*, for that matter?

The woman before him smiled and offered a jug of water, which he gladly accepted.

"The Legion bids you most welcome," she said, just as he'd taken a long swig.

He nearly spat it out and stared wildly at her.

"T-the Legion?" he asked, voice raspy. "Of Loren?"

The woman looked confused and shook her head.

"No, I'm sorry. You've only just arrived, you see."

Danny closed his eyes, feeling another wave of nausea wash over him, this time tinged with panic. He felt nervous fingers take the jug from him, and he surrendered it with a low moan as he laid his throbbing head gingerly into his hands. Then a thought occurred to him.

"W-who are you?" he asked, looking up at her. Strangely enough, something told him he already knew the answer.

"My name is Tammy," the woman said, smiling kindly. "Tammy Altman."

SEE WHERE THE JOURNEY BEGAN...

FREE for Newsletter Subscribers!

www.hbreneau.com/thecantor

One life at an end, another just beginning.
Chaos looming in the distance.

See where the journey began in this prequel to *Chaos Looming*, Book 1
in The Legion of Pneumos series.

THE STORY CONTINUES IN...

Haven Enduring

That which was undone may be reborn.
But only at the price of chaos.

Book 2 in The Legion of Pneumos series.
Order Now!

Read on for a sneak peek...

HAVEN ENDURING

CHAPTER ONE

242 Marian Era (M.E.)

The heat washed over her, falling in waves that pushed her deeper into the mud of the jungle floor. Keira drew a ragged breath, feeling the moisture of the air settle heavily in her lungs. *Any minute now.* A mosquito buzzed incessantly around her nose, and it took every ounce of her deeply held willpower to resist the desire to swat at it. Instead, she held perfectly still—muscles tensed and ready to strike.

She glanced at the Bellators that surrounded her—statues in the midday heat. Red cloaks abandoned and faces smeared with camouflaging mud, they crouched in perfect silence, awaiting a quarry that had yet to show its face. Her heartbeat thrummed in her ears; the familiar tang of adrenaline settled on her tongue. She let it wash over her, pushing down every thought and jagged memory along with it. There was nothing beyond this—the hunt. She reveled in it.

And yet still they waited, the lingering seconds stretching into even longer minutes. The marauders that had been terrorizing the Southern Shield for months had embedded themselves deep within its tropical jungles, carving out fortresses that were impenetrable to any outward assault. In truth, they had no reason to face the Bellatorio on equal terms, not when they merely had to wait.

The gentle cracking of a twig immediately grabbed her attention, and her ears perked to catch the spongy sucking sound of the muddy jungle floor, confirming her suspicions; someone was out there. Her fingers twitched toward the sword at her belt, but she resisted the urge. She couldn't give away their position until the last possible moment.

Keira could feel the tension in the air, a palpable thrill that coursed through her body.

This is it.

Slowly, ever so quietly, she allowed her fingers to inch toward her gilded hilt, the cold steel of its pommel firm under her curling fingers. Still more twigs snapped, and she felt the hairs on the back of her neck rise.

They're practically on us.

On instinct, Keira reached within herself to feel the pulsing ball of energy behind her stomach. She flitted on the edge, desperately wanting to send feelers out, to calculate how many of them there were and find out their strength. But an all-too-familiar sensation of panic bloomed in her belly, and she quickly released the ball of energy. *I can't*, she thought, *not without—*

She bit her lip. It didn't matter. Besides, her pneuma still required a whistle to guide it. To cast it out required sound, and sound was the one thing they could not afford, not yet, at least.

Another moment passed, and then a strangled roar emerged from her compatriot only a few yards away, quickly followed by the cries of the entire patrol. Keira surged to her feet, meeting the startled eyes of a frightened marauder, who barely had time to react before her blade pierced his chest and he crumpled to the ground.

From the corner of her eye, she noticed one young Tiro cry out as he stumbled, crashing to his knees. The marauder he'd been skirmishing with let out a strangled yell of triumph as he lunged toward the fallen Bellator.

Keira leapt over her fallen comrade, barely registering the sharp ring of metal as her sword collided with the marauder's blade. She was close enough to see his yellowing teeth, to feel his stale breath. Spittle flew from his mouth, and her stomach lurched as it struck her face. She ignored the sensation and disengaged, repositioning to come at him again from the side.

He parried, and she deftly twirled their blades through the air in a shearing clang of sliding metal—making a full arc before they released. She staggered back, trying to regain her footing as she glared at the hulking man.

A flicker of movement made her drop to a crouch as the whistle of an arrow hissed just overhead. Glancing around, she couldn't make out a likely source in the mayhem of clashing blades, the Bellatori patrol fully engaged now against the marauders.

Spinning back to her initial quarry, Keira found him gone, disappeared through the dense overgrowth of jungle. She swore and started after him.

She'd made it about three steps when the cry of a young Bellator drew her attention, and she watched as he collapsed to one knee, gripping a deep slice to his side as his assailant's blade arced up and over—coming in for the kill.

Keira's legs moved of their own volition, and she lunged forward, slamming her shoulder into the marauder. They tumbled to the ground in a heap, and Keira squirmed, desperate to disengage, before a crushing blow to her abdomen knocked the wind out of her. She rolled, dry-heaving her nonexistent breakfast as she scrambled to her feet. She barely got her sword up in time to parry as the man surged toward her.

Their blades met with a force that sent an ache through her arm, her fingers instantly going numb. She dodged to the side, aiming for his exposed flank, but he was too quick. He spun with her, forcing her back until she felt the press of gnarled bark against her spine. She let him advance, waiting for the last possible moment as a cruel side cut flew toward her. She dodged, letting his blade slice deep into the tree, where it lodged. It was just a moment before he wrenched it free, but it was one moment too long.

She slammed into him, thrusting her dagger into his belly once . . . twice . . . before he collapsed in a heap, blood gurgling from his throat.

Keira stood, chest heaving as she stared down at him, his eyes slowly dilating into the ghoulish surprise of death. But in her mind, she was seeing another body—face swollen and hair matted with blood . . . *Danny.*

Keira squeezed her eyes shut, willing the image to burn free of her retinas, and her breath came in shallow gasps. She forced her body into submission, breathing through pursed lips as she steadied her shaking hands on the tree beside her. When she had control, her eyes flickered open—darting around as she searched for whatever threat beckoned. But from where she stood, all the marauders lay dead—their bodies already being looted by the surviving Bellators. Whoever remained must have fled for safer ground.

"Th-Thank you."

She turned to find the young Tiro she'd saved staggering toward her, arm still gripping his side as he stared at her in wide-eyed gratitude. Keira felt a flush stain her cheeks, and she waved him off, turning to stalk away. His face fell as she slid past, but she kept moving. She felt her adrenaline fading and moved faster, desperate to outrun the hollow exhaustion she knew would follow in its wake. She pushed aside the underbrush until she could just make out the muddy tracks left by the fleeing marauders.

"They went this way!" she called, before taking off through the dense vegetation, not caring who, if anyone, followed her.

Branches tore at her clothes and hair as she pushed her way through the underbrush, leaping over snarled roots the size of her thighs that snaked up from the ground. Somewhere in the back of Keira's mind, she wondered if she was even headed in the right direction, or if she was only pushing deeper into the heart of the jungled island. She wasn't sure she cared. The adrenaline in her stomach burned out any doubt or worry before it could take hold as her legs carried her forward. She was beyond worry.

Crashing through a wall of foliage, Keira stepped through to dazzling tropical sunlight. She blinked against the rays that reflected off the white sands and shielded her eyes, scanning the horizon for any sign of the fleeing marauders.

There!

Footsteps trailed away from the jungle's edge, making for the port town of Albé. Cursing, Keira started toward the village, fighting the drag of her boots as they sank into the powderlike sand.

Reaching the edge of the town, Keira slowed to a walk, not wanting to attract undue attention, but she soon realized the effort was pointless. With her pale, sunburnt skin and blue eyes, not to mention the sword strapped to her hip, she couldn't have been more conspicuous. Keira kept her head down as she moved along the streets, but she could feel the islanders' dark eyes following her, narrowed and tense.

A figure crossed her path and Keira tensed, reaching instinctively for her sword. But it was only a middle-aged woman, slobbering baby bouncing on her hip as she looked Keira up and down scornfully. The woman eyed Keira's sword, and she quickly dropped her grip on its hilt.

Relaxing, the woman sidled closer, speaking in a hushed murmur. "The one you be looking for? He came tru' not ten minute before you, be making for the stables right off."

Keira glanced around eagerly. "Where are they, then?"

The woman pursed her lips and raised her dark eyebrows pointedly at Keira's waist satchel. Keira's eager grin twisted into a scowl as she fished out a handful of penarii, the copper coins that saw most business done on the islands. She dropped them into the woman's palm, who pocketed them with businesslike efficiency before gesturing to the west.

"You be following this road, but stop before you be reaching the blacksmith. The stables being just to the right."

Keira turned to thank the woman, but she'd already pushed past, baby still bouncing on one hip, her other arm firmly wrapped around a large basket. Tightening her sword belt, Keira set off at a near-jog down the road the woman had pointed to, hoping she wasn't already too late.

The stable itself was an airy building, built on strong balsané wood stilts to elevate it above the ever-present threat of flood. Keira peered past the half dozen horses tied under the three-sided exterior overhang toward the open door beyond. Inside, the stablemaster argued with a man whose back was to her. She froze. Though he wore a cloak with the hood pulled up, her gaze traveled down to his boots, to the thick jungle mud caked up the sides.

She broke into a run.

Maybe it was the sound of her footsteps, or the slide of metal as she unsheathed her blade, but the cloaked man suddenly turned and caught her gaze. It was him.

Shoving the stablemaster aside, he made for the row of horses tied under the overhang within the inner corral.

Oh no, you don't, Keira thought, veering toward a horse that stood tied outside a nearby building. Keira saw the marauder's knife flash as he unfettered the reins of a sorrel mare and leapt onto its back. Wheeling the horse around, he barreled toward the open side. Keira was still a few yards away from the nearest horse, but as she glanced toward the entrance to the stable complex, she felt the breath punch out of her in a whoosh.

There was only one way in or out of the corral, and a group of children crouched just beyond, their view of the marauder blocked by tall hay bales as they skipped smooth pebbles across a circle drawn in the sand that blew across the wood planks of the street. From the angle of the doorway, Keira knew there was no way the marauder would see them in time. She had a moment's indecision as she glanced at the waiting horse in the opposite direction. Then she was running.

The children shrieked as she came upon them, but she ignored their squeals. Scooping up the two smallest children in one arm, she yanked a slightly older girl to her feet, hauling them all out of the horse's path.

The two youngest came willingly enough, no doubt stunned by the shock of it all, but the oldest writhed and kicked as Keira dragged her out of the road.

"My necklace!" the girl shrieked, wrestling her way out of Keira's grip and dashing back toward the circle. She lunged for the glinting object that lay amid the stone as the marauder's horse came barreling toward her.

"What are you doing!" Keira cried. Dropping the squalling children, she lunged for the older girl—tackling her just as the sandy circle erupted under flying hooves.

It took a moment to disentangle themselves. Coughing, Keira shot a rueful glance at the marauder's back before rounding on the girl. Rising from the ground, the girl brushed sand from her dress and carefully peeled open her fingers. Cradled in the center of her palm lay a perfectly spiraled sea shell fixed to a broken piece of twine. Keira glanced at it, noting the speckled rose pink that stood out against the girl's warm brown skin. It was beautiful, Keira had to admit, remarkable in its perfect symmetry and the way the sunlight twinkled off the grains of sand embedded in its surface. But it was certainly not worth dying over.

"What on earth were you thinking?" Keira asked, glaring at the top of the girl's head, where strings of dark brown curls escaped her twin braids. The girl met her gaze, glaring right back with the most piercing eyes Keira had ever seen.

Keira blinked.

They really were extraordinary, their shade almost white-green, the color of seafoam or a choppy wave. They'd be a unique feature in any company but were striking among the Udánma, the native people of the Southern Shield. Keira knew they took pride in the dark warmth of their eyes, often ringing their lids with light hues to make them stand out all the more.

"You really should be more careful," Keira said, shifting awkwardly as she realized she'd been staring at the girl for a bit too long.

The girl glowered back, either not noticing the pause or else too used to gawking to care. She muttered something in the native language of the islands that Keira couldn't understand, although she definitely picked out the word *grelún* uttered with a surprising amount of condescension for someone who likely still had some baby teeth.

Keira was about to reprimand her again when the girl spun on her heels and scampered away, gesturing at the two younger children, who quickly chased after her.

Jaw clenched, Keira glanced back in the direction the marauder had gone but saw no sign of him. *Great*, she thought, *no doubt spreading word of our camp position.*

Keira stretched, feeling the adrenaline eking out of her muscles as a familiar wave of exhaustion washed over her. With it came the emptiness, that hollow void and accompanying panic she kept at bay through sheer force of will and the ever-present distraction of combat. She quickly shoved the feeling away. There was still a job to do, and she clung to that thought. She had to warn the Bellatorio. The next attack would be swift and precise. Pneumos help them if they were caught off guard.

Haven Enduring

That which was undone may be reborn.
But only at the price of chaos.

Book 2 in The Legion of Pneumos series.
Order Now!

ABOUT THE AUTHOR

H.B. Reneau is an author of fantasy and contemporary fiction. Author, physician, and proud dog mom, she is known for her character-driven, genre-crossing fiction that draws on her experiences in both medicine and the military. She has a particular love for strong female characters who face up to adversity and manage to subvert some expectations along the way.

To learn more, head over to her website at www.hbreneau.com. There you'll find her books, blog, and fun extras. Or reach out directly! Follow on social media and sign up for the monthly newsletter to receive receive free gifts, awesome discounts, and updates on all her latest projects.

If you enjoyed this book, please consider leaving a review at your favorite online storefront!

facebook.com/hbreneau

twitter.com/HBReneau1

instagram.com/h.b.reneau

ALSO BY H.B. RENEAU

<u>The Legion of Pneumos</u>

Chaos Looming

Haven Enduring

<u>The Legion of Pneumos: Novella Collection</u>

The Cantor

The Centus

The Rebel

The Remnant